SUSPICION

6/2016

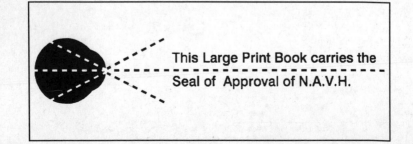

SUSPICION

JOSEPH FINDER

THORNDIKE PRESS
A part of Gale, Cengage Learning

GALE
CENGAGE Learning®

Farmington Hills, Mich • San Francisco • New York • Waterville, Maine
Meriden, Conn • Mason, Ohio • Chicago

GALE
CENGAGE Learning·

LIBRARY OF CONGRESS CATALOGING-IN-PUBLICATION DATA

Finder, Joseph.
    Suspicion / Joseph Finder. — Large print edition.
        pages cm — (Thorndike Press large print basic)
    ISBN 978-1-4104-6749-2 (hardcover) — ISBN 1-4104-6749-X (hardcover)
    1. Single fathers—Fiction. 2. Drug traffic—Fiction. 3. Large type books.
I. Title.
PS3556.I458S87 2014b
813'.54—dc23   2014015405

Published in 2014 by arrangement with Dutton, a member of Penguin Group (USA) LLC, a Penguin Random House Company

Printed in the United States of America
1 2 3 4 5 6 7 18 17 16 15 14

For Dan Conaway

PART ONE

1

Sometimes the smallest decision can change your life forever.

Abe Lincoln's bodyguard decides to stay for another drink at the bar at Ford's Theatre during intermission.

The archduke's driver makes a wrong turn in Sarajevo because he refuses to ask for directions. (Men, right?)

You finally listen to your know-it-all brother-in-law and invest everything you have with a guy named Bernie Madoff. Steady returns, dude. A no-brainer.

The tyranny of small decisions, someone once called it. The gate of history turns on small hinges.

Danny Goodman's nightmare began with a quick handshake and a friendly smile.

Whenever he drove up to his daughter's private school, the Lyman Academy, Danny couldn't help thinking of stately Wayne

Manor, the baronial mansion outside Gotham City where Batman lives as Bruce Wayne. If only he were driving the Batmobile instead of a 1997 Honda Accord.

Lyman was the most exclusive private girls' school in Boston, and most of the other cars in the pickup line were gleaming luxury SUVs: Range Rovers or Mercedes-Benzes or Land Cruisers. Today, though, Abby would be spared the public humiliation of an Accord sighting, because her father had arrived twenty minutes early for the afternoon pickup. He had an appointment with the head of the Upper School, Tinsley Thornton, whom everybody called Lally.

Lally. No wonder the place made Danny uncomfortable.

He parked in the side lot, where the teachers parked, and where his dented old Honda didn't look quite so out of place.

The office of the head of the Upper School was at the end of a long corridor next to the headmaster's office and Admissions, which might as well have been labeled RE-JECTIONS. You either had to know someone — several someones — to get into Lyman or be able to write a check sizable enough to build a new library. Danny had been fortunate: The foundation his late wife, Sarah, had worked for was endowed by a guy who also happened to be chairman of Lyman's board of trustees.

Lally Thornton welcomed him to her large, oak-paneled office with a concerned look, clutching his hand in two of hers. Her steel-gray hair was held back with a black velvet headband. She wore a black turtleneck, a double strand of pearls, and perfume with the strong floral smell of urinal cake. Her air of lethal graciousness always reminded Danny of that socialite girls'-school headmistress who shot the diet doctor years ago.

"Is everything all right with Abby at home?" she asked with hushed concern, settling into a low brocade chair while Danny sat on the couch at a right angle to her.

"Oh, yeah, she's — doing well." He swallowed hard.

"It must be so difficult for her."

He nodded. "But you know, Abby's a strong kid."

"Losing a mother at her age. What a terrible thing."

Danny nodded. She must have just reviewed the file. "I had a quick question about the Italy trip," he said.

She lit up. "It is *such* a profound experience," she said. "You'll see. It changes them. They come back different people — more aware of the world, more appreciative of different cultures, and, well, it seems to just dissolve all those cliques, all those silly tensions between the girls. I'd even call it transformative. Abby — oh, she's going, isn't she?"

"Well, see, that's the question."

"She must. She absolutely *must*. It's the trip of a lifetime."

He blotted his damp palms on the knees of his suit pants. "Right, I know, I've heard. . . . But Abby — well, you know how idealistic these girls can be at that age. She's sort of concerned that some of her classmates might find it difficult to go."

"Difficult?"

"The five thousand dollars, I mean. Not everyone can afford it, and, you know, that bothers her." Danny tried to sound casual. As if he were a hedge fund tycoon with a social conscience. Instead of a writer whose advance on his latest book had run out months ago.

What Lally apparently didn't know was that he was more than a month late with this semester's tuition. He had no idea how he could possibly come up with it — let alone five thousand bucks for a trip to Italy

12

on top of that. Lyman had the biggest endowment of any private school in the United States. He was fairly certain they'd squeak by a bit longer without his lousy sixteen thousand dollars.

He imagined her reply: *Why, that five-thousand-dollar fee, that's merely a* sugges-tion, *a* recommendation. *Of course it's waived if it's a hardship for any family.*

He felt a single fat bead of sweat trickle down behind his left ear, then down the side of his neck, and under his shirt collar.

"Isn't that thoughtful of her? Well, you tell Abby that if any of her friends aren't going to Italy because of the money, their parents should say something to Leah Winokur right away. We have scholarships for deserving minorities."

"Of course." He'd come here to try to finagle something that might enable Abby to go to Italy. A price break, maybe. A loan. Something. A scholarship for minorities didn't exactly help. The only minority that Abby Goodman, blond-haired and blue-eyed, belonged to at this school was Girls Whose Parents Didn't Have a Summer House. "You know, I do wonder whether it might be difficult for other parents, too — not minorities but not, you know, the very wealthy. To pay that kind of money on top of everything else."

"I doubt most Lyman parents would consider that a hardship. After all, no one *has* to go to Italy."

With a smile as cold as a pawnbroker's, she said, "Was there anything else?"

2

The halls were crowded with teenage girls. It rang with squeals and shouts and laughter. Some of them walked arm in arm or hugged one another. Danny often marveled at how affectionate girls that age were and couldn't help contrasting them with teenage boys, who smelled like old gym socks and zit cream and expressed affection by punching one another on the shoulder.

He waited for Abby with a deep sense of dread.

Not going on the Italy trip, she'd said, would be social death. She'd be a pariah. He'd told her he'd think about it. He'd see what he could do.

Meeting with Lally Thornton had been a desperation move, a Hail Mary pass that didn't complete. No need to let Abby in on just how bad things were. How they were basically living on fumes. He wanted her life to be as normal as possible, given the circumstances.

She was doing better than a lot of girls her age would have done. She was strong, but her mother's death had hit her hard. For months, her default expression had been a Darth Vader mask of anger. Who could blame her?

He didn't look forward to giving her the bad news about the one thing she was looking forward to.

From behind him came a rumbling basso profundo. "Oh, Danny boy, the pipes, the pipes," sang a school security guard, Leon Chisholm. He was a black man of about sixty with close-cropped white hair and a wide, open face. He wore wire-rimmed glasses and had a gap between his front teeth; the vibe was part professor, part prizefighter. He'd spent twenty years with the Boston Police Department, so he was probably able to handle a few mean girls in Lululemon yoga pants.

"Officer," Danny said with a grin, and clapped him companionably on the shoulder. When Leon's oldest daughter, Rebecca, had graduated from Bunker Hill Community College — the first in the family to go to college — Danny had helped her get a job with a publisher in Boston. Leon liked Danny, one of the few Lyman dads who said hi and actually chitchatted with him. To most other Lyman parents, Leon was invisible.

Then Danny caught a glimpse of Abby near the front lobby — her silvery metallic fringed scarf, then her face. Smiling, which surprised him. He couldn't remember when he'd last seen her smile. She was walking arm in arm with her new BFF, Jenna Galvin.

Jenna Galvin seemed to be Abby's polar opposite: She was small and dark-haired and chubby, where Abby was slender and graceful and blond. Jenna seemed sour, aloof, even arrogant, whereas Abby was sweet-natured and sociable. Or had been, anyway, until six months ago. Jenna had just transferred to Lyman as a junior, which was unusually late to start a new school, and had apparently been an outcast there. Abby, empathic as ever, and maybe also a bit rebellious, had felt bad for the new girl and befriended her. Now they were inseparable.

Abby's face lit up when she saw her father, which was disorienting — was she smiling at someone else? She maneuvered nimbly through the teeming horde of girls and threw her arms around him.

First uncoerced hug in eleven months, Danny thought. *But who's counting?*

"Oh my God, Daddy, thank you!"

For what? he wanted to say.

She hugged him even harder. He still hadn't gotten used to how tall she'd grown. "Thank you thank you thank you. I just saw my name on the Italy trip list. I *knew* you'd let me go. You are so *awesome.*"

"Abby, honey —"

Jenna touched her arm. "My dad's here, come on." A sleek silver-haired man in an expensive-looking camel-colored suit entered the lobby and gave Jenna a kiss.

"Abby, wait — what are you talking about?" Danny said.

But Abby didn't hear him. She'd turned around and was talking to Jenna. Abby said, "I know, right?" before turning back to her father.

"Daddy, is it okay if I go home with Jenna?"

He felt a flash of irritation. She never seemed to want to spend time at home. But he said only, "Well, I don't know. I'd rather not have to drive out to Weston to pick you up."

"Esteban will take her home," Jenna said.

Esteban was the Galvins' driver. Jenna's father was some kind of investor and had a lot of money, even by Lyman standards.

"Abby," Danny said, but then someone tapped him on the shoulder. He turned.

18

The silver-haired man. Thomas Galvin.

He appeared to be in his late forties. His blue-gray eyes were like steel against his deep tan. His suit was exquisitely cut, his pale blue shirt perfectly pressed, his tie neatly knotted. Everything in place. Danny's crappy sport coat, which he'd bought off the discount rack at the Men's Wearhouse Black Friday sale, felt itchy.

"Just wanted to introduce myself," the man said, offering his hand. "Tom Galvin."

"Dan Goodman."

Abby was already out the front door with Jenna.

"Nice to meet Abby's dad. She's terrific."

"Most of the time," Danny said with a grin.

"Jenna couldn't ask for a better friend."

"Well, it's great to meet you, too."

"Listen, thanks for letting me kick in on that Italy thing." He had the accent of a kid out of Southie.

"Kick in?"

"Abby has been a lifesaver for our Jenna. You have no idea."

"Hold on a second. You paid for *Abby's* trip to Italy?"

"For totally selfish reasons, trust me." He lowered his voice to a confidential mutter. "This is Jenna's fourth school in three years.

19

She was already begging to leave until she started hanging out with Abby. And she sure as hell doesn't want to go with the class to Italy if Abby's not going."

Danny's cheeks grew hot. He was astonished, and embarrassed. And angry, though he rarely let anyone see his anger.

How much had Abby told her friend? She couldn't possibly know how bad their financial situation was, but she must have said something. This was beyond embarrassing; it was demeaning. This rich guy was treating them like a charity case.

"That's extremely generous of you," he said, "but I can't accept it."

"Please. It's for my daughter."

"I'm sorry. I'll call the bursar and set them straight. But I really do appreciate the thought." He smiled, then turned and pushed through the front doors.

The sun dazzled his eyes. A gleaming black Maybach limousine was parked at the curb. It had to belong to Galvin. A man in a uniform of black suit, white shirt, and black tie approached Abby and Jenna with a cardboard Starbucks take-out tray and handed them each a cup. Galvin's chauffeur must have gone on a Starbucks run.

"Thanks, Esteban," Abby said. She turned as Danny emerged, beaming excitedly, her eyes shining. "Everything okay, Daddy?"

He beckoned her over. "Boogie," he began quietly, using the pet name he never used around anyone else.

"Oh God, I'm so so *so* excited," she interrupted. Then followed a torrent of words — *pasta* and *gelato* and *shopping* — that Danny couldn't quite follow. She grabbed both of his elbows. "I'm going to *Italy*!" she almost sang.

He hadn't seen her this happy in years. Dimples had appeared on her cheeks, her smile so wide it looked like her face might crack in two.

Now what? Tell her there'd been a mix-up?

Danny had once made the mistake of opening a link a friend had sent him. It was something called a crush video. It showed a woman stepping on a tiny kitten with her stiletto heels. It was one of the sickest, most disturbing things he'd ever seen, and he wished he could *unsee* it.

Telling Abby the Italy trip wasn't going to happen would feel a bit like that.

"Dan," Galvin said by way of greeting as he came out the front door, lowering his BlackBerry.

Danny approached and said, in a low voice, "I can only accept this if you'll let me pay you back."

Galvin's eyebrows shot up. He nodded solemnly. "If you don't, I'll send my goons after you." He gave Danny a wry smile.

"I mean, no offense, but it's a little awkward. We don't even know each other."

"Which is crazy, right? Given how close Abby and Jenna are? Listen, come over for dinner tomorrow night, wouldja? The boys are home from college, and they love Abby, and Celina is making her famous *arroz con pollo.*"

What could he say? The guy was shelling out for his daughter's trip to Italy. Dinner with his family was the least he could do.

Much later, he'd replay that moment over and over again in his head.

He thrust out his hand and smiled. "Sounds great," he said. "Thanks a lot."

3

When Danny opened the door of the two-bedroom on Marlborough Street, he was greeted by the loud thumping of a dog's tail against the floor. Rex, their arthritic chocolate Lab, struggled to get up from his bed near the kitchen.

"That's okay, buddy, no need to get up for my sake," he said, coaxing Rex back down onto the plaid dog bed, stroking his graying coat, massaging his haunches. Rex was thirteen years old, which was old for the breed. His muzzle had gone silver, his amber eyes clouded with an opaque cataract haze. He'd belonged to Sarah, went with her after the divorce, and then had moved in with Abby. The old boy, profligate with affection, had heroically gotten Abby through her mother's death.

The red message light on Danny's phone was blinking.

Eight voice mails. Seven from one particularly odious and persistent collections agent named Tony Santangelo of Asset Recovery Solutions, who seemed to have trained at the Bada Bing school of debt collection. His "solution" was to "garnish" Danny's wages.

Garnish. Such a benign-sounding word. Like parsley sprigs and radish roses.

And what wages?

He'd replayed, over and over, that odd exchange with Tom Galvin. *Thanks for letting me kick in on that Italy thing.* Who was the guy, really? In the age of the Internet, the information had to be out there, and Danny, if nothing else, was an ace researcher.

Sitting at his desk in the small alcove off the living room that was now his "study" — his office had become Abby's bedroom — Danny opened a browser on his old MacBook Pro. LinkedIn had a long list of Thomas Galvins. Halfway down that roster was a Thomas X. Galvin who'd graduated from Boston College, worked for Putnam Investments, and was the founder, chief executive, chief investment officer, and managing director of Galvin Advisers on Saint James Avenue in Boston.

Bingo.

Rex, who was now curled atop Danny's shoes, heaved a long soulful sigh and nuzzled even closer.

Galvin Advisers of Boston, Mass. The website was nothing more than a secure portal, a page showing an overhead view of Boston's Financial District, and a log-in box that asked for user name and password. Above it, the words: *This website is intended solely for the employees and investors of Galvin Advisers.*

Danny's girlfriend, Lucy Lindstrom, arrived with dinner in a white plastic bag. Takeout from a place on Newbury Street: a salad for her and linguine with shrimp scampi for him. He could smell the garlic, the warm olive oil, oregano, a vinegary bite.

She leaned over to stroke Rex's face, causing him to close his eyes in bliss. Then she gave Danny a squeeze and a kiss. Her hair gave off a faint whiff of cigarette, which told Danny she'd spent the day doing outreach. She was a psychiatrist for the Boston Health Care for the Homeless Program, and she spent two days a week on the streets of Boston, trying to bribe and wheedle homeless people to come in and get treated.

She wore a pale gray turtleneck under a blue V-neck sweater with black jeans and a great old pair of black leather boots that Danny loved seeing her in. She was wearing

25

her chunky black glasses, which Danny was convinced she used to make herself plainer, and thus less vulnerable, at work. It gave her a sort of winsomely studious look.

They'd been going out for three years, but they'd known each other since freshman year at Columbia. Back then, before life had kicked them both around, Lucy Lindstrom seemed unattainable. To Danny, she was the It Girl of his college class. She had blond hair that came down in unruly ripples to her shoulders, a sharp nose and chin, blue-gray eyes, a dazzling smile, an endearing overbite.

Back then, she'd been way out of his league. Frankly, she still was.

The two decades since college had etched faint lines around her mouth and vertical worry lines between her pale eyebrows. It wasn't just the years; she'd also survived an unhappy first marriage.

Danny knew she was overly sensitive about the signs of aging, indoctrinated like most women by fashion magazines.

Danny couldn't care less. He thought Lucy was more beautiful now than when she was a freshman.

She set the round foil take-out pans on the dining table and eased off their cardboard lids.

"Hard day?"

"Mostly a lot of walking around. I need a shower." Lucy never complained about her work. He admired that.

"Glass of wine first?"

"Sure, why not?"

He pulled the cork out of a chilled bottle of Sancerre and poured them each a glass. They clinked. The wine was crisp, citrus and chalky.

"Street outreach?"

She nodded. "There was this guy at South Station today, sleeping on a bench. He looks like he's seventy, but he could be ten years younger — you know how the street ages them. Well, the police tried to take him to one of our day shelters, but he refused to go. Really fought with them. So I tried."

She looked pained, as if reliving the moment. And at the same time tender, transported. She felt a deep connection with the homeless guys. As far as Danny was concerned, they were vagrants and bums, but they were Lucy's children, her wards, not her patients.

"I told him it's getting to be really cold at night and he should sleep at the Night Center, not out on the street. But he said people were tampering with his food and they'll get to him if he goes to sleep. He

27

started babbling — all kinds of nonsense. Word salad."

He nodded. "Paranoid schizophrenic." He found her work fascinating but also fundamentally baffling: How could she bear taking care of people who didn't want her help?

"Probably. We need to get him on Risperdal, but first I need to get him to talk. So I asked if I could sit with him and he said no. I said I just wanted to help. He said, 'What the hell can you do for me?' So I said, 'Well, I have cigarettes.' And he said, 'Oh, okay.' " She took a sip of wine.

Danny laughed. "Suddenly you couldn't shut him up."

"I gave him a five-dollar gift certificate for McDonald's, a cigarette, and a pair of white tube socks."

"So he's coming in to see you?"

She shook her head. "Later, maybe. First I have to get him to trust me. But you know, there's something really . . . moving about this guy."

"How so?"

"There's an intelligence in there. A really great, interesting mind locked away, deep inside. It's sort of heartbreaking."

The phone rang.

No, he thought. *Don't let it be Tony Santangelo from Asset Recovery Solutions again.*

He was about to let it go to voice mail when he checked the caller ID: 212 area code and the name of his literary agency, Levitan Freed Associates.

His agent, Mindy Levitan, rarely called except when she was in the middle of negotiating a deal for him.

It couldn't be good news.

"How's life in the salt mines?" Mindy said. She had a raspy voice from years of smoking, which she'd only recently been able to quit with the help of a Russian hypnotist.

"Excellent," he lied. "Deep into it." For several years now, he'd been working on a biography of a nineteenth-century robber baron named Jay Gould.

"Good, good. That's what I like to hear." She said it without enthusiasm. "So listen, Danny. Sorry to call you at suppertime, but I just got into my country house and checked my messages. And I got a call from Louisa." Louisa Penniman was Danny's editor. She was a legendary editor of "serious" nonfiction. She'd made her bones on "inside the Beltway" books about politics and a couple of presidential memoirs. She was widely feared and even more widely disliked.

"You're breaking up," Danny said. "I'm losing you."

"Nice try. We're both on landlines. Listen, this is serious, Danny. She wants to cancel the book."

4

Danny felt his mouth go dry. "She wants to cancel because I'm a few months late?"

"First, kiddo, it's not 'a few' months, it's *fifteen* months —"

"Okay, but —"

"You know how bad things are in the industry. Publishers are all freaking out about e-books. They're looking for any excuse to cancel contracts these days."

"Was there ever a time when things *weren't* bad in publishing?"

Mindy gave a quick, rueful laugh, more a bark. "Louisa Penniman doesn't screw around."

"This isn't just a threat? I mean, you think — she's actually serious?"

"As cancer," Mandy said. Then, quickly, she added: "Sorry. Bad choice of words."

Mindy Levitan had gotten him a bigger advance for his biography of Jay Gould than he'd ever expected. It helped that his first book, *The Kennedys of Boston,* had been a finalist for the Pulitzer Prize, even though it didn't sell particularly well. Or actually win the Pulitzer, for that matter.

Also, he had to admit that his proposal had been damned good. Even better was Mindy's pitch to publishers: *No one knows who Jay Gould is anymore,* she'd written in her cover e-mail. *Yet no one had heard of some Olympic track star shot down in World War II, but* Unbroken *was a massive best-seller. Nor had anyone heard of a serial killer who menaced Chicago during the World's Fair, which didn't stop readers from buying* The Devil in the White City: *It's all in how the story is told.*

And Danny knew how to tell the story. Jay Gould was a railroad speculator and a strikebreaker and one of the richest men in America, an inside trader and a virtuoso at bribery, a scammer and a liar who actually bragged about being "the most hated man in America."

Random House, HarperCollins, and Simon & Schuster had all bid, but Louisa at Triangle had topped them all. The money sounded good at first — until you subtracted Mindy's fifteen percent and spread the payments out over the three years, at least, it would take him to write the book. Plus, a big chunk of the money wouldn't come in until the trade paperback was published, at least a year after the hardcover. Not that he was complaining: He got to do what he loved, and if he lived frugally and didn't go on any trips to the Caribbean, he could have made it.

But then came the call from Sarah.

His ex-wife had just gotten the results of a biopsy. There'd been no lump, nothing on a mammogram. Just a little warmth and redness in one breast she noticed one day. The skin felt different, hard and taut like an orange. Her lymph nodes were enlarged. Her doctor had told her it was probably an insect bite, and he'd prescribed antibiotics.

Her doctor was wrong.

The survival rates for inflammatory breast cancer weren't great. She was a single mom, and she was frightened.

One minute Danny was researching the Great Southwest Railroad Strike of 1886, and the next he was Googling estrogen receptors. Sarah's second husband had taken a job at a firm in Manhattan, and their eventual breakup had been acrimonious. And the guy was a jerk, as Sarah had finally come to realize. She needed Danny's help.

He began eating a lot of cafeteria meals at the Dana-Farber cancer center.

For the first time in years, his daughter actually seemed to need him around, too. She needed a steadying presence. She also needed someone to drive her to dance practice and play rehearsals and sleepovers. While he waited in the cramped back room of the dance studio, he researched chemo-therapy and radiation and hyperthermia and raw apricot seeds and vitamin B17.

And Jay Gould moved to the back burner.

Because Mr. Gould, as fascinating as he was, wasn't as important as Danny's daughter, or his ex-wife, whom he'd never stopped loving even when she stopped loving him.

"Danny?"

"What?"

"I said, we need to figure out what's next. How soon can you get me a hundred, hundred fifty pages? To see if we can keep them on the reservation. Keep her from canceling."

"You think that'll do it?"

"Might. Who knows? It's the only card I have to play. So you'll do it?"

Danny wasn't even close to having a decent hundred-plus pages, and he wouldn't be for at least a month. But if the book was canceled, there went his entire income stream.

Danny swallowed hard. "No problem," he said.

5

Lucy looked at him, arched her brows, and smiled sadly. "How bad?"

"Very."

He told her what Mindy had to say. And about his meeting with the head of school.

And then about the surprise loan from Thomas Galvin.

"Oh," she said. "That's generous." She didn't sound enthusiastic.

"Lucy."

She avoided his eyes.

"Let's hear it," he said.

"Well, are you sure that's really a good idea?"

"Why not?"

"I just think it's weird for this guy who doesn't even know you to pay for your daughter to go on a trip."

"It's unusual, I'll give you that. Though he invited us over for dinner tomorrow night."

"I work tomorrow night. I mean, if I was even invited. Does Abby know about this?"

"I don't think so."

"Never underestimate teenage girls. They notice everything. And they can be manipulative. Believe me, I used to be one."

"Maybe."

"I just think it's not a good idea to borrow money from this guy you barely know. It just — well, it sends up a red flag."

"You know what's not a good idea? Charging five thousand bucks for a friggin' school trip to Italy. The way this school just takes for granted that parents can shell out that kind of money."

"You're just figuring this out?"

"No, but it still annoys me. What it's doing to Abby."

"So we're really talking about Abby's new friend."

"Abby gets driven home from the Galvins by a Hispanic servant wearing a chauffeur's uniform, okay? There's something wrong with that."

"I wouldn't mind it."

"She's a kid. And it's not her life. It's someone else's."

"Exactly. That's not her life, and she knows it. That kind of thing isn't going to turn her head."

"How could it not? It's like when someone says to you, 'Doesn't that tag inside the neck of your T-shirt bother you? Doesn't it itch?' And all of a sudden, what do you know? — it *does* itch. That tag starts driving you crazy."

"The itch being — what? Living with a father who adores her but doesn't happen to be a zillionaire?"

They heard the squeak of the front-door hinges, the thud of Abby putting down her backpack, the *thump-thump-thump* of Rex's tail against the floor. Abby was talking to the dog as if he were either a young child or a moron. "How was your *day,* Rex? Have you been a *good* boy? Oh, why is your collar still on?" The dog's prong collar jingled. "Let's ask Daddy if he remembered to take you out for a walk."

When she walked to the kitchen, she looked more like a woman, less like a girl. In the couple of months since she'd become best friends with Jenna, she'd started dressing differently. Instead of her everyday uniform of light blue Juicy sweatpants and a plaid fleece-lined flannel shirt, untucked, she'd wear preppy-looking twin sets and leggings. She'd started using makeup. He wanted to tell her to stop, slow down. You have your whole life to be a grown-up. You only get to be a girl for a few years.

"For you." She pulled an envelope from the pile and dropped it on the table. He recognized the cream-colored paper stock of a Lyman Academy envelope. "Looks like another bill," she said. "Are we behind on the tuition again?"

"We're fine," he said. "Nothing to worry about. You have dinner yet? I've got some shrimp and linguine left, if you want it. Or I could make, I don't know, macaroni and cheese?"

"No, thanks," she said, her tone softening a bit. "I ate at the Galvins'."

"Great," he said, trying to sound upbeat. Lately she'd been having dinner most nights with Jenna and her family. Who could blame her? Dinner with just the two of them was often strained, punctuated by long silences. But still . . .

"I guess I get to meet them tomorrow night."

She nodded. "I know. You'll like them a lot."

"Hey, Abby," said Lucy, coming up from behind and giving Abby a quick peck on the cheek. "I love those flats. Tory Burch?"

Abby looked uncomfortable but, at the same time, pleased. "I guess."

Danny used to worry about how his

daughter would get along with his girlfriend. But she and Lucy seemed to be friends. Maybe it was because Lucy never tried to take Sarah's place. Maybe it was because Abby wanted another mother figure in her life. Maybe it was because Sarah had married a man Abby didn't like.

"They're so cute," Lucy said.

"Are they new?" Danny asked.

Abby's face reddened. She looked around theatrically and said, "What is this, like, the Style Network? Um, can I go do my homework now, please?"

"In a moment," Danny said. "We're talking."

Abby folded her arms and compressed her lips, making it clear how much talking she planned to do.

"I asked, are those shoes new?"

Abby looked at him steadily for a long moment, as if deciding how to reply. Finally, she said, "They're a gift from the Galvins, okay?"

"That's so nice," Lucy said, trying to calm the waters. She busied herself at the dining table, which was piled with books and papers and junk mail. She was smart enough not to get involved any further.

"A gift? For what occasion?"

"Occasion?" Abby's eyes widened. "I

mean, for standing there like a dork, watching Jenna buy stuff when we were at the Natick Mall this afternoon, because I don't have a credit card and I don't have any money, and she probably just felt sorry for me."

"She felt *sorry* for you?"

"She has her own Platinum American Express card and I don't even have, like, a debit card."

"That's terrible. How can a girl show her face if she doesn't have a Platinum AmEx card?"

Abby smoldered silently.

"If you wanted to buy something, you could have called me. You know that."

"And you would have said no."

"Maybe yes, maybe no. But at least you should have asked."

"Oh yeah, sure, I could see that. Like, 'Hi, Dad, I just saw the cutest pair of Tory Burch flats and Jenna just bought a pair and can I have two hundred dollars to buy them, too?' Like you would have said yes? At least why don't you be honest with *yourself*?"

"Two hundred dollars?" Danny said. "You're damned right I would have said no."

"See?"

Obviously, his daughter didn't mind receiving charity from the Galvins. "You

41

girls spent the afternoon at a shopping mall? What about your homework?"

"I didn't have my laptop with me."

"Why not?"

"You're talking about that MacBook that weighs, like, a thousand pounds? I don't think so."

"You carried it around all last year and didn't mind."

"And the year before and the year before and the year before. It's a dinosaur. It should, like, be on *Antiques Roadshow* or whatever."

He tried not to laugh. "If you need a new laptop, we can talk about it," he said. "Until then, why don't you invite Jenna over here sometime? Maybe you two can actually get some homework done."

Abby stared with incredulity. "Are you serious?"

"If you're concerned about privacy, I can go out and work somewhere while you girls are here. Find a Starbucks, whatever."

"You don't get it, do you?"

"What am I not getting?"

"You think I want her to see this . . . this *veal cage* we live in?"

Danny couldn't help bursting out laughing.

"It's not funny!" she protested.

"Of course it's not, sweetie," Danny said. When her mother was well, before her second marriage broke up, Abby had lived in a rambling old six-bedroom Victorian in Chestnut Hill that belonged to her stepfather, a partner in a big Boston law firm. Now she had no stepfather — not that she minded that — and no rambling house, and no mother.

He came closer, tried to put his arms around her, but she bucked away. "I just want to make sure you give yourself enough time to do your homework. This is a really important year. You know that. This fall, you'll be applying to colleges, and —"

"Seriously?" she said, stiffening. "Seriously?" Then, yelling: "I don't *believe* this!"

She spun around and ran into her bedroom and slammed the door.

Lucy glanced up from the dining table, gave a sad smile. She didn't need to say anything. She felt bad for both father and daughter; she understood the complexity. Her marriage, to an architect, had broken up, though amicably; her son, Kyle, was a sophomore at Bowdoin. She'd been through all this.

She ran her fingers through Danny's hair. "No one ever said teenagers were easy," she murmured.

6

Lucy woke early and made coffee for the two of them before leaving for work. Danny managed to get in a solid hour of writing before he heard the music coming from Abby's room.

Thumping, floor-vibrating bass, some kind of hip-hop. It wasn't so long ago that Abby awoke to some sweet twangy ballad by Taylor Swift or one of her many clones. Now everything she listened to sounded the same: Auto-Tuned vocal tricks and rants about being "on the floor" in "the club."

Twenty minutes later, he was sitting at the dining table reading *The Boston Globe* and sipping coffee from an oversize white mug that said *I ♡ My Daddy* in the spindly printing of a five-year-old. The *Y* looked like Poseidon's trident. Abby had made it at a friend's birthday party at a clay workshop in Brookline where kids decorated ready-made pieces of ceramic pottery. More than a decade ago, and he remembered it as if it were a few months.

Abby emerged from the bathroom in a steam cloud, wearing a bathrobe, hair wet from the shower. She came over to the small kitchen without acknowledging his presence and poured herself a bowl of Cinnamon Roll Frosted Mini-Wheats, doused it with Lactaid milk, and brought it over to the dining table.

"Any left for me?" she asked as she sat down.

"Any what?"

"That." She pointed at his coffee mug.

He grinned. "You're too young to get hooked on caffeine."

She slid the pile of mail in front of her and began flipping idly through the envelopes. "I mean, it's so not a big deal when I sleep over at the Galvins'. Celina always makes *café con leche* for Jenna and me."

"Celina is their housekeeper? Or their cook?"

"Keep up, Dad. She's Jenna's mom." She picked up the cream-stock envelope from Lyman and slid a finger under the flap. He didn't want her looking at the reminder note — no need for her to worry — but he also didn't want to make too big a deal of it, so he said nothing.

45

"Well, you're not at the Galvins', are you?" he said, and he couldn't hide his smile.

He'd solemnly sworn, when Sarah and he first saw that whooshing heartbeat on the fetal monitor, never to say all those trite, predictable things that all parents seem to say. Like: *As long as you live under my roof, you'll live by my rules* and *Because I said so* and *I don't care what the other kids do* and *Don't make me stop this car.*

He put the milk away in the refrigerator, and then he heard a high-pitched sound, a stifled cry, and he whirled around.

Abby was holding the Lyman letter in a trembling hand. The paper rattled. Her face had gone pale.

"Hey, don't worry about it," he said. "The check's a little late. I have to move some money around."

She was crying with an abandon that Danny had seen her do only once before, in the hospital room right after Sarah had died. There was barely any sound. Like she was gasping for breath. Or hiccupping. Her eyes were wide, her mouth open and down-turned. She looked almost in shock. Tears streamed down her cheeks.

Danny felt his insides clutch. She was overreacting, but he couldn't stand seeing her in pain. "Boogie," he said softly, coming

46

over to her and circling his arms around her shoulders from behind. "Abby. Baby, what's wrong?" He glanced at the letter and felt his stomach drop. Even though he glimpsed only fragments of sentences, it was enough to understand:

. . . *regret to inform* . . . *leave us no choice* . . . *immediate payment is received.* . . . *Abigail's school records* . . . *assist in the transfer to another school* . . .

Unless Lyman Academy received sixteen thousand dollars by five P.M. on Friday — three days from then — Abby would have to leave the school.

He squeezed her tight, her tears scalding his forearm, her chest heaving.

"Listen," he said, softly yet firmly, "that's not going to happen, okay?"

Then came a rush of words in one terrible anguished sob, most of which he couldn't make out. Just the words *all my friends* and *Daddy.*

The shape of her mouth when she'd let out a cry was precisely the same as it had been seconds after she'd been born, when the nurse had taken her, all of six pounds, from the obstetrician's gloved hands, swaddling her expertly in a blanket, and put her down on the warming table. Then this tiny infant had curled her tiny hands into fists and let out a great big gusty cry, the first of her life, announcing, *Hey, I'm here!*

And he knew he'd always do everything in his power to protect this little creature.

"Sweetie," he said. "Listen to me. Don't even think about it. That is *not* going to happen. You have my word."

But he knew his assurances were hollow, his promises empty, and he wondered whether she knew it, too.

7

Danny had been late with the tuition once before: last semester, in fact. But the bursar's office had let him slide for a few weeks. They must have gotten marching orders from the administration to be compassionate, since Abby's mother had died over the summer.

But Lyman's compassion apparently had its limits.

He had no pull at the school. The guy whose foundation Sarah had worked for, who'd been chairman of the Lyman board, had died of a stroke a couple of years ago.

So he decided to go straight to the top.

"I'm having sort of a silly little problem I thought you might be able to help me with," he told Lally Thornton when he finally got her on the phone. "Seems I'm a bit late with this semester's tuition — it's mostly a matter of liquidity. Moving money around and such. But I should have it cleared up in a week or so."

He paused, waited for her to say something reassuring. But there was only silence. Then she said, "And?"

Finally, he went on: "I thought you might be able to reassure the bursar's office for me."

"I'm sorry, I don't follow."

"You know, we got a form letter about Abby having to leave Lyman if the bursar doesn't receive a check by Friday or whatever. They're being pretty hard-line about it."

"Well, I'm not sure I understand why you called *me,* Mr. Goodman. This is a matter for the bursar's office. Not for the head of the Upper School."

"I've already spoken with them —"

"So I understand." Her tone had become downright icy. "You're not asking that an exception be made for you, I trust."

"Not an exception per se, but — well, a little leeway is all. A little compassion, really."

"I'm sorry, Mr. Goodman. I wish I could help. Please ask Abby to send me a note once she's settled at her new school, tell me how she's doing. I really am so fond of her."

Even if he could bring himself to ask Lucy

to lend him money, he knew she didn't have it to lend. She was barely getting by herself. So that was out.

His parents, Helen and Bud, lived modestly and always had, in the same small house in a development in Wellfleet, Massachusetts, on Cape Cod, where Danny had grown up. His dad was a contractor and a finish carpenter and a decent man, but he was irascible. He was a man who didn't take guff. He was always pissing people off. At the same time, he was a good person; he always paid his construction crew better than anyone else. Whenever any of them ran into trouble, he'd bail them out, lend them money and not keep track of what he was owed.

When he retired, he had hardly any savings. He and Danny's mother lived off Social Security.

Danny had no one to borrow the money from. At least, no family or friends.

He tried to remember why he was so uncomfortable about accepting a loan from Thomas Galvin for the Italy trip. Pride? That didn't seem like such a compelling reason anymore. He imagined a balance scale with his pride on one side — looking like some raw, shapeless, pulsing, purplish internal organ — and Abby's happiness on the other; he imagined Abby as a chubby, laughing baby wearing only a diaper. The chubby baby easily outweighed the pulsing blob. What had he been thinking? If he had jewelry to pawn, or anything of value to sell, he'd do it in a split second. If he knew a Vinny Icepick, he'd borrow sixteen large.

He had to find some money somewhere, somehow . . . and soon.

8

The town of Weston, ten miles west of Boston, was where a lot of the really rich Bostonians lived. Some of the houses out there were true McMansions, but the biggest ones were hidden from view by great swaths of forest, marked by nothing more than a street sign or a mailbox.

Danny drove past the entrance to Galvin's property three times without seeing it. There were no lights or stone columns or pillars or plaque. Just a simple aluminum mailbox with a number painted on it, not particularly large.

He turned down an unmarked road and followed its winding path through the woods until a set of tall wrought-iron gates, filigreed with ornate scrollwork and attached to tall stone columns, appeared in a clearing. He came to a stop. The gates were closed. Mounted to a column were a call box and a CCTV camera.

He cranked down the car window and pressed the CALL button. After a few seconds, a woman's voice crackled over the intercom, "Please come in."

The gates swung inward as low lights came on, illuminating another stretch of driveway, here paved with cut stone. The road curved gracefully around until suddenly an immense house loomed into view, like a castle appearing out of the mist.

It was Georgian, built of fieldstone with a slate roof. Its façade was perfectly illuminated by floodlights on the ground. It had graceful lines and was three stories high and almost half as long as Danny's block on Marlborough Street. Danny had been expecting a gaudy McMansion. But Galvin's house, though vast, was actually beautiful.

Off to one side was a full basketball court. Danny remembered clearly the day his father had installed an in-ground basketball hoop on a pole next to the blacktop of their driveway. How all the neighbor kids thought that was as cool as it got and wanted to use it at all times of day.

In front of the house was a circular drive. He pulled around, got out, slammed the door. Its rusty hinges squeaked.

The front door came open. It was a huge slab of ancient-looking oak that looked like it came from a castle in Spain. Galvin, in suit and tie, stood there with his wife. She was dazzling. She had glossy straight black hair and big brown eyes and a radiant smile and reminded him of Penélope Cruz, only a few years older. She was small and slim and wore a clingy, deep blue sheath that showed off a long waist and the swell of a voluptuous bosom. She didn't look old enough to have a kid who'd graduated from college.

Behind them, a couple of little rat-dogs skittered and yapped. They were tiny, hairless, and dark gray with outsize ears like a bat's. "Loco! Torito! Quiet!" the woman said. "I'm so sorry. They think they're protecting us, they're keeping us safe. I'm Celina."

Danny had expected a servant to open the door, a butler in livery. Not the hosts themselves. He introduced himself and handed her a bottle of wine in a metallic-looking red Mylar gift bag that someone had left in his apartment a couple of years ago when he still had people over for dinner.

Celina pulled the wine out of its bag and admired it as if it were a rare and expensive Bordeaux instead of an $8.99 special from the bargain bin at Trader Joe's. At least he'd sprung for the one with the fancy label instead of the Two-Buck Chuck.

"Châteauneuf-du-Pape!" Tom said. "Nice!" He nodded and gave Danny a sly smile. "That's red, right?"

"Not sure," Danny said, smiling back.

"Like I can tell Château Whatever from Welch's grape juice, right?" Galvin said. "But I can tell the fancy kind, because they're in French." He put a hand on Danny's shoulder, guiding him in, while Celina took his coat.

"Your daughter is in the kitchen, helping cook," Celina said.

"She knows how to do that?"

"Oh, Abby is a fantastic helper," Celina said, half scolding. "She does everything. She's like I have another daughter. I'm sorry, but you can't have her back." Her smile was dazzling. "We're keeping her."

"We do have an attractive long-term leasing plan," Danny said.

"Lina's always wanted another daughter," Tom said. "After two sons, she feels she's earned it."

Celina gave him a playful swat.

"No problem getting here?" Tom said.

"Actually, I think I might have made a couple of wrong turns on your driveway," Danny said. "Thank God for GPS." The Accord didn't actually have a nav system, but whatever.

Galvin cracked up. "Come say hi to the girls." The rat-dogs yapped and pranced alongside as they headed to the kitchen.

"I don't think I've ever seen dogs like that before," Danny said. "What's the breed?"

"Xoloitzcuintli," Celina said.

"I'm sorry, *what?*" All he could make out was something that sounded like *show* and maybe *queen.*

"Xolo," she said slowly. She pronounced it like *show-low.* "They're extremely rare. Mexican hairless. The ancient Aztecs thought they had magical healing powers."

"Oh, yeah?"

"They also ate them," her husband said.

"That is not true," Celina said sharply. "Why do you always say this?"

"It's true," Galvin said. "There are these Spanish accounts of huge banquets with platters heaping with Xoloitzcuintlis. I read it somewhere."

"Oh," she said. She sniffed. "Will you excuse me? I think they burn the garlic." She hurried down the hall.

"Probably tasted like chicken," Danny said.

Galvin roared with laughter. "I'm going to do you a big favor and not tell Lina you said that."

"I appreciate it."

"Hey, you didn't need to bring wine."

Danny shrugged. "Not a problem."

In a low, confiding voice, Galvin said, "Man, I love Trader Joe's. Ever try the Two-Buck Chuck? Not bad at all."

9

Busted.

Danny smiled, but winced inwardly.

It wasn't as if he'd tried to pass off a nine-dollar bottle of wine as a two-hundred-dollar Bordeaux, but now it looked like he'd been somehow sneaky about it. Anyway, how the hell did Galvin know about Trader Joe's? No way did a man who had his own home basketball *court* buy two-dollar bottles of wine.

But maybe that was the point. Maybe Galvin wanted to show he was just a regular guy.

Or maybe he was just ribbing Danny, the way guys do with their buddies.

In any case, Galvin obviously didn't miss a trick.

"I figure our girls are spending all this time together, we ought to get to know each other," he said.

Somewhere deep within the house, someone was practicing a classical piano piece, imperfectly but well. He heard Abby's laugh, smelled garlic and maybe fried chicken.

"Love your house," Danny said. "The layout is perfect."

"That's Celina. She worked with the architect. Made all the decisions. I didn't do squat."

Yeah, right, Danny thought. *All you had to do was shell out fifty million bucks for it.*

"Hey, so Abby says you guys live right in the city."

"Yep."

"You're lucky, man. Back Bay, huh? I've always wanted to live there. Walk to work. All that scenery. The college girls walking around in shorts."

"It's not bad."

"Celina likes the whole suburban thing. I just do what I'm told." He shrugged broadly.

Their kitchen was magnificent, bigger than any restaurant kitchen he'd seen. Copper pots hung from racks over two large islands topped with black stone. There were several wall ovens, and an enormous, gleaming burgundy commercial gas range with copper trim, looking like an antique steam engine. Danny's father had built a house in Wellfleet for a software magnate who'd

60

specified this same La Cornue range.

The vaulted ceiling was crisscrossed with hand-hewn beams that could have come from a medieval castle. The floor, ancient-looking limestone scarred and worn to a velvety patina, might have been salvaged from the same castle.

Jenna stood over a giant round skillet that was sputtering and smoking.

"*¡Ay, Dios mío!*" Celina said, rushing over to her daughter. "Don't burn the chicken, *mija*! Just brown it." The dogs scrabbled around the kitchen, yapping hysterically.

"I'm not burning it!" Jenna protested.

"Hey, Daddy," Abby said. Her smile faded a bit when she saw him. She avoided his eyes. She stood at one of the islands, mashing something in a bowl. Obviously, she was still upset or angry or both, still worrying about whether she'd have to leave school. She didn't believe her father had things under control, and he couldn't blame her.

"Hey, baby." Danny entered the kitchen, gave Abby a hug. "What're you making?"

"Guacamole. Nice kitchen, huh?"

If she intended a dig at their own, minuscule kitchen, he chose to ignore it. "Amazing." Bravo could film *Top Chef* here with room for a studio audience. "Make sure and mash those lumps out, huh?"

61

"No, Celina says it's not supposed to look like you used a blender."

Celina quickly came over, placing her hands on Abby's shoulders from behind. "In Mexico we make our guacamole always with little chunks in, just like she's doing." Danny could smell her perfume, something spicy and exotic. "That's perfect, *mi hija.* Ooh, I want to *keep* this girl! Can we have her?"

The second time it wasn't quite so funny, Danny thought.

Furtively, Danny ran a hand along the edge of the island. This wasn't granite. Its surface had the delicate crazing pattern of Pyrolave, glazed lava stone, ridiculously expensive. The software magnate in Wellfleet had ordered Pyrolave. Galvin's stone fabricator had done an awfully slick job, because you couldn't see a seam anywhere. Then he realized there was no seam because it was one huge slab. Holy crap, what that must have cost.

And that crazy little idea that had been tickling the back of his mind, drifting like tumbleweed way back there, suddenly lodged itself front and center.

He thought: *The guy probably spends sixteen thousand bucks a month on ties.*

I already owe him five thousand. What's

sixteen thousand more, really?

Seriously. Why not?

What was there to lose?

He looked up and caught Galvin watching him. Their eyes locked. Galvin smiled. Danny smiled uncomfortably back.

"Hey, were you feeling up my countertop?"

Embarrassed, Danny said, "I didn't know lava stone came that thick."

"You just do a renovation or something?"

"My dad was a contractor. I used to work for him."

"Yeah? My dad was a plumber."

"In Southie?"

"How'd you know?"

"I used to see those trucks around. Galvin Brothers Plumbing, right? The green shamrock?"

"See, I knew I liked this guy," Galvin said.

10

The two Galvin sons appeared from wherever they'd been hiding to join the family at dinner. Both of them were tall and rangy and good-looking: dark-haired and light-eyed, heavy brows and strong jaws. Brendan, the younger one, wore a Boston College sweatshirt, Old Navy sweatpants, and flip-flops. Ryan wore scruffy jeans and a Ron Jon Surf Shop T-shirt and was barefoot. He looked almost like Brendan's fraternal twin, only he was somehow more finished, more refined, his jawline sharper and his face more angular. Apart from the eyes, they both looked a lot more like their mother than their father.

"Brendan comes home once in a while to get a decent meal," Galvin said. He'd removed his jacket and wore gold suspenders over his white shirt. He'd loosened his tie. "Ryan, what's your excuse? Laundry piling up?"

"Very funny," Ryan said.

"I told him he can bring home all the dirty clothes he wants," said Celina, "but Manuela's not going to do it for him. He can do his own laundry. We're not a hotel." She clapped her hands together briskly in front of her a few times to emphasize her point.

Brendan was a sophomore at BC, and Ryan had graduated the year before and was doing some sort of scut work at a TV station. It sounded to Danny like he was supporting himself. His father, the gazillionaire, wasn't paying the rent. That was interesting.

Abby seemed to fit right in, as if she were the Galvins' second daughter. She and Jenna whispered about something, and Abby giggled. Their plates were piled high with chicken and rice and beans, the most delicious *arroz con pollo* Danny had ever tasted.

"So you're a writer, huh?" Galvin said.

"Yup."

"Very cool." Galvin sat at one end of the long oak farm table in the kitchen, his wife at the other. The sons sat across from the two girls. They shifted in their chairs and feigned interest. The dogs slept under the table.

"Well, I don't know about *cool,* but . . .

it's a job."

"You write under your own name, or do you have a pen name?"

"Under my name. Daniel Goodman." Danny got asked that a lot. It was a polite way of saying *I've never heard of you.*

"I've always wanted to write a book, but I can never find the time. I got stories to tell. Maybe when I retire."

Danny was always amused when people told him they'd love to write if only they had the time. As if the only thing that held them back from a successful writing career was a lack of leisure.

"Yeah, well, I guess I'm just lucky enough to have all this free time on my hands," he said.

Galvin chuckled. "Ya got me there. So, you write novels or what?"

"Nonfiction." He clarified: "Biography."

Galvin held up the bottle of wine Danny had brought and waggled it. "No, thanks," Danny said. Galvin topped off his own glass.

"Anything I've read?" Galvin said.

"The Kennedys of Boston."

"Huh. That sounds familiar. About Jack Kennedy and his family?"

"More about Jack Kennedy's grandfather, 'Honey Fitz' Fitzgerald, who used to be mayor of Boston a hundred years ago. The

66

founder of the Kennedy dynasty. A colorful character."

"*Colorful* usually means corrupt," Galvin pointed out.

Danny smiled. "Exactly. Corrupt yet beloved."

"Working on one now?"

"Always."

"What's it about?"

Danny hesitated. The phrase *robber baron* might not sound so good to Galvin's ears. Especially if Danny were about to ask him for a loan. "A biography of a nineteenth-century businessman."

"Yeah? When can I get my copy?"

"Mom, will you tell Brendan to give me back my shoe?" Jenna said.

"Give your sister her shoe," Celina said.

"I don't have it," Brendan said, poker-faced.

"He, like, took it off with his feet," Jenna said. "He's like a *monkey.*"

"All of you, *ya basta*!" Celina said. "Are you six year old?"

Danny was grateful for the interruption, but Galvin didn't give up: "When's your new book go on sale? Maybe I'll pick up a copy."

"You'll have to wait a while," Danny said. "I'm still writing it."

"Going well?"

"A little slow, frankly. Life gets in the way sometimes."

"You ever get writer's block?" asked Ryan, the older son.

"Nope. It's a job like any other. Plumbers don't get plumber's block, right?"

"I like that," Galvin said. "You hear that, kids? That's called a work ethic. No one tells him to work. He just sits down every day and makes himself write, whether he likes it or not."

Danny nodded uneasily.

A sudden blast of music came from somewhere. Danny recognized the opening guitar riff from "Sweet Home Alabama" by Lynyrd Skynyrd, rendered tinnily as a ringtone. Galvin got up and took a BlackBerry out of the breast pocket of his suit coat hanging on a peg. He glanced at the number, answered it. "I'm at dinner," he said abruptly. A long pause. "It's dinnertime. I'm having dinner with my family." Another pause, then he snapped: "I *said* . . . I can't."

Danny had the feeling he'd just seen a side of Galvin he didn't like to show.

Galvin jabbed at the BlackBerry to end the call. "Man oh man, ever have one of those days when it feels like everyone wants something from you?"

Danny swallowed hard. "All the time."

Maybe asking him for a loan wasn't such a good idea after all.

"How's the job search going, Bren?"

Brendan shrugged. "I don't know."

"Let me know if I can make some calls for you."

"It's okay."

"You don't want to spend the summer on the beach in Nantucket again, do you?" his father said, a glint in his eye. "Be one of those losers in wet suits who spend all their time surfing?"

"I'm trying," Brendan said sullenly.

"Aw, he's in college, Tommy," Celina said. "He can play. It's okay for him to get a job after college."

"What's wrong with spending the summer on the beach in Nantucket?" asked Jenna, indignant. "Why does he *have* to get a job?"

"That's right," said Celina, "why?"

Galvin grinned. "Now the girls are ganging up on me. Help me out here, Danny. Give me some cover."

Danny shook his head, unwilling to be lured into a family tiff. "Sorry, man, you're on your own."

"Danny, you guys go to the Cape for the summer, right?" said Galvin. "How long have you had a house in Wellfleet?"

"Wellfleet?" Danny didn't remember telling Galvin that his parents lived in Wellfleet, that he'd grown up there. And he definitely hadn't said anything about summers.

"Your summer place. Abby told us all about it."

"Summer place in Wellfleet?" he said sardonically. "Yeah, I wish —"

Then he caught a glimpse of Abby twisting uncomfortably and blushing.

He realized she'd been trying to impress the Galvins by turning her grandparents' modest tract house in Wellfleet into something it wasn't, the place where she "summered" every year.

And then he quickly finished the sentence: "— wish it didn't take so long to get there."

"Cape traffic's brutal on the weekends," Galvin agreed.

But Danny could see the amused detachment in his eyes and knew that Galvin had picked up on his slip.

Galvin didn't miss a thing.

After dinner, Galvin excused himself to take another call in his study. There was no kitchen help in sight. Danny wondered whether this was the maid's night off or something. Then Abby and Jenna tried to

70

teach Brendan some kind of complicated dance as a song came blasting over speakers concealed throughout the kitchen, something about "party rock" being "in the house tonight."

Brendan and the two girls hopped up and down, running in place, pivoting from one side to another, dipping low and then high. They shuffled and slid and moonwalked. Brendan scooped up one of the dogs and tried to manipulate its paws around to simulate dancing, but it struggled and growled menacingly, and Abby and Jenna dissolved in a fit of laughter.

She seemed genuinely happy here. Danny finally understood why she was so drawn to the Galvins. It wasn't their wealth. It was the big and warm, chaotic and welcoming Galvin clan that she longed to be part of.

She wanted to be a member of a family.

Galvin returned to the kitchen after a few minutes. He stood next to Danny for a moment, watching the kids dance.

"Cute, huh?"

Danny nodded.

"She's such a good kid, your daughter. She brings out something in Jenna we haven't seen before. In years, anyway."

"Hmm," Danny said and nodded again. "They both seem happy."

"That's what I mean. Hey, how about we step away? Feel like a single malt?"

Danny hesitated for a moment — he'd already had a glass of bad red wine and had to drive home on the turnpike — but before he could reply, Galvin said, "I need to ask you a favor."

11

Tom Galvin poured them each a few fingers of whiskey from a bottle whose label read THE MACALLAN 1939. He stood at a wet bar in his study. The walls were lined with leather-bound volumes that were probably purchased by the yard and had never been read. Everything smelled like cigar smoke.

"Not everyone gets the good stuff, you know."

A quiet knock at the door. They both turned. It was Esteban, the driver. Danny realized he'd never heard him speak.

"Eh, Mr. Galvin, will I be driving your guests home?" Esteban's voice was soft, his speech halting. He was unusually tall and broad, but his black suit fitted him perfectly. He had a large head, pockmarks on his high cheeks, and Bambi eyes. A large mole on the right side of his neck in the shape of Australia. A strange-looking fellow, neither ugly nor attractive, but somehow gentle and kindly seeming.

"Go to bed, *mi amigo*."

"Thank you, sir." Esteban made a slight bow, more a nod of the head, and was gone.

Galvin finished pouring and handed Danny a cut-glass tumbler. They clinked glasses. "Here's to our wives and girlfriends," he said. "May they never meet."

Danny smiled and nodded. In the back of his mind he wondered what "favor" Galvin could possibly want from him.

"Your daughter is Jenna's only friend, you know," Galvin said.

"I know they're close."

"She's such a good influence on Jenna. I mean, Jenna's actually doing the assigned reading for school without bitching and moaning about it. Like, she actually read *To Kill a Mockingbird,* and we didn't have to nag her once."

"I read it out loud to Abby when she was probably too young for it, but . . . yeah, she's a reader. Nice to know they talk about books, not just hip-hop or dubstep or whatever."

"It's like . . . if you surround yourself with good people, it makes you a better person. Brings out the best in you. Surround yourself with bad people, it brings out your worst. Every other school she's gone to, last couple of years, she always seemed to fall in with the druggy, no-good kids. Bad influence. But Abby brings out the best in her. You have no idea how amazing that is." Galvin's eyes shone, as if they might be moist.

"That's great," Danny said, not knowing what else to say, surprised by the unexpected intimacy of the moment.

"You're doing something right, brother."

"Me? Nah, I just try not to get in her way too much. I don't know what I'm doing. I screw up all the time."

Galvin smiled. "So you're raising Abby yourself? How the hell do you do it?"

"Hmm," Danny said, half smiling, scratching the side of his face. He looked up and said musingly, "You know those old disaster movies when the airline pilot has a heart attack and the flight attendant has to fly the plane?"

He smiled. "Karen Black in *Airport 1975*? Or maybe it was *Airplane!* and it was Julie something. . . ."

Danny smiled back. "Exactly. Whatever. You know, suddenly I'm supposed to know how to fly this thing? But you don't have a choice."

Galvin shook his head. "Man, I gotta hand it to you. If it wasn't for Celina, I can't even

75

imagine . . ."

He beckoned Danny over to a couple of overstuffed leather chairs in front of a cluttered antique desk, where they sat. From a low table next to his chair, he lifted a glossy black lacquer box with gold lettering on top that said COHIBA BEHIKE. He lifted the lid and pulled out a couple of cigars, fat as sausages, and offered one to Danny.

Danny nodded, and the solemn ritual began. Galvin handed him a cigar cutter. Danny snipped the end of his cigar, then handed the cutter back. Galvin lit his cigar with a lighter whose hard blue flame looked like it could cut steel. He took a few puffs, and handed the lighter to Danny.

They smoked silently for a minute or so. Danny remembered why he never liked cigars. He thought about complimenting Galvin on the cigar. But what could he say, that it made him only mildly nauseated? Instead, he pointed his cigar at a wooden presentation case on the desk. Seated in a bed of red velvet flocking was a bronze medal that said COLLEGIUM BOSTONIENSE.

"You're a distinguished alum of BC?"

He nodded. "President's Medal for Giving a Shitload of Money."

Danny laughed. Galvin was self-effacing

about it, but he still kept the medal on display.

"Wanna know something?" Galvin finally said, contemplative. "I'm just a lucky son of a bitch. I know that sounds like some kind of bullshit false modesty, but believe me." He looked up at the ceiling. "Ever drive somewhere and you're pressed for time, but you just hit all the green lights, one after another? You know, boom boom boom — you just hit 'em all right? You just luck out?"

Danny nodded.

"Well, that's me. God's honest truth. Hand to heart." He placed a palm over his heart. "Look up *right place, right time* in the dictionary, you're gonna see my picture."

"I doubt that, but . . . okay."

"Now, I don't want you to take this the wrong way. But listen to me when I tell you: I've been rich and I've been poor."

"Let me guess which one's better."

"Not gonna argue with you there," he said with a grin. He pulled something out of his inside breast pocket and handed it to Danny: a folded slip of paper.

"Here's the favor," Galvin said. "Take this without giving me a hard time."

It was a check for fifty thousand dollars, written on Galvin's personal account at J.P. Morgan Private Bank.

Danny looked up. "What's this?"

"A year's tuition at that damned over-priced girls' school, plus some breathing room."

"What — what are you . . . ?" Danny was momentarily at a loss for words.

"Lyman is Jenna's fourth school in three years. We've pulled her out of Winsor and Milton and BB&N and — jeez Louise, I can't keep 'em straight. She always falls in with a bad crowd. Or they all think she's stuck-up. . . . The word gets out that her daddy has some money, and the kids go all *Mean Girls* on her. I don't get it. Now, finally, she has a close friend who's a really good person, and I don't want anything to screw that up."

"But . . . but what made you . . . how do you know . . . ?"

"I have my sources."

Danny's head was spinning. A few minutes ago he was weighing whether to ask Galvin for a fraction of this, and now . . . Abby must have said something to Jenna; that had to be what happened. "I can't possibly accept this. I mean . . . and anyway, this is way more than I need."

"So don't spend it all."

"I don't know when I can pay you back. I mean, I have some money coming from my publisher . . . at some point, but I —"

"Pay when you can."

"I — I don't know, I'm uncomfortable about this." Not so uncomfortable, of course, that he'd turn it away. But it seemed like the right thing to say. He recalled how upset Abby looked earlier, in the kitchen. How she'd cried when she'd opened the letter from Lyman telling her she'd have to leave school.

"For Christ's sake, don't get all, like, WASPy and uptight on me. You and me, we're not like that. Believe me, I deal with guys like that all the time. I could buy and sell most of these snotty a-holes in the Financial District, but God forbid they should let me into the country club, right?"

Danny smiled and nodded. He assumed Galvin was talking about an exclusive place actually called The Country Club, outside of Boston. It sounded like he'd applied and been turned away, or been blackballed or something.

Danny nodded. "When someone told Mark Twain that Andrew Carnegie's money was tainted, he said, it sure is — 'tain't yours and 'tain't mine."

Galvin guffawed. "There you go. Yeah, we come from the same place, you and me. My dad busted his butt to raise ten children.

Your dad was a contractor. Neither one of us was born with a silver spoon in his mouth."

"This is incredibly generous of you."

"Way I see it, this fifty thousand bucks won't even fill the fuel tanks of my boat, okay? If Abby leaves Lyman, I really don't know what the hell Jenna's gonna do. So if you don't think I'd spend fifty thousand dollars to ensure my daughter's happiness, well, you don't know me." His stare burned into Danny's eyes. He looked almost angry. His tone was grave. "I would consider it an honor if you would accept this."

Danny studied the pale blue check. Tears welled up in his eyes, which usually only happened when he remembered Sarah's last days. "Can I ask you something?"

"Of course."

His cheeks were burning. "Do you think you could wire it instead?"

12

The fifty thousand dollars hit Danny's bank account by noon the next day.

He checked the balance online. Refreshed his browser a few times. He wanted to make sure it was really there. That it wasn't an illusion. It was there, and it stayed there.

It was real. Tom Galvin was as good as his word.

Fifty thousand dollars. A lot of money. Not enough to pay off everything he owed, certainly. That would be like trying to put out a house fire with a glass of water. But it would quench enough of the fire to clear a path out of the house, to let him escape the burning wreckage.

Most important, to protect Abby.

He called the Lyman Academy and asked to speak to the bursar, Leah Winokur. The woman whose calls he'd been avoiding for weeks.

She sounded surprised to hear his voice,

and not pleased. He told her he was going to drop off a check when he picked Abby up in a few hours.

Haltingly, Leah Winokur replied, "I'm sorry, but today's the deadline. Five o'clock today."

"And I'll see you at two thirty."

"I'm afraid that's going to be too late, Mr. Goodman. Technically, the funds have to be received in the school's bank account by five o'clock today. A personal check won't clear in time. Unless it's a cashier's check, or —"

"I'll wire it to you right now," he said. "Will that do?"

On the way home from school, he said, "Abby, I wanted to set your mind at ease. I got things straightened out with the bursar's office."

She let out a breath. "Oh my God. Oh my God. Oh, thank you, Daddy. Oh my God. Thank God."

No, thank Galvin, he thought but didn't say.

"I love you, Daddy," she said in a small voice, barely audible.

"I love you, Boogie."

At home, Abby disappeared into her room to do homework, while he sat at his laptop and tried to work on the book. Distracted, he Googled the name of the cigar Galvin and he had smoked in his study. A limited edition Cohiba Behike from Cuba. Maybe he'd buy Galvin a box as a thank-you gift.

He did a double take. Only four thousand of these particular cigars had been produced.

They cost over four hundred dollars *each*.

He had smoked a cigar that cost four hundred dollars, and he didn't even like it.

Then he Googled the single malt Galvin had poured, the 1939 Macallan 40 Year Old. And did another double take.

Over ten thousand dollars per bottle.

Abby emerged from her bedroom around seven. "What's for supper?" she said.

"How's pasta?"

She shrugged. "Whatever."

The phone rang, and Abby picked it up.

"Daddy, it's for you." She covered the phone's mouthpiece. "Someone from something to do with . . . stamps?"

He took the phone. "Yes?"

"Is this Daniel Goodman?" A man's voice, cordial and professional.

"Who's this?"

"Mr. Goodman, my name is Glenn Yeager. I'm with the United States Postal Service in Boston."

83

"Um . . . yes?" he said warily. "What's this about?"

The man laughed. "I'm with the postmaster general's office, and one of my responsibilities is administering something called the Citizens' Stamp Advisory Committee. You may have heard of it?"

"No, I'm sorry."

"Well, I'll keep this brief. The committee meets four times a year to decide what goes on postage stamps."

"There's a committee for that?"

"Quite an illustrious committee, in fact. It's made up of fifteen prominent citizens — artists, musicians, writers, corporate leaders, historians. Public figures. The meetings are held in Washington, and of course all your expenses are covered. And there's a generous per diem for expenses."

"I'm sorry, I don't understand. What does this have to do with me?"

"Well, Mr. Goodman, Doris Kearns Goodwin had to drop out at the last minute — a tight book deadline, I think it was — and your name came up. We wanted a writer with expertise in American history."

"You're kidding."

"The reason I'm calling at this late hour is that we need to fill this vacancy immediately. We were wondering whether you might be able to come by our offices in Boston tomorrow morning."

"I — tomorrow?" Danny paused. "Sure, that's fine. What time?"

"Say, eleven. And it won't take more than half an hour. Just some routine questions for the press release and forms and what have you. I know this is terribly last-minute, but if it's at all possible . . ."

"Sure," Danny said. "No problem."

"Wonderful," Mr. Yeager said. "We're all excited to meet you. I'm a big fan of your Kennedy book, by the way."

"So you're the one," Danny said, one of his standard jokes.

Mr. Yeager chuckled, and gave directions. "One last thing," he said. "I need to ask you to keep all this confidential until the official announcement. The government, you know."

When he hung up, Abby said, "What was that all about?"

"Some — government committee," he said. "They want my input on who gets put on postage stamps." He shrugged.

Maybe the old saying was right: Good news really did come in bunches.

When it rains, it pours.

13

The next morning, Danny wrote more than he had in a year. He was on fire. His fingers flew at the keyboard, the sentences spewing out of him like tape out of one of those old stock tickers. By the time he stopped, at a few minutes after noon, he'd written eighteen pages.

It was that drink with Galvin that did it.

The way Galvin had talked about how those snooty blue-blood types had looked down on his money. Galvin, the plumber's son who'd made a fortune, thought of himself as an outsider and always would.

Something had flicked a switch in his brain, because he finally understood Jay Gould. The problem had been that he didn't like his subject. Because he didn't quite understand him. But Gould was no worse, really, than any of the other business titans of his time. He gave to charity, gave money to his employees and to all sorts of people in need. He just didn't publicize it. Jay Gould's career was your classic rags-to-riches story. He was born on a farm in upstate New York and went to New York City with five dollars in his pocket. After he hit it big, the newspapers of the time trashed him, and he didn't bother to defend himself. He let his enemies write his biography. That was his strategic blunder.

Buzzing with satisfaction, Danny called a taxi and got a ride to downtown Boston, to the big ugly building called One Center Plaza, where the stamp commission had its offices, along with a bunch of other government agencies. He got there fifteen minutes early. He had his laptop with him in a shoulder bag, in case he needed to do some work.

The offices were on the second floor. There was no sign on the door, just a number: 322. The gray wall-to-wall carpeting was soiled, a large blob of a stain at the threshold of the office door.

A pretty young African American secretary was sitting at a cheap-looking government-issue L-shaped mahogany-laminate reception desk. She smiled and held up an index finger to signal she'd be with him shortly. After a minute or so she said, "I'm sorry, Mr. . . . Goodman, right?"

He nodded, smiled.

"Would you like to have a seat? I'll let them know you're here."

He sat in one of a row of chairs against one wall under the DEA seal, which showed a stylized eagle's head in gold on black. Most Wanted posters lined the walls, offering MONETARY AWARDS for MAJOR TRAFFICKERS.

About two minutes later, she said, "He'll be right out."

The door to the inner offices opened and a squat, slump-shouldered man in an ill-fitting navy suit emerged. He had a large bald head a size too big for his body, almost no neck, and a fringe of wispy gray hair that reached his collar. With his thin downturned mouth, he vaguely resembled a frog. He had a bristly mustache and a face that bore the scars of serious teenage acne. He wore steel-rimmed bifocals and looked to be around fifty.

"Mr. Goodman, thank you for coming," the man said. "I'm sorry to keep you waiting. Special Agent Glenn Yeager."

Danny rose slowly, and they shook hands. "Did you say 'Special Agent' . . . ?"

"Come on in. We'll have a talk and I'll explain. This shouldn't take long at all," the man called Yeager said, holding the door open for Danny.

They went down a long corridor. Yeager seemed to have a slight limp. The walls were curved, following the curve of the building's façade, and painted government-agency white. The floor was covered in ugly gray indoor-outdoor carpeting.

Yeager stopped at the first open door. A man was sitting at a round conference table in a small windowless room, talking on the phone, papers and folders spread out in front of him. He put down the phone's handset when he saw the men, and got to his feet.

"Mr. Goodman, this is Special Agent Philip Slocum."

Slocum was slim and had shoe-polish-black hair parted on one side and an athlete's wiry build. He was whippetlike. His face was sharp and inquisitive, foxlike, lean and lined, with a heavy five-o'clock shadow. He looked coiled, compact and restless. Instead of offering his hand, he showed Danny a black leather badge holder.

The badge was gold-colored metal. The words DEPARTMENT OF JUSTICE over an eagle and, below it, the words US DRUG ENFORCEMENT ADMINISTRATION and SPE-CIAL AGENT and a number.

"You guys are DEA?" Danny said. "Now

I'm totally confused. What's this got to do with postage stamps?"

"I trust you haven't mentioned this meeting to anyone," said Yeager. He spoke in a precise, almost scholarly tone you wouldn't expect to emanate from that froglike mouth. He sat at the round table, and beckoned Danny to do the same.

Danny remained standing and gave a barely perceptible nod. "What's going on?"

"It's for your own protection."

"My *protection*? The citizens' stamp committee —"

"Was a pretext to get you in here, Mr. Goodman," said Yeager. He glanced at his colleague, who slid a sheet of paper across the table to Danny.

"Do you know what this is?" Yeager said. He seemed to be the one in charge.

The paper was covered with columns of figures. At first glance it meant nothing. When he looked closer, he saw his name and his bank's name and his checking account number.

Then: *WIRE IN* and a series of numbers and the words *T. X. GALVIN* and more numbers and *$50,000.00*.

"Is that your bank account?" Yeager said.

"Yes."

"This record is accurate? Thomas Galvin

paid you fifty thousand dollars?"

"He didn't 'pay' me anything. It's a loan. Anyway, what the hell kind of invasion of privacy — ?"

"Do you have paperwork for this 'loan'?"

"Paperwork? A guy lends a friend some cash, he doesn't make you go to a notary."

"Thomas Galvin gave you fifty thousand dollars without any paperwork?"

"He's a friend. He trusts me."

"I'll bet he does," the other one, Slocum, said. His raspy tenor had the harsh sound of metal grinding against metal. His right leg vibrated, pistoned.

"You mind telling me what this is all about?"

"Thomas Galvin is the target of a DEA investigation."

"Drugs? You seriously think . . . ? He's an Irish Catholic guy from Southie, for Christ's sake."

"Ever hear of the Sinaloa cartel?" said Yeager.

"Mexican drug ring? What about it?"

"We have reason to believe that Thomas Galvin is working on behalf of the Sinaloa cartel."

Danny stared in disbelief. Then he erupted in laughter. "Ah, now I get it. The Mexican wife. Sure. He's married to a Mexican woman, so he *must* be connected to a drug cartel. Because, of course, all Mexicans work for the drug cartels, right?"

"Celina Galvin's father was Humberto Parra Fernández y Guerrero," Yeager said.

"Am I supposed to know who that is?"

"The former governor of Michoacán, one of the Mexican states, and later on a major player in the narcotics trade."

"Oh, for God's sake. This is insane. Galvin's an Irish guy from Southie. He doesn't seem like the kind of guy who'd get involved in the drug business. Not at all."

"And you know this . . . how?"

Danny paused for a long moment. "He just doesn't seem the type."

Yeager gave him a long stare. "Neither do you."

"Excuse me?"

"Please sit down, Mr. Goodman."

Danny's heart was beating crazily, though he wasn't sure whether out of panic or out of anger. He stood with his arms loosely folded. "What's this all about?"

"You are directly and financially linked to the international narcotics trade."

"That's ridiculous," said Danny.

"That money links you," Slocum said. "You are now officially a coconspirator."

"Hold on a second," Danny said, raising

his voice. "Tom Galvin was nice enough to lend me money for my daughter's god-damned private-school tuition!" He paused, looked at each agent one at a time, then went on more quietly. "Two hours after I received the money from Galvin, I wired sixteen thousand dollars to the Lyman Academy. So maybe you can tell me how that fits into your theory."

"It makes no difference what you did with the funds," Slocum said. "I don't care if you gave it all to an orphanage in Rwanda. You received a wire transfer of dirty money, which means you're implicated."

"Yeah?" said Danny. "And how was I supposed to know that?"

"Look up 'willful blindness' or 'conscious avoidance,' " Yeager said. "The court assumes you didn't ask any questions because *you didn't want to know* where Galvin's money came from. You deliberately closed your eyes to the crime."

"Which means," Slocum said, "you can be prosecuted even if you claim you didn't know a thing."

Danny swallowed hard. The room seemed to tilt one way, then the other. "*Prosecuted? For what?* For innocently accepting —"

"Please listen closely," said Yeager. "We are a phone call away from making an appointment with the US Attorney. Once that happens, the toothpaste's out of the tube."

"What the hell *is* this?" Danny's mouth had gone dry. He was having difficulty getting the words out.

Slocum gave a small, nasty smile. "This is conspiracy to commit money laundering, mail and wire fraud, and bank fraud. And that's just for starters. You're looking at thirty to forty years in prison."

"That's federal time," said Yeager. "Know what that means? No parole."

"Then again," said Slocum, "I don't think you'd last very long in prison. Our Mexican friends are going to worry about how much you know, whether you're going to start co-operating. They have guys in our prisons everywhere. We can't protect you."

"You don't seriously think you can prosecute me on these bogus, trumped-up charges, do you?" said Danny.

"I like our odds," said Yeager.

Slocum shrugged. "Even if these charges don't hold up in court? You really want to spend the next five years of your life fighting the system? We're the government. We've got hot-and-cold running lawyers and all the time in the world. You, on the other hand? You hire a half-decent lawyer to try to get you out of this, your legal bills could reach a couple million dollars by the time all's said and done. Doesn't look like you have that kind of money in the bank."

"And I wouldn't count on your friend Galvin to bankroll your defense," said Yeager.

"Not once we seize his assets," said Slocum. "And yours. Your condo, your crappy car, and that thirty-two K in retirement money? Gone. Poof."

"Sure, in the end, you might be able to persuade a judge and jury to acquit you," Yeager said. "Though I wouldn't want to bet on it, since the Department of Justice rarely loses a case. In the meantime, you and your family will be dragged through the gutter. Good luck trying to get your good name back. Your poor daughter — Abigail, right? — having to live under that shadow? Terrible thing to do to a kid."

Dazed, his head reeling, Danny sank down into a chair. "What the hell do you want?" he said.

14

"Your help, that's all. We just want your co-operation," Yeager said.

"On what?" Danny said.

"Access to Galvin. You seem to be one of the few people he spends time with."

"I barely know the guy," Danny said. "Before last night, I don't think I'd said ten words to him."

"Yeah?" said Slocum. "What happened to 'he's a friend, he trusts me'?"

"Your daughter certainly spends a lot of time with his daughter," said Yeager.

"Keep my daughter out of this."

"I wish we could. But if you refuse to cooperate, we'll have no choice."

Danny felt nauseated. "Meaning what? What kind of cooperation are you talking about?"

Yeager looked like he was about to reply, but then he fell silent. He slid a piece of paper across the table toward Danny.

Then Slocum said, "As soon as you sign the cooperation agreement, we'll get into the weeds."

Danny scanned it quickly. It said *Confidential Source Agreement* and *DEA form 473.*

It felt almost unreal, as if he'd stepped out of his ordinary life and into another world. *Confidential source. The Drug Enforcement Administration.*

It was sickening.

He tried to steel himself, to gather the resources necessary to fight back. "What do I get if I sign this?"

Yeager said slowly, "A pass on prosecution. A chance for a happy ending."

Danny's heart thudded and he felt acid rising in his gullet. Was there actually a way out of this nightmare? "But . . . what do you want me to do?"

Yeager turned to Slocum, who nodded, almost imperceptibly.

Slocum said, "We need an ear inside Galvin's house."

Danny looked at him for a few seconds. "Jesus Christ. . . . You want me to wear a *wire*?"

"Sign the form and we'll talk specifics," said Slocum.

He shook his head. "I want to talk to a lawyer. I have that right."

Yeager shrugged, palms up. "Be our guest. But one word of warning?"

Danny looked at him and waited.

"You might want to be careful who you talk to."

"Actually, I'll talk to whoever the hell I please."

Yeager shrugged. "Of course you will. But there's a reason we brought you in the way we did. These cartels have eyes and ears everywhere. If the word gets out that you've been meeting with the DEA, your value as a CS is blown."

"CS?" asked Danny.

"Confidential source," said Yeager.

"If they find out you met with us," said Slocum, and he sliced a finger across his throat. He gave a leering smile. "So you might wanna be careful who you confide in."

For a long moment, Danny examined the floor, the worn gray industrial carpet. His head swam. He needed to gather his thoughts, get some topnotch legal advice, be very careful about his next move. Whichever way he decided to go, the consequences were serious and permanent.

"If I decide to sign this," he said, "how do I get in touch with you? Just . . . come back here?"

"Absolutely not," said Yeager. "This is a satellite office for our group. A gray site. Undisclosed working location."

"Think about it like this," Slocum said. "The cartel keeps a close watch on the main DEA headquarters in the JFK Federal Building — who comes and goes. They see someone associated with Galvin going in for a meeting at DEA? They're gonna do something about that."

Yeager wrote a number on the back of his business card and handed it to Danny. "Call this number when you want to come back."

Slocum said, "You really don't want to take your time about it."

"Or what?"

"Or the deal's off the table. And we come after you with handcuffs."

15

Danny stumbled out of One Center Plaza into the blazing sunlight. He felt numb.

He found a Starbucks and got a coffee and sat for a while and thought. He was, it seemed, well and truly screwed.

He signed on to the Internet. Googled "sinaloa cartel."

Google's autocomplete feature suggested a few similar searches:

sinaloa cartel *chainsaw*
sinaloa cartel *members*
sinaloa cartel *news*

Unable to stop himself, he selected "sinaloa cartel **chainsaw.**" He clicked on that link and clicked ENTER to confirm he was eighteen years of age or older, and a video started to play.

It showed a couple of paunchy shirtless guys in Mexico. Talking in Spanish. Probably dope dealers or hit men for the Sinaloa cartel. Very bad guys, looking scared as children, tied up on the ground, against an adobe wall.

Then someone comes out wearing military camo fatigues and starts up a chain saw, the kind you'd use to cut down a tree. In a few seconds, he beheads both of them. Once second they're alive, the next they're decapitated.

They were snitches, the caption said.

A confidential informant was a kind of snitch.

This video had a sound track. A type of Mexican folk song called *narcocorrido:* guitars and trumpet and accordion, set to a polka beat. *Narcocorrido* ballads were odes to the murderers and torturers of the drug cartels. The folk heroes.

Somehow that made it worse, the jaunty, galumphing happy *narcocorrido* sound track instead of the victim's screams.

Within a couple of minutes he'd seen photographs of fourteen cartel soldiers chainsawed into sections, legs and heads and torsos, arrayed on the ground like the parts of an expertly carved Thanksgiving turkey.

Well and truly screwed.

He needed to talk to someone, an expert. A criminal defense lawyer. But he didn't know any.

Sarah's ex-husband was a lawyer. His ex-wife's ex-husband. That was complicated and fraught enough to make his head hurt.

No, thanks.

Lucy's college roommate was a corporate lawyer, a big shot in DC. Lawyers always knew other lawyers. Sometimes they knew only other lawyers. He took out his cell phone and hit the speed dial for Lucy.

Then hit END before the call went through.

Telling Lucy what kind of trouble he was in was a major decision, one he couldn't undo. He needed to think that over.

Not yet.

He knew someone. A guy who'd lived across the hall freshman year. Jay Poskanzer spent most of his life in Butler, Columbia's great library. Nerdy, tightly wound, brilliant, acerbic. He'd gone to Harvard Law and clerked for a Supreme Court justice and later became a hotshot lawyer in private practice.

His specialty, Danny was pretty sure, was criminal law.

He needed someone in criminal law. Someone really good.

He picked up his phone again and made the call.

16

Jay Poskanzer was considered one of the best criminal defense attorneys in Boston. He regularly appeared on *Boston* magazine's list of the city's Top Power Lawyers.

He was a partner at Batten Schechter, a powerhouse firm on the forty-eighth floor of the Hancock Tower. From the plate-glass windows of his office, you could see the Back Bay and the Charles River and the Financial District, arrayed in miniature like a raised-relief map. His office was cluttered with sports memorabilia: signed broken baseball bats, framed signed photos of Red Sox players in action, a framed piece of the old Boston Garden parquet floor.

Poskanzer had frizzy reddish-brown hair with a lot of gray in it, balding on top. He had tortoiseshell glasses, a nasal voice, and a caustic manner. He was a successful lawyer now, but he was still every bit the nerd he'd been as a freshman in college.

There was the obligatory small talk about their families. Poskanzer had a couple of sons a bit younger than Abby, one at Fessenden and the other at Belmont Hill, both private boys' schools, "brother" schools to Lyman.

"Hey, listen, I owe you a thank-you," Danny said.

"For what?"

"For . . . Sarah — you know, your contribution. Sorry I didn't have my shit together enough to send you a note."

At Sarah's funeral, guests were asked to make donations to the Breast Cancer Research Foundation, in lieu of flowers. Poskanzer had given something like a thousand dollars in Sarah's name.

"Don't worry about it. I mean, least I could do and all that. You still . . . seeing . . . Lucy Lindstrom?"

Danny nodded. He wondered if even Jay Poskanzer had privately lusted after the It Girl back in the day.

"Lucky guy."

"Don't I know it."

"So," Poskanzer said behind his glass-topped desk, tenting his fingers. "I can see you're nervous, Danny. Why don't you tell me what's going on."

Danny took a deep breath, leaned forward

in his chair, and started in, telling Poskanzer about the events of the past couple of days — his money troubles, the loan, the mysterious call, and the stunning discovery that the DEA was monitoring his bank records because of an ongoing investigation into Tom Galvin.

"Wait a second," Poskanzer said. "Thomas Galvin?"

Danny nodded, unsettled by the urgency in Poskanzer's voice.

"You know him?"

Danny nodded again.

"So they're saying — so Galvin is suspected of laundering money for *Sinaloa* — a Mexican *drug* cartel?"

"Something like that."

Poskanzer put a hand out like a traffic cop. "Sorry, I'm trying to wrap my mind around that."

"It's crazy, right?"

He gave a low whistle. "Oh, Jesus, Danny. This isn't good, Danny. This is bad."

Not what Danny wanted to hear. It hit him like a punch in the gut. Of course it was bad, but it was ominous to hear a criminal defense attorney say that. "What do you mean, exactly?"

"When Galvin transferred the funds, did you give him any kind of written understanding, a note, something?"

"It was a loan. I'm going to pay him back."

"You have it in writing?"

Danny shook his head slowly. "A friend lends a friend money, you usually don't sign a contract, right?"

"So the fifty thousand — it could be anything. A payment of some kind."

"It could be, but it's not."

"You can't prove it was a loan?"

"They can't prove it *wasn't.*"

"They don't have to." There was a long pause. "If the government suspects Galvin of laundering money for the Sinaloa cartel, or trafficking, or whatever — they're going to use every weapon in their arsenal. Which means that sometimes the innocent by-stander gets caught in the thresher."

"I don't understand."

"You borrowed money from the wrong guy."

"Okay, but I don't know the first damned thing about drugs or Mexican cartels or . . . I didn't do a damned thing wrong! Isn't that all that really counts here?"

He exhaled slowly. "Unfortunately, no. You got caught in a major drug-trafficking investigation that has nothing to do with you. Like I said, the government's gonna use every weapon they have, and in this case

106

it means pressuring you until you agree to cooperate. The power, the advantage — it's all on their side. It's unfair, but there it is. You're in a no-win situation. That's the ugly truth."

Danny swallowed hard. "Jay, you're supposed to be the best lawyer in Boston."

Poskanzer allowed himself the ghost of a smile. "Arguably."

"So you're saying, what, we can't fight this?"

"Danny. Of course we *can* fight it. I'm here for you — whatever you want to do, I'll do. But let me lay out the plain facts. The way the law works in this case, you do business with a criminal, the presumption is you're a criminal. You can fight it, sure. But the odds are against you. When the US government decides to prosecute someone on narcotics charges? *They almost always win.* Look, I'm not going to sugarcoat it. Do you know what the federal narcotics conviction rate is?"

Danny shook his head impatiently.

"Over ninety percent." Poskanzer turned slightly and began tapping on his keyboard. "Here it is — ninety-three percent. That means ninety-three percent of people charged with 'drug trafficking,' however that's defined, got convicted. Almost *all* of

them did prison time. That means you have a nine in ten chance of ending up in prison. That's the reality."

Danny almost leaped out of his chair. *"Prison?"* he sputtered. "Did you say *prison*? Are you freaking *kidding me*?"

Poskanzer shook his head slowly. "Danny, come on, sit down, okay? All I'm saying is — if we choose to fight it in the legal system, the odds are extremely high you end up in prison."

Bitterly, Danny said: "So basically, I can get prison time for . . . just accepting a loan from a guy?"

"When they call it a racketeering offense, you sure can." Poskanzer swiveled his computer monitor around so Danny could read the screen. "Take a look."

A table of some kind. Words and numbers. "What is it?" Danny asked.

"These are the federal sentencing guidelines for RICO offenses. Racketeering, as they call it. Given the amount of money involved — fifty thousand dollars — and the fact that it falls under the category of narcotics-related conduct, you could get three hundred twenty-four to four hundred months in prison."

Danny stared in mute terror. "I don't even know how long four hundred months is."

Poskanzer didn't even hesitate. "Thirty-three years."

He swallowed. "This is bullshit!" He tried to summon indignant outrage, but instead it came out like a plea. "This is total bullshit."

Poskanzer bowed his head for a moment, as if praying or lost in thought. Then he lifted his head and said, "Do you remember that time we got onto the roof of Low?"

Danny nodded. "Roofing" — getting onto the roofs of campus buildings — was a venerable Columbia tradition. You had to pick locks and shimmy through windows, and there was always a chance of getting caught, which could mean being thrown out of school. But that just gave it an illicit thrill. In their freshman year, he and Poskanzer had once sneaked onto the roof of Low Library in the middle of the night. The view was spectacular. Far below, the quad twinkled and sparkled.

Danny nodded, wondered what his point was.

"That was cool," Poskanzer said.

"It was."

"I hated freshman year. My roommates were assholes. You were one of my few friends."

Danny was moved. He'd had no idea. He

nodded and smiled. "I'm honored."

"Listen to me. I could take your money. I'd be happy to. Well, my firm would be happy to. But we're friends, you and me, so I'm not going to lie to you. Fighting the US government is an incredibly expensive undertaking. We'd need a retainer of two hundred fifty thousand dollars, to start."

"Jay, I don't have that kind —"

"And they know that, believe me. The fact is, a competent defense may end up costing you a million, maybe even two million, by the time all is said and done." Danny recalled one of the DEA guys saying something like that. "Also, it'll tie you up for years. And then, like I said, the odds are way against you. You'd have a nine-in-ten chance of going to prison. For up to thirty-three years."

"Jesus."

"Look, if you were my brother, my dad, my best friend, I'd tell you to cooperate. But you're also a single dad. You're Abby's only parent. You gotta think about that. You'd be ruining your daughter's life. I mean, have you appointed a guardian for Abby?"

"A . . . *guardian*?"

"In case you end up in prison. In case you have to go away. Because that's *probably* what's going to happen to you. Unless you cooperate with them. You really want to spin that roulette wheel? I don't think you do."

"I don't *believe* this!"

"Go get a second opinion, Danny. And a third, and a fourth. Ask any lawyer experienced in dealing with the feds. They'll all tell you the same thing — only maybe they'll soft-pedal the odds against you. Plenty of lawyers would be happy to take your money and bankrupt you. But I don't want to do that. I'm advising you — as a friend — to cooperate. You want to fight, I'll fight for you. But I can't recommend that course of action, not with a clear conscience."

"But . . . say I *do* cooperate. Then what happens to me?"

"You sign a deal with the government . . ."

"No, that's not what I mean. Let's say I do whatever they want. I become a confidential informant, or confidential source, whatever they call it. Wear a wire or record my phone calls with the guy. And let's say this leads to Tom Galvin's arrest. *Then what happens to me?*"

Poskanzer hesitated. "You . . . you're a free man."

"Have you ever watched any of those videos of the Sinaloa cartel beheading snitches with a chain saw?"

Poskanzer shook his head.

"If information I provide sends Tom Galvin to prison, and if he really is working for the Sinaloa cartel, who the hell's to say I don't end up in one of those videos?"

There was a long, long silence.

"I don't think you have a choice," Poskanzer said. "I'm really sorry, but I don't think you have a choice."

Danny took the elevator down in a daze. He barely noticed the other passengers. Somehow he found himself in the lobby of the Hancock Tower and then out the revolving doors.

He had no doubt that Jay Poskanzer was giving it to him straight. If a lawyer like him — arrogant, brilliant, and with a chip on his shoulder the size of Nebraska — didn't see any point in taking on the Department of Justice, what use was there in trying to fight a battle he couldn't win?

Poskanzer was right, he was a single father. He had to think about Abby.

Standing outside the office building, blinking in the bright sun, he took out the business card that one of the DEA guys had given him and dialed the number.

■ ■ ■ ■

PART TWO

■ ■ ■ ■

17

Special Agent Yeager was holding a Black-Berry against his ear when Danny returned.

"Yeah, it's me," he said. "Yeah. Yeah."

He glanced at Danny quickly, like he was a dead mouse his cat had just brought in. "Well, that's not going to happen," he said into his phone.

Yeager waved Danny in without looking at him again.

When the door clicked shut behind them, Yeager ended his call and stuck out a hand. He shook Danny's hand with a paw like a broken-in baseball glove.

"You're doing the right thing."

Danny said nothing. *Like I have a choice.*

"Let's get your signature on the dotted line so we can get moving," Yeager said, guiding Danny down the hall. A burnt-toast smell lingered in the air as they passed a break room: microwave, small cube refrigerator, a Keurig coffeemaker, a jumbo box of coffee pods from a discount shopping club. Boisterous laughter came from behind a closed door across the hall. A staff meeting of some sort.

The agent with the shoe-polish hair, Slocum, was sitting at the table in the same conference room where they'd met before. This time he was sorting through a sheaf of papers arrayed in front of him like playing cards in a game of solitaire.

"Well, look who's back," said Slocum. "Have a seat. Get comfortable. This is going to take a while. We need to take a complete personal history."

"For what?"

"For our debriefing report to headquarters," Yeager said. "We gotta make a case for how we think you can help us."

"What's to debrief?" asked Danny.

"Standard procedure for all sn— uh, confidential informants," said Slocum.

"You almost said *snitches.*"

"Old habit." He smiled nastily.

"Kind of hard for me to be a snitch if I don't actually work for the cartel," Danny pointed out.

Slocum let out a long sigh.

After forty-five minutes and a stack of multipart forms, they'd finished the biographical questions. Then they asked him to sketch out a floor plan for Galvin's house, or at least as much of it as he'd seen. They asked him to recall as many details about Galvin's home office as he could: door placement, windows, how many computers, what kind of electronic equipment. Every single item on top of Galvin's desk. Danny was quietly pleased at how much he was able to recall. The two agents took turns. One asked the questions while the other went for coffee or water or a potty break.

"Why do you need to know all this?" Danny asked at one point.

Slocum, the bad cop, said, "Why don't you let us ask the questions."

"Did you ever see him place a call on a landline?" Yeager asked.

"Actually, no. Just his mobile phone. His BlackBerry."

"And you're sure it was a BlackBerry? It didn't look bulkier or different in any way?"

"I didn't get that close a look."

"Do you have his cell number? Of his BlackBerry, I mean."

Danny nodded. He took out his iPhone, went into his contacts and read off Galvin's number.

"Did you notice whether he did any texting?"

"I don't think I could tell the difference

between texting and making a call," Danny said. "Why? What do you need to know all this for?"

"We need to know who he's talking to and what he's saying," said Yeager.

"So tap his phones."

"Brilliant idea," said Slocum, getting up. "Why didn't I think of that?" He shook his head in mordant amusement and walked out of the room.

"What makes you think we haven't done that?" said Yeager. "The problem is, the cartels have gotten too smart. They never discuss business over phone lines that aren't encrypted."

"Did it ever occur to you guys that maybe the reason Galvin doesn't talk cartel business over the phone is because he's not doing any cartel business?"

Yeager seemed to be suppressing a smirk. "We've picked up an encrypted signal going out over one of his landlines, probably in his home office."

"So?"

"There's a reason he's using encryption."

Danny shrugged. "You guys can't break it?"

"Not so simple. You've been reading too many spy novels."

"No such thing as reading too many spy novels."

They asked for his iPhone and installed a couple of apps on it. One was ChatSecure. It used an encryption protocol called Off-the-Record. It allowed them to send and receive text messages securely.

"We've given you a Gmail account to use."

"I already have one."

"Don't use it. Not for messaging us. Use this one." He wrote on a yellow Post-it: *JayGould1836@gmail.com.*

"If you want to use Google Talk for messaging, use that account."

"Jay Gould," Danny said. "You've done your homework."

"And 1836 —"

"Is the year he was born, yes, I know. And what makes you think Galvin's going to open up to me?"

"We don't think that," Yeager said. "Of course he won't."

"So what do you need me for?"

"For this."

Slocum's voice, triumphant. He'd appeared in the doorway, a white cardboard box in his hand instead of a cup of coffee. He swooped in and put the box on the table in front of Danny. It looked like a bakery box, like it was intended to hold pastries, maybe a half dozen cupcakes. He opened the flaps and pulled out a little sculpture. A cheesy-looking repro of Rodin's *The Thinker,* the kind of thing you'd find at a flea market. It even had a fake patina of green over black to make it look like the bronze original in the Musée Rodin, oxidized from decades of Paris rain. It was meant to be used as a bookend. It was a curio. It was a piece of crap.

"What's this?" Danny said.

"A gift," Slocum said. "You're going to give it to Galvin as a token of your gratitude for the generous loan."

"A . . . bookend? Is it at least part of a pair?"

"What you see is what you get," Slocum said. "It's a room bug. There's a GSM listening device built in. Transmits over cellular service."

Yeager said, "Since we can't decrypt the phone signal, our best hope is to plant a listening device in the room itself. Listen to his end of the conversation at least. We'll monitor it for thirty days. Then we're required to report back to the court."

"A single bookend," Danny said. "Why would I give him a bookend? That's weird."

Yeager shrugged. "It's a . . . a thing. A piece of art or whatever. It's what the technical boys came up with."

"You guys are serious about this? I'm sup-posed to give him this garage-sale, flea-market piece of junk as a thank-you gift? You think he's going to put something like this on his desk? You must think he's some goombah out of *The Sopranos.* The guy has sophisticated tastes. He's not going to put this on his desk. This is an embarrassment. It's not even a good copy."

"He won't want to offend you," Yeager said. "He'll keep it on his desk in case you look for it next time you visit."

"He barely knows me. He's not afraid of hurting my feelings. He'll toss it before I pull out of his driveway."

"Possibly," conceded Yeager. "Or not."

"You got a better idea?" said Slocum, a challenge.

Danny shrugged. "At least make it an eagle."

"An eagle." Slocum gave a scornful laugh.

"The Boston College mascot."

"That's a thought," Yeager told Slocum. "Not a bad idea."

"That'll delay us a couple days at least," Slocum replied. "The tech boys have to locate an eagle and then fit it."

"It's worth the wait," Yeager replied.

"Forget it," Danny said. "He isn't likely to

put it on his desk anyway."

"I'm inclined to agree," Yeager said. "This is going to take some rethinking in any case."

"Why do you need me anyway?" Danny asked. "Don't you have a team that can do some sort of covert entry into the Galvins' house one night when they're out and plant listening devices?"

"That option was considered and discarded," said Yeager. "Galvin's house is never unoccupied, even when the family's gone. There are always servants. Plus a state-of-the-art security system."

"And you guys can't get around that?"

"It's not feasible," Yeager said. "No way to do a B&E without detection in that house. Plus, the moment they suspect an intrusion, they'll have the place swept and sterilized. Whenever you do an operation like that, you have to be extremely careful about the law of unintended consequences."

"Meaning what?" said Danny.

"Sometimes things go to shit," said Slocum.

Danny swallowed hard. "You don't want me doing this. It's way too risky. Talk about unintended consequences. You want a professional. I don't have the right skill set."

"Actually, you've got the single most

important qualification," Yeager said. "Access. The man seems to trust you."

"My only 'qualification,' as you put it, is that my daughter's a friend of his daughter's. But frankly, if what you say is true, I don't like the idea of her spending time over there anymore."

Yeager leaned over and placed his catcher's-mitt hand on Danny's wrist. "Absolutely no changes. This is crucial. It's extremely important that you don't alter any patterns. If you suddenly won't let your daughter go over to the Galvins', he'll get suspicious."

"And what happens if he catches me planting some bug in his office — what then? What if he somehow discovers the transmitter? What happens to me? What happens to my *daughter*?"

"So don't get caught," said Slocum.

Yeager said, "Nothing's going to happen to your daughter."

"And what if the word gets out that I'm cooperating with the goddamned DEA? If you guys have a leak? What if someone blabs to someone and Galvin gets wind of it? And he finds out I've planted a bug inside his house?"

"Don't borrow trouble," said Yeager. "We'll worry about that if and when it happens. But it won't. Everything will be fine."

"What happened to the law of unintended consequences?" Danny said.

Both DEA agents fell silent for a long moment. A smile played about the corners of Slocum's mouth.

"There's absolutely no reason to worry," Yeager said.

But even he didn't sound convinced.

18

The text came two days later.

On his laptop, actually. A tritone sounded, reverbing fuzzily like a vibraphone. A window opened on his laptop's screen, asking whether he'd accept a digital fingerprint, an encryption key. The window was full of gibberish, a block of meaningless characters.

The sender was AnonText007@gmail .com.

He clicked yes, and then a text message popped right up: 7 p.m., IHOP, Soldiers Field Rd, NE corner pkg lot.

A meet had been set for the parking lot of the International House of Pancakes in Brighton.

Danny had already begun to hope the DEA had lost interest in him. That they'd finally realized it wasn't such a good idea to press such a rank amateur into service. Too risky. Too many unintended consequences.

With a sense of foreboding he typed *OK,*

and clicked SEND.

He knew he couldn't tell Abby about the DEA.

She was a teenager, a member of the Oversharing Generation who documented their every move on Facebook or Twitter or Instagram. She could never be expected to keep a secret like this. Her best friend's father was a financier for a Mexican drug cartel? Her own dad was being blackmailed into gathering information on the Galvins? She'd be incredulous, then outraged, and most of all buzzing with excitement. Her need to tell Jenna would be an uncontrollable reflex.

Lucy was a different story. She was the soul of discretion. He trusted her absolutely. She'd never gossip; she knew how to keep a secret.

But when he called her that afternoon, he found himself unable to tell her the astonishing latest.

"Luce, baby, I'm going to be late for dinner tonight."

"What about Abby?"

"Home, as far as I know. Not at the Galvins'."

The complexities of their living arrangements had been worked out over time. With her son, Kyle, away at Bowdoin, Lucy was an empty nester. She disliked rattling around her Brookline condo, making dinner for one. She preferred spending time as a family with Danny and Abby on Marlborough Street.

She wasn't Abby's mom, and she wasn't a substitute. She was Daddy's girlfriend, not an authority figure. Yet in a sense she was Abby's girlfriend, too: kind of a big sister. What might have been awkward in another family seemed to work fairly well, maybe because Lucy was a psychiatrist and knew where the land mines were and how to sidestep them.

"Okay," she said. "I'll fix something with Abby, then. What's up?"

He was ready with a lie. "An old friend of mine's in town and wanted to pick my brain. He's got some idea for a book. I think he wants publishing advice, which generally means how he can get an agent."

"Who's that?"

"You don't know him — guy named Art? Art Nava?"

"I don't know the name. From Columbia?"

"Nah, I met him through Sarah. A million years ago. Anyway. You two just go ahead and have dinner without me."

Art Nava was a high school friend of his from Wellfleet, someone he hadn't talked to, even thought of, since high school graduation. Why he'd chosen that name, he had no idea.

All he knew for certain was that he wanted to protect Lucy from the dangerous swerve his life had taken, to keep her innocent and uninvolved. To take this on alone and not endanger the woman he loved so much. It felt like the right thing to do.

But it was the first time he'd ever lied to her, and he was sure it wouldn't be the last.

At five minutes before seven that evening, Danny was sitting in his car in the parking lot of the International House of Pancakes in Brighton. The lot was mostly empty: The pancake chain's "eat breakfast for dinner" campaign had never worked in a big way — but a steady trickle of cars came in and out. The white noise whoosh of traffic from Soldiers Field Road was rhythmic, almost lulling. Or it might have been lulling, in another setting, at another time.

Because he didn't know what to expect, and he hated uncertainty. He was to park in the northeast corner of the IHOP lot by seven o'clock.

They would find him.

128

He waited. A few spaces away, a red Jeep Grand Cherokee was parked. It probably belonged to an employee, maybe a manager. The other cars in the lot were clustered much closer to the restaurant.

Whenever a car pulled in, he looked up, watched to see if it was headed toward him. By 7:05 he'd watched a total of five cars enter the lot and three leave. None of them came anywhere near. The agent he'd talked to on the phone — Yeager, the less obnoxious of the two — had been emphatic about punctuality. He'd give them another five minutes and then leave.

His cell phone made a strange bling sound. It displayed the words ENCRYPTED CHAT RECEIVED. He unlocked the phone and read the message. Look to your right, it said. Take the side door. No key necessary.

He looked to the right, saw no one and nothing.

For a moment he didn't understand. Then he saw, maybe twenty feet away, a motel. The CHARLES RIVER MOTEL, a sign said. A black side door with white trim. He hadn't paid any attention to the building, but there it was, closer than the IHOP.

Then another bling, and a new text message: Room 126. First room on your right.

He got out, slammed the car door, looked

around briefly. A low set of concrete steps leading into the motel, bracketed by hedges. You were supposed to insert a key card into a slot to open the door, but when he pulled the handle toward him, it came right open. Someone had jammed the door lock. The hallway was dim and smelled of diapers. He could hear babies crying, multiple babies in multiple rooms. He wondered if this was one of those hotels that the state had taken over for overflow low-income housing. The first door on the right was numbered 126. He knocked once, and it came right open.

Slocum, the one with the Just for Men Jet Black hair and the pointed face of a fox, at the door. Danny entered, and Slocum closed the door behind him without saying a word. Yeager was sitting in the corner. The curtains were closed, and the only light came from a single desk lamp.

"Daniel."

"Seven o'clock sharp, huh?" Danny said. "I guess you meant government time."

Yeager shook his head slowly, and said, "The precautions are for your own safety." He held out a small, dark blue velvet bag.

Danny took it. Something heavy but small was inside.

"Careful," Yeager said. "It's just been calibrated. We don't want it to get out of whack."

Danny tipped out a large metallic disc that looked like a coin. It was a bronze medal that bore the inscription COLLEGIUM BOS-TONIENSE.

"Look familiar?" Yeager said.

Danny nodded. "I think so."

"It's an exact replica of the Boston College President's Medal he's already got, only it's made from resin."

He weighed it in his palm. It was heavy and cold, even felt solid, like a real medal. "This is a transmitter?"

Yeager nodded once. "A GSM-based monitoring device. Sound-activated. Calls us when it detects sound in the room so we can listen in. But you get the hard job. You have to swap it for the original."

"How am I supposed to do that?"

"Figure it out," Slocum said.

Danny turned and said to Slocum, "I've been in the guy's home office exactly once. Call me crazy, but if he really does cartel business in there, I have a feeling he might not want me wandering around in there by myself."

Slocum gave a sour smile and looked away like he was bored.

Yeager said, "It shouldn't take you more than a few seconds. You just need to find the right opportunity."

"Simple as that," Danny said. They were an odd duo, he thought, the two DEA agents. Yeager's manner was studious to the point of affectation, but beneath it, like traces of old paint, a palimpsest, was something rough-hewn, crude, and nasty.

"Notify us when you've placed it," Yeager said.

"How?"

"Secure text message. Use your Jay Gould account. We'll reach out to you the same way."

"Then am I done?"

Slocum folded his arms. "If we get what we need, sure."

"And what if he catches me?"

"Don't get caught," said Slocum.

"Thanks," said Danny. "But I'm an amateur. I've never done anything remotely like this."

"It's not difficult," Yeager said. "We'll give you step-by-step instructions."

"Wonderful," Danny said in a flat tone. "But you still haven't answered my question. What if I get caught?"

"I wasn't kidding," Slocum said. "Try real hard not to get caught. These Sinaloa guys, they're careful and they're ruthless. There's a reason Galvin's driver doubles as his body-guard."

"That guy's his bodyguard?" Danny said. "Who's Galvin afraid of?"

"The competition," said Yeager. "Other cartels. These guys don't screw around."

"Just be prudent," Slocum said, "and you have nothing to worry about."

19

Rex's tail thumped against the floor when Danny returned home. He was curled up at Lucy's feet as she sat on the couch working. He didn't even try to get up.

"That didn't take long," Lucy said. "I hope you didn't scare him off."

"Scare who off?"

"Art Whatever. Your friend the wannabe writer."

It took Danny a moment. His nerves were still vibrating like a plucked string. "Oh, right. No, he just wanted to know some basic stuff, you know — how to get an agent, all that. The usual."

"What kind of book does he want to write?"

Lying to her was bad enough, but now having to elaborate on the lie was even worse. "I don't even think I could tell you. He didn't have a very clear idea himself. Hold on, let me say hi to Abby." He'd noticed her backpack on the floor.

Abby was sitting on her bed, MacBook in her lap, tapping away.

"Hey, Boogie, how was school?"

"Hey, Daddy," she said without looking up. "It was all right."

"How was precalc?"

"It was great. I won the Nobel Prize for calculus."

"Yeah? Do you have to go to Oslo or Stockholm for that one? I always forget."

She shook her head distractedly, done with the game.

"Am I interrupting your homework?"

"Yeah, but it's fine."

"Writing a research paper about Facebook?" He could see enough of the screen to recognize the Facebook logo.

"Did you want something, Daddy?"

"How's Jenna?"

"Fine."

"You planning on going over there tomorrow?"

She looked up. "I don't know, why?"

"Because I'd love to be looped in on your social plans."

"Ha ha ha. Is this about how I'm spending too much time over there? I mean, I was home for dinner and you weren't, so I'm just saying."

"Someone's being a little oversensitive." He could see this starting to spin into an argument, so he tried to reel it back in. "They're great, aren't they? I can't blame you for wanting to hang out with them."

"I don't 'hang out' with them, I hang with Jenna."

"Chillax, baby."

" 'Chillax'? What are you, like a bro now?"

"I meant it ironically. So what's Esteban like?"

"Their driver? I don't know. I don't think I've ever talked to him. He's a good driver, if that's what you're worried about."

He was about to ask whether Esteban carried a gun, but then thought better of it.

"I'm sure he is. He doesn't have to take you home all the time. I can pick you up, some days."

"I thought you don't like driving out to Weston, and losing your parking space."

"I'm happy to pick you up. We need to spend more time together, you and me."

She shrugged, went back to her tapping. "Whatever."

"Anyway, I'll be doing some research at Wellesley College, so it's convenient."

She nodded.

Somehow he had to get himself back inside the Galvins' house. He couldn't exactly invite himself over. There was no plausible reason for him to see the inside of Tom Galvin's home office again any time soon.

Unless he could think of an excuse. A reason to come over again that didn't sound contrived or bogus.

The right opportunity. He hoped it would come soon.

20

The next day, Abby texted him from school: ok if I study with Jenna after school?

Instead of the usual, mild annoyance, he felt a strange sort of relief. Home for supper? he texted back.

Her answer came almost immediately: Sure!

He texted back: I'll pick you up.

Her answer came half a minute later: Thanks! But that's ok, Esteban can drive me home.

He thought for a moment, then texted: I'll be out there anyway, remember?

Adults tended to text, Danny had noticed, like they were sending a telegram: short and terse. Kids, who had no idea what a telegram was, texted as if they were writing e-mail, conversational and slangy. Then again, Abby and her friends considered e-mail as archaic as writing on foolscap with a quill.

Her text came back: ok?

Meaning: Okay, if you insist, though I don't really get it. She'd forgotten that he'd told her he was doing research at Wellesley College. Or maybe she didn't hear it the first time. It was like the old *Peanuts* animated cartoons, whenever a teacher or parent talked to Charlie Brown or his friends. You never heard actual words. You heard the *mwa mwa mwa mwa* of a trombone. Half the time, that was how Danny suspected his voice sounded to Abby.

He texted back, Pick you up @ 6.

Thanks! came her reply.

Then, at around five thirty, when he was about to leave for Weston, his iPhone made the tritone fanfare announcing the arrival of a new text. He glanced at the screen. It was from Abby: OK if I stay for dinner?

Danny thought for a long moment. He could always say no, pick her up at six as planned. If he said yes, it wouldn't be plausible that he'd still be in the area later on. She'd want to have the Galvins' driver, Esteban, take her back to Boston.

The phone nagged a tritone reminder.

He decided not to reply. He'd learned how the mind of a sixteen-year-old worked. She'd assume the answer was yes unless she was told otherwise.

■ ■ ■ ■

At just before six, he was standing in front of the Galvins' castle door. He rang the bell. As he waited, another tritone text bleated. He didn't look at it. He knew it had to be from Abby. Only Lucy or Abby ever texted him.

The door opened after a minute or so. Celina Galvin was wearing skinny jeans and a purple V-neck sweater. At her feet, the bat-faced hairless dogs scurried and scampered and yapped.

"Oh, Daniel, I'm so sorry! Abby didn't tell you she's having dinner with us?"

"Is that right?" A delicious smell wafted from the interior.

He knew exactly what she was going to say next. At some houses, you'd never hear the words. But Celina was Mexican, and Mexican hospitality is legendary.

"Can you stay for dinner?" she said. "Please?"

It was just four of them: Celina, Jenna, Abby, and Danny. Brendan was back at his dorm room at BC, and Ryan had returned to his apartment in Allston, where he lived with a girlfriend he still hadn't brought around to meet the parents and probably never would. ("For me it's fine," Celina said. "He knows she's not the right one, so why do I have to waste my time being nice to her?")

They all sat at one end of the long farm table. The family cook, a stout gray-haired woman named Consuelo, ladled *sopa de frijoles,* black bean soup, into colorful ceramic bowls.

"Daddy, I'm sorry, I definitely texted you!" Abby said.

"Oh, when I was in the archives I put my phone on Do Not Disturb mode. Must have missed it. It's no big deal. Anyway, I get to have another great dinner at the Galvins'."

"Abby," Celina said, "you know Esteban will take you home. Your father shouldn't have to come all the way out here to pick you up."

"Not a problem," he said. "I was in the area anyway." Before she could ask why, he said, "Is Tom still at work?"

"He has a client dinner in town. Oh, what kind of hostess am I? You are a big wine drinker, yes? Consuelo? *¿Podría obtener una buena botella de vino tinto para el caballero?*"

"I'm fine. I don't have wine every night."

A few minutes later, he asked to use their bathroom.

He hadn't seen one off the kitchen, but there were a lot of rooms and a lot of doors and it was always possible a bathroom adjoined the kitchen. But he didn't think so. "It's just out there down the hall, on the right." Celina waved at the corridor along which Galvin had taken him to his home office. "Oh, let me show you. People get lost sometimes. It's very confusing, this crazy house."

"Not at all," he said firmly. He got up and pulled out his iPhone. "If I get lost, I'll call for directions."

The half bath was only twenty or thirty feet down the hall. Its door wasn't visible from the end of the farm table, where everyone had been sitting. He passed it, went a little farther down the hall and then took a right. Another fifty feet or so and he'd reached Tom Galvin's study.

The door was open.

The lights were off. The waning sun cast an amber light. Dust motes hung in the air.

The medal sat in its case near the edge of Galvin's desk, the side that faced visitors. Danny wondered how many people came to visit him here. And who. Was it here that he did his cartel business?

If he did any.

He entered the room, braced for the spotlights overhead to go on, activated by motion. But it didn't. The room remained shadowed. He didn't want to risk putting the lights on.

He took out his iPhone, set the flash function on the camera to ON, and snapped a few quick pictures of Galvin's desk and the area around it. With each shutter sound, a pale light danced and blinked.

Galvin's medal was smaller than he remembered. He hoped the decoy in his pocket, the one he was supposed to swap it for, was the right size.

His heartbeat sounded thunderously loud.

He reached out a hand and grasped the edge of the medal with trembling fingers. It was cold, and thicker than he'd expected.

It wouldn't come out of its case.

The blood rushed in his ears, so loud now that he could hear nothing else. Just the whoosh of blood and the rapid, accelerating tattoo of his heart. His fingers closed around the medal and grabbed it and tried to turn it, tried to pry it loose, but it was seated firmly. Too firmly. Was it somehow cemented down, not meant to be removed?

He felt a cold, unpleasant prickling at the back of his neck.

It came loose. Finally, it came out. The

medal was thick and heavy and cold. He slipped it into the right breast pocket of his suit jacket.

From his left pocket he took the replacement, warm from his body heat, and noticeably lighter than the original.

The tremor in his fingers had become even more obvious.

Please, God, he thought, *let it be the right size.*

He placed it over the round inset in the red velvet and saw that it was a fraction of an inch too big.

It didn't fit in the case.

His heart raced wildly. He felt nauseated.

Now what? Give up? Put the original back in the case and tell the DEA agents they'd screwed up the measurements?

When would he ever have a chance like this again?

With both thumbs he pressed down hard on the fake medal, tried to seat it into the round inset, which refused to yield. He pushed harder — was he wrecking the delicate electronics of the listening device? — until it went down all the way, right into the inset, mashing it slightly.

But it was seated snugly. The red velvet around it puckered downward slightly, like the lines around an old man's mouth.

The medal was slightly turned. The *D* in the Roman numerals at the medal's outer edge, *MDCCCLXIII*, should have been centered on the midline, but it was off slightly so that the third *C* was at the centerpoint.

But he didn't dare take it out and reposition it. There wasn't time — with every second the chances that someone would catch him in here increased — and taking it out and mashing it down one more time might mangle the red velvet noticeably.

Then he realized that he hadn't paid any attention to how the medal had been placed in there originally. Maybe it was turned one way or another. He had no recollection.

But would Galvin notice a tiny detail like that? It seemed unlikely.

He let out a long, silent breath. Backed away from the desk.

And heard the familiar raspy voice.

"Can you believe Grill 23 was closed tonight?" said Tom Galvin.

21

Danny felt his entire body jolt. He let out an involuntary cry, a sort of strangled yip.

Galvin laughed. "Didn't mean to startle you like that."

"Hey. You had — I thought you had a dinner with a client."

"The guy had his heart set on Grill 23 — some friend of his said they serve the best steak in Boston — and I kept telling him, you know, Abe & Louie's, you can't go wrong there, I like their steaks even better, and you can't go wrong with Capital Grille, either. But no, he says his wife won't let him do red meat more than once a month, and he's not wasting his monthly allotment on any steak except Grill 23's. So we had a drink and rescheduled."

"Well, since you've caught me skulking around your office, I might as well come out and ask."

"Ask . . . ?" In the gloom, Galvin's eyes

were inscrutable.

"I wanted to surprise you. Those amazing cigars — what are they called again? I wanted to get you a box of them. Least I could do to thank you."

Galvin switched the overhead lights on and took a few steps into the room. He gave a small, crooked smile. "They haven't moved." He gave a casual wave toward the overstuffed leather chairs in front of his desk. Danny glanced. On the end table next to one of them was the black lacquer box, COHIBA BEHIKE in gold letters on its lid. The gold glittered in the overhead spotlight. "I appreciate the thought, but you don't really want to spend half the money I lent you on *cigars,* now do you? That box cost close to twenty thousand bucks, Danny boy. It was a gift — I wouldn't spend that kind of money on *cigars.* Come on."

"O-o-oh, I see. No, I don't think so." He chuckled.

"Appreciate the thought, though. I hope you're staying for dinner."

Danny couldn't decide if he was pleased or dismayed at how smoothly he'd just lied. Maybe both.

But that strange feeling was quickly overwhelmed by a low hum of anxiety. He was certain Galvin knew he was lying.

22

"You left the lights on," Abby said.

As he put the key in the lock, he noticed the spill of light under his apartment door.

Then he remembered. Yesterday, Lucy had offered to pick up sushi for the three of them — California roll and such for Abby, no raw fish — for dinner tonight.

"Oh, shit."

Lucy was on her laptop at the dining table. Arrayed around her were clear plastic trays with decorative green plastic blades of grass and rows of sliced sushi rolls. The remains of a glass of white wine.

"I'm guessing you guys already ate."

"I screwed up. My bad, Lucy. I'm sorry."

She didn't look angry or even particularly annoyed. She smiled as if secretly amused, shook her head. Maybe a little annoyed. "There's plenty left. But it won't be any good tomorrow. Unagi, Abby? It's cooked."

"I'm good," she said. "Daddy, you didn't

tell her you were at Wellesley College?"

"Why Wellesley?" Lucy asked.

"Yeah, there's an archive there . . ." His voice trailed off. Another lie.

"The Jay Gould archive," Abby announced.

Thanks, kid, he thought. *You basically have no idea what I do for a living and suddenly you're doing the play-by-play color commentary?*

"There's a Jay Gould archive at Wellesley?" Lucy said. "You're kidding. That I never would have expected. The letters of Elizabeth Barrett Browning and Jay Gould, together under one roof. Who knew?"

"It's just the letters between Gould and one of his wives," Danny said, and added hastily, "How was your day?"

"It was fine," Lucy said distantly, but the way she furrowed her brow made Danny's stomach do a little flip. She knew him too well.

With both his daughter and his girlfriend at home, there wasn't much privacy. He waited until Abby had gone into her room and Lucy was in the shower, then he sat down at his desk in the living room, loaded a program the DEA agents had given him called Adium, and signed on to the

JayGould1836@gmail.com account.

He composed a text to AnonText007@gmail.com. Just three words: device in place. He stared at it for a few seconds.

A window opened: OTR FINGERPRINT VERIFICATION. The encryption "fingerprint" for the DEA agents. A box of gobbledygook popped up on his Gmail page. Fortunately, he didn't have to know what the hell he was doing to make it work. He assumed it meant that his text messages to them were automatically encrypted, and theirs back. He clicked ACCEPT.

ENCRYPTED CHAT INITIATED. In other words, the text had gone through successfully.

Then he remembered about the pictures. He e-mailed to himself the photos he'd taken of Galvin's desk. Saved them to his computer's desktop. Then sent them to AnonText007@gmail.com.

And he was done.

The DEA boys would get the evidence they needed to arrest Tom Galvin. They'd arrest Celina's husband, Jenna and Ryan and Brendan's father.

He didn't want to think about that, though. It came down to a very simple choice: Galvin's family or his. That wasn't exactly a difficult decision, was it?

Not that he cared about what might happen to Galvin. He hardly knew the guy. Even the man's wife and kids — he didn't know them, either. If Galvin were truly involved in criminal activity, he deserved to go to prison.

He signed off.

But he hated lying to the two women in his life.

He hadn't lied to Abby since Sarah's death. And then he'd had no choice. Sarah had insisted.

Sarah had wanted Abby to go to Camp Pocapawmet, on Cape Cod, that last summer, just as she'd gone every summer since she was eleven. And he'd gone along with it, but he'd said, *You don't want her around for . . .*

Tearfully, Sarah had shot back, *This is not the way I want her to remember her mommy. I don't want her to remember me as a sick, dying woman. I want her to enjoy being a kid. A couple of weeks of just being a kid. Carefree and happy. Because when I go, everything will change for her.*

But he didn't want to lie to her.

Call it protection. Call it protecting her childhood. I don't want a shadow to fall over that girl until it really has to.

So he'd lied, of course. Mommy had an infection in her lungs. She had to spend a little while in the hospital, and then she'd get better.

Meanwhile, Sarah went through round after brutal round of chemotherapy. Anthracycline and taxane. The chemo had to come before surgery. But it was stage-four cancer. The cancer had spread to the lymph nodes. The prognosis was poor.

There wasn't even time for surgery. It all happened too fast.

And when everything turned for the worse at the beginning of August, when it had become clear that Sarah had days left, not weeks or months, Danny had picked Abby up at camp and told her Mommy was sick.

Abby lay in the hospital bed next to her mother, her arms around her mother's belly as Sarah slept, the machines wheezing and beeping, both of them crying. For two days.

Danny knew that Sarah waited to die until Abby had gone home for the night. Danny knew she couldn't bear to depart this earth in the embrace of her child.

So Abby'd had four worry-free weeks at camp before the shadow fell over her life.

At the time it felt like the right thing to do.

■ ■ ■ ■

Danny loathed being trapped in this pointless lie about Jay Gould: one more lie he'd have to keep track of. But he decided not to speak of it again unless and until it came up.

Which of course it did, later that evening, as they lay in bed. Danny was rereading — well, reskimming, actually — an old book by Gustavus Myers called *History of the Great American Fortunes,* and Lucy was working on her laptop.

"He was married only once," she said.

"Huh? Who?"

"Jay Gould. You said 'one of his wives,' but he married once, to Helen Day Miller, who died like three years before he did." Wikipedia's page for Jay Gould was open on her computer screen. She gave him a sidelong glance.

Why had he told her such an idiotic, sloppy lie? It was just the first thing that had sprung to his mind. He hadn't given it a thought. "What made you look that up?"

"I remember when you first started working on the book, I read something about him, I was wondering why he was considered such an evil jerk, and I noticed he only

153

married once. Not six times or something, which you'd expect. These days, anyway. And I thought, well, I guess the times were different then. Or maybe he was a good husband at least."

"Did I say 'one of' his wives'? Long day. I misspoke."

She flipped the laptop closed. "No, you didn't, Danny. There aren't *any* Jay Gould archives at Wellesley and —"

"Sweetie, listen. I told Abby I was doing work out there because I wanted to take her home myself. That's all. I'm not comfortable with her being driven around by a chauffeur."

"So why not just tell her that?"

"Obviously, I should have. I didn't feel like setting off another argument."

"God forbid you should get into an argument with someone."

He shrugged. If you don't want to be psychoanalyzed, don't date a shrink. Lucy understood, long before he did, that he had a problem with anger. His problem was something that he never thought could possibly be considered a problem: He never gave in to anger. He felt it, sure, plenty of times. But he prided himself on his ability to suppress it. When an argument began, he'd always de-escalate. Holding anger in this way required great self-control, but he'd taught himself that self-control since childhood.

He'd learned by example. For years he'd thought that his father, Bud, had a short fuse.

But putting it that way, so bland and benign, made it sound normal. Bud Goodman in fact had no fuse. He was one of those chemical compounds, like liquid nitroglycerin or mercury fulminate, that would explode on impact. Danny had learned how to avoid the triggers that would set his father off, and there were many of them. Disobedience was one. Dishonesty. A raised voice.

Bud, who was a great carpenter, a fine craftsman, was constantly losing subcontractors. He'd tell them off, or just go after them in a hot flash of anger, until they quit. He lost plenty of clients that way, too. One lumberyard in Wellfleet refused to do business with him because he once tore into the yard manager, though Bud insisted that they were selling him short lots.

If you listened only to Bud Goodman's side, his subs were a capricious and moody bunch, every last one of them. Danny learned quickly that there was always another side of the story, usually involving a

Bud Goodman tantrum that ended in a mushroom cloud of rage.

Even when Sarah moved out, he didn't understand that maybe he'd gone too far in the opposite direction. "For God's sake, what's wrong with you?" Sarah had snapped one day. "Do you not care what happens to us? Do you not even give a shit?"

"Come on," he replied, making her point. "Let's talk this through reasonably. No need to shout."

Lucy once told him about a psychologist and marriage therapist named John Gottman who had identified what he called the Four Horsemen of the Apocalypse. These were the four most destructive behavior patterns that, if exhibited by a spouse, spelled doom for the marriage. This psychologist claimed that within the first three minutes of observing a couple, he could tell with ninety-four percent accuracy whether they would be divorced in the next five or six years. One of the most destructive of the Four Horsemen was "stonewalling" — tuning out, evading, avoiding conflict.

Didn't all men do that?

No, Lucy had insisted.

"Well," he replied, "I'm not the angry sort. Sorry about that, but I'm just not."

"What are you not telling me?" she asked.

"Lucy, come on, you're making a whole lot out of nothing."

"Are you still worried Abby spends too much time at the Galvins'?"

He shrugged. "Not especially. I mean, I wish she spent more time with her other friends. Given how volatile friendships between girls this age can be."

"So you're no longer worried about her head being turned by their wealth?"

"Their kids seem to have a good set of values. . . ."

They're good people, he almost said. *Nice family.* But he caught himself.

He didn't know what to think about the Galvins.

"Maybe I'm not as concerned about them as I used to be," he said.

He slipped out of bed — dressed in an old pair of gym shorts and a Bruce Springsteen T-shirt (Tunnel of Love Express Tour, 1988, purchased at the concert at the Worcester Centrum) — and went out to the kitchen to grab a glass of tap water.

Abby was still awake — no surprise; she was a night owl — and was standing against the refrigerator, spooning Ben & Jerry's Red Velvet Cake ice cream out of the container. She held out the spoon. "Want some?"

"No, thanks." He gave her a quick hug. "I

love you, Boogie."

"I love you, Daddy."

He took a water glass from the cabinet over the sink, held it under the faucet, and lifted the handle.

"That ice cream won't keep you up?"

She shook her head.

"Don't forget to take Lactaid."

"I know." She paused. "Hey, um . . . you didn't go to BC, did you?"

"Boston College? I went to Columbia. You know that. But BC's an excellent college." Was she actually thinking about which colleges she might go to? This was a historic moment.

"I know, I thought . . . I mean . . ." She hesitated a beat. "So why do you have a Boston College medal? I don't get that. Did they give that to you or something?"

He froze. He watched the water brim over before he remembered to pull down the lever to shut off the flow.

He'd left his jeans on the floor outside the bathroom, setting, as always, a lousy example for his daughter. But why was she going through his pockets?

"Did I drop that thing somewhere?" he asked.

"My pen died, so I wanted to borrow one of yours and I didn't want to knock on your

158

bedroom door, you know, and *disturb* you guys." An artful roll of the eyes. "So how come you have it?"

He shook his head vaguely. He was too weary to concoct a plausible lie and didn't want to come off as defensive or angry and provoke her suspicion. "It's a long story," he said. "Boring and complicated. Now, come on, isn't it your bedtime?"

"What?" she protested.

"And, Boogie — let's not poke around in each other's things, okay?"

23

Two days later, at a few minutes after five in the morning, Danny was awakened by the triumphal tritone plink of a secure text message on his iPhone. Lucy stirred in her sleep, mumbled, "What?"

"Sorry," he whispered.

He grabbed the iPhone from the bedside table. He slid it unlocked, saw that the message was from AnonText007. Meet 9am 75 West Broadway, South Boston. Take T.

Another meeting? He'd thought he was done with them. Now what was the problem?

The T was, in Boston slang, the subway. For some reason they didn't want him to drive. What was that about?

He was too keyed up to go back to sleep, so he went into the kitchen to make a pot of coffee.

By the time Abby awoke, he was wide awake and jittery.

She sat in silence in the front seat during most of the ride to school. Every half a minute or so, she'd change radio stations, dissatisfied with all of them. Her favorite hip-hop station was all talk. When she wasn't changing radio stations, she was busy texting.

Ever since she'd become a teenager, Danny had given up trying to read her moods in the morning. She could be pouting or seething, or she could be just fine. She wasn't a morning person. Anyway, sixteen-year-olds weren't biologically programmed to get up at six thirty. He'd read that somewhere.

She hadn't said another word about the Boston College medal she'd found in his jeans. Of course not. What had struck such fear in Danny's heart was just one more minor scuffle between Abby and Dad, another one thrown on the pile, already forgotten.

"I hate this!" Abby said suddenly.

"What do you hate?"

The length of the drop-off line at school they'd just pulled into?

"This . . . stupid piece-of-shit flip phone!"

"Hey. Language."

"Sorry. Piece of crap. It's so hard to text on this thing. How come I can't get an

161

iPhone?"

"You want a Mercedes-Benz with that?"

"No, I'm serious. I hate it! None of my friends have flip phones anymore."

"I know, life can be so cruel. First there's that genocide in Darfur, then there's the famine in Somalia, and then, worst of all, Abby Goodman is forced to use a last-year's-model LG flip phone."

Abby smoldered and didn't reply. Too easy, Danny thought. Shooting fish in a barrel.

A car pulled up in the line behind him. Galvin's chauffeured Maybach. Tom Galvin sat in the front seat, talking on his Black-Berry.

"We must be right on time," Danny said. "We're ahead of the Galvins."

Abby turned, saw Jenna, waved.

"That's not Esteban," she said.

Danny glanced in the rearview mirror. "You're right."

"Maybe Esteban is sick. He must get sick sometimes."

"Sure."

When they pulled up to the front entrance of Lyman Academy, Abby allowed herself to be kissed, though on the top of the head, not offering a cheek.

"Have fun, Boogie."

"How could I not," she replied drily.

She pulled open the door and slinked out.

The high beams on Galvin's car pulsed on, then off. "Danny," called a man's voice. Abby slammed the car door and scampered over to Jenna.

Danny turned to his right, then turned around, and saw Galvin's hand out the window of his limo, waving at him.

"Got a sec?" Galvin called.

Danny pulled forward into the short-term parking area, off to one side, and the Maybach pulled alongside.

Danny got out, tense and smiling. His mouth was dry.

The driver had gotten out and come around to open the passenger's-side door for Galvin. It definitely wasn't Esteban. This one wore the same uniform, the billed cap and black suit and tie, but it fit him awkwardly, like something he'd taken off the rack at a uniform shop. He was around the same height and breadth as Esteban, but his build seemed more exaggerated: arms like ham hocks, a torso that tapered sharply. He looked brutish, like a wrestler or maybe a boxer who'd spent too much time in the ring. He had a small, sloped head atop a neck that was as wide as the head it supported, thinning black hair, deeply inset

163

raisin eyes. His face was spiderwebbed with broken capillaries. His lips were purplish and fat, like two slabs of liver, and seemed permanently parted even when his teeth were clenched.

Galvin got out, nodding at his bodyguard.

He looked terrible. His eyes were bloodshot, with deep circles underneath and lines on his forehead Danny hadn't noticed before. Galvin, who normally looked so polished and serene, looked like he'd been up all night.

He shook Danny's hand.

Danny felt fear wriggle in his belly.

"Danny, I'd like you to meet Diego, my new driver. Diego, this is Mr. Goodman. He's a friend of mine and, more important, the father of Abby, Jenna's best friend. Danny and his daughter are very important people in our lives." His left eye twitched almost imperceptibly.

Diego bowed his head and smiled somberly, exposing the glint of gold molars, then returned to the driver's seat.

"Gotta make sure the new guy knows the key players in my life," Galvin said.

"What happened to Esteban?"

Galvin's left eye twitched again, very slightly. If you didn't know him, you might not have noticed it. He seemed to have

164

developed a tic. He sighed. "Esteban had to go back home to his family in Mexico. Not a good time to break in a new driver, but there's probably no convenient time."

"That's a bummer."

"Didn't you say you play squash?"

"Well, I haven't played in a while."

"That's okay. My squash partner canceled on me, and I need the workout. Would you be free for a game after work today?"

"I'm not a great player."

"Neither am I. It's just for fun."

"I've got to do an interview this afternoon," Danny lied. "Maybe some other time."

He was almost positive he'd never told Galvin he played squash.

24

The location for the meet with the DEA guys was a diner in South Boston that looked like an authentic old diner out of the 1950s. Its exterior was shiny diamond-plate metal siding. A neon sign said MUL'S. Inside, it looked even more authentic, with red leatherette booths and stools, Formica-topped tables, and white-tiled walls. Behind a long counter edged with ribbed aluminum, a couple of line cooks were frying eggs and turning pancakes the size of dinner plates. Everything smelled like bacon and coffee and maple syrup.

Glenn Yeager was seated at one of the corner booths, facing the entrance, chowing down on a huge breakfast. Next to him was an open laptop, a black Toshiba. The booth looked to be strategically located. No other tables were close. They could talk openly.

"Where's Bad Cop?" Danny asked.

Yeager replied through a mouthful of egg,

"Change of plans."

Danny sat down at the booth as a waitress appeared with a menu and a glass carafe of coffee and filled a chunky white mug. "Change?"

Yeager gulped down a few swallows of orange juice. Cleared his throat. He closed the laptop. "Phil's checking out a lead. He might join us later."

Danny shrugged. He wasn't going to complain about Slocum not being there.

The waitress, copper-haired and big-busted, said, "Know what you want, honey?"

"I'm all set with just the coffee," Danny said.

"Come on, Daniel, order something. Best breakfast in town."

Danny shook his head and waited until the waitress gave up and left. "What's this about? I thought I was done with you guys."

"We've got a problem. We're not picking up a signal."

"The transmitter?"

Yeager nodded solemnly.

"That's not my problem. I did everything right, on my end."

"Unfortunately, it's very much your problem. Until we get what we need on him, you belong to us."

167

And here, Danny thought, was the flaw in their arrangement. He had no way of knowing whether they were telling him the truth. Maybe the bug in the dummy Boston College medal was working just fine but they wanted him to keep planting surveillance devices on Galvin. More and more of them, more brazenly, until he got caught.

Unless he'd already been caught. That thought had lodged in his head like a half-chewed bite of steak stuck in your craw. What if Galvin knew?

"Isn't the thing voice-activated?"

Yeager nodded again.

"Maybe it's not transmitting because he hasn't been talking in his office recently."

"But he has." Yeager sounded almost mournful. "We're picking up signal traffic on his home-office landline. Encrypted, so we don't know what he's saying, but we know he's made several calls."

Danny shrugged, shook his head. "I don't know what to tell you. I did my job."

"Maybe you mishandled it. These little pieces of electronics can be delicate."

"I didn't even open the thing." Slocum had opened the dummy medal for him and showed him the component inside. But he hadn't shown Danny how to open it himself, since he didn't need to.

"I believe you. Maybe it got jiggled. These things happen. Point is, it's not transmitting."

"Well, no way am I going back to his study," Danny said. "He caught me in there — he came home unexpectedly when I was placing it, and . . . What if he figured out what I was doing? What if he opened the medal or just destroyed it, or . . . ?"

Yeager blinked a few times but said nothing. He looked at Danny with dead eyes.

"Is it possible he discovered the bug?" Danny asked.

Yeager watched him a little longer. "You're alive, aren't you?"

"Jesus."

"Maybe his security people did a sweep." He shrugged. "The fact that you're alive indicates they don't know you're the one who planted it."

"Well, I'm not going back into his study and planting something else. Absolutely not. I can't."

Yeager pointed with his fork to a reddish hillock on his plate. "They make the best corned beef hash here. Big chunks of brisket. Not that stuff that tastes like cat food you get everywhere else."

"I'm not hungry."

"You want to try something that'll take

the top of your head off, get the homemade cinnamon bun muffin and ask them to grill it for you. I mean, it's life-transforming."

The waitress topped off his mug of coffee, even though he'd maybe taken two sips.

"He has a new driver," Danny said.

"There you go." Yeager shrugged and gave him another dead-eyed look. "The driver took the fall for you. He probably goes into Galvin's office from time to time to get things for his boss, drive them into town. He's a logical suspect."

"So Galvin didn't know it was me."

"Clearly. Nothing was wrong with the transmitter. Safe guess his security people found it in a routine sweep."

"And this poor guy gets killed."

"Collateral damage. Better him than you, right?"

"Great," Danny said, unable to muster much enthusiasm.

Yeager pulled a small black nylon Nike gym bag from the floor and set it on the table. He unzipped it partway and shoved it toward Danny.

He looked inside. There was a gadget inside not much bigger than an iPhone. He looked at Yeager. "Now what?"

"That little doohickey is called a MobilX-tract. It's made by an Israeli company for law enforcement and intelligence agencies, and it costs a buttload of money. Handle with care."

"What does this have to do with me?"

"It's the only move we have left. We tried downloading a software agent to his Black-Berry, but no luck. This way is far more likely to succeed. All you have to do is plug it into Galvin's BlackBerry and touch a few screen prompts, and in three or four minutes it'll download everything. E-mails, text messages, contacts, you name it. Idiot-proof."

"*All* I have to do?"

"We get the information on his Black-Berry, we've got the case against him nailed down."

"That thing never leaves his hands."

"I doubt that."

"I'm supposed to just grab it from him and start downloading . . . ? This is insane."

"It's easy. All you need is the right op-portunity."

"No such thing. Look, it's not my fault that your transmitter was discovered. I did my part. I don't see why I have to risk my neck again because your plan didn't take into account the possibility that Galvin's security people would do a sweep."

Yeager shrugged and took a heaping forkful of hash. He chewed for a few seconds and then said, through a mouthful of food, "You get points for trying. But until we have enough on him to justify an arrest warrant, you're still on the hook."

"Why did you want me to take the T here anyway? Why not my car?"

"Security."

"Like I might be followed?"

"Or there's a tracker on your car. It's all possible."

"If there's a tracker on my car, that means they suspect me," he reasoned. "Right?"

Yeager shrugged. "Maybe they're doing their due diligence. Watching you, seeing who you meet with. Making sure you're not working for the DEA."

"And if they find out I am?"

"That's why we're taking measures to protect you."

"What happens if they find out I'm meeting with the DEA?" Danny persisted.

"Why do you keep obsessing about this? You're, like, picking a scab. Don't keep thinking worst-case scenario, or you'll be too scared to function effectively."

"Yeah, well, he invited me to play squash with him."

"You see? He definitely trusts you. That's a great opportunity. Please tell me you said

172

yes. I'm thinking he's not going to be bringing his BlackBerry onto the squash court. Your opportunity has just presented itself."

"I said no. Anyway, that's not my point. He said I told him I played squash. I never told him that."

"So?"

"How would he know I play squash? I don't even know where my racquet is anymore."

"Isn't that an Ivy League kind of sport? You went to Columbia. That's an Ivy League school, last I heard. He just figured."

"Listen to me —"

The waitress appeared again to top off his coffee mug. "You sure you're not going to have breakfast, sweetie?"

"I'm good," Danny said.

The waitress looked disappointed, but she smiled and sidled away.

"He knows things about me I never told him," Danny said. "It's like he's had me checked out. Like he's been briefed about me. That thing about the squash, that was a slip."

"And that surprises you? Your daughter spends a lot of time with his daughter, he lets you into his house, into his family's life — you think he's not going to be careful? He's not going to have a backgrounder done on you? This is not a guy who trusts a lot of people. In his position, he can't."

Danny exhaled slowly through his nostrils. "Maybe that's all it is."

"That's all it is," Yeager said. He turned his head and smiled. "There's your buddy."

Danny turned and saw Phil Slocum approaching the booth, a beat-up leather portfolio in one hand. He looked grim, even grimmer than usual. He sank into the booth next to Yeager without even giving Danny a glance.

"You look like someone stole your lunch money," Yeager said.

Slocum unzipped the leather portfolio, took out a brown file folder, and handed it to Yeager. "The body checked out."

Yeager's smile faded. He pulled out several 8 × 10 glossy photographs. "Dear God in heaven," he said. "Goddamned animals."

He handed one of the photos to Danny. "I would say they discovered the bug."

It was a photo of a body so disfigured, the carnage so gruesome, that at first glance it didn't even look like a human being.

Only when he saw the mole in the shape of Australia on the right side of what remained of the neck did he recognize Galvin's driver.

25

"It's him," Danny said. "It's the driver. Esteban." Hot prickles of sweat broke out on his forehead, on the back of his neck. Hot acid burned his gullet, and he felt queasy, as if he might vomit. "Where did you find the . . ."

"The body was found in an alley behind a bar in Brighton. Covered by a plastic drop cloth. It was obviously a drug-related execution, and it looks like he was tortured, so the Boston Police drug unit caught it."

Danny lurched from the booth, clattering his fork to the floor, and rushed outside, where he threw up on the sidewalk. A young couple carrying matching Under Armour gym bags were passing by at that moment. The guy shoved his girlfriend away from the trajectory of the vomit.

Danny remained bent over for a minute or so, head ducked, the world spinning and wobbling.

The photos depicted a work of sculpture made by Satan. An arrangement — a derangement — of a human body in parts. The man in the photo, though it was but a torso, was holding his own severed head, as if he were clutching a soccer ball. The head looked like Esteban's head, but it also looked like one of those hyper-real latex Halloween masks, except for the horrific bloody innards of his neck and trachea that hung down raggedly, a torrent of dark blood.

The eyes were open slightly, as if he were falling asleep.

Stuffed into the head's mouth, like discarded gristle on a butcher's counter, was what appeared to be his own dismembered penis.

Danny returned unsteadily to the diner and stood at the booth.

"Was he one of yours?"

Yeager's eyes widened. He glanced to either side. "Sit down, please."

The booths on both sides of them were still empty. Danny slid into the booth, slowly and reluctantly.

Slocum said, "You really think if we'd turned Galvin's driver, we'd be wasting our time with you?"

"Don't shed a tear for Esteban," Yeager said. "He was a low-level *sicario* for the cartel."

"Meaning?"

"Enforcer. Hired gun."

"Well, that could easily have been me."

"It wasn't," Yeager said.

"Who did it?" Danny asked.

"The cartels have cells scattered around the country," Yeager said. "There's no shortage of muscle. We put out a BOLO and this report of a body came back. And checked out."

"Isn't this just going to lead back to Galvin?" Danny said. "As soon as the body's identified. I mean, the driver to some rich investor is found tortured and murdered —"

"The body won't be identified," Yeager said. "Their security people will do their tricks with ID cards and fake passports. This guy here" — he tapped a pudgy forefinger on one of the glossies — "is a John Doe."

Danny nodded, bit his lower lip. "Well, I'm out."

Slocum made a slight movement, as if he were about to say something threatening, but Yeager put a hand on Slocum's arm.

"This is not going to happen to you."

Danny laughed bitterly. "Oh, right, of

course not. How could I possibly think that?"

"If anything, this guy's death is your protection. You're off the hook."

"But you guys have made it clear I'm still very much on the hook. You think you can keep pushing and pushing me until I'm found in pieces, rolled up in plastic somewhere?" He shook his head. "Uh-uh. I'm not meeting with Galvin again. That relationship is over."

"Just like that?" Slocum said. "Suddenly you're gonna cut off all contact? You don't think *that's* going to look suspicious? They find a transmitter, they finger the driver, and suddenly you've disappeared? They'll *know* they got the wrong guy. You'll just turn the klieg lights on yourself, buddy."

Danny smiled unpleasantly. "Oh, no, it won't be anything that obvious. I'll be sick for a while. Then I'll be way behind on a deadline, and I'll make excuses. After a couple of months, he'll give up. Relationship's over. That's all it takes."

"And your daughter?" Yeager asked.

Anger flared up in him suddenly, a lighted match tossed into gasoline. Calmly, he replied, "My daughter has no idea what's going on. Her relationship with Galvin's daughter is innocent, and no one's going to think different."

Their waitress swooped in. "He's the only one eating today? You boys aren't hungry?"

Danny shook his head.

"I'd love the workingman's special," Slocum said.

"I'm sorry, honey, that's only available till nine. Something else?"

"Then I think that crème brûlée French toast has my name on it."

The waitress beamed.

"Danny," Yeager said when she had left. "Who else do you think is going to protect you and your daughter?"

Danny felt his cheeks go hot. "What kind of protection are you talking about? Like those murderers are going to give you advance warning?"

"It's highly unusual for them to target the DEA. They don't want to go there."

"But they do, don't they? I've read about —"

"It has happened," Yeager admitted. "But it's rare, and the Sinaloa boys, well, they may be brutal, but they're also smart enough to know not to take out DEA agents. They do, they're in a world of shit."

Danny stared at him with incredulity. "They thought Esteban was working for you guys."

Yeager said calmly, "They executed the driver because he was a Mexican, Daniel. They thought one of their countrymen was a traitor, so they had to send a message. But they hardly ever do that sort of thing to us or to our people."

"So what happens if I'm caught next time? How are you going to protect me then?"

"We'll get you out of there. You and your daughter."

"Like, the witness protection program?"

Yeager nodded once.

"You've got to be kidding. I'm not going to do that. I'm not going to live that way. I'm not going to ruin my daughter's life."

"That's the worst-case scenario, Daniel. It's not going to happen."

"Can you guarantee that?"

Yeager and Slocum were both looking at him now, but neither said a word.

"Right," Danny said. "Look, I'm the only parent my daughter has. I'm not going to orphan her, you understand? You want to prosecute me for money laundering or whatever bullshit crime you come up with, go for it. Have at it. The fact that your little device got discovered, that's not on me. That's your screwup. I did exactly what you asked me to do. I acted in good faith. I co-operated."

"Exactly," Slocum said. "You cooperated."

"Uh-huh. What's that supposed to mean?"

"You don't realize the position you're in, do you?" Slocum said. "You don't seem to get what we have on you, Danny boy."

"What you *have* on me . . . ?"

"You're not pulling out now, my friend," Slocum said. "Like the bank says, 'substantial penalty for early withdrawal.' "

"Is that supposed to be a threat?"

"Sometimes the DEA leaks," Slocum said. He took a long swallow of coffee. "I really hope that doesn't happen in your case."

And suddenly Danny understood what kind of position he was in. They would rather tip the Sinaloa cartel off that he was a DEA informant than let him get away.

He stood up.

"Daniel, please," Yeager said.

Slocum put down his coffee cup. He reached into his pants pocket, pulled out his wallet, and took out two crisp new hundred-dollar bills. "Here," he said. "Take Galvin up on that squash game. And buy yourself a decent squash racquet."

26

The executive conference room of Harmonics Global, Inc., looked like a thousand other executive conference rooms in corporations around the world. Since the headquarters of Harmonics Global was located in San Diego, though, it had a kind of California feel. There was blond wood and large windows, a lot of glass and steel and copious light. A large Cisco TelePresence screen took up most of one wall. On the opposite end was a projection screen that retracted with a touch of a button. Twenty high-backed leather chairs ringed a gleaming elongated oval table made from African mahogany with purpleheart border inlay.

Harmonics Global was a large private portfolio company whose holdings included fourteen separate companies, ranging from auto parts to contract food services to insurance to freight.

Very few people knew who really owned

Harmonics Global.

At the head of the table sat the CEO of Harmonics, a formidable woman named Laurie Hornbeck. Laurie knew that most people didn't consider her a warm person. She was often called no-nonsense. Her division chiefs were afraid of her. Her blond hair was cut in a short, efficient bob that her detractors called mannish. She wore one of her habitual brightly colored suits over a white silk shell. Today's color was sapphire blue. The only jewelry she wore was gold stud earrings and an onyx choker.

But Laurie Hornbeck was not running the meeting. That was the job of the chief financial officer, Allen Hartley, because the agenda this morning was the budget. It didn't help that Hartley spoke in a monotone. His presentation, Laurie thought, was verbal chloroform. He talked about "optimized distribution networks" and "improved supply chain visibility." He talked about an "end-to-end ROI-driven solution." He talked about "deliverables" and "dollarizing" approaches and taking a "deep dive" into the data. Al Hartley droned as he went through his charts and graphs, and the directors of each division took notes on their laptops, and Laurie Hornbeck furtively checked her BlackBerry.

The rule at the monthly budget meeting was that all participants had to switch off their cell phones. Laurie Hornbeck, being the CEO, was exempt.

About halfway through the meeting, Laurie's BlackBerry buzzed. She put on reading glasses and looked down at the text message that appeared. She cleared her throat and looked up. "Tony, Karen, Barry — in my office right now, please. My apologies, Al. I need fifteen minutes."

She rose from the table.

Laurie Hornbeck's office was flooded with light from the floor-to-ceiling windows overlooking the Pacific. Her office was as efficient and as spare as her hairstyle. Her desktop was empty except for a few photos of her son, her laptop, and two phones, one of them secure. A clean desk meant an orderly mind. In one corner of the room was her bag of golf clubs. On the walls hung several paintings of Taos, New Mexico, by Helmuth Naumer, vivid pastels of pueblos and canyons. Laurie was from New Mexico and kept a vacation house in Taos and got back there whenever she could.

She kept her face calm, because a good leader must stay calm and confident. But she was acutely aware of the acid splashing the back of her throat. Of how violently her heart was pounding. This whole nightmarish development was all she'd been able to think about for days.

Two weeks chilling in Belize, she thought glumly. And now, back in the office just a few days, it was as if she'd never gone.

"It's Omaha. We've sprung a leak," she said. She kept her expression neutral, but she fidgeted with her onyx choker.

"What do you mean, a leak?" said a thin, dark-haired woman with a mournful look. She was the controller of Omaha Logistics, one of Harmonics Global's top holdings. It provided freight-forwarding services to an array of corporate clients, transporting truckload freight in containers and trailers by land, sea, and air.

To almost everyone outside this room — occupied by the top three officers of Omaha Logistics — it looked like a legitimate company.

"One of our cargo jets was seized yesterday in Fresno."

"Jesus Christ," said Omaha's chief operating officer, a pasty-faced, chipmunk-cheeked man with a potbelly. "Fully loaded?"

Laurie nodded. "Then yesterday a banker in the San Francisco office of Pacific Commerce Bank disappeared."

"Mother of God," the controller said quietly, her face growing ever more mournful. "It's Toth."

"What do you mean, disappeared?" asked the chipmunk-cheeked COO.

"He didn't show up for work," Laurie said. "He's not at home. We pinged him and he hasn't replied."

"Do you think he's in the wind?" asked Omaha's chief financial officer, a handsome Latino-looking man with a light brown complexion and thick black hair combed straight back.

"Look, maybe he'll turn up on a beach in Playa del Carmen with a nose bag full of coke and a bevy of barely legal hookers. But I doubt it. That's not his speed."

"But do we have any reason to believe he's been arrested?" the Latino CFO asked with alarm.

Laurie shrugged. "We sure as hell better hope not. I don't even want to think about that possibility. Because if he has . . ." Her voice trailed off. Her stomach roiled with acid. She needed a Tums. Lately she'd been chewing them like candy.

A breach, a leak — that was the nightmare scenario they all dreaded. If the truth were ever to come out about Omaha, they'd all go to prison.

Or — given who their true employers were — worse.

"We have to find the banker at once," the CFO said. "Before he spills anything." In times of stress like this, his Mexican accent became more prominent.

"Obviously," said Laurie. "But by far the more important matter is the leak. We need to find out where it's coming from. Or who it's coming from. And then it has to be plugged. By whatever means necessary."

"Toth has to be found and prevented from talking," the controller said, her voice rising sharply. "Can we get to him? Stop him?"

Laurie looked at Omaha's CFO but said nothing. She wanted this to come from him.

He picked up on her cue. "If we act right away, we can contain the damage. We have a contractor."

The other three corporate officers fell silent. The chipmunk-cheeked COO shifted in his chair.

"This can't be traced back to us," the controller said.

"Obviously," the CFO said. "He is reliable and discreet. This is a job that requires a great deal of finesse. He is in fact a surgeon."

"Are we all in agreement?" Laurie asked.

Everyone but the CFO seemed to be avoiding her eyes.

"This is not going forward unless we're unanimous," she said. She waited. A course of action as fraught with danger as this, she wanted everyone's sign-off.

"Yes," said the controller at last.

"All right," said the COO.

Laurie Hornbeck turned to the CFO. "Then make the call," she said.

27

Riding the T from Broadway to Park Street, he texted Abby: pick up @ 3? He never called her at school, of course. Nor did he send e-mails; e-mails were for old people, she insisted. Abby texted throughout the day, between classes and even during some classes. She texted with the speed of a court reporter. She used abbreviations and jargon he didn't understand.

She replied within two minutes: Thanks but going over to Jenna's, OK?

No, not okay. No way. Danny texted back: Not today. I want you at home.

The train went through a tunnel, and cell service was unavailable, and by the time he reached the Park Street stop, he had a voice mail. From Abby. He didn't even bother listening to the message. He knew she'd be pleading or squawking, or some combination. Only desperation would cause her to resort to the spoken word.

As he crossed the platform to board the Green Line train to Arlington Street, he called her back.

"Daddy," she answered, voice taut. "Jenna and I are going to study precalc, I swear. I promise we'll be working." In the background a girl squealed.

"You can do that at home," he said.

"But we're studying together. I mean, like, why do I have to be at home when we're just going to be on chat?"

"I'd like you to be at home today."

The DEA guys were right: He couldn't abruptly pull out of Galvin's orbit without raising all kinds of suspicion. But Abby was a different story. She was the connective tissue. If she stopped hanging out with Jenna, then he could part ways with Galvin naturally, no questions asked.

He felt like he'd pulled the pin from a grenade and hadn't yet tossed it.

"I mean," she said, her voice getting high, "I could ask the driver to take me home at, like, seven, so we can have dinner, okay?"

He could see Esteban's mutilated head, and he felt nauseated.

"I'll pick you up at three," Danny said with finality, and pressed END.

Then he called Tom Galvin at his office. "You still free for a game of squash?"

28

Danny had walked past the grand old brownstone hundreds of times and had always wondered what was inside. It was a federal-style mansion with a white granite façade, on the steep stretch of Beacon Street facing the Public Garden. The building was wider than its neighbors, with a double bow front.

Its porticoed entrance was unmarked. Just a burnished oak door with a polished brass knob and brass mail slot. Most of the buildings on this block were private residences; Danny had always assumed it was one of those mansions that had been in some Boston Brahmin family since the days of Oliver Wendell Holmes.

It turned out to be the Plympton Club, Boston's oldest social and athletic club. He'd heard about it but didn't know anyone who belonged. Until now.

Inside, the creaky floors were covered with

oriental rugs, the walls covered with oil paintings of boats and birds. A couple of racks of deer antlers were mounted on the wall. Display cases held yellowed antique squash racquets and sepia photographs of players from early in the last century. According to a piece in *Boston* magazine he'd read online, the Plympton Club had six squash courts, a saline pool, and a court-tennis court, known by racquet snobs as a real tennis court. There was a library and an ornate dining room.

He waited on a hard sofa, gym bag on the floor, and tried to act nonchalant.

His discomfort at being in the Plympton Club was nothing, however, compared to his fear of the device in his gym bag being discovered. And how the hell was he going to get five minutes with Galvin's Black-Berry? It never seemed to leave his hands.

And if he got caught . . . ?

What happened to Esteban could just as easily happen to him.

Danny found it hard to believe that Tom Galvin, who seemed an affable, genial type, was in any way involved in the unspeakable murder-torture of his own driver. Maybe he didn't even know about it.

But the people Galvin worked for were brutal and cold-blooded and terrifying.

They wouldn't hesitate to do to Danny what they'd done to Esteban.

If he were caught.

He had to be extremely careful. If there was the slightest chance of being caught, he had to back out of it.

The young blond woman behind the reception desk smiled at him and resumed stamping forms or something with an old-fashioned date stamp. A couple of middle-aged business types came in, laughing heartily about a "triple bogey." They both wore blue blazers with brass buttons. One wore green pants with whales on them. The other wore khakis. They greeted the woman behind the desk, and she waved them through a doorway.

"I kept you waiting," Galvin called out as he entered from the street.

Danny flinched, startled by Galvin's voice. "Hardly," he said, though it had been fifteen minutes.

The twangy guitar riff from "Sweet Home Alabama" played suddenly. Galvin fished his BlackBerry out of the breast pocket of his charcoal chalk-stripe suit.

"Marge, let's push that up an hour," he said loudly into his phone. "What? Hold on, the reception here sucks . . . exactly." He ended the call and shook his head. The young woman behind the desk seemed to give him an annoyed look. "Sorry about that. Just one of those days. You got your gear?"

Danny lifted the gym bag by way of reply. "Everything I need. What's with the ringtone, by the way? Some Alabama connection or something?"

He shrugged. "I like Lynyrd Skynyrd. 'Gimme Three Steps'? 'Free Bird'?"

Danny smiled. "Sure."

"Didn't you ever want to play guitar in a rock 'n' roll band?"

"Sure, who hasn't?"

They rode a small elevator down.

"Cell phone use is officially frowned on here," Galvin muttered, sounding chastened. "It's *not done.*" He affected the lockjaw used by Thurston Howell III in *Gilligan's Island.*

"Impressive place," Danny said.

"I prefer to use the word *insufferable,*" Galvin said. "But it's convenient to my office."

"*My* gym doesn't have antlers on the wall."

"Well, this place doesn't have blacks, Jews, or women. Or Italians or Irish. With the glaring exception of me. Man, having me as a member is such a hair up their ass." He beamed.

194

"Whose?"

"The stiffs who run this mausoleum."

"They let you in."

"They had no choice. They had to."

Danny looked at him. The elevator descended sluggishly, juddering.

"You know, you can't even apply for membership here. You get 'tapped.' You get nominated, and then they sound you out, then they interview you. You have to have dinner with the whole damned governing board, one at a time. Like an endless goddamned colonoscopy."

"I guess you charmed them."

"Charmed them? I saved their butts. This place was going under. The roof was literally caving in, but they didn't have any funds in reserve to repair it, and the old boys refused to increase membership fees. They were talking about selling off part of the building or even shuttering the club altogether. So I stepped in and bailed them out. Made a long-term loan on generous terms."

"In exchange for membership," Danny said, smiling. "An offer they couldn't refuse."

Galvin grinned. The elevator opened on a low-ceilinged corridor that smelled faintly of eucalyptus. "Turned out I had all the right qualifications." He lowered his voice, even though there didn't seem to be anyone within earshot. "These a-holes think they're better than anyone else because they didn't have to work for their money. Great-grandfather earned it, which makes them aristocrats or something. Whereas guys like me from Southie, went to BC, whatever whatever, who have the chops to earn our own money, we're gonna get black-balled. . . ." His voice trailed off as a silver-haired older man passed by in a madras jacket with plaid pants. The man nodded and said, "Tom."

Galvin nodded back.

"I saw that e-mail about the Galvin Fitness Center at Lyman," Danny said. A notice had gone out from Lally Thornton's office announcing plans for the new pool, track, and athletic facility, thanks to a generous gift from Thomas and Celina Galvin.

Galvin pushed open the heavy door to the men's locker room. He sighed, grabbed a couple of towels, and tossed one to Danny. "Sometimes you gotta grease the wheels. No other school was willing to take her in for junior and senior years."

He stopped at an attendant's desk.

"¿Hola, José," he said, "que tal?"

"Pues muy bien, Sr. Galvin," the moon-

196

faced, chubby attendant replied, handing Galvin a locker key on an elastic loop. *"¿Y usted?"*

"¡Bien, bien . . . ya sabes como va la vida!"

Danny wasn't surprised that Galvin spoke Spanish, being married to a Mexican woman. But he seemed to speak with the fluency of a native. That surprised him.

"Sweet Home Alabama" came on again. Galvin pulled his BlackBerry out of his suit, gave José an apologetic smile, and headed toward a long bank of lockers.

"An hour, an hour and a half at the most," he said into the phone. "We good? Okay."

He hit END and put it back into his suit jacket pocket. "That's how the world works," he said, as if the conversation had never been interrupted. "Sorta like your robber barons. Vanderbilt and Carnegie and Rockefeller and Morgan — it took a couple of generations to wash the stink out of that money, right?"

"True."

"Why are those guys 'robber barons,' anyway? Why aren't they entrepreneurs?"

"Excellent question."

"I mean, were they any different from Steve Jobs or Bill Gates or the guys who founded Google? And didn't Rockefeller give away billions of dollars? I bet they all

197

did, right?"

"One man's robber baron is another man's entrepreneur. Or philanthropist. What about you?"

"What about me?"

"Robber baron or entrepreneur?"

Galvin waggled his head to one side, then the other. Like he was about to deliver a clever reply. But then thought better of it. "I'm an investor."

"What kind of investor?"

"Private equity. It's boring."

"Not to me. Or probably to you."

He heaved a sigh. As if he'd given this answer a hundred thousand times before. "I manage money for a very wealthy family."

"Yeah? Who's that?"

Galvin shrugged. "Do you know the names of the ten richest families in Mexico?"

"No," Danny admitted.

"Then I don't think the name would mean much to you."

The locker room smelled of burnt towel lint from a dryer nearby, mixed with the smell of some kind of old-fashioned hair tonic, like Vitalis, and underlying it all the odor of musty gym clothes. There was a TV mounted high on the wall in a small lounge area. A stainless-steel refrigerator with glass doors containing an arsenal of dewy water bottles. A long sink counter equipped with combs in tall glass Barbicide jars bathing in blue disinfectant. Disposable razors, cans of Barbasol shaving cream. Rows of old-looking lockers made of dark wood, some with keys in their locks, metal tags dangling from their elastic lanyards.

The locker room was not quite deserted, but close to it. A few voices came from a distant locker bay. As far as Danny could tell, the only employee working the locker room was José the attendant. Not a lot of staff seemed to be employed at the Plympton Club, which fit the profile of a club under some financial duress.

A bull-necked guy in his seventies, powerfully built and covered in gray fur, strutted by totally naked, everything hanging out, towel around his neck.

Danny took note of Galvin's locker, number 809, and found an available one nearby. Galvin's gym clothes, he saw, were already in his locker, neatly folded. The club apparently did members' laundry. A canister of Wilson yellow-dot squash balls on a shelf, a racquet on a hook. Galvin removed his suit jacket and draped it on a wooden coat hanger.

His BlackBerry was still in the breast pocket.

Danny changed into a white undershirt and an old pair of Columbia gym shorts. Galvin's clothes looked brand-new: white shorts and a red-and-black shirt, both bearing the Black Knight logo. A blindingly white pair of Prince squash shoes.

The two middle-aged businessmen who'd come in before them were now leaving the locker room, squash racquets in hand, still talking golf. They wore old rumpled T-shirts (Harvard Crew and Phillips Exeter) and gym shorts with sagging elastic waistbands. Like they got their clothes from a heap in the homeless shelter where Lucy worked.

"Nice togs, Thomas," Harvard Crew said.

"Thank you, Landon," said Galvin.

"Very sharp. Are you playing in the US Open?"

Galvin smiled mirthlessly. He gave Danny a knowing look. Danny was familiar with that kind of faux-friendly rich-guy backstab. He heard it at Lyman, too. Two minutes later the guys would be privately mocking Galvin for his nouveau riche attire. For trying too hard.

Galvin slammed his locker door and turned the key to lock it.

The BlackBerry inside.

29

Galvin placed his stuff — his zippered racquet case, his locker key, a new can of balls,
a towel — on the ledge outside the glass
wall at the back of a court. Danny dropped
his racquet case and towel right next to
them and kept his locker key in his pocket.

Their warm-up was bumpy. Danny
couldn't settle on a grip. He kept mis-hitting
the ball, either wildly high or too low. From
the next court over, indecent grunts and
moans echoed, like in some porn flick.

Danny was convinced you could tell a lot
about someone by how he or she played
sports. Was she a ball hog or a team player?
Was he a mild-mannered guy who turned
into a psycho on the court or the field?
Spontaneous, or analytical?

Tom Galvin was deadly serious about his
game. That easy wit, that contrarian sense
of humor — it was all gone. He was a fero-
cious player. Not just that he was skilled,

which he was — he had a pro's sense of strategy — but he just didn't give up a point. In his goggles, Galvin even looked like some kind of evil insect, a praying mantis.

Granted, Danny didn't put up much in the way of competition, at least not at first. Once he'd been a decent player, at Columbia, but that was too many years ago. He was hardly in peak condition anymore. He was slow. He didn't maintain control of the T. His serves were too easy.

Whereas Galvin's serve was killer. He lobbed it in a perfect high arc: a lethal parabola that plopped down in the back corner far behind Danny, hit the nick, and died a nasty little death. Danny lost the first two games in short order before he began to figure out how to answer such a powerhouse serve.

In the third game, Danny finally pulled even with Galvin. Eight all. Then one of Galvin's shots bounced twice, no doubt about it at all, which gave the serve to Danny and maybe even the winning point. To Danny's surprise, Galvin picked up the ball and marched to the service box with no discussion.

"Uh, I'm pretty sure that was a double bounce," Danny said.

"No, it wasn't," Galvin said flatly.

"Actually —"

"Ready?" Galvin moved into position to deliver another one of his killer serves. Danny almost persisted, almost said, "I *saw* it," but decided it wasn't worth it. Galvin knew damned well the ball had bounced twice. No point in arguing. His club, his ball, his rules.

It occurred to him that, with two guys as competitive as they were, playing squash wasn't exactly a formula for camaraderie.

On the next point, Danny somehow managed to hit a soft drop shot from the forehand side, in the front right corner. Galvin, a half second late, came crashing into Danny's left shoulder a split second after the ball hit the nick. He was obviously too late to have retrieved the ball anyway.

"Let," he said.

Danny laughed. "No way you would have got that."

"Dude. I called a let. You were in the way."

His club, his ball, his rules. Danny let it slide.

After Galvin won the third game in a row, he said, "Best of seven?"

"Sure," Danny said. "But how about a water break first?" He was dripping with sweat. The grip on his racquet was slippery.

"You're trying to break my rhythm, aren't you?" Galvin said. Twin rivulets of sweat coursed down either side of his face. "I think you're trying to mess with my momentum."

"Hey, whatever it takes."

Galvin smiled and pushed open the glass door. The air outside the court was chilly, and it felt good against Danny's face. Galvin grabbed his towel, jingling the locker key, and blotted his face with the towel. He gestured with a floppy wave toward the drinking fountain and headed over there himself.

"Actually," Danny said, setting his racquet on the floor, "I'll grab us a couple of cold water bottles, if you don't mind."

Galvin waggled a hand without looking back.

Danny stooped down, picked up Galvin's locker key in what he hoped was one fluid gesture — *an innocent mistake,* he could claim — and went into the locker room.

He didn't hear or see anyone else there.

He tried locker number 809 and found it locked.

Maybe that's why they're called lockers.

The locker room was still. In the silence he became aware of ambient noise from distant machinery: the wheezing and clattering of an industrial washer and dryer, maybe in a utility room nearby. The rush of water through the ancient sclerotic pipes. The muted whoosh of the ventilation system. A showerhead dripping, plinking, into a puddle on the tiled shower floor.

And over it all, his heart thudding. Faster than normal, but steady. He'd rehearsed this whole thing, had gone through it mentally over and over again, considering every angle he could think of, every possible hitch.

He turned the key and pulled it open, a sense of queasy dread coming over him. Galvin's locker was orderly. His splendid chalk-stripe charcoal suit hung neatly on a hanger, which had been placed on a hook. On the top shelf was the spare can of Wilson yellow-dots and two neatly folded T-shirts, both new-looking. A very nice pair of cordovan cap-toe brogues, buffed to a mirror shine, had been carefully placed on the locker floor, both toe-in. Inscribed on the tan insole was a signature, John Lobb, probably the shoemaker.

The BlackBerry was in the left inside breast pocket of the suit.

Still no one around.

He couldn't resist peeking at the label sewn on the inside pocket:

MADE IN ENGLAND BY
ANDERSON & SHEPPARD LTD
SAVILE ROW TAILORS
32, OLD BURLINGTON STREET, LONDON

Then there were some kind of numbers that looked typewritten, and a date: 22/08/11. Danny didn't know much about the sort of clothes rich people wore, but he knew enough to recognize that a Savile Row tailor was a big deal, and those numbers and that date meant the suit was custom tailored.

Danny slid the BlackBerry out of Galvin's suit jacket. It was on, but the display said DEVICE IS LOCKED. Meaning it was password-protected.

But he'd expected that.

Yeager had assured him that the MobilX-tract was able to circumvent passcodes. He glanced at the time. Only two minutes had gone by, which wasn't bad. Grabbing a couple of water bottles from the cooler in the locker room lounge would be a matter of a minute, a minute and a half. But add in a quick potty break, and four minutes wouldn't provoke Galvin's suspicions. Much longer than that, and Galvin would wonder what had happened and might amble back to the locker room to look for him.

So far, so good.

Then he was startled by a sudden blast of music.

The "Sweet Home Alabama" ringtone seemed louder than before. No doubt because it had pierced the stillness. He didn't remember how to silence the ringer. He didn't want to answer the call, just wanted it to stop playing Lynyrd Skynyrd. It keep blaring while he grabbed the phone wildly, hitting every button he could find on the sides and on top. Finally the music stopped.

When he heard the voice, he jumped.

José the attendant stood no more than ten feet away. He was a quiet one.

"Can I help you, sir?" hc said.

30

Galvin's BlackBerry felt warm in his grip.

He slipped it into the front pocket of his gym shorts and said, turning back to the locker, "There they are."

Ignoring José, he took the canister of squash balls from the shelf, popped off the plastic lid, upended the tube, and dropped one into his palm. He affected an indifference to the attendant. As if the kid was a distraction, an annoyance. Nothing more.

He pocketed the ball, then looked around at José, as if he'd just noticed him. Now his disinterested expression turned supercilious. Danny had learned from his time as a Lyman parent. "Mr. Galvin would like a bottle of water. Uh, you know, *agua*? Could you please get me a couple? Thanks very much."

As if the locker room attendant were his personal retainer. Which was probably how most of the club's members regarded him.

In the arsenal of human expressions, arrogance was an effective weapon of offense. Whether or not José suspected Danny was rummaging around in Tom Galvin's locker, he had a job to do. That was his first priority.

José shifted uncomfortably. He looked wary. "Yes, sir," he said. "Of course."

He could see Danny had opened Galvin's locker. But was he there at Galvin's behest? José would have to assume it. Whatever he thought, he would never dare accuse a guest of such petty criminality. Job security trumped loyalty every time.

The moment José was gone, Danny closed Galvin's locker and raced to his own. Before Galvin's phone could ring again, Danny unlocked his locker and set Galvin's phone on top of his Under Armour gym bag.

Now José had returned, a water bottle in each hand.

"Thank you," Danny said, taking them, setting them down on the bench. He smiled.

José nodded but didn't smile back.

After José had circled back to his desk, Danny again opened his locker. He unzipped the end compartment of his gym bag and took out a wadded-up shirt, inside of which was the little oblong device.

Standing in front of his locker now, he worked quickly. He connected the MobilXtract gadget to the micro USB port on the side of Galvin's BlackBerry. He'd already set up the MobilXtract as much as he could in advance, entering the model number of Galvin's phone, selecting the option for working around the password, selecting EXTRACT ALL. Now all he had to do was press the START button on the thing and let it go to work.

The MobilXtract's display came to life. It said DETECTING . . . CONNECTING . . . and then EXTRACTING CONTENTS.

A green progress bar came up. Yeager had told him it would take anywhere from forty-five seconds to three or four minutes, depending on how many photos Galvin kept on his phones. Photos, videos, and ringtones were the main memory hogs, Yeager had said.

But the progress bar seemed stuck. It was just a little sliver of green. It wasn't moving. He waited. No voices in the locker room. Nobody else in sight.

He checked his watch. Four minutes had gone by. That was a lot of time, but he could finesse it. He'd got the water and used the john. Why not?

He looked again at the green progress bar, watched it inch along. Actually, *inching* wasn't the right word. *Millimetering,* maybe.

Slowly, slowly, almost unbearably so.

But at least it was moving, if incrementally. It was working. But this wouldn't be finished in a minute or two. It looked like the job was going to take a while. Maybe five minutes. Maybe more.

He couldn't stay here while the transfer happened.

He had to leave Galvin's BlackBerry connected and go back to the squash courts.

It was a risk. A fairly big one, actually.

If Galvin abruptly decided to return to the locker room . . . ?

But he had no choice.

Danny handed Galvin the bottle of water. His stomach was tight, but he managed to keep his facial expression relaxed.

"I'm all set," Galvin said. He set it down on the floor, not far from where he'd earlier deposited his squash case and his key. The key that was no longer there.

Galvin's key was in Danny's pocket.

Looking at his watch, Galvin said, "Ready to rock 'n' roll?"

Danny nodded. Somehow he had to get back to his locker, disconnect Galvin's BlackBerry, and put it back.

Before Galvin noticed his locker key was missing.

Or decided he needed to use his Black-Berry, damn the club's rules.

Powered by nervous energy, but even more by simple competitiveness, he played better and more forcefully than he had before the break. Maybe because he was beginning to learn Galvin's serve, or maybe he just got lucky, but Danny returned the serve, hit a drive, and Galvin hit a drive back. Then Danny hit a backhand drop shot and scored a point. He'd pulled even. Eight all.

Then came a long rally. Not just a long rally, but the Bataan Death March of rallies. A cramp emerged in his left side, spreading and blooming, its raptor claws clutching and twisting his insides. The only noise in the court was the squeak of their gum soles on the floor and the *th-pock th-pock th-pock* of their racquets hitting the ball.

Galvin began panting.

Then Danny backed away from the ball and bent deeply, stepping back as if clearing space for a big backhand drive. But at the last second, he hit the ball softly. It kissed the side wall, barely touched the front wall, and there it died.

Galvin had lost the point and the game. He laughed loudly. "Ha! The old trickle boast! Nice!"

"Thanks."

"Good job of — deception there." Galvin gasped. "Ya got me."

"Thanks." Danny scooped up the ball to serve, but Galvin put up a hand to stop him. He was breathing heavily.

"You almost killed me."

Danny smiled.

"All — right," Galvin said. He leaned over, bracing himself with his palms on his thighs. He looked up at Danny, face dark, glowering. "The hell did you — do in the locker room?"

Danny's stomach did a flip. "What?"

"That break you just took," Galvin said. "I know what — you were up to."

"Hold on . . ."

"That wasn't a water break. You went — you found some Red Bull, right?" He attempted a pallid grin. "PowerBar, maybe? I mean, you musta taken *something* back there. Now, that — was a *game.*"

Relief flooded Danny's body like a warm bath. He smiled, nodded. "Damn near killed myself. Listen, my bladder's about to explode. Gotta use the bathroom real quick. This time I won't take as long. Promise."

"Gonna take another hit of that Red Bull, is that it?"

Danny chuckled. "Be right back." It would

take only about a minute to disconnect Galvin's BlackBerry — the gizmo had to be finished hoovering up the data — and return it to Galvin's locker.

"Know what?" Galvin said. "I think — it's nature's way — telling us it's quitting time."

Danny's mind began spinning, a hamster on a wheel. He had to get back to his locker before Galvin opened his own and noticed his BlackBerry missing.

Before — *oh God* — Galvin realized his locker key was missing.

Screwed, he thought. *Now I'm screwed.*

"No way. I'm making a comeback."

"Three to one — Danny — don't know what kind of miracle you're hoping for."

"I thought we said best of seven."

"Naaah, I've got to get back. Got an afternoon from hell ahead of me."

"I'll make it quick. You can spare ten more minutes, right?"

"Sorry, man. I'm — done. You're welcome to stay and — do drills or whatever."

"That's all right. See you in there," Danny said, hoping to get there ahead of him. When he reached the swinging doors to the locker room, he heard Galvin groan loudly.

"My damn locker key."

Danny froze. Swiveled his head toward Galvin. "Oh, jeez. Sorry, man, I must have spaced out, grabbed yours." He fished Galvin's key out of his left pocket, held it out sheepishly, then tossed it to Galvin, who caught it in the air. "No wonder I couldn't open my locker."

"So where's yours?"

"I got both. Don't ask."

Galvin looked baffled, shook his head. "Whatever."

Danny pushed his way into the locker room ahead of Galvin. Galvin followed a few seconds behind, still breathing hard.

Danny went to his locker, unlocked it, and planted his body between the open locker and Galvin's line of sight. The MobilXtract had finished. The entire contents of Galvin's BlackBerry had been downloaded.

Now all that remained was to get Galvin's phone back where it belonged.

Galvin was standing before his own open locker, staring inside. His breathing was slowing. His brow was furrowed. Like something was puzzling him.

Like he was looking for something.

Danny reached in, yanked his dress shirt off its hook and draped it over the Black-Berry and the MobilXtract. He held his breath, bracing himself for Galvin to notice the missing BlackBerry.

And if he did, then what?

He'd assume his memory was faulty. Anyone would. He'd be thinking that he didn't really put his BlackBerry in his suit pocket. He just thought he did. When you reach middle age and you start to forget things, your memory's no longer an unimpeachable witness. Maybe he left it somewhere, misplaced it. He wouldn't be suspecting theft, not here, not in the Plympton Club.

He'd search his locker. Then look around to see if he'd dropped it.

Maybe he'd go ask José.

Instead, Galvin didn't seem to be missing his phone at all, at least not yet. He was disrobing. So Danny did, too.

And realized the hitch in his plan.

Because if Galvin locked his locker and took his key with him to the shower, Danny wouldn't be able to return the damned BlackBerry.

But would he lock up? You would at a gym whose clientele was sketchy. Not here.

Galvin didn't.

He slammed his locker just before Danny did, and they headed for the showers.

But then "Sweet Home Alabama" came on. Muffled, but still audible.

Danny cursed silently.

Galvin stopped, turned, as if listening to

the tune.

Or as if deciding whether to answer his phone.

Then he turned back and kept on going, and Danny, exhaling, followed. The showers were next to the restroom area with the sinks and toilets and urinals. Danny hung up his towel and entered an old-fashioned shower stall across the aisle from Galvin's. It had once probably been deluxe but was now just old. White subway tiles covered the three walls, floor to ceiling, with little hex tiles on the floor. Brass shower mixer handles and escutcheon and a sunflower rain showerhead the size of a dinner plate.

Danny let the water run for all of ten seconds, the world's fastest shower. It didn't even have a chance to get warm. Then he shut it off, grabbed his towel off the hook, and rushed through the restroom area toward the locker, as if he'd forgotten his shampoo or something. Even though each shower stall had shampoo and soap dispensers.

He heard a *squee squeee squee squee* and glanced up to see José.

The damned locker room attendant, who seemed to have a sixth sense for when Danny didn't want him around, was pushing a big yellow mop bucket and wringer on squeaky casters. He didn't look up when Danny went by.

Danny needed ten, at most twelve, seconds to make the switch.

He had counted it out. Open his locker, take the BlackBerry, over to Galvin's locker, open it, reach into Galvin's suit jacket, slip it into the pocket.

Six quick moves. Twelve seconds, max.

He found his locker. Opened it.

Heard loud voices reverberating against hard walls.

"¿Como le fue el partido?" José speaking.

"Mas o menos." Galvin. He, too, must have taken a brisk shower. José probably wouldn't be talking to him if he were still bathing. That meant Galvin was out, maybe toweling off.

But maybe he'd take his time drying himself. Or stand in front of the mirror and comb his hair.

Danny opened his locker, yanked the USB cable out of the phone.

"¡Chinga, espero que el pegó fuerte!" said José.

He spun, located Galvin's locker.

Then Galvin's voice, louder and markedly closer. *"¡Si, le gané bien facíl! ¿Como esta Andrea?"*

Pulse racing, he opened Galvin's locker. A

sudden worry: What would he say if Galvin saw him? *Sorry, wrong locker? I opened yours instead of mine?* Preposterous and not credible.

Galvin's chalk-stripe suit hung neatly on its wooden hanger.

Now José: *"Pues si,* señor, *está muy bien, gracias a Dios."*

Without even looking, Danny jammed the BlackBerry into a pocket, the inside breast pocket of the suit, and —

Shut Galvin's locker door just as Galvin hove into sight, towel around his waist, whistling.

He clearly hadn't seen what Danny had just done.

Sweat broke out on Danny's scalp.

"So what's up for you now?" Galvin asked, opening his locker. "Back to work?"

"Gotta pick Abby up at school."

"Right, right, it's almost that time, isn't it?" He put on an undershirt and then his crisp white shirt. "Sometimes I like to pick Jenna up, but today doesn't work."

They finished dressing. Galvin put on his suit coat. "This was fun. We should do it again. You're a whole lot better than you kept telling me. Man, I mean, a trickle boast, right?"

"Sweet Home Alabama" came on. Galvin

reflexively reached his right hand into his left inside breast pocket.

The tune kept playing. Galvin looked baffled. Fumbled around. His left hand reached into his right inside breast pocket.

His eyes narrowed.

"Strange," he said, grabbing his Black-Berry. "I always keep it on that side."

He answered the phone: "Yep?" Then, "I should be there in ten minutes."

He ended the call. "I must be losing my mind," he said.

As if he knew something was amiss.

31

Danny drove up to the pickup line at Lyman right on time, but he didn't see Abby in the knot of girls hanging out in front of the school's main building.

Nor was she among the girls trickling out of the front entrance. She was normally punctual. Maybe she was talking to a teacher. Maybe she'd misplaced something.

By the time Danny's car reached the curb, the crowd of girls was thinning out, and still no Abby.

Leon Chisholm, in full traffic-cop mode, gave him a wave and a smile. "Haven't seen her," he said. Danny smiled back, hit her phone number on his iPhone.

It rang once and went to her voice-mail message, high-pitched and singsong. "Hi, it's Abby, you know what to do!"

Leon waved him out of the queue, toward the short-term parking area just off the circular drive. "If you don't mind," he said.

"So I can keep the trains running on time."

"No problem." Danny felt a flash of irritation. Normally, she couldn't wait to get the hell out of school. It was possible, sure, that she had a good reason for being late. But she should have texted to let him know.

After five minutes or so waiting with the car running, he switched it off and walked into the school building. He saw a girl he recognized from one of Abby's birthday parties a few years back at a Build-a-Bear Workshop where the girls made their own teddy bears. She was tiny and had a mop of curly hair and a sour disposition and was in the middle of an animated conversation with a much taller girl in a Lyman Crew warm-up jacket.

"Shira?"

The girl turned away from the crew jock. "Yeah?"

"You see Abby?"

"You mean, like, in school?"

"I mean, like, recently."

Shira shrugged, shook her head, and turned back to her friend.

Danny checked his phone for a text message, maybe a voice mail that might have come in without the phone making a sound. That happened sometimes when the reception was spotty. Nothing there.

He didn't remember what her last class was or where it took place. He didn't remember where her locker was. But the school secretary-receptionist in the front office would know where she was supposed to be. It occurred to him that she might be sick, might have gone to the school infirmary. But the school was supposed to call him and say so. Maybe it had just happened.

All that speculation was pointless, he then decided. She was probably loitering at the lockers — wherever they were — with Jenna.

Though, come to think of it, he hadn't seen Galvin's Maybach limo in the pickup line, and there was no way the new driver was going to be late picking her up.

He looked around, fully expecting Abby to appear, sheepish or defensive or some combination of both.

But she wasn't there.

The school secretary, Mrs. Gifford, a grandmotherly white-haired woman with apple cheeks who was probably ten years younger than she looked, smiled at him as she finished a conversation and then hung up the phone.

"Looking for Abby?" Mrs. Gifford said. She knew the names of all the school's students and could identify all the upper classmen by face.

"She didn't sign out early, did she?"

She donned a pair of reading glasses on a chain around her neck and consulted her computer screen. "She was here today, but you knew that. And, no, she didn't sign out early. Unless she left early and forgot to sign out as they're supposed to."

"Where was her last class?"

"Well . . . human sexuality, in Burke 203."

"How do you get there?"

It was a long trek through the main building and into the adjoining one, Burke Hall, a maze of jags and blind alleys and staircases up and down and up and down again. He saw a pretty black girl named Carla who was a friend of Abby's, or at least used to be.

Carla had seen Abby at lunch but had no idea where she was now.

Abby wasn't in or near the classroom where her last class had been held. Danny checked his iPhone, obsessively now, for a text or a voice message or an e-mail. He called her mobile phone and it went straight to voice mail.

She was nowhere in school to be found.

So maybe she had disobeyed his order and gone home with Jenna, before dismissal. Somewhere in his call log he had the

Galvins' home number, he was sure. He'd called the house once or twice. Celina Galvin had called his cell once, he recalled. But when he located her incoming call in the call history, it was marked BLOCKED. He searched for the outgoing calls he'd made to their house but didn't find any. Maybe, in fact, he'd never called their landline. Celina had called him once, and he'd called Abby's cell when she was over there. No use in trying directory assistance to find their home number. It would be unlisted for sure.

Well, Galvin was never without his Black-Berry. He called that number, and it went right to voice mail. Damn. Using his phone's browser, he found the phone number for Galvin Advisers in Boston and called it. He got one of those infernal voice-mail prompt menus that tell you to enter the four-digit extension of the person you want to speak with, or press 9 for a company directory. He pressed 0, then pressed it again, until an operator came on the line, and he asked for Tom Galvin's office. A woman answered Galvin's line and said he was out of the office and she had no information on when he was returning, and she had no way of reaching him, and would he like to leave a message? He did. He said it was urgent.

He called Lucy, on the off chance that she might know something.

"I haven't talked to her," Lucy said. "Was she upset about something?" Traffic noise was loud in the background wherever she was. On Danny's end, in the school hallways, it was getting quieter.

"No. Well, yes, maybe. I told her to come home after school and not go over to the Galvins'."

"Oh, really?"

"She naturally wasn't happy about that."

"Did she refuse?"

"Refuse? No."

"Did she sound upset?"

"Annoyed, maybe."

"Angry at you?"

"Probably, but what else is new?"

"So maybe she took the T home."

"She knew I was picking her up, like always."

"Sure, but maybe she felt insulted. Belittled, as if you were questioning her judgment."

"Of course I was questioning her judgment. She's sixteen."

"Maybe she felt infantilized."

Infantilized. Shrink talk. But he knew better than to point it out.

"So she rebelled by taking the train home,

to remind you she's not a kid anymore. Or to punish you, show you she didn't want to get a ride with you."

"Infantilized." It just slipped out.

"Danny. If she was on the T when you called and the train was underground, she wouldn't have cell phone reception and you'd get voice mail. Just try her again."

"Yeah, well . . ." He'd called her five or six times by now. Unless her train was stuck underground, she couldn't still be on the subway. "If you hear from her . . ."

"Of course. You're not scared something might have happened to her, are you?"

"Gotta go," Danny said.

But he couldn't keep that image from violating his thoughts, that grotesque photo of Galvin's chauffeur Esteban, horribly butchered. Abby was the most precious thing in his life, and what's most precious to us is our greatest vulnerability. If someone had taken her, kidnapped her . . .

But he couldn't allow his thoughts to veer off that way.

He felt oddly remote from the halls around him, covered with drawings and projects. Bulletin boards about club activities and games, and cubbyholes for the younger girls. Unsettling self-portraits on the wall, executed with creepily disproportionate features, a gallery of present and future body-image issues. It was like he was floating in midair, seeing everything through the wrong end of a telescope.

He returned to his car and got in and tried to clear his head, to think of what to do. He checked and rechecked his phone for voice mails, for texts that might have popped up, might have slipped by unnoticed, but there were none.

He flashed back to an incident he didn't like to think about, years ago when Abby was three, maybe four. He wondered whether all parents had something similar happen to them. Sarah had some function after work, so he'd taken Abby to the Prudential mall.

Her favorite store was an overpriced candy shop with a display case of chocolate truffles and chocolate-covered pretzels and white chocolate peppermint bark and dried pineapple crescents enrobed in milk chocolate. A revolving rack of huge multicolored lollipops. But Abby was always drawn to the Plexiglas bins of radioactively hued jelly beans.

He had said no, no candy today, and they went to the food court to get her a slice or two of pizza. Standing in a long line, he turned, and she was gone.

He looked around, gripped with panic. She wasn't there; she was nowhere in sight. Heart racing, he walked through the hordes of tourists, didn't see her, knew she'd been abducted. *I looked away for a second,* he'd say later.

He found her two minutes later at the candy shop, shoveling red jelly beans into a clear plastic bag. The longest two minutes of his life.

Maybe that was all that had happened. Red jelly beans. Because if what had happened to her was anything like what he feared, he didn't know what he'd do. He couldn't go on living.

Leon Chisholm approached, stiff-legged, and Danny rolled down the window.

"Abby in trouble?"

In trouble? he thought. *What's he implying, what does he know?* And then, the realization: "Oh, no, she's not being kept after school, no."

"You look shook up."

"I'm fine, everything's . . . I just don't know where the hell my daughter went." He tried to sound annoyed, not scared.

"The junior and senior girls, a lot of them go over to the food court down the block after school. Where the hospital is? They get pizza or ice cream or have a bagel or what have you. I see them heading over there in little gangs."

"But you didn't see Abby, right?"

He shook his head. "Nor her friend Jenna."

"It's the damnedest thing."

"I'm sure it's nothing."

"I'm sure you're right."

He texted her: Where R U????? and waited for her reply, but nothing came. He waited for the word *delivered* to appear in little letters under the text, a reassuring confirmation. But it hung there in a green balloon, a dialogue bubble in a comic strip. And nothing came back. He called her cell again.

Finally, he realized, stupidly, that he hadn't called the one, most obvious place: home. She must have gone home on her own, sulking, and turned off her phone. She had a house key, after all.

No answer.

In the old days of answering machines, he could have spoken after the beep, and if she was there, she would have heard. And picked up. But that didn't work in the age of voice mail.

He pulled out of the circular drive and drove the few short blocks over to the medical area. The traffic was heavy and there were no parking spaces. He double-parked and raced into the food court, moving from the bagel place to the pizza place to the coffee place to the ice cream place, and she wasn't there. The tables were crowded with people, a few tables of girls just a few years older than Abby, some looking Abby's age, but none of them Abby.

He returned to the car with his heart pounding in his ears and found a Day-Glo orange parking ticket tucked under a windshield wiper. He didn't care. He got into the car and gunned the engine and barreled through a yellow traffic light, and drove to Marlborough Street.

No parking spaces there, either. He double-parked and ran up thc front steps of his building. Keyed himself in and took the stairs to the second floor, and as he put the key in the lock, he rehearsed the angry words he was going to speak.

But she wasn't home.

He collapsed onto the couch, gripping his iPhone, feeling at once hollow and nauseated.

He was finding it hard to keep the terrifying thoughts from intruding now. The simple logic of the cartel's enforcers taking his daughter. Of course they would. He cursed himself for ever having let himself get involved in this. He should have taken his chances with the lawyer and the court system, and his daughter would be here with him, instead of . . .

He called Galvin's cell again and it went to voice mail, but he didn't leave a message. He called Galvin's office and asked for Galvin and got the same unhelpful secretary. "He must have left early for a meeting out of the office, Mr. Goodman. I don't know what else to tell you."

Danny found it hard to believe that Galvin's secretary couldn't locate him precisely at any moment, but he said, "I'm a friend. As I told you. What's his home number?"

"I'm sorry," she replied quickly. "We don't give that out."

"You see, the problem is that my daughter's missing, and I need to know whether she might have gone home with Jenna. My daughter is Abby Goodman. Can you at least call Celina and ask if she's there?"

A pause. "Certainly, can you hold?"

In a little over a minute, she returned to the line. "I'm sorry, Celina's not home. None of the family is there. I wish I could help you. I know how worried you must be."

"Thanks for trying," he said, and hung up.

He called Abby's phone and called it again and again. He texted her again. He searched his call log for missed calls.

You heard things like the first thirty-six hours after a disappearance were the most important. Or was it the first twelve hours? He didn't remember.

But he knew he should call the police and report her missing, that was the first thing to do.

File a missing-persons report with the police and look forward to that moment, maybe an hour from now, when his phone rang and it was Abby, and there'd been some sort of misunderstanding, and he'd have to call the police back sheepishly. He would be delighted to be made a fool of.

He just wanted her back.

If . . . if the cartel enforcers had done . . . something . . . (he wouldn't let himself complete that thought. Just . . . something) they would contact him and make a demand.

And he would instantly comply, whatever they wanted.

If they wanted blood, he would gladly offer himself up. If they would let her go, he'd submit himself to the same torture they'd inflicted on Esteban. Just as long as they let her go.

His iPhone rang, and he heaved a big sigh until he looked at it and saw it wasn't Abby.

Heart hammering.

"No," he said to Lucy. "Nothing. I looked everywhere. You didn't hear from her?"

"This is weird, Danny."

He just exhaled.

"It's not like her."

"No."

"She wouldn't have, I don't know, gone somewhere on her own, right? I mean, a pretty sixteen-year-old girl, she's not —"

"Don't, Lucy. Just . . . don't go there."

"I'm sorry. Danny, you should probably notify the police."

"You're right."

"I mean, it's just a formality, the sort of thing you're supposed to do, because I'm sure she's on her way home, and it was a big misunderstanding, that's all."

"Right," he said dully, and at that moment, he heard a key turning in the lock.

32

"Where were you?" he said. Torn between towering relief and towering anger, he tried his best to keep his tone neutral. But there was no disguising the quaver in his voice.

Abby seemed smaller, as if she had shrunk into herself, the way a pill bug rolls itself up into a tight ball when threatened. Her cheeks, normally brushed with pink, were bright red, but that could have been from being outside in the cool air. Her metallic-glinting scarf was wound around her neck several times. Her fine blond hair flew away in wild hanks.

"Shopping with Jenna," she said. "What's the big deal?"

He got up from behind his desk and approached slowly. "What's . . . the big deal? What's the big deal? You didn't get my phone messages or my texts?"

"I turned off my phone."

"You turned off your phone." *Steady,* he

told himself. *Cool it.* "When have you ever, I mean ever, turned your phone off? What the hell did you have it off for?"

She shrugged. "I was trying to save the battery."

"That thing has never been turned off since I bought it for you, not once."

"That's not true." She kept looking to the side, as if avoiding his eyes, as if afraid he'd see through her. She unwound her scarf.

"Can I see your phone, please?"

"For what?"

"I want to see the times of the text messages you sent. I want to see if you were on your phone during the last couple of hours when I was desperately trying to reach you, when I thought something bad might have happened."

"Like I'm some kind of criminal, that's why you want to look at my phone? Like you don't believe me?"

"How come you won't look at me?"

She pulled off her jacket, head still turned away. She circled around to her right and walked toward the bathroom. "I have to use the bathroom, okay?"

"Hold on a second." She kept walking. "Will you stop, please? We're talking."

Without turning to look at him, staring at the bathroom door, she said, "What . . . do you want . . . to know?"

"You didn't know I was picking you up at school?"

"Oh, I see, so you're pissed I didn't tell you I was going to walk around Newbury Street with Jenna?"

"I told you to come home."

"I'm home, aren't I? You didn't say I had to come home the second school was out."

"Any reason you didn't tell me what your plans were? So I didn't have to waste my time driving over to Lyman and waiting in line and then spending half an hour asking everyone at school where you'd gone? And thinking something had happened?"

She stared straight ahead. She still wouldn't meet his eyes. "I'm sorry, okay? I'm sorry. I screwed up. I should have told you but I forgot, okay? What do you want me to do now? Am I going to get grounded for a year or something?"

"Look at me."

"Can I please just use the bathroom? I'm, like, about to pee my pants."

"Look at me."

She turned to her left ever so slightly. "Okay? Can I go now?"

"Turn around all the way. What are you hiding?"

She compressed her lips, furrowed her

brows. Then she turned so she was looking straight at him.

"What the hell is that on your nose?"

"What does it look like?"

"Is that . . . ?" He came closer. "Is that a ring in your nose? Did you pierce your nose?"

Quietly now, she said, "Obviously."

A small metal ring ran through her right nostril and through the side of her nose. He stood a few feet away. "You pierced your nose?"

"So?"

"Did we ever talk about this? Did you ask my permission?"

"It's my body. I have the right to do whatever I want."

"No, you don't, actually. You do not have the right to get piercings or tattoos or anything of the kind, anything permanent, without clearing it first with me. Are you out of your mind?"

"You would have said no anyway."

"You're damn right I would have said no. What the hell gives you the right to pierce your nose, like a, a . . ."

"Hey, it's done, okay? Keep up."

"I don't believe this. I don't believe you defaced your body, put a ring through that beautiful nose. I mean, for God's sake, that's going to leave a permanent scar."

"No, it's not. I asked her, and she said if I ever decide to take it out, it's going to leave a little freckle, that's all."

"Where did you have this done? Do you realize what kind of infection you might have?"

"Oh, come on, is that what you're worried about? She was almost like a *doctor.* I mean everything was sterile and she uses a disposable needle and changes it every time, and she was, like, totally anal about, oh, you have to clean it with salt water and you have to put in the right kind of earring, not sterling silver, only fourteen-karat gold or surgical steel or titanium. I mean, she was totally totally crazy sterile about *everything.*"

"Oh, Jesus," he said, and he thought, *She's right here, she's alive, nothing happened, no one took her.* Tears came to his eyes. "Don't ever do that again."

She noticed his tears and looked at him with alarm.

"This isn't just about piercing. Don't you *ever* ignore my phone calls and text messages. Ever. Do you hear me?"

"What is the big deal? What are you afraid of?"

"Two pretty sixteen-year-old girls going around the city by themselves, going into

239

body piercing places or whatever, you're a target."

"Oh, please. That's ridiculous. It was daylight and we were on a busy street with a lot of people around me. Nothing's going to happen."

"Jesus, Boogie." He came close and put his arms around her, flooded with relief. She kept her arms stiff at her side, didn't hug back, her mouth downturned in anger. "I was scared out of my mind, sweetie. Don't ever do that to me again."

Finally, she put her arms around him, her face pressed against his chest. "I'm sorry," she said, her words muffled.

"It's okay."

She sniffed. "Actually, I really do need to use the bathroom."

He released her.

When she came out, he was sitting on the couch, waiting for her. "Boogie, come over here for a minute."

"I have homework."

"It can wait. Come over here and sit down." He patted the sofa next to him. She sat down in a chair on the side of the sofa.

"What?"

"Listen. We need to talk about the Galvins."

"What about them? You didn't say I

couldn't hang out with Jenna. You just said I couldn't go over to their house tonight."

"I don't want you going over there any-more. I don't want you getting a ride in Mr. Galvin's limousine."

He'd made a decision, finally. Earlier it might have raised eyebrows, his keeping her away from the Galvin family. But Danny could handle it, let Galvin know the loan had nothing to do with it. He'd just say it was about strengthening the father-daughter relationship.

"What is this? All of a sudden you don't like them? I thought you liked Jenna."

"I do, absolutely. She's a great friend. I don't mind if she comes over here, or —"

"I am not inviting her over here to see this place. You saw what their house is like."

"If she's really a friend, she's not going to judge you based on the fact that your daddy isn't rich, all right?"

"What's the difference if I go to her house or she comes here?"

"You've been going over there way too much, and you know it."

She paused, frowned. "So I won't go over so much, okay? Is there, like, something you don't like about them? Like they're a bad influence?"

"I'd like to spend a little time with you

241

once in a while, you know?"

She shrugged. "I mean, it's not like we have a lot to talk about."

"Ouch," he said. "I don't agree, but if you feel that way, let's work on it."

"It's too intense. It's like being under interrogation every time we have dinner, like you want to know every last thing about what I'm doing and how I'm feeling. . . ."

"So I won't interrogate you so much. We'll just keep it lighter."

"Is this because you think Jenna made me get my nose pierced? Because that totally wasn't what happened at all. We both did it. She didn't *make* me do anything."

"That's not it. I just don't want you going over to their house anymore or riding in their limousine. Okay? Are we clear?"

"I know what this is about. I know about the loan."

"Loan?"

"He lent you, like, a hundred thousand dollars or something, right? Because you're going broke." She turned to face him, accusingly. "You're just embarrassed about it. You don't like me seeing how they live, and we live like this. Isn't that what it's really about?"

He felt a flush of shame and a quick pulse of anger. He hadn't told her anything about

242

the money Galvin had lent him. What if Galvin had told Jenna he'd taken care of the Goodmans' money problem, don't worry about it . . . ? If he had . . . well, he just shouldn't have. That really wasn't her business.

"Abby, that's not it at all. I just don't want you going over there anymore."

She stood up, staring at him furiously, smacked her hands against her thighs. "Why don't you just admit it's punishment? You're pissed off I didn't ask your permission to get my nose pierced and now you're punishing me by trying to keep . . ." Her words came all in a rush now, high and run together and indecipherable. Her face was red, and tears glinted in her eyes.

"Boogie. This is not punishment."

"— the one thing that makes me happy, my best friend, and you want to take her away from me!"

"Abby!"

She turned and ran to her bedroom. He sat back in the couch and folded his arms and stared into space.

He almost wished he could tell her what was really going on.

Almost.

■ ■ ■ ■

PART THREE

■ ■ ■ ■

33

Danny tried to read in bed but couldn't make any headway. Maybe he was too much of a wimp to be a dad, but he couldn't stand watching Abby cry. He hated the fights and the struggle that came with having a kid. Generally, he tried not to give in to emotional blackmail, or to be a pushover — kids needed to be given boundaries and limits. Maybe not as much as his own parents had done. But you couldn't go too far in the other direction, either. Kids, he decided, were like iPhones: They didn't come with an owner's manual.

He wished he could be open with Abby, tell her the truth — that her father had gotten involved in some very scary stuff, that her best friend's father worked with people who murdered without hesitation. That he couldn't allow her to be a hostage.

But he couldn't say anything about it. He didn't trust her to keep a confidence.

Certainly not from her BFF.

Lucy came into the bedroom after almost an hour in Abby's bedroom. She looked tired. He could see dried traces of tears on her cheeks.

He looked up, raised his brows.

She shook her head. "She's still upset. I told her to forget about homework, and she didn't fight me on it. She basically cried herself to sleep."

"Oh, Jesus."

"I think the nose piercing looks kind of cute on her." She slipped out of her jeans, then pulled her shirt over her head.

"Oh, come on. She can mutilate her body after she turns eighteen."

"Whoa, what happened to Cool Dad?"

"I never claimed to be Cool Dad."

She unlatched her bra and her breasts swayed. "She did it. Okay? That was her little act of rebellion. Believe me, there are far worse ways for kids her age to rebel."

"She could have pierced her septum and had one of those little horseshoes coming out of her nose."

"Worse than that. But that's not what pissed you off, really."

"That wasn't the only thing. She went off the grid for three hours. This girl, who sleeps with her phone in her hand and probably posts things on her Facebook page during math class. She just went dark. How would you have felt?"

She settled onto the bed. "You over-reacted, okay?"

"I was scared something might have happened to her. She knew I was picking her up at school, and she just vanished."

"When we were kids, we could go for almost the whole day without talking to our parents, right? On a summer day, you'd go out in the morning, the screen door would slam shut behind you, and you spent the day riding bikes or hanging out with your friends, and there were no cell phones. You didn't have to check in."

"It's a different world. There're abductions and child molesters and sickos with chloroform driving panel vans."

"There's no evidence that kids are more endangered these days. That's a media myth. Anyway, that's not even the point."

"Which is what?"

"You know, I always resented it when people tried to tell me how to raise Kyle. Especially when I was a single mom. Everyone always had advice. *Don't be so strict, don't be so lax. Don't let him watch TV, don't make TV the forbidden fruit. Don't let him play computer games or video games.* I mean, it drove me crazy. Even when people were right. From the very beginning, when you and I first started seeing each other, I told you I was never going to play shrink. Never going to tell you how to be a dad."

"I asked you to go in there."

"And I'm flattered she wanted to talk to me. It means a lot. I mean, it's complicated, navigating our relationship. I'm not her mom, and she doesn't want that."

"So tell me what she said. How bad is it?"

"Look, Danny, you're a terrific father."

"But?"

"But nothing. You are."

"And?"

She shrugged. "Why are you doing this, Danny?"

"She's over there too much. Let's not you and me argue, too."

"You're cutting her off from her best friend."

"It'll be good for her."

"I don't get it. You don't mind if Jenna comes over here, you just don't want Abby going over to the Galvins' house?"

"Something like that."

"Why?"

He exhaled, frustrated at his inability to tell her the real story. "Spending all that time over there is just giving her unrealistic expectations. It's warping her."

"But that's not what you told her. You said she can never go over there."

"Well, for the time being."

"You need to think about why you're doing this."

He reached over, stroked the silky skin of her breasts, gave a nipple a gentle squeeze. She folded her arms.

"What?" he said.

"There's something you're not telling me about the Galvins."

He shook his head, didn't hesitate, and came right out with the lie. "Not true."

"There's something. Something about them you don't like. What is it?"

"That's not it at all."

"Cut the crap, Danny. I *know* you. I can read you like a book. That time when you claimed you went to the Wellesley College library and you so clearly didn't?"

"You're not still on that, are you?"

"There's something going on. Something about Galvin. Why don't you tell me?"

"There's nothing to tell," he said, and he rolled over and switched off the bedside lamp. "Nothing to tell."

She looked at him for a long time, but she left it there. The conversation was over. He awoke some time later, realizing he'd forgotten to send a text message to the DEA confirming that he'd done the deed. He got out of bed as quietly as he could. The floor creaked, and Lucy stirred in her sleep.

In the living room he switched on the lamp on one side of the couch, opened his laptop, and waited for it to join the wireless network.

He signed in to the JayGould1836@gmail .com account and began composing an encrypted text message, when he saw there was already a message waiting for him:

Nice work, it said. Meet 10 a.m. tomorrow morning to return equip. location tbd.

He wondered how they knew he'd managed to upload the contents of Galvin's BlackBerry. He'd only told them he'd try. How did they know he'd succeeded? Maybe it had been uploaded automatically; was that possible? Probably.

How much did they know about him? How closely were they watching?

And when, he wondered, would they finally leave him alone?

34

During the ride to school, Abby gave him the full-on silent treatment.

"Let me guess," Danny said after a moment. "You're pissed about this Galvin thing."

She stared straight ahead.

"Abby, talk to me."

Silence.

"I hate seeing you like this, Boogie. Let's talk."

She opened her mouth, looked like she was about to let loose a stream of invective. Instead, very carefully, she said: "No."

But he kept at it. His working assumption was that she'd tell everything to Jenna anyway, so he had to be mindful of what he told her. "Look, the Galvins are great people. A totally great family. And Jenna is terrific." He was willing to exaggerate for the sake of family harmony. "But sometimes people just need to take time off, even best friends. I want us to spend time as a family again. You and me, or you and me and Lucy. Okay?"

She stared straight ahead and didn't reply. When they reached the drop-off point in front of the school, she hefted her backpack, opened the car door, jumped out, and slammed it without saying good-bye.

Have fun, Danny thought.

Five or six cars ahead in line he saw Galvin's Maybach limo. Just seeing the car made his stomach clutch. Galvin knew something, suspected something, about him. He had to. Danny prided himself on being a careful observer of people — most writers were — and he'd seen the suspicion dawn on Galvin's face when he found his BlackBerry in the wrong pocket. It wasn't exactly subtle.

Though that didn't mean Galvin would connect Danny to the DEA. That was a logical leap even a highly suspicious person wouldn't easily make. Galvin had brought Danny into his orbit; Danny hadn't wormed his way in. And Danny didn't have the profile of a man working with the Drug Enforcement Agency.

Unless Galvin had other sources. That was possible. Assume Galvin had protection, people working for the cartel who watched out for him. People who stayed in the background and kept an eye on whoever he came into contact with, as Yeager had said. Was that such a stretch? Galvin was an important player for the cartel. Of course they'd take care of him, keep an eye on him. Make sure he wasn't being compromised in some way.

Maybe Galvin had other sources. Maybe, finding that his BlackBerry had somehow moved to the wrong suit pocket, he'd asked around. Maybe the cartel's people had turned their scrutiny on Danny and found out — somehow — what Danny was up to.

That wasn't impossible at all, was it?

As he rounded around the circular drive, he saw that Galvin's limousine was parked on the shoulder of the road by the school gates. Right by the exit. As if waiting.

Danny was tempted to gun the engine, get the hell out of there. But then Galvin's new driver — what was his name, again? — stepped out of the car and waved him over.

Keep going? Ignore the guy?

He couldn't. He couldn't just drive by. That in itself would have been suspicious. He slowed, pulled over. Lowered his window.

"Mr. Galvin he like talk to you," the driver said.

Danny parked the Honda behind the Maybach and got out. He approached the limousine, trying to appear casually curious. The rear passengers' door came open.

"Get in," Galvin said, looking grim.

35

"Something wrong?"

"We have to talk," Galvin said.

Danny's mind raced, trying to compose a plausible-sounding explanation. But nothing came. Only a flat-out denial. *You serious? You think I took your BlackBerry? Why the hell would I do that? How? Come on, man, get real. Jesus.*

"What's the problem?"

Inside, it was even more luxurious than he'd imagined. It looked like a private club and smelled like expensive leather. The passenger compartment was large enough to contain two big, comfortable-looking seats in back, facing forward, and three facing rear.

Galvin, sitting in one of the two rear seats, patted the one next to him. He was wearing another one of his very expensive-looking suits, this one a nailhead worsted. Clambering in, Danny could smell Galvin's cologne, something subtle and peppery, and he realized for the first time that this smell made him anxious. It smelled of power. It smelled vaguely toxic.

"I don't have a lot of time," Danny said. The seat was deep and comfortable, the leather buttery.

Between the rear seats was a console, its surface some kind of tropical wood veneer. Galvin touched it and it popped open. He pulled out two cold water bottles and handed one to Danny.

"Diego," he said with a quick motion of his left hand, and a glass divider slid up between the passenger compartment and the cockpit.

"Come on, let's take a quick drive. Just leave your car here for a while. We can talk, and I can show you my boat."

"Your what?"

"My boat. My yacht. I'm heading over to the harbor now. Check out my new nav system."

"I really should work."

"Come on — take us half an hour. I'm launching it early this year so we can sail down to Anguilla over spring break."

"Where is it, down in Quincy?"

"Boston Yacht Haven. Right here. Come on."

Danny nodded. He unscrewed the cap from the water bottle and took a sip. "Okay. Sure."

Ten minutes later they were pulling over a series of speed bumps and into a private marina in the North End, on Commercial Wharf on the Boston harbor. Danny waited for Galvin to bring up whatever it was he wanted to talk about, but he just chatted away, small talk.

"You can just wait right here, Diego," he told his driver. "Shouldn't be more than ten, fifteen minutes."

"*Si,* señor."

Danny could barely keep up as Galvin led the way around the side of the rambling, angled clubhouse and along a dock. The air was crisp and clean and tinged with salt. A gentle breeze came off the water. Moored to the pier were several yawls and a small boat — it was too early for most people to put their boats in the water — and on the other side of the building was what had to be Galvin's boat. It was a big, beautiful, streamlined thing, cream and white, all swooping lines and aggressive angles. Painted on its bow was EL ANTOJO.

"That yours?" Danny said.

"Yep," Galvin said. He stopped at a black-painted security gate on the dock and swiped a key card and pulled it open. Danny followed Galvin down a gangway to the slip.

"El Antojo?"

"It's sort of an inside joke in our family. It's one of those Spanish words that's impossible to translate. It means 'whim' or 'craving,' something like that. When I bought it, Lina and I had a big fight — she said she couldn't believe I'd dumped millions of dollars on an *antojo* — a caprice, a whim."

"It's a beauty, though. For an *antojo.*"

"Thanks. The Italians know how to build them."

Standing on the slip, watching the yacht bob gently in the water, Danny experienced the momentary illusion that the dock was rocking, not the boat.

"What kind of boat is it?"

"It's a Ferretti. Their Custom Line — the Navetta 26 Crescendo. Took almost three years to build."

"It looks fast."

"Not especially. Cruising speed is twelve, thirteen knots. She'll get up to fourteen knots. But she's sporty. And she can go all the way down to Anguilla without refueling. And she's smooth. Semidisplacement hull. Know anything about boats?"

"I grew up in Wellfleet, remember?" Some-

260

where a distant ship's horn sounded. A jet passed by low overhead, taking off from Logan Airport.

"Right, right." Galvin climbed a short ladder onto a wide main deck. Danny followed him up another set of stairs to a spacious sky lounge.

"Do you drive it yourself, or do you have a crew?"

"Depends. For long trips I usually hire a captain, but most of the time I take it out myself."

"It's gotta be more exciting to drive it yourself, right?"

"Exciting? Lemme tell you something. Exciting is the one thing you *don't* want when you're at sea. Exciting is when you hit an iceberg or sail into a hurricane or have your bilge pump fail. Or hit a rocky shoal. I'll take boring anytime."

"Ever come close?"

"To what, sinking?"

Danny nodded.

"No. Not that I know of."

Danny looked down at the water, green-tinged black with a surface that looked like velvet. "When I was a teenager, I helped scuttle a ship."

Galvin looked at him, head tipped, half smiling, unsure whether this was a joke.

Danny could hear the hum of the fuel barge nearby. The pilings underneath the marina were exposed, like the mouth of a cave. It was low tide.

"Remember when they sank this big old navy warship in Cape Cod Bay to use for target practice?" Danny said.

"Sure, like twenty years ago or something."

"The demolition guys hired to do it were one of my dad's subcontractors. So when I was sixteen, I got a job helping place the explosive charges along the hull."

"Really? Cool."

"It was nasty work, actually. We had to put all these shaped charges on the hull below the waterline so when they went off, it was like cutting a line all the way around. And a twenty-thousand-ton ship went down like a rock in less than two minutes."

"Must've been cool when it all went boom."

"A bunch of little thuds, actually. They time the explosions. The trick is to keep the boat upright as it sinks so it'll settle straight down onto the ocean floor."

"Blowing shit up is fun no matter how old you are. It's a primal instinct. Legalized violence."

"Sure. Instead we watch hockey or football

or boxing and compete in business. We don't actually take part in the violence ourselves anymore. We're civilized."

"Yeah," Galvin said, but he sounded like his thoughts were somewhere else. "Yeah."

They both fell silent for a moment, peering at the horizon, the scudding clouds, the seagulls diving and swooping and cawing. "You know," Galvin said, "sometimes when you're out on the boat in the middle of the ocean, with nothing around for miles, nothing in sight, nothing but water, you realize how insignificant we are, in the scheme of things. You find yourself thinking, you know — O Lord, be good to me. Your sea is so wide and my boat is so small."

"Hmph," Danny said. "Not all that small, actually."

"Okay, asshole," Galvin said, feigning annoyance but visibly pleased. "I guess it's all relative. The big fish doesn't look so big to the even bigger fish."

"Guess so."

"Danny," Galvin said. "So this thing I wanted to talk to you about?"

"Yeah . . . ?"

"Look, you told Abby she can't come to our house anymore. I want to know why."

So that was it. Not what he'd expected at all.

"It's complicated, Tom."

"They've become close. Best of friends. Does that concern you?"

Was Galvin onto him, somehow? Did he *know* why Danny wanted to keep Abby away?

"It's not the closeness that concerns me." Danny said. "It's . . . I want her home more often."

"That all?"

Danny felt his guts constrict. "That's all," he said. "Nothing more than that, really."

"Be straight up with me. This isn't about that nose piercing, is it? I mean, yeah, Jenna never should have taken Abby to get her nose pierced. That was wrong. Celina shouldn't have just assumed that Abby had permission. Just because she said so doesn't make it true. I know how angry you were about that, and hell, if I didn't have the two older boys, I'd probably be freaking out, too. But —"

"I — Abby said she had permission?"

"And Celina should have checked with you. I don't know what else I can say but that she screwed up. She meant well, Celina did, but she screwed up. *We* screwed up. In loco parentis, all that crap."

Danny couldn't help laughing with relief. "I've already cooled down. I mean, I was angry last night, but, well, if that's the extent of her teenage rebellion, I'm lucky. She's not pregnant, and she doesn't have a tattoo on her butt or something."

"As far as you know."

Danny groaned comically.

"My parents wouldn't let my sister Linda get her *ears* pierced until she graduated from high school."

"I don't get the whole piercing mania anyway, to be honest."

"Danny, listen, I'm not one for deep talks, you know? *Feelings* and all that? Not my department. But you and I both know this isn't just about the piercing. Right?"

Danny felt trapped. He heaved a sigh of frustration. He couldn't keep pretending that this was all about a nose piercing, not anymore, not face-to-face with Galvin. He hesitated.

Galvin went on: "It's about the money, isn't it?"

No, Danny was about to say, but then he caught himself. "Maybe that's it." His iPhone emitted the tritone text alert, but he didn't dare check it.

"You know, I was afraid this might happen. That's why I never lend money to friends. I made an exception in your case because I saw how desperate things were

265

for you. But it almost always causes tension in a friendship. I'm a man, you're a man, I get it. You feel somehow embarrassed that you had to take money from me. Now you feel obligated. There's just no way around it. Maybe I didn't handle it the right way. I don't know."

"No, Tom," Danny said. He shook his head, fell silent. Of course he felt awkward about it, who wouldn't? But if only that were the problem. "It was incredibly generous."

His iPhone made another text alert sound.

"Danny, you gotta understand something. Abby's like family. What she's done for Jenna — I can't even begin to express my gratitude. Your girl, her heart, her friendship — she's —" Danny was quite sure that Tom Galvin's eyes were moist. "I don't want anything to happen to that bond between the two girls. It's too important to her. It's too important to *me.* So listen. Whatever I'm doing that makes you uncomfortable, we have to sort this out. Okay? Whatever it is."

"Of course."

"I have an idea. We've got a place in Aspen. How about we all go out there this weekend, just the two families? You guys and us. Bring your girlfriend, too. We'll take my plane; it'll be fast and easy and a good time. My two sons both have other plans, so it'll just be the girls. You and I can hang out, schmooze, talk this thing through. For the sake of our daughters, huh? What do you say?"

36

The little boy was screaming. He was afraid of the big vaccine needle. And the young woman aide clearly didn't know how to stick the needle in without inflicting pain.

Dr. Mendoza saw this and placed a gentle hand on the nurse's shoulder. *"¿Puedo probar?"* he said. *May I try?* He never liked to make the aides feel inadequate.

"Por supuesto, Doctor," the young woman said right away, nodding, handing him the hypodermic.

The boy, who looked to be around three, was yowling and bucking in his mother's strong arms. And who could blame him? To little children, all hypodermic needles looked big and scary. "What is his name?" he asked the mother.

"Santiago," the mother said. She was missing most of her front teeth.

"Santiago, I'd like you to meet my friend Nicolás." He pulled from the front pocket of his white coat an orange rubber toy with colored knobs for eyes and ears. "Nicolás is a Martian. He's very, very scared of needles. Look."

Santiago stopped struggling for a moment and looked warily at the toy. His cheeks were wet with tears, and a dribble of mucus ran down from one nostril.

Dr. Mendoza moved the hypodermic needle near the toy, touched the needle against the orange rubber skin of the toy's tummy, then squeezed its belly. Its eyes and ears bugged out in comic fear. Santiago burst out laughing and reached for it, and Dr. Mendoza let the boy have it. He had a dozen more in the back room of the clinic. Every time he visited the United States, he bought them at a toy store in San Diego. The children loved them.

"Can you help Nicolás? He needs his shot to make him all better."

Santiago was happily squeezing the rubber toy's belly, making the eyes and ears pop out, and laughing delightedly.

"Now maybe you can show him what a brave boy you are. Can you close your eyes and count to three, very slowly?" asked Dr. Mendoza.

He held the needle just above the boy's shoulder.

"Uno . . ."

The needle's point touched the shoulder.

"Dos . . ."

Then Dr. Mendoza inserted the needle lightning fast, and it was over.

"Tres," the boy said, squeezing his eyes tight, bracing for the shot that had already come.

"We're done!" Dr. Mendoza said. "You did it! You did such an excellent job!"

The boy opened his eyes wide. "Really?"

The clinic was located in the outskirts of Culiacán, the capital of the Sinaloa state in Mexico. The neighborhood was desperately poor, and the people couldn't afford to see a doctor. So they queued up for hours, sometimes all night, to see a doctor without charge. Some days, there were dozens waiting when he arrived at seven in the morning. Some brought tortillas for their lunch.

Dr. Mendoza volunteered here two days a week. It was a good break from his surgical practice at the private hospital in downtown Culiacán, where all his patients were well-heeled. He felt it was good karma.

It had been a long and busy day. A man of around seventy, complaining of tenderness in his groin, had a bulge the size of a lemon. It had been there for more than a year. It was a right inguinal hernia that was incarcerated but not, thank God, strangulated. Dr. Mendoza scheduled the man for an outpatient procedure.

A young man had accidentally slashed one of his wrists with a machete while chopping weeds in a coconut grove. He'd come in with the laceration bound in a dirty, bloody handkerchief, blood dripping everywhere. A little girl had stepped on a sewing needle at home, and her mother, a seamstress, had tried to pull it out but succeeded only in breaking off one end. A teenage boy's arm had been broken for three weeks, had been reset wrong, and Dr. Mendoza had to yank it into place to reset it properly. An adorable little baby girl with tiny stud earrings, wearing a pink sweater, was screaming in pain. Her eyes were red. He reassured the baby's nervous parents that their child had nothing more serious than a bad case of conjunctivitis, easily treated with ophthalmic Cipro.

The waiting room bustled with patients and their families, people dirty and sweaty from working in the fields or the *maquiladoras,* many of whom had no teeth and no last name. With the squalling of infants and the screams of children and the shouting of the adults, you could barely hear yourself think. But Dr. Mendoza didn't mind it at all.

Even though he was a surgeon, most of the work he did at the free clinic was general medicine. He was vastly overqualified. But that was fine. He believed in balance. He believed that the good he did here two days a week compensated for . . . his other work.

Then he noticed the clamor of the waiting room subside. Something had happened to quiet all but the youngest. He stepped out of the examination room and saw a man standing at the entrance to the waiting room. He wore snakeskin boots and jeans and a gaudy silk shirt. He wore a little gold AK-47 on a gold necklace, and a black cowboy hat. A tattoo covered most of his neck.

Everyone in the room was frightened of the man. They recognized his type. He was a *gavillero,* a trigger man for the cartel. A killer. The man squinted, his shrewd eyes scanning the room, then falling on Dr. Mendoza. Heads turned toward the surgeon and back toward the *gavillero.*

Dr. Mendoza beckoned him in with a flick of his hand.

Away from the eyes of an audience, the *gavillero* seemed to become another person.

He was polite and deferential, almost obsequious.

"Don Armando," he said, bowing his head. "I come with a message from *el gran jefe.*"

Dr. Mendoza's eyes bored into the *gavillero*'s.

The younger man handed the surgeon a folded slip of paper and gave another nod.

Dr. Mendoza took it, glanced at the name and telephone number, folded it, and slipped it into the breast pocket of his white coat.

"Tell *el gran jefe* I will take care of this tonight. After I see my last patient."

"Yes, sir," the *gavillero* said with another nod.

"Well?" Dr. Mendoza said.

"Sir?"

"You may go," Dr. Mendoza said. "I have patients waiting."

37

Galvin's invitation, the more Danny thought about it, was baffling, even nerve-racking.

Was it some sort of mind game? Was Galvin toying with him? On two occasions he'd caught Danny in compromising, or at least highly questionable, circumstances. That time when he returned home unexpectedly to find Danny loitering in his study. And when he noticed his BlackBerry had unaccountably migrated to the wrong suit pocket. His driver had taken the fall for the transmitter discovered on his desk. But how could Galvin not suspect Danny? He'd have to be oblivious or hopelessly naïve — neither of which described Thomas X. Galvin.

Or playing him in some patiently twisted way. Why else would he have invited Danny to spend a weekend in Aspen, to burrow even deeper into the bosom of his family — unless he was three steps ahead of Danny.

and was playing the long game. Some complex scheme in which Galvin would confront him, trap him, expose him.

Or worse.

On his way back home, he called Lucy and told her about Galvin's invitation. He half expected her to react negatively, or at least skeptically. He always trusted her instincts. She'd been right, probably, to warn him against accepting a loan from Galvin, even though she had no idea what the terrible cost would be.

"Aspen!" she said. "Are girlfriends invited?"

"Expressly."

"Aspen sounds great."

"Really? I'm surprised."

A secure text message alert interrupted the call, that strange plinking sound. It was from AnonText007: 10 a.m. McDonald's Central Square, Cambridge

"I've never flown in a private plane," she said.

"You don't mind all this?"

"All what?"

"Extravagant, conspicuous wealth."

"Why should I mind it? It sounds fabulous. I haven't been skiing in years, ever since Kyle started snowboarding."

"How about all that time up close and

personal with the Galvin family?"

"It'll be fascinating."

"You have no idea."

"Aren't you and he becoming best buds?"

"I wouldn't put it that way. We get along."

"Well, let me remind you, I'm a trained psychiatrist. Maybe I'll gain some useful insights into Abby's relationship with the Galvins."

"I'm surprised."

"What, you expected me to tell you not to go?"

"I expected you to agree with me that it might not be a good idea."

"Is there some reason I'm overlooking?"

He exhaled. He was keeping so much from her now that he was finding it hard to keep track of what he'd told her and what he hadn't, what she knew and what she didn't.

"I suppose not," he said.

Central Square in Cambridge was barely a mile away from Boston's Back Bay but a world apart. The Back Bay was wealth and European sophistication: harmonious Victorian architecture, redbrick sidewalks, tree-lined streets, gas streetlamps, stratospheric real estate prices. Whereas Central Square, just across the Charles River, was seedy and shambling, perennially run-down, in a state of constant urban decay.

Danny had driven past this McDonald's probably a thousand times before but had never noticed it. As soon as he pulled into a space on Mass Ave, half a block away, he had a fairly good idea why Slocum and Yeager had selected it for a meeting. The restaurant was inconspicuous and was on the corner of Mass Ave and a narrow side street, with plate-glass windows on either side, a glass box. If you were sitting inside the McDonald's, you could observe everyone coming on both sides.

It was also the kind of place where you could sit at a table and hang out indefinitely without being disturbed. The counter staff were talking among themselves and taking the occasional order from a customer.

Danny entered, grabbed a corner table, set the gym bag on the floor. The whole place smelled like French fries, which was not unpleasant. The DEA guys weren't there yet. Two young men were speaking Portuguese, one wearing a Red Sox cap. An Asian kid in an MIT sweatshirt was devouring a Big Mac, wearing giant headphones, and fiddling with his iPod or iPhone at the same time. No one else was there.

He glanced at his watch, brushed a

crumpled drinking-straw wrapper off the table along with the crumbs of the last patron's meal, touched a splotch of something sticky.

The side entrance, on Douglass Street, opened, letting in a rush of cold air. It was Glenn Yeager, in a black North Face fleece ski jacket and an oversize pair of sunglasses. He went right up to Danny's table without looking around.

"Bad cop," he announced in a low, guttural voice, "will not be joining us. In answer to your question." He removed his sunglasses. His eyes looked slightly out of focus.

"Bummer," Danny said.

Yeager removed a glasses case from a zippered side pocket of his fleece, took out steel-rimmed bifocals, put them on as delicately as a surgeon doing microsurgery. He glanced down at Danny's feet, at the gym bag containing the device. "See, I told you that thing was idiot-proof."

"How did you know it worked?"

"It uploaded the data remotely, right after you finished." He shimmied his hands. "The magic of the Intertubes."

"So now you have everything you need," Danny said brightly. "You have the mother lode."

"Well, we have some, anyway. But a lot of

the contents of his BlackBerry were en-crypted."

"That surprises you?"

"Not at all. The cartels have gotten really sophisticated about their comms. And they don't use BlackBerrys for the really sensi-tive stuff. They use the Internet. Still, they like to use BlackBerry's PIN-to-PIN mes-saging system for routine communication because it doesn't go through a server. Doesn't leave any digital bread crumbs. We didn't capture much of his e-mails, but at least we got the phone numbers of contacts in his address book."

Danny shrugged. "So we're done here." A statement, not a question.

Yeager smiled thinly. "We were delighted to hear about Aspen."

"To hear *what* about Aspen?"

"That you're joining the Galvins there this weekend."

Danny stared at him for a few seconds. Then he hunched forward. "If you have some kind of bug in his limo, what the hell do you need me for?"

Yeager's face was impassive.

"I didn't give Galvin an answer. I haven't decided yet."

Something about Yeager's eyes.

"You son of a bitch," Danny said. "Did

you plant some kind of bug on *me*?"

Yeager shook his head slowly. "Come on. Anyway, point is, he's meeting someone in Aspen. We think it's someone quite high up in the cartel hierarchy."

"In Aspen?"

"The ski weekend is probably just a cover. They're extremely careful about locations and venues. If they've chosen to meet in Aspen, it's because they know they can do it without being monitored. Any trackers will be spotted at a distance. They'll stand out. The terrain in Aspen works well that way."

"So why don't you fly out there and tail him? You don't need me."

"That's not how it's going to play out. You'll be with him. You'll have access to him. We want to know who he's meeting. If we get that, it's huge. The definitive link between Galvin and the cartel we've been trying to nail down for three years now."

"You don't get it, do you? This is a family ski weekend, not some Iron John initiation. Tom Galvin and I aren't going to be sitting around nude in a drum circle in the snow, howling at the moon."

He smiled. "He trusts you."

"I'm not doing it. I almost got caught downloading his BlackBerry. The fact that

I'm still alive is a miracle. I'm not doing any more."

Yeager spread his hands on the table. His left hand drew back when it touched the sticky gunk. "Danny, you're understandably nervous. I get that. But if he were suspicious about you, he wouldn't have invited you to spend time with his family."

"Unless he has some other plan."

"Come on, now. You're overwhelmed, I can see that. I completely sympathize. Every confidential informant I've ever worked with goes through a crisis of nerves. Look, Danny, you're not alone. You have the full force of the US government behind you."

"And that's supposed to reassure me? The fact is, the more often I do this, the greater my odds of getting caught. I got you the contents of his BlackBerry. Now I'm done. *We're* done."

He stood up. There was a steady stream of people entering and leaving, getting late breakfasts or early lunches. The MIT kid was gone. A couple had taken a table nearby, both of them in their midforties with matching bushes of Chia Pet hair.

"Sit down, please."

"I've cooperated with you more than was reasonable. More than was safe, frankly."

"You're done when we say you're done,"

Yeager said, softly but with steel in his voice. Then, more gently: "You've signed a contract. If you renege, our deal is off. The agreement's dead. You'll be indicted and charged and you'll have no leverage whatsoever."

"Hold on —"

"You'll be in the worst of all possible worlds. Not only will you be indicted, but the cartels — they're going to realize you cooperated. And we're not going to be able to help you. Not at all. No witness protection program. No protection at all. If you're lucky, you spend your life in jail. But far more likely, you get killed. Is this really what you want?"

"The information I already got you? That doesn't count?"

"Read over your copy of the agreement you signed. Until we have enough to justify an arrest warrant for your friend, you're still on the hook. You don't get to walk away until we're finished. You quit now, it's like you never cooperated in the first place. You agreed in writing to testify."

Danny sat back down. "Testify? Do you have any idea what would happen to me if ever I testified in court? If I even make it that long? My daughter would be without a father."

"In all my years, I've never had an informant killed. Never. Not once."

"It's happened. You know it."

"Listen to me, Danny. We're in the process of building an overwhelming case against Galvin, a case that's going to be so strong that he'll have no choice but to plead out. These cartel guys, they never go to trial. Once you get us what we need — once we have probable cause and we get an arrest warrant for that asshole — we'll have enough to put him away. It'll be so strong that I doubt we'll even *need* you to testify. We'll do everything we can to minimize your role in this. We're not going to put you in harm's way. I mean, look — you do us no good dead."

"That's sweet."

"On the other hand, you walk away now, you're committing suicide."

"Because you're going to leak, is that it?"

"No. You walk away, we'll have no choice but to indict you, and it's going to be all over the indictment — which is, by the way, a public document — that you cooperated with us. It's like painting a target on your chest."

"And if I do this? Is that it? The end?"

"Absolutely."

"How do I know you're not going to

charge me anyway?"

"We're not interested in you. You're not just a small fish, you're *plankton,* for God's sake."

"I want that in writing. I want a letter of immunity."

"We can't get you a letter of immunity if you haven't been indicted."

"But the US Attorney can."

"And what makes you so sure of that?"

Danny waggled his hands. "The magic of the Intertubes."

"Well, let me assure you, that never happens. Maybe on TV, but not in reality. You're going to have to take me at my word. You're going to have to trust us."

Danny stood up again. "Well, I don't."

"This is not going to end well."

"I'll take my chances," Danny said, and he walked out without turning back.

38

Dr. Mendoza entered the lobby of the Executive Suites Hotel in Oakland, California. Off the lobby was the bar-lounge, a dismal and subdued place, and sitting at the bar — a long, shallow half-moon topped with fake granite — was a somber collection of people. A couple in their late sixties, both florid-faced, who appeared to be married and bored with each other. Three businessmen in their thirties, probably here for some convention, all staring blankly at the football game on the TV mounted just above them. They all seemed transient and lonely.

Dr. Mendoza found a seat at the bar next to a pinch-faced, middle-aged businessman type, hunch-shouldered, in a navy blue golf shirt and khakis. The man was alone, drinking a Scotch and soda and staring into space.

"How's the game?" Dr. Mendoza said, indicating with a wag of his head the football game on the TV.

The man turned to him and shrugged. "I have zero interest in football."

"Nor I." Dr. Mendoza was relieved, since he knew almost nothing about American football and had no interest in learning anything about it. "If only my investments gave me time to watch sports."

He let that hang for a few seconds until the man next to him replied, as Dr. Mendoza knew he would. "What sort of investments?" he said, trying to sound casual.

"Oh, mostly for myself and my family," he said airily, glancing up at the TV set as if he'd suddenly developed an appreciation for football.

They chatted for a while. Dr. Mendoza remained tantalizingly vague about the nature of his fortune while letting it be known that it was substantial. He was more interested in learning about the real estate market in and around the Bay Area. The businessman had gotten a lot more talkative. Dr. Mendoza had been transformed, in his eyes, from an annoyance to a potential client. Of course, the man didn't say why he was staying at the hotel, and Dr. Mendoza was careful not to ask.

When the man got up from his stool and excused himself to use the restroom, Dr.

Mendoza said, "Please allow me to buy you a drink."

"I think I've had all the Scotch I need for the night, but thanks anyway."

"Just one more drink? I need to pick your brain a little more about real estate in this area."

"Well . . . I suppose just one more drink. After all, I don't have to drive home."

The businessman returned a few minutes later, settled himself on the bar stool, and saw the fresh drink in front of him. "Thank you kindly," he said. He raised his glass to Dr. Mendoza's.

"To a long life," Dr. Mendoza said.

They each took a drink. "Your accent," the businessman said after a while. I can't place it. . . ."

"Argentina," Dr. Mendoza said, beaming. "And after all these years in Portola Valley, I thought I'd lost it."

"I knew it was Spanish or Mexican or something." He made a tiny grimace as he swallowed, and Dr. Mendoza worried that the Scotch wasn't adequately masking the acrid taste. But then the man took another sip, and Dr. Mendoza was able to relax. "Argentines speak Spanish, huh?"

"Indeed," said Dr. Mendoza. "Of course there are differences between the way we

287

speak and the way the Spaniards speak. Just as there are differences between the way they speak in, say, Oaxaca and the way they speak in, say . . ." — he paused to let the name slide into place with a satisfying click — "Sinaloa."

The banker stiffened, just as Dr. Mendoza expected. He was an emotionally volatile man. The cartel's dossier indicated that he took medication for a heart condition. A volatile temperament like his would not long withstand the DEA's pressure. With trembling hand he set down his tumbler.

But he had drunk more than enough of the chemical.

Panicked, he said, "Who the hell are you?"

"I am the angel of mercy, Mr. Toth."

Toth closed his eyes for a moment. "Oh, dear God in heaven, I don't know what you've been told, but I haven't said anything to anybody."

Dr. Mendoza nodded patiently. "Of course not."

"How — how did you find me here?"

Dr. Mendoza shrugged. The banker had gotten sloppy. The DEA had stashed him under a false name at this hotel, and then he'd used his credit card to order out for Chinese food.

"I told them there was no point trying to

hide me. I told them you people could find me anywhere. But you need to understand something." He wielded a stern index finger. "I told them nothing. *Nothing,* do you understand?"

Dr. Mendoza shrugged.

"The 'angel of mercy,' you said —"

"You are a drowning man and I am your life raft."

"I never said a word, not — not a goddamned word!"

"Of course not."

"They — they came to me!"

"Of course they did."

Dr. Mendoza's placid unconcern rattled Toth more than any explicit threat might have done. "Never — I never gave them — didn't say a goddamned word! They moved me here" — he looked around with distaste — "said I needed protection. I never made — never cooperated — I didn't — say anything! You have to — believe me!"

"I'm sure you haven't."

"And I won't — won't say *anything.*" He masked his pleading tone in steely emphasis.

"I believe you."

"You — your employers have made me a lot of money and — I mean, why the hell — I wouldn't turn myself in to the DEA! Why would I?"

"Perhaps because you fear them less than you fear us," Dr. Mendoza suggested gently.

"I'm not an *idiot!*" Toth was beginning to gather his wits, to speak in an aggrieved tone. "I know you people can get to me anywhere — I mean, the fact that I'm here doesn't indicate *anything*. They threatened me. I don't know how the hell they knew about me, but I never told them a *thing*. Why would I? That would be *insane.*"

"It would indeed."

"Why — why are you here?"

Dr. Mendoza shrugged again. "Just for a friendly chat."

"Well, let me make it absolutely clear to your —" Something suddenly occurred to him. Toth smiled, lifted his head, eyes wide with desperate enthusiasm. "I hope you've considered the possibilities here. I hope your . . . your employers realize that we can use this situation to our advantage. To plant disinformation. To *mislead* the DEA, do you understand? This could be a brilliant strategy. The DEA will think they have a co-operating defendant, but what they won't know . . ." He closed his eyes. "I need to lie down for a . . . I think I overdid . . . the Scotch. Feeling a little lightheaded . . ."

"This is because your blood pressure is dropping," Dr. Mendoza explained. "You take a vasodilator for your heart condition, do you not?"

Toth looked surprised. "What does that have to do with . . . ?"

"No one who takes a vasodilator should ever take Viagra," Dr. Mendoza explained. "It is quite dangerous. Your blood pressure will drop to zero."

Toth could barely keep his eyes open. "Viagra? I've never taken —" The tumbler of Scotch slipped from his grasp and thudded on the bar.

He looked down at it, and he knew.

"This will not be painful, not at all," said Dr. Mendoza. "This will go quite easily." Dr. Mendoza rose from the stool and placed a hand on the man's shoulder. "I told you, I am the angel of mercy."

There were far, far more painful ways to die than to imbibe thirty milliliters of sildenafil citrate suspension mixed with whiskey. Even if he had drunk no more than half, that was still, for him, a lethal dose. No one would ever suspect foul play. It would look like he'd foolishly got hold of some Viagra and didn't know how dangerous it was for him to take any of the stuff.

It was quite clever, actually.

"Good evening," Dr. Mendoza said. He left the bar without turning back once. He didn't need to. He heard the banker slump to the floor as he lost consciousness.

To die in such a painless manner was indeed a mercy.

Particularly given the alternatives.

39

Tom Galvin's private plane was a Challenger 300, made by Bombardier. Its exterior was white and shiny and glinted in the sun on the tarmac at Hanscom Field in Bedford, Mass.

He'd driven Lucy and Abby in the Honda. They'd parked in the lot at eight thirty A.M. and rolled their bags into the general aviation terminal to wait for the Galvins.

On the dot of nine, the Galvins arrived. Through the plate-glass window in the terminal, Danny watched the Maybach limo pull right up to the plane. Tom, Celina, and Jenna got out of the car while Diego, the chauffeur, unloaded their luggage. A short staircase popped open, and everyone climbed in like they were taking a shuttle bus. Danny noticed the Galvins didn't bring any skis. Presumably, they left them at their house in Aspen. Danny, Lucy, and Abby all planned to rent skis when they got there.

Celina turned and waved them over.

"We don't have to go through, like, security?" Abby asked.

"I guess not," Lucy said.

No tickets, no security lines, no taking off your shoes or stuffing a Ziploc bag with liquids.

It was good to be Galvin.

When they'd boarded the plane, Danny introduced Lucy to the Galvins. Celina greeted him and gave her a kiss. Abby and Jenna went off together so Jenna could give her the tour.

The cabin was roomy, over six feet tall and around seven feet wide. In the forward part of the cabin were four big beige leather club chairs, two facing two. In the aft was a long couch facing a couple of club chairs. There was no flight attendant.

"Not bad," Danny said, trying not to look impressed.

"It's better than the Green Line," Galvin said with a laugh. He turned, saw the two girls sitting in the club chairs up front. "Hey, move it, those are the grown-ups' seats!"

"Can this thing go to Aspen without refueling?"

"It can fly to Europe without refueling."

"This is awesome," Abby said, a big smile

on her face. She didn't bother pretending to appear nonchalant. "Do we have to turn off our cell phones and stuff?"

"Yeah, right," Galvin replied. "What a crock, huh?" With a smile, he called to Danny, "The only hitch is, they won't let me smoke my cigars in here."

"Wanna watch a movie?" Jenna asked.

"Don't you girls have homework?" Celina said.

"They're not allowed to assign homework on a three-day weekend," Jenna answered.

"What about your *Prejudice* paper?"

"It's *Pride and Prejudice,* Mom, and it's not due till Tuesday."

"I want you to work on your paper for at least one hour," Celina said. She waggled an index finger. "After that, you can watch a movie." She turned to Lucy. "These girls, they can't be without a screen in front of them or they go crazy with boredom."

"Speaking of screens," Galvin said, "we've got Wi-Fi on board and a coffee machine in the galley kitchen." He pointed aft.

"I'm good," Danny said. "Sorry your sons can't join us."

"Yeah, well, Brendan has exams, and Ryan and his girlfriend are doing . . . whatever they do."

"Thomas," Celina said warningly.

"They're probably screwing," said Jenna.

"Hey!" Celina said. "I don't want to hear these word out of your mouth!"

"Sorry," Jenna said quickly.

"All right," Galvin announced. "Let's all get seat-belted and get this show on the road." He and Danny sat in the club chairs next to each other in the front of the cabin, and Celina and Lucy took the other pair. Lucy took a book out of her handbag — a new biography of Cleopatra — and set it in her lap. The pilot gave a safety briefing over the PA system, and a few minutes later the plane took off.

The chairs were white leather and far more comfortable than any airplane seat he'd ever sat in. Hell, maybe more comfortable than any chair he'd ever sat in, period. Galvin was working on a laptop on a pull-down table. Danny had set up his laptop on the table in front of him, too, but he was far too tense even to think about working.

All he could think about was the DEA. How much of their threats was bluster, and how much was for real? He had no way of knowing. He had no one to talk to about it.

A low hum of anxiety had taken hold of him. It knotted his stomach. He felt like he'd drunk ten cups of strong coffee.

He wanted to stop cooperating with the DEA but didn't know how he possibly could. *You walk away now, you're committing suicide,* Yeager had said. He'd be painting a target on his chest. Once the word got out that he'd been working with the DEA against the cartel, he wouldn't be alive much longer.

Why? Because if he walked away, they'd move to indict him, and that indictment would detail his cooperation with the DEA against Thomas Galvin. And the cartels would learn the details from the indictment.

Or so the DEA warned him.

But maybe that threat was hollow. Maybe.

Thanks to a few hours on Google late the night before, Danny had his doubts.

For one thing, a federal indictment could be sealed. The details didn't have to leak out.

Anyway, the DEA wasn't going to move against him until they'd nailed down their case against Galvin. He'd read through all sorts of stories on federal prosecutions until he had a good idea of how the government tended to move in big drug cases.

They wanted the big kahuna, not the big kahuna's insignificant little buddy. They weren't going to screw up their case by tipping off Galvin and the cartel. That would be just plain stupid.

And then there was the fact that he was here, sitting on Tom Galvin's private plane. If Galvin was really working for the Sinaloa cartel, and if Galvin had any reason to believe Danny was a DEA informant . . . well, Danny and Galvin's wife and daughter wouldn't be here. Simple as that.

At least, if Danny's reasoning was correct, anyway.

He wondered whether he should meet again with Jay Poskanzer, and try to figure a way out. Or some other lawyer. Get a second opinion.

He looked up and noticed Galvin watching him. He felt a wriggle of fear in his gut.

"Not bad," he said, his hands outspread, indicating the airplane they were sitting in. "Mind if I ask, do you own this?"

"Nah, charter. Told you, they won't let me smoke my stogies in here. Owning is a huge pain in the butt. You gotta have full-time pilots on payroll, lease a hangar, all that crap. I don't really fly often enough to justify it."

Danny nodded. Lucy and Celina were talking animatedly. They seemed to have bonded right away.

"Plus, whenever we fly to Aspen, I always insist on the most experienced pilot they have," Galvin said.

"Why's that?"

"Aspen's a scary place to fly in and out of. It's in the middle of a mountain range, the runway's only five thousand feet long, there's just not much room for error. If you miscalculate, you could slam into a mountain."

"I see," Danny said. Air disasters were not his favorite topic while flying.

"When the ceiling's less than a thousand feet, the pilot can't see the runway. You're flying four hundred miles an hour, and —"

"Got it," he said curtly.

In a lower voice, Galvin said, "Your girlfriend's great. Really cool."

"Yeah, thanks."

"They look like they're getting along." An hour into the flight and Lucy and Celina hadn't stopped talking. "How does she do with Abby? That's got to be a tough gig."

"Well, actually. Better than me." Danny was surprised at Galvin's question. Most guys wouldn't notice something like that, let alone remark on it.

"Your wife — she passed, right?"

"Last year. She was my ex-wife by then."

"Breast cancer?"

Danny was certain he hadn't given any details of Sarah's death. Maybe Galvin had heard from Abby. Danny rarely talked about Sarah's cancer or the terrible days before and after her death. He'd never have expected Galvin to ask about something so personal.

Danny nodded.

"Poor Abby, huh?"

"It's been a rough couple of years," he said sadly.

"Rough for you, too, I bet."

Danny looked at him. "Yeah."

There was a long pause, and then the moment seemed to have passed. Galvin looked at his laptop screen. Danny wasn't sure whether Galvin had gone back to whatever he was working on, or had just fallen silent, not wanting to dig further.

Then Galvin said crisply, "Could I ask you something?"

Danny looked at him, glimpsed the grave expression, felt his stomach tighten. "Okay . . ."

Galvin looked over at the women, who were still deep in conversation. Then back at Danny.

"My security people found something on my BlackBerry." His gray eyes locked into Danny's.

"*Security* people?" Danny felt his face grow hot. He wondered whether his face was flushing visibly. He hoped not.

Abby and Jenna laughed again, and Celina got up from her seat and went to where the girls were watching a movie.

"My clients — I told you, they're an extremely wealthy family, right? Well, they're really private. I mean, almost paranoid. Part of my deal with them is, I agree to regular security audits and intrusion detection systems and communications security, all that. I mean, real crazy, over-the-top stuff."

"Okay . . . ?" Danny shrugged, palms up, with a mystified what-does-this-have-to-do-with-me? look.

"They found an attempt to access my BlackBerry."

Galvin paused. Danny wasn't sure if Galvin was waiting for a response. So he said, "Huh." His throat had dried up. He swallowed a few times. "Weird."

"So I need to ask you something."

Danny cleared his throat, swallowed. "Sure."

"I never put the thing down. Celina calls it my electronic pacifier. I always have it with me. In bed, in the crapper, everywhere. And I'm trying to remember when the last time was it wasn't in my hands. And it comes to me." He paused. "It was when we played squash a couple of days ago."

"At the Plympton Club?"

Galvin nodded.

"I don't remember," Danny said smoothly. "You sure you didn't take it with you onto the court?"

He shook his head slowly, deliberately. "They don't allow you to bring cell phones into the squash courts."

Danny shrugged. He felt a rising tide of panic. His mouth was so dry now, he could barely swallow. His heart was pounding. He tried to look unfazed, or maybe even bored, but he knew it wasn't working.

"And then — I know this'll sound nutty to you — but when I got back to my locker after the game? The phone was in the wrong pocket."

Danny laughed, once, a dry, brittle laugh.

"I know, I know — like, how OCD is that, right? But it's just a habit. I'm right-handed, so I keep my BlackBerry in my left inside pocket." He touched the left side of his chest, right over the left breast pocket of his suit jacket. "You know, like how Buffalo Bill always kept his gun holster on his left side or whatever. So I can draw fast."

Galvin smiled casually but watched Danny's eyes.

Damn it to hell, Danny thought. *Just come out with it. Stop toying with me. Accuse me;*

*get it out there so I can bat it away with a
casual denial.*

*Don't act defensive. Don't act angry. Act, if
anything, bored.*

*An innocent person won't take a wild ac-
cusation like that seriously.*

Danny broke the silence. "You think
maybe one of the snotty club members is
engaged in corporate espionage? Like maybe
the Exeter T-shirt guy?"

Galvin was no longer smiling. "The security people say the time when someone tried
to access my BlackBerry — well, it was
when you and I were playing squash."

"Bizarre." Danny was starting to feel
queasy.

"So help me out here," Galvin said. He
was no longer looking directly at Danny. He
was staring past Danny's right shoulder at
the window.

"Okay."

"You went to the locker room when I was
on the court."

"I did?"

"You went to get some water. Some bottles
of water."

"I vaguely remember."

*I pretended to take his locker key "ac-
cidentally." He barely seemed to notice at the
time.*

"Remember that kid, the Hispanic kid, José? In the locker room?"

"The one you were speaking Spanish to?"

"Yep. Him. You didn't see him near my locker, did you?"

Danny blinked a few times. He couldn't decide whether to continue acting bored or look like he was trying hard to remember something so minor, so obscure, that no one could possibly be expected to recall.

He opted for the eye squint, the furrowed brow. The trying-as-hard-as-I-can-to-remember look.

Trying not to show the relief that washed over him.

And now what? Accuse the locker room attendant of loitering near Galvin's locker, of breaking into Galvin's locker? That innocent kid? So he'd end up like Esteban, the chauffeur, sliced and diced in a Dumpster somewhere? Anyway, what would a locker room attendant want with Tom Galvin's BlackBerry? That made no sense.

Or did it? What if José made a regular habit of ransacking members' lockers, stealing pocket change here and there, and for some reason — not beyond belief, not at all — he picked up Galvin's BlackBerry to make a call, or just to look at it? Out of good old-fashioned curiosity?

That was a plausible explanation. But Danny knew that if he pushed that lie, and the cartel believed that some kid from the Plympton Club locker room had tried to get into Tom Galvin's BlackBerry . . .

Would the kid really end up carved into a dozen pieces?

Galvin fidgeted. He drew a long breath.

Then something occurred to Danny. "The locker room attendants have access to all the locker keys, I bet."

"Huh." Galvin looked dubious.

"Then again . . . I don't know, he seemed like a real nice kid."

"You never know. You think you know someone . . ."

"Well, who else would have access to your locker?"

"I don't know what to believe. You wanna know the truth, I don't care. But my clients — man, do they ever care."

He looked like he was about to go on when Celina appeared behind him. "Tom, do you know the girls were watching *Knocked Up*? I told Jenna that's not for kids. I told her, no more movies or TV for her for the rest of the day."

Galvin shrugged. "Ah, Celina, she's got a guest this weekend. Let's give her a break."

"No," Celina said severely. "She has to

learn, she breaks the rules, there are consequences."

A few hours later they landed at Aspen/ Pitkin Airport, where they were picked up by a driver, a different one, in a black Chevy Suburban.

This one was armored, too.

40

If he hadn't known it was a private house, Danny would have assumed they were pulling up in front of a deluxe ski resort. It was an immense, rambling contemporary structure with a Japanese feel to it, built of stone and logs, a short drive north of town in a part of Aspen called Red Mountain. The curves and peaks of the roof were dusted with drifts of snow like powdered sugar.

The floors inside were blond wood, the walls rough-hewn stone and glass. Mostly glass. There were cathedral ceilings, a huge stone fireplace, and floor-to-ceiling picture windows that looked out onto the steeply canted mountainside: an astonishing view.

The driver — a sour-looking, barrel-chested man of around forty — carried everyone's bags inside. He wore a necklace of colorful wooden beads and seemed to speak no English and talked only with Celina, in Spanish.

"Let me show you two to your room," Celina said, taking Lucy by the elbow. "Jenna, Abby can sleep in your room, okay? But don't let me catch you watching videos! Read books! You remember what is books?"

Jenna rolled her eyes. "I'm taking her to the Bowl."

"The Bowl! Abby, *querida,* are you a very strong skier?"

"Sure," Abby said.

"No," Danny broke in. "She's not."

"Dad!"

"You haven't skied in three years," Danny said.

"It's not like you forget," Abby said. "It's like riding a bike."

"You two go to Buttermilk." Celina waggled a finger.

"That's for babies!" Jenna protested.

"Don't argue with me," Celina said. "Anyway, don't they have that superpipe?"

"True," Jenna said. "Can we take the Vespas?"

"No," Celina said sternly. "Alejandro can take you. No more talk." She pointed toward a hall off the main sitting area. "Go."

"And I've got work to do," Galvin said to Danny. "You guys settle in, you can rest, take it easy, whatever."

"No," said Celina, "I want to take Lucy

cross-country skiing out behind the house. Danny, is okay if I borrow your beautiful girlfriend later this afternoon? After you have a little rest?"

"Sounds wonderful," Lucy said. "Where can I rent skis?"

"No problems. We have skis for everyone in the mudroom in the back," Celina said. "Everything you need."

Danny's iPhone sounded a text message alert. He saw it was from AnonText007 and slipped it quickly back into his pocket.

When they got to their room and Celina had left, Lucy sank down on the king-size bed, covered in a moss-green-and-gold-striped comforter, and let out a long, throaty sigh.

"You have a good talk with Celina?"

"I like her a lot," Lucy said. "She must be lonely out there in the burbs, just doing the mom thing."

"Well, she doesn't have to work, that's for sure."

"She wants to have lunch when we get back to Boston."

"You gonna do it?"

"Sure. She wants to talk about the home-less center."

"You gonna hit her up for a donation?"

"The idea's crossed my mind."

"Maybe not such a great idea."

She gave Danny a curious look. "Why not?"

"It's already sort of awkward, all the money he's lent me."

"Yeah, the homeless aren't as worthy a cause as a five-thousand-dollar trip to Italy."

"Lucy. No fair. You know damned well what that was about."

"I'm sorry. Cheap shot. But I didn't twist her arm or anything like that. She kept asking about what I did, wanted to know more about it, and she said she wanted to get more involved."

"Just what we need — get more involved with the Galvins."

"He says, standing in the Galvins' Aspen house," she teased.

Danny exhaled. She was, of course, absolutely right. "It's . . . complicated. It would just put us even deeper in their debt."

"Can we change the subject?" She tugged at his belt. "Come lie with me and be my love."

He smiled and turned to the enormous window, the stunning view of Aspen Mountain. There were no drapes or blinds.

"You think anyone can see in?" she said.

"Not without a telescope," Danny said, "and if they're that determined to watch us

310

make love, they deserve a free show."

She laughed, and he felt the first tug of arousal.

Lying naked in bed, Lucy said, "I don't think she's terribly happy in her marriage."

"Why do you think that?"

"Just from the way she talked about Tom. There's something not quite right."

"How long have they been married?"

"It's not just the normal stuff, the stresses and strains of a long marriage. Something else. I barely know her, and she was unburdening herself. She comes from some plutocratic Mexican family."

"Plutocratic, as in rich?"

She nodded. "I always assumed their money came from her husband's investment business."

"She actually told you her family is super-rich?"

"No, of course not, not like that. I inferred it. But her father was the governor of one of the Mexican states — Veracruz, I think? She went to some convent school in Paris and traveled a lot as a kid, had servants, lot of horseback riding, all that."

"She told you all this?"

Lucy nodded. "Oh, and do you have any idea how Galvin makes his money?"

"Just that he invests money for some very rich family."

"Three guesses who that family is."

Danny smiled. "Holy crap. He's working for his in-laws, huh?"

There was a knock on the door.

"Lucy, it's Celina. You are ready for some skiing?"

"Be right out," she said.

Dinner was at a place called Munchies Grill, which was a wealthy ski resort's idea of a burger place. Rustic wooden picnic tables inside and curls of wood shavings and sawdust on the floor and cutesy neon signs. Its hamburgers were made from grass-fed beef from a small local supplier, rib meat, ground with bone marrow, stuffed with pork shoulder, and served either on house-made pretzel bread or house-made English muffin. Instead of mashed potatoes, they offered "smashed" Yukon gold potatoes. Not plain old French fries but truffle curly fries with roasted garlic aioli.

Their burgers took forever. After two Diet Cokes, Danny excused himself to use the restroom, at the back of the restaurant.

As he stood at the urinal, he heard the door bolt slide into place. Then, immediately behind him, a familiar baritone, a voice with a metallic rasp.

"You didn't really think you could just walk away, did you?"

41

Danny finished his business and zipped up and turned to face the DEA agent, Philip Slocum.

His heart pounded, but his voice was steady. "You didn't follow us here," he said. "I was watching since we left Galvin's house. There was no one behind us the whole way." He turned slowly. It was only him and Slocum in the restroom. The door was bolted.

"So you're a countersurveillance expert now?"

"You put a tracker on the Suburban."

"What difference does it make, as long as we're together?" Slocum gave a leering smile.

"Sorry you've wasted a trip. Maybe you can get in some skiing while you're here."

The side part in Slocum's jet-black hair was a broad line of pale white scalp. His eyes were dark and hard.

"How about we go out there and say hi to Tom Galvin?" said Slocum. "Let him know we're old friends, you and I. That we've been working together for several weeks now. I could hand him my business card."

"I doubt you want to screw up your investigation."

"Yeah, hate to have him think the DEA is looking at him closely." Slocum smirked. "I'm sure that would never occur to him."

"What do you want?"

"Pictures. Photos of whoever Galvin's meeting with."

Someone was trying the door. The knob twisted. Then, from outside, a muffled voice: "Sorry."

"And for that you need *me*? Won't the DEA spring for a good telephoto lens?"

"We don't know when and where he's meeting. Whereas you're spending the weekend with him."

"He's not on a leash. You expect me to stalk him? Follow him everywhere he goes?"

"Pretty much."

"Well, unless you want me to use my iPhone to take pictures, I'm afraid I can't help you."

"I'll have a camera for you tomorrow morning."

"What, you're going to drop it off at

Galvin's house?"

"No. You're going to meet me in town early tomorrow morning. Seven A.M. Place called Sweet Tooth on South Galena. It's a coffee shop. You're an early riser, and you need your coffee."

"I don't have a car."

"You don't need one. You'll walk into town."

"And what happens if the mister or missus happens to be awake and says, where're you going, coffee's on?"

"You say thanks but no thanks, you need to clear your head to start your writing day. You're a writer — make something up. Tell 'em you like to take walks. It's not even two miles. Shouldn't take you more than half an hour. Any longer than that, you're in lousy shape and you really do need the exercise."

42

Dr. Mendoza was perplexed.

He had stanched the flow of blood but hadn't yet discovered the cause of the bleeding.

Eliminating the banker had been an urgent necessity, of course. If the man had spilled, the consequences would have been immense. Truly catastrophic for the cartel.

But his employers had bigger worries. The question was how the Drug Enforcement Administration had even learned of the banker's existence. Obviously, someone on the inside had tipped them off.

An informant. A "confidential source," as the DEA called a snitch.

But who?

Surely, it was someone close to Thomas Galvin, the cartel's US-based investor. Someone in his office, perhaps. Or on his personal staff. Someone who had access to his home.

Unfortunately, the cartel had reacted to the leak with customary crudeness. They'd thought they had identified the culprit and sent their *gavilleros* armed with knives and machetes.

But they'd guessed wrong.

Well, Dr. Mendoza knew where to find out. Maybe the leak was in Boston, maybe not. But the *identity* of the source would without question be in Washington, DC. At DEA headquarters.

Like all government bureaucracies, the DEA kept records, great masses of paper, with a manic compulsion. Even on their most closely held sources they kept notes, papers, documents. Naturally, these files were sealed and locked away. But files always needed to be updated and indexed and accessed. Such was the nature of a bureaucracy, its lifeblood. And that work was always done, without fail, by low-level file clerks.

And here was the DEA's weakness. The human factor, always.

Low-level file clerks were extraordinarily easy to turn.

He needed to fly to Washington, DC.

He could barely remember a time when he wasn't in the employ of the Sinaloa cartel.

318

He had been barely thirteen on that sun-scorched afternoon when the big black Lincoln pulled into the gas station/bodega where his mother worked as a cashier. The heat shimmered up from the asphalt. He ran to the pump and took the driver's order. The man spoke in Spanish. In that part of San Diego, everyone spoke Spanish.

"Okay, kid," the driver said, handing him a twenty, "a pack of Winstons, two packs of Marlboro unfiltered, couple cans of Pepsi, and today's paper."

"Do you have a quarter?" Armando Mendoza asked.

"I just gave you a twenty, kid."

"Yes, but it's not going to be enough."

The driver looked skeptical. "How the hell do you know that?"

Mendoza had shrugged. How to explain simple arithmetic? "Well, it's sixteen ninety for the gas, the three packs of cigarettes is one eighty-nine, and with the Pepsi and the newspaper, that's twenty dollars and twenty-four cents. So, I mean, this is close, but . . ."

"You some kind of math genius?"

"I just added it up."

"In your head?"

He nodded. He was showing off, of course.

The driver said to a man next to him in

319

the front seat, "You see this?" Then he stuck his elbow out of the window and leaned closer to the teenager. He removed his mirrored sunglasses. "How much is 239 plus 868 plus 102?"

"That's too easy."

"How much, huh? You can't do it, can you?"

"One thousand two hundred and nine."

"Hold on, hold on." The driver turned to the other man. "Your watch has a calculator on it, right? Okay. Kid, what's 7566 plus 8069? Quick, now."

Mendoza smiled. He paused for a few seconds. "Fifteen thousand six hundred thirty-five."

"That right, Carlos?"

"Nope," said the other man.

"Nice try, kid," the driver said. "You almost had us there for a while."

"Hold on, hold on," the other man said. "Fifteen six three five. He's right."

"That's what I said," Armando protested.

"Jesus, kid."

Later, his mother was furious when she heard he'd gotten into the backseat of the Lincoln. Just a few months earlier, a kid in New York City had gone missing, and his face appeared on milk cartons. She'd told him this story as if to inoculate him from the possibility of anything so terrible happening to her only child.

But all they'd done was to take him to meet their *jefe,* to show off his math skills. *El jefe,* the great Héctor Luis Palma Salazar. El Güero as he was called: the Blond One. El Güero was impressed and made him an offer. They would rescue him from the barrio. They'd even send him to college. They'd train him as an accountant, and then he'd work for the cartel.

But even at the age of thirteen, Armando Mendoza knew he wanted to be a doctor. A surgeon: That was his true desire. Not an accountant.

El Güero didn't argue. There was need for medical talent as well. He was farsighted, a brilliant organizer who had built the Sinaloa cartel into the most powerful drug-trafficking organization in history. El Güero Palma needed someone utterly reliable to enforce discipline, ask questions and get answers, conduct "interviews," as Mendoza began calling them, whatever it took. And administer justice when it had to be done: with a scalpel and not an AK-47.

Dr. Mendoza was young — too young — but his time would come. The cartel would pay for medical school in Guadalajara and support him during his surgical residency.

In return, he would belong to the cartel. He would provide them with surgical services as needed. Later, after he became a surgeon, he asked them to underwrite the clinic in Culiacán. If he was going to work for the cartel, much of the work unpleasant, he wanted to do good works, too.

His work for the cartel, his nonsurgical work — his special work, as he thought of it — this gave him no pleasure. He was not one of those miscreants who took sadistic pleasure in such things. He simply believed that it was better that a job be done well than poorly, and in his hands, it was always done well.

It was also a fact that he had saved many more lives, through his work at the clinic and at the private hospital in Culiacán, than he had taken. He had alleviated at least as much pain as he had caused.

Dr. Mendoza felt the need to remind himself of this, since very soon, he was quite sure, he would be inflicting a great deal of pain.

43

At six o'clock the next morning, Danny's iPhone alarm went off. The bedroom was dark and a bit overheated, and for a moment Danny, woozy, nearly gave in to the temptation to go back to sleep.

Until he remembered.

Lucy mumbled, "Why are you getting up?"

"To do some work," Danny said.

"What time is it?"

"Six. In Boston, it's eight o'clock."

She murmured, "We're not in Boston," and rolled over.

No one else was up, which was a relief. Before the grown-ups had retired for the night, Galvin had announced that they weren't crack-of-dawn ski types and everyone should feel free to sleep in. But Danny was prepared in case Tom or Celina were up — he knew the girls wouldn't be — and offered him coffee and wondered why in the world he was headed out so early. He'd say he was mentally outlining the next chapter of his book. Fresh air always helped him think clearly. Who'd question that? Writers were an enigma to most people anyway.

The front door sounded a chime when he opened it, but it wasn't alarmed. Outside it was dark and cold and the snow crunched and squeaked underfoot. The frigid air stung his cheeks and earlobes as he walked along the shoulder of the road.

There was hardly any traffic, with the exception of a Jeep passing by, blaring a snatch of something hip-hop and unmelodic. Gung-ho skiers, probably, on their way to sample early-morning corduroy.

The walk to town took just over twenty minutes. Gradually the sky began to brighten.

Sweet Tooth was exactly as Danny had expected, a hipster coffee shop/bakery that offered chai latte and gluten-free brownies and organic fair-trade coffee roasted by hand in small batches. Something by Ray LaMontagne was playing on the speakers. The only patrons were an exhausted-looking young dad with a squalling baby in a stroller, and, sitting by himself on a beat-up leather couch, Philip Slocum.

Danny ordered a small black coffee, which set him back four dollars, and joined Slocum on the couch.

An idea had just occurred to him, and he took out his iPhone.

"Hold on," he said, feigning annoyance at some dull task he had to get out of the way.

It wasn't easy to snap a photo of Philip Slocum furtively. But he muted the phone's volume and then held it up vertically as if trying to get a better view of something on the screen.

And hit the CAMERA button. No sound, no flash. Just a half-decent, fairly in-focus picture of Slocum's face.

"Did anyone watch you leave the house?" Slocum asked.

"I doubt it. Everyone was asleep. Why?"

He slid a small black nylon pouch across the sofa toward Danny. "Because you didn't leave the house with this, so you might not want to flash it around."

Danny unzipped the pouch. Inside was what looked like just the lens for an SLR camera, a small black barrel. But on second glance he could see it was an entire camera, extremely compact, its body dwarfed by its lens.

"And where's this meeting taking place?"

"We don't know. Just that it's going to be fairly remote. They're concerned about tracking devices and surveillance."

"I told you, I don't have a car."

"You don't need a car. Galvin's not taking a car. Too easy to be tracked."

"So maybe they're meeting at Galvin's house."

"Doubt it."

"Then, what? — he's walking?"

The baby let out an ear-piercing shriek. Danny sometimes missed having a little kid — Abby was a heart-meltingly adorable little girl — but he sure didn't miss having an infant that age.

"Most likely it'll be a location where cars can't drive to — where you can't park a van. Where you can't point a parabolic microphone. And where the cell phone coverage is so unreliable, or nonexistent, that no concealed transmitters are going to work. It'll have 360-degree visibility, so they'll be able to see anyone approaching."

"Including me," Danny said. "So they can pick me off with a sniper rifle."

"No," Slocum said patiently. "You're a friend. A houseguest. If for some reason you're spotted, Galvin will vouch for you."

"And when is this supposed to happen, this meeting?"

Slocum shrugged. "This weekend. Today or tomorrow. That's all we know."

"And it could be anywhere. Anywhere he doesn't need a car to get to."

"Right. So try not to leave his side."

When Slocum had finished his instructions, Danny stood up.

"Hey," Slocum said. "Buy some muffins and scones to take home to the Galvins. Be a nice houseguest."

Danny jammed the camera case into the outside pocket of his down parka. He bought an assortment of scones and muffins. With a white paper sack in his hand — SWEET TOOTH printed on it in the same typeface the Grateful Dead used to use on their albums — he left the coffee shop.

The first thing he noticed was a black Suburban.

Standing a few feet from the coffee shop, smoking and watching the front door, was Galvin's driver.

44

The Suburban passed Danny on his way back.

He half expected Alejandro to pull over and offer him a lift. There was no question they'd recognized each other. The chauffeur had looked away too quickly.

Of course, it was possible that the chauffeur genuinely didn't recognize him. But if he did, and if he'd witnessed the transaction between Slocum and Danny, had seen Danny pick up the camera . . . ?

By the time he got back, the Suburban was parked in front of the house, its engine block ticking and creaking as it cooled. He glanced around. Alejandro was nowhere to be seen.

And through the glass front door he saw a light on that hadn't been on before. He stamped his boots on the welcome mat, unlaced and removed them when he entered. In stocking feet, he followed the light into the kitchen.

Galvin, in a white bathrobe, his back to Danny, sat at a high chair at a long granite island. Coffee had just been brewed.

Danny held up the Sweet Tooth paper sack by way of efficient explanation. "Good morning."

"Good morning," Galvin said heartily. He laughed and pointed to an identical paper bag on the counter by the coffeemaker. "Alejandro just got back from there."

Had the driver gone into the shop right after Danny had left?

"Great minds think alike," he said.

"You went all the way into town on foot to get coffee?" he scolded. "I told you guys to make yourself at home. *Mi casa es su casa.*"

"I guess I'm still on East Coast time." He set the bag down on the island. "The terminally hip barista said their cinnamon buns are to die for."

"Well, no one's going to complain about seconds."

"Amazing view," Danny said, pointing at the enormous picture window. "You probably take it for granted by now."

Galvin pushed back his chair and stood up. "That view is what sold us on this property. That and the fact that there's a cross-country trailhead close by. We can just put on our cross-country skis and take off from the backyard if we want to. In town's a lot more convenient — you can walk pretty much everywhere — but you don't get the view."

"What are we looking at?" Danny approached the window, and Galvin joined him.

"Snow," Galvin said.

"Thanks." The comfortable sardonic banter of a couple of buddies. "Is that Aspen Mountain?"

"Aspen Highlands Bowl." He pointed. "Steeplechase. That's upper Castle Creek valley."

"Beautiful." There was no backyard, really. No fence defining property lines. Just a few stands of birch trees jutting up from the snow and lines of scrub pines. And a blanket of snow that went on for as far as he could see. And no other houses in view.

"Anytime we're not here, you guys are welcome to stay. Otherwise it just sits here empty."

Danny nodded. "Thanks." They both stood admiring the scenery.

"And when we *are* here, too, of course. Celina and your, uh, girlfriend look like they're becoming fast friends. Abby and

Jenna are inseparable. And you're not so bad yourself." Galvin clapped an arm on his shoulder. "Seriously, the first time I met you, I knew you."

"Knew me?"

"Recognized you. Like you were a kindred spirit among all those phonies at Lyman, all those hoity-toity types."

"I don't exactly belong," Danny said.

"Neither of us does."

"Except you're —"

"Rich?"

"You could put it that way, yeah. As long as you've got beaucoup bucks, Tinsley Thornton couldn't care less where you come from."

"*Lally*, you mean. Please." A tart grin. "See, Danny, that's where you're wrong. She knows who I am and where I'm from. To her, and to everyone at that school, I'll never be more than a blue-collar kid from Southie who got lucky. As far as they're concerned, I'm no better than some jamoke who works at a gas station and just won three hundred million bucks in the lottery. I'll always be, you know" — he extended a pinkie and mimed drinking a cup of tea — "below the salt, as they'd say. They're happy to take my money, sure, but I don't have any illusions about the kind of smack they

331

talk about me at board meetings."

Danny shrugged, grinned. "*Jamoke.* My dad's favorite insult."

"You grew up on the Cape, right?"

"Yep. Wellfleet."

"But not McMansion Wellfleet, I'm betting."

"Not even close."

"I forget if you told me, he was a plumber like my dad, right?"

"Contractor. Carpenter, really — that's what he most loved doing."

"Bet he was good at it."

"He was great. A real craftsman. Meticulous. But a lousy businessman."

"My dad was a good businessman but not exactly meticulous." He laughed. "But everyone loved him. Did you say your dad passed?"

"No, they're both alive."

"Lucky. Mine are gone. Funny how the relationship changes when they get old. You start giving them advice. They even listen to you once in a while. They need your help, and you don't need theirs anymore."

Danny nodded.

Galvin went on, "Whatever stuff you went through, whatever ticked you off about your mom and dad, you just move on from that. You take care of them, because that's what you do."

Danny nodded. "Dad's starting to lose it, you know, so we may have to put him in a home pretty soon. But he's gonna go kicking and screaming."

"I see the way you look at Abby. I see it in your eyes. You'd do anything to keep her safe."

Danny felt tears spring to his eyes. "You know it."

"I mean, I'd kill to protect my family. Bet you'd do the same."

Danny nodded, uncertain what he was getting at. He looked Galvin in the face, just as he heard Celina say, "What big trouble are you two plotting?"

"Morning, babes," Galvin said as they kissed.

"Good morning," Danny said.

He thought about what Galvin had just said. He'd kill to protect his family. From anybody else, that would be a figure of speech.

From Galvin, though, it sounded awfully like a threat.

45

Celina made French toast and bacon for breakfast, which they had along with the pastries from the coffee shop, and then they all suited up and took the Silver Queen Gondola to the summit of Aspen Mountain, six of them in one cabin. The sun glinted off the snow trails, dazzling ice-encrusted trees, the skinny pine trees far below like the bristles of a coarse brush.

The three Galvins were wearing expensive ski outfits. Jenna had on a gold down jacket and ski pants that looked like blue denim but weren't. Her mother wore a long silver metallic coat with a fur collar, too high fashion to be practical on the slopes. Tom had a bright yellow Salomon parka that resembled a rain slicker with a high collar. A bright green-and-yellow-striped knit cap with a pompom. With that outfit, Danny thought, he should be easy to spot at a distance.

The girls sat on the bench facing the adults and didn't stop talking the whole way. Abby wore the hot-pink Helly Hansen ski parka that Sarah had bought her a couple of years ago, a little worn and a size too small.

Lucy held Danny's hand. She leaned in close and said, under her voice, "She really looks happy, doesn't she?"

Danny nodded. In the bright light, he could see a few faint freckles across Lucy's nose. She hated her freckles, usually hid them with makeup. He thought they were adorable. She was wearing a light blue down jacket with a blue scarf and white pants that made her great legs look even greater.

Abby paused in midsentence and looked at them. She had the hearing of a bat, at least when she was the subject of conversation.

"We've never skied before, have we?" Lucy said.

"This is a first."

"You know I'm pretty good at this sport, right?"

"I'm not surprised. You're good at most sports."

"You're not going to be embarrassed, I hope."

"At what?"

"At how much better a skier I am." She said it with a coy smile, almost flirtatiously.

"Not at all. I'll be inspired, more likely. You make me a better man."

"That's for sure," she said with a laugh.

But Danny wasn't thinking about skiing.

He was thinking about a way out. The DEA had him in a corner, it was true, but that didn't make him powerless. If he were actually able to snap a picture of whoever Galvin was supposed to be meeting with, then he'd have something the DEA wanted.

You want the pictures? How about I get a letter of immunity? Signed by the DEA and the Department of Justice and whoever the hell else was necessary to make it ironclad. The president, if need be. A guarantee that he would never be indicted for anything to do with Galvin.

That would finally banish the threat hanging over his head, which kept them coming back and coming back. He was fed up with being a marionette. The only way to cut the strings was to be ruthless.

But how safe would it be to trail Galvin? If he were actually meeting someone from the Sinaloa drug cartel, he'd take precautions against being followed. And Danny was a writer, not a spy. Not a trained intelligence operative. He didn't know the first

336

thing about surveillance. From everything he'd read on the subject — mostly, he had to admit, spy thrillers — following someone without being detected was a skill acquired by a professional after long practice. Not a skill he had. No way.

Short of chaining himself to Tom Galvin's ski boots, there was simply no way to make sure Galvin didn't go off somewhere during the course of the afternoon. Galvin could ski down the mountain and disappear into the streets of Aspen. He could meet someone at a café, a restaurant, a bar, and Danny would never know about it.

All he could do was keep Galvin in sight as long as possible. And hope he got lucky.

At the top of the mountain, they got off the gondola, snapped into their skis, and gathered to confer.

"There aren't any green trails?" Abby asked, trying to sound casual. She swallowed hard.

"Just intermediate and expert," Danny said. "You can snowplow for a while until you get used to it. It'll all come back to you. Wasn't it you who said it's like riding a bike?"

"The blue trails really aren't so scary," Jenna said.

The girls didn't want to ski with the

oldsters, and who could blame them? Abby pulled her goggles into place, and the two of them started down the slope, a blue trail called Easy Chair, which didn't in fact look particularly easy.

Celina said, "Everyone: One thirty at the Sundeck for lunch?" She pointed at the building behind them. "Okay? Girls? Yes?"

Jenna waved an impatient acknowledgment to her mother, and the two girls were off. If Abby was nervous about her skiing ability, she was no longer showing it.

A minute or so later, the adults set off down the same slope, giving the girls enough of a head start to be on their own. Galvin was nimble and graceful, clearly an expert. Lucy was even better. Celina was good, about on par with Danny.

They quickly came to a juncture with a black trail.

"What do you think, Danny?" Lucy said. "Stay with the blue?"

Galvin said, "I'll probably be doing mostly black trails. Don't worry about trying to keep up with me."

There was no way to explain to Lucy why he needed to stay with Galvin at all times. He hesitated a moment, then said to Galvin, "I'll be fine," and he followed Galvin toward the expert trail, leaving Lucy and Celina behind.

The black trails weren't easy. They were scary at times, with some incredibly steep runs, but Danny managed to keep up with Galvin, more or less, for the next two hours or so. They skied on black diamond trails, but not double black diamond ones. The difficult ones, but not the "expert only" ones. He took a few spills, wounding just his dignity. He worried about the camera, hoped the down padding would protect it from damage.

A few times he spotted Abby and Jenna on the chairlift or cruising down the slopes. Abby seemed to be doing just fine. Twice he and Galvin met up with Lucy and Celina on the Shadow Mountain chairlift line. If Lucy was annoyed about being left behind in favor of Galvin, she didn't display it.

At a few minutes past one thirty, the adults all gathered out behind the Sundeck restaurant by the picnic tables to wait for the girls. They stashed their skis in a rack. Galvin lit up a cigar. He waggled it at Danny with a questioning look.

Danny shook his head. "Thanks anyway."

A few diners at the picnic tables were giving Galvin poisonous glares, but he didn't seem to notice, and if did, he didn't care.

Something about him seemed different. He was unusually preoccupied, pensive. Maybe he'd made a bad trade at work. Lost a couple hundred million dollars. Maybe he and Celina had had a fight.

Maybe that was all.

Anyway, how well did he really know the guy? They'd had a couple of friendly chats. They'd bonded over their similar backgrounds. Men don't sit around sharing their feelings. They do stuff together. They don't cry together or gossip; they watch football on TV, maybe play poker. They drink together, rib each other.

Maybe he was preoccupied. Or maybe he really was about to meet his contacts from the Sinaloa cartel.

"Hey, you," Lucy said to Danny. "You took off."

"I'm sorry about that. I guess I just wanted to push the edge of the envelope. My bad."

"Men and their competitiveness," she said, shaking her head, amused.

Danny made a stop in the men's room, clomping, with his ski boots on, like Frankenstein's monster.

When he returned, Galvin was gone.

"Tom went back to the slopes," Celina said. "He said he wasn't hungry." Something

340

about the way she spoke, the way her eyes wouldn't meet his, prickled Danny's suspicions.

"Which way did he go?" Danny said. "I think I'll join him. I don't mind skipping lunch."

"I saw him going that way," Abby said. She pointed vaguely toward the uncleared back section of the mountain, away from the blue and black trails, down the hill on the other side of the gondola landing.

"Oh, stay with us," said Lucy.

"Knowing Daddy," said Jenna, "he'll be doing one of the double black diamond runs."

"I wouldn't mind trying a couple of double black diamond runs," Danny said.

"I think maybe Tom is just wanting to ski by himself," Celina said. Her tone was brittle. She gave Danny a quick but penetrating look.

Danny, pretending not to hear her, headed toward the uncleared area.

"You're not staying for lunch?" Lucy said. "You sure?"

"I'm good," he said.

And he set off in search of Tom Galvin.

46

On this side of the mountain, beyond the railing, were yellow signs on tall posts warning SKI BOUNDARY. The area was cordoned off with a pink neon rope. A diamond-shaped yellow caution sign: DANGER — NO SKIING BEYOND THIS POINT. Another one read WARNING! HAZARDS EXIST THAT ARE NOT MARKED — SKI WITH CARE. Just beyond that, a red sign mounted on a pole declared: THIS IS YOUR DECISION POINT. BACKCOUNTRY RISKS INCLUDE DEATH.

There were no marked trails here. There were no trails at all. This was the off-piste, ungroomed section, reserved for the most adventurous expert skiers, the hard-core powder heads and freeriders, the rippers and the shredders.

He could see a few lone tracks from skis and snowshoes. Also the parallel corduroy tracks laid down by the teeth and tread of a Sno-Cat, the snow vehicle that could climb up or down the mountainside. People generally didn't ski terrain this rough on their own. Adventurers usually went in groups led by guides on Sno-Cats.

Had Galvin really taken off down this side of the mountain? It didn't seem likely.

It didn't seem at all likely that Galvin had gone this way. Abby must have been mistaken.

Then he noticed something dark and gnarled and malodorous in the snow a few paces ahead: the discarded butt of a cigar, like the turd of a small dog.

He peered down the mountainside, hoping to catch a glimpse of Galvin's yellow parka among the glades. Nothing. But that didn't mean he hadn't skied down this way. He might just be out of sight, down a gulley, on the far side of a swell.

The sunlight reflecting off the snow dazzled his eyes. He put on his goggles and took a deep breath and stood at the lip of a cornice.

The snowdrifts looked seriously deep. Based on the diameter and taper of the tree trunks, he estimated that the snow was as deep as six feet in some places. This was not terrain he was used to skiing. Untouched, ungroomed runs like this, with such a deep snowpack, were meant for backcountry skiers.

Not him.

He briefly weighed making a desperation move — attempting a controlled descent, carving long turns side to side, zigzagging to slow his speed. But standing on the ledge and looking down, he realized what a preposterous idea it was to try skiing this side of the mountain. He turned his skis to one side — and felt the ledge crumble beneath him.

Suddenly he was plummeting, rocketing down the steep decline. He found himself whooshing through powder a foot deep, unlike the hardpack on the other side of the mountain, where the snow was flattened by hundreds, maybe thousands of skis every day. Here the snow was fluffy and lighter than air. It was like gliding through a cloud.

But the wide-open bowl quickly gave way to a more densely forested area, the tall pines scattered on the mountainside. Now he found himself weaving in and among and around the trees, picking up speed. Pines popped up before him like the looming obstacles in a video game. He carved a hard turn to one side, swerved to the other, slaloming between closely set tree trunks. From somewhere deep in his memory he recalled that the best trick for swooping between the trees was to focus on the white spaces in between, aiming carefully.

He swooped and carved, faster and faster, propelled down the hill by gravity and momentum, and he tried to slow himself down. But the only way to do that was to carve back and forth, shift his weight from one side to the other. And that he couldn't do. Because he was catapulting downhill so fast, with so little clearance between the trees, he couldn't afford an unnecessary turn even a few degrees to one side or the other. His skis shuddered. His legs and thighs burned from the unaccustomed muscular exertion. And the terrain between the trees was wildly inconsistent. In some places the snow was deep and fluffy; in other places were sheer patches of ice, and every so often he hit a rocky knuckle. His face felt frozen solid. He caromed faster and faster, always aware that the slightest miscalculation would send him crashing into a tree trunk.

Suddenly his skis crunched against something, which he realized only too late was a ridge, a cliff.

Midair, soaring, he felt time slow. He could see the sharply pitched slope, the rocky chasm directly below, and he knew that if he dropped too quickly, he would hit the rocks and be instantly killed.

He knew his fate was outside his control. He couldn't alter the force of gravity or the trajectory of his descent. He'd vaulted down an icy chute into a twenty-foot drop, a vertical rock wall, with nothing but slippery boards strapped to his feet and no brakes.

And yet, for one brief passing moment, it was exhilarating. To feel nothing below him. Airborne, free falling, a human projectile, a missile. It was thrilling. Like nothing he'd ever experienced before. The wind howled in his ears.

He was just a few seconds, and one wrong turn, away from the finality of death.

And he realized at the deepest level of his consciousness how thin the margin was between extreme, awesome, energizing terror — and death. For the first time in his life, he understood thrill seekers, extreme skiers and mountain climbers. Hang gliders and skydivers and tightrope walkers. He finally understood the intoxicating sensation of defying death, of facing down our hardwired instinct for self-preservation.

And then, just as quickly as this realization had come over him, another kind of understanding seized him. That he might actually meet his death on the rocks below.

And the instinct for self-preservation reasserted itself.

This might have taken as much as two seconds. Certainly no more. He bent his knees, squatted, braced himself —

— and landed hard on the ground, absorbing the impact, a blow to his entire body all at once. He catapulted forward. He'd lost control.

The tip of his right ski caught on something. He flipped over and landed, hard, on his back, and for a moment everything was absolutely quiet. He'd come to an abrupt stop.

He tasted blood.

He twisted, felt pain shoot through his limbs, then throughout his entire body, jagged, like the crackle of lightning.

Icy snow bit his ears, his eyelids, the back of his neck. He tried again to move, wriggled, and found he could move his legs, his arms. He felt bruised all over, but nothing seemed to be broken. Then he remembered how to get up with skis on. He tucked his feet in toward his butt and leaned his knees to the left side. He realized he'd lost both skis. Slowly, carefully, he rolled over. Felt something twang in his lower back, a pizzicato pluck of nerve endings. A tendon? A pulled muscle? He hoped it was nothing more serious than that. For a moment he needed to rest, so he sank down, his face buried in the snow, which felt strangely warm, and then icy cold.

Then, bracing himself on his elbows he pushed up, the exertion sending more daggers of pain through his arms and shoulders. He pushed through the pain and got to his knees. He tasted more blood, probed the inside of his mouth with his tongue, realized he'd bitten his lower lip during the fall.

Unsteady on his feet now, he saw something maybe two or three hundred feet away. An old shack, it appeared, built from logs. It couldn't have been more than ten feet by ten feet. Squat and sturdy and old, with a shingled roof. It looked like an old mining hut, left over from the mining boom at the end of the nineteenth century. He knew that Aspen had once been a silver mining camp, the largest in the country, until the day Congress repealed the Sherman Silver Purchase Act, demonetizing silver; in a matter of months, Aspen was a ghost town. But many of the old buildings remained, dotting the mountainside.

Through a small window on the side facing him, Danny could see a flickering amber light within. And silhouettes moving inside. Instinctively, he sank to the ground, sat in snow. He rooted around in his pockets until he located the nylon pouch that held the camera.

He yanked it open, the ripping sound of the Velcro closure loud in the muffled silence.

He trained the strong lens on the window, dialing the focus in and out until a face came into focus.

Galvin's.

Even this far away he could smell one of Galvin's cigars.

Galvin seemed to be rocking back and forth. No, he was pacing. Behind him was a man, or maybe two men, both of them wearing dark coats. One of the other men was bald. Danny refocused on the bald man. A plump, cue-ball round face with a goatee festooning a double chin. A heavy brow, unshaven-looking. He heard the crack of a tree branch, and he turned to look.

A man in a black parka and ski mask was lunging toward him. Before Danny could scramble to his feet, something crashed into the side of his head, an almost inconceivable explosion of pain, and the white light had bloomed to blot out his entire field of vision, the blood bitter and metallic, like copper pennies in his mouth, and then everything was absolutely quiet.

47

Later, the paramedics told Danny that he'd probably lost consciousness for no more than twenty or thirty seconds. But whatever happened in the hour that followed, he had no recollection of it. Later he was told he kept asking, over and over, "Where am I?" and "What happened?" He had nothing more than fleeting strands of memory, swirling like the streamers of yolk in a partly scrambled egg.

One minute he'd been staring through the camera lens at an old log cabin. The next minute, he was lying flat on his back in some sort of large barnlike room with plywood paneling. He had no idea where. Faces swam in and out of his field of vision. One face loomed directly above his, upside down, the funny-looking harp of a mouth forming nonsense words.

The cadence made the gobbledygook sound like a question, but the words meant nothing.

He tried to look around, but he could barely move his head. The room was over-heated. Stifling hot, actually. He felt drenched with sweat.

Again he tried to look around, to figure out where he might be and how he'd ended up there, but his head wouldn't move, his neck wouldn't swivel. With a flutter of panic, he tried to lift his entire torso, but he was totally immobilized. His legs, his arms, his hands, and feet — all were frozen in place. Nothing would move.

He was struck with a terrible realization: *I'm paralyzed. I'm a quadriplegic.*

". . . the United States," said a voice.

"What?" Danny said. *I can't move my limbs, can't even move my head. I'm frozen in place, locked in. I'm paralyzed.*

"Who's the president of the United States?" The upside-down face, the harp mouth. A raspy baritone.

Danny stared up at him in disbelief. *I'm a quadriplegic, and you're wasting my time with ridiculous questions like that?*

"Calvin Coolidge," he said.

The upside-down face swam out of his field of vision. Someone chuckled and said, "Wiseass."

"At least his sense of humor is intact."

Galvin.

An image came back to him. Galvin and someone else in the window of a small log cabin. The other person in the cabin was someone he'd never seen before. Cue-ball head. Spherical. A goatee floating in the middle of a double chin. Heavy brow.

How long ago had that been? Hours, maybe? Galvin meeting with some unidentified person in an old slopeside hut. But now he and Galvin were here.

"Where am I?" Danny said.

"America in 1925 or whatever, I'm guessing." Galvin again.

"I can't move," Danny said.

"Hey, baby." Lucy's face was close, her eyes wide. She looked scared.

"Hey, you. Will *you* tell me where I am?" He smiled with relief, with gratitude, with love.

"Ski patrol hut at the base of the mountain. Sweetie, do you remember falling and hitting your head?"

"No . . . not really."

"You remember going off to ski the uncleared side of the mountain?"

"That was sort of an accident. I didn't mean to."

"How's your head? Do you have a headache, or are you dizzy, or . . . ?"

"I can't move."

"Guys, there's no reason for him to be strapped down like that," Lucy said. "Come on. This is silly."

"I'm strapped down? That's the best news I've gotten in years."

Now the same voice that had just asked him about the president of the United States said, in a hoarse baritone, "I'm going to insist he go to Aspen Valley Hospital to have a CAT scan."

Danny could hear noises, snaps and buckles and something rubbing against something. The sharp pain of something squeezing against his wrists. Then he could feel his hands, tingling and heavy. He could move them.

Then the same thing with his ankles and his feet, which also tingled from a loss of circulation. He wriggled his fingers and found they worked just fine. His toes as well. A strap came off his chest, and a pair of hands helped him to sit up.

Lucy's hands. She leaned in and kissed him. A warm swell of love lapped over him. "Do you have a headache?" she asked again.

He moved his head side to side gingerly and didn't reply.

The front of his head, his temples, began thudding, hard. Truth was, he had a terrible headache. Like his brain was sliding back and forth in his skull. The pain seemed to be centered just behind his eye sockets. The thudding kept time with his heartbeat. If he could only grab the front of his head and detach it at the temples, he felt as if he could remove the headache and hold it, blood-slick and throbbing, in his hands.

"Seriously," she said.

"Yeah, some," he said.

Everything was bright and blazing with fierce color. He saw a few men in red-and-black parkas marked with white first-aid crosses, obviously members of the Aspen Mountain Ski Patrol. A few others he didn't recognize mulling around. Galvin standing behind them, his bright yellow down jacket unzipped.

Next to him, in a black parka with the zipper partway down, stood his driver, Alejandro. He was an odd-looking man, Alejandro. His head was unusually wide, but his face was narrow, the features clustered close together. A pale line in his upper lip looked like the trace of an old scar. His necklace of green and black beads had a pendant dangling from it that looked, from this distance at least, like the Virgin Mary.

But it was the black parka that chimed something in his memory.

Danny noticed his ski boots had been removed. He was in stocking feet.

One of the men in the red-and-black parkas leaned forward. "Your pupils look normal, and your vital signs seem to be fine," said the raspy-voiced one who seemed to be in charge. "You passed all the cognitive tests. Except the one about the president.

"Fact is, you got knocked out. Might have been for only a few seconds, but you were disoriented for a long time afterward, and that's something you have to take seriously."

Danny nodded, carefully. It hurt to move his head.

"You're a very lucky guy. Your friend here happened to see you and called us immediately." He glanced at Galvin. "If it wasn't for him, you might have frozen to death out there."

"Thank Alejandro, not me," Galvin said. "He's the one who found you."

Danny turned to look at Galvin, then at Alejandro, and then back to Galvin. He remembered a black parka and a black ski mask. Galvin said something to his driver, and Alejandro left the ski patrol hut.

Something about the black parka stirred a vague, fragmentary recollection.

The ski patrol guy said, "We're going to

give you a ride over to Aspen Valley. You might have a skull fracture or internal bleeding, so you need to have a CAT scan at the very least."

"I think I'm okay. I hate hospitals."

"You don't want to fool around with head injuries."

"I understand. But I think I'll be okay. Thank you guys so much for everything." He looked at Lucy. "Where's Abby?"

"The girls are skiing with Celina," Lucy said. "Let me help." She reached for his elbow.

"Really," Danny said, "I'm fine."

Galvin said, "Alejandro's getting the car. I'm going to take him home. We'll see you guys in front of the lodge." He gave a quick wave, a flip of his hand, and went outside.

"I'm sorry," Lucy said to the patrollers.

Even though he didn't need any support, he took Lucy's hand. She helped him put on his sneakers — she, or someone, must have retrieved them from the rental area.

"You don't look so good," Lucy said when they were outside. "Do you hurt all over, honey?"

He smiled. "Just my head."

"I know you hate hospitals, but you should go. If you start babbling nonsense, I'm taking you in. No debate."

"You sure?"

"About what?"

"Sure you'll be able to tell if I'm babbling nonsense? Worse than usual, I mean."

"You have a point. Any idea how you got knocked out?"

"I really have no idea, Luce. I can't remember much of what happened."

But he did remember, more than he wanted to say. He hadn't fallen. He'd been knocked out.

By the man in the black parka and the black ski mask.

Who must have been Galvin's driver, Alejandro.

He needed to sit down. The throbbing behind his eyeballs started up again. If he kept his head steady as he walked, he found it hurt less. It didn't feel as if his brain was thumping back and forth.

"Are you feeling sleepy?"

"Not sleepy. Just . . . I don't know, crappy."

The black Suburban was idling at the curb in front of the Little Nell. Tom Galvin got out of the front seat and opened the middle passenger door. Lucy came around between Danny and the Suburban to help him in. "I'm fine, really," he assured her.

When he was seated, Lucy began climbing in, but Galvin stopped her with a gentle hand on her shoulder. "Would you mind staying with the girls?"

"I think I should stay with Danny."

"Celina needs to meet a friend for coffee for some fund-raiser they're cochairing. She's not crazy about leaving the girls out there on the slopes alone. Don't worry about our boy. I'll get him straight home. He's in good hands."

She gave Danny a kiss on the lips, one that lingered a few seconds longer than usual. Her eyes, meeting his, radiated concern. "All right," she said, and reluctantly waved good-bye.

When they'd pulled away from the curb, Danny waited for a long moment. The only sound was the purr of the Suburban's 320 horsepower and V8 engine.

Then he said: "We both know what happened."

Galvin didn't reply. Danny wondered if Galvin had heard. Maybe not.

He was about to say it again when Galvin turned around and looked right into Danny's eyes. "I think it's time we talk."

48

Galvin gave his driver a sidelong glance. Alejandro nodded, barely perceptibly.

Danny's forehead thrummed as fast and as violently as his heart.

"You're right," he said. "It's time."

Another long silence. The Suburban pulled into a gas station parking lot, by-passed the pumps, and executed a U-turn. No one said anything. After a moment, Danny noticed the terrain changing, unfamiliar. "Aren't we heading back to the house?"

"Not just yet," Galvin said. "There's some Motrin back there in the seat compartment. You should probably drink some of that water there. You'll feel better."

"I'll be fine when I get some rest."

"First we're going for a drive," Galvin said.

Danny felt his stomach flip over. He started to protest, then sat back in his seat.

He heard the whine of the Suburban's

automatic transmission as it shifted gears.

They were heading northwest on Highway 82, Danny noticed. Galvin didn't speak. Neither of them did.

Finally, when the silence had gone on long enough, Danny said, "Where are we going?"

"Somewhere we can talk in private."

"You want to talk, let's talk. Pull over."

A long pause. "There's a place I want to show you."

"Some other time."

He wondered whether Galvin was planning a talk. Or something else. He tried to suppress a surge of panic. He thought about texting Slocum and Yeager to let them know what had happened, how he'd been knocked out. . . .

Which reminded him about the camera Slocum had given him. He was pretty sure he hadn't taken any pictures of Galvin meeting with whoever he was meeting with. He hadn't gotten the chance before someone — was it in fact Alejandro the driver? — struck him, knocked him out. Which meant the camera was still in his pocket. He patted the pockets of his down parka, then rummaged through them but found nothing. The camera wasn't in the zippered pocket. Or had he been holding it when he'd been knocked out? Probably so.

Making it likely that someone — Alejandro? — had taken it.

Galvin turned around, looking at Danny. "I want us to talk in private," he said. His eyes slid toward the driver and back again. Was Galvin saying he didn't want his driver to hear? "We're gonna go for a walk."

They kept on driving for a while. Danny had no sense of how long it was. He'd grown sleepy, lulled by the monotony of the road, yet he was too apprehensive to doze. A few cars passed, but not many. Then the Suburban signaled left and turned onto an unpaved road. Not just a dirt road, but rock-strewn: The vehicle canted and crunched and sidled and shuddered. They came upon a yellow diamond-shaped sign:

4-WHEEL DRIVES ONLY PAST THIS POINT

That was followed by another sign, bigger and rectangular and more urgent:

ATTENTION DRIVERS
EXTREMELY ROUGH ROAD AHEAD
VEHICLE TRAFFIC DISCOURAGED
4×4 WITH EXPERIENCED DRIVERS
AND NARROW WHEEL BASE ONLY

"What's the plan?" Danny said uneasily.
"You'll see," Galvin said.

361

The road quickly grew narrower, lined on either side with trees and wild shrubbery: spindly spruce and fir trees caked with snow, dense stands of barren aspens, wind-deformed willows and scraggly branches, snow-dusted scrub oak and pines.

Another road sign loomed into view:

THIS IS THE LAST CHANCE
TO TURN AROUND OR
PASS ANOTHER VEHICLE FOR MILES.
NARROW ROAD WITH STEEP DROP OFFS.
IF YOU ARE NOT ON FOOT,
A BIKE, OR AN ATV
YOU SHOULD TURN AROUND NOW!

In another five hundred or so feet the road ended. A ROAD CLOSED sign, striped with orange reflective tape and screwed on to a couple of ground-mounted I-beam supports, barricaded the way. It didn't look temporary. It looked seasonal. The road was closed for the winter.

Danny now had a fairly good idea what kind of walk Galvin intended to take him on, and he was finding it hard to breathe.

There was no one around, no one within sight, no one within earshot. For miles, probably.

Lucy was the only one who'd seen Galvin

leave with Danny, and as far as she knew, Galvin was dropping him off at home. He'd made a point of saying so, Danny now recalled.

The Suburban pulled over to the side of the road, next to a downed paper birch.

Galvin said something to his driver in rapid Spanish.

"Tom," Danny said.

But Alejandro had switched off the engine and gotten out, then came around and opened the middle passenger door and reached in to get him.

49

Something in the set of the driver's grim expression told him not to bother struggling. He got out of the car and said, "What's going on?"

"I told you. I want us to go for a walk."

"I'm not really up to it, Tom."

"I want to show you something."

Alejandro went around to the passenger's side of the front seat and opened the door for Galvin, who also got out.

Galvin crossed in front of the Suburban and put an arm around Danny's shoulder and walked with him toward the ROAD CLOSED sign.

"What's this all about, Tom?"

At the barrier, Galvin stepped ahead of him, between a fence post and a coil of orange plastic road barrier mesh that looked like it had been just tossed there. Danny looked back, saw Alejandro standing by the car, waiting.

Reluctantly, he followed Galvin.

Just up ahead, he saw, the mountain road juked at a sharp angle.

"I want you to see one of God's miracles," Galvin said. He leaned down, picked up a stone, and hurled it.

Danny didn't hear it drop.

When he rounded the bend, he saw why. The road was no longer a road. It had become a narrow ledge that ran along the side of a jagged, rocky canyon cliff.

A cliff that dropped straight down forever.

The canyon wall below the path was a sheer, straight drop, virtually perpendicular. It looked like a shelf that had been blasted out of the rock face. He didn't see how even a small four-wheel-drive vehicle could fit all four of its tires on the one-lane road. Or how a car approaching from the opposite direction could possibly get by.

There was no guardrail. There were patches of snow and ice.

His heart began hammering.

Galvin was wearing Timberland boots; Danny wore sneakers. It wouldn't take much for Danny to lose his footing on the ice or the rubble-covered ledge and slip and plummet a thousand feet into the ravine.

The body probably wouldn't be recovered until the spring. The assumption would be clear: out-of-town hiker, inexperienced and on his own.

An unfortunate accident.

He's going to kill me, Danny realized.

It was perfect.

Galvin beckoned him on. His face was grim. "Let's go. Come on."

"I can see quite well from here, actually."

"Come on. I won't let you fall."

"I can see it great from here."

"This is my favorite place in the world."

"Yep, it's nice."

"No, Danny boy. It's not 'nice.' Get over here. Do I have to ask Alejandro to *carry* you over here?"

Danny hesitated, but only for a few seconds. A scuffle on the edge of a cliff would be risky for Galvin, though not as risky as for Danny. But Danny was determined to put up a struggle. If he was going over the edge, Galvin was coming with him.

He thought of the old Hitchcock movie in which Joan Fontaine is convinced that Cary Grant is trying to kill her. He brings her a glass of milk, and Hitchcock supposedly put a little battery-powered lightbulb in it to make it glow ominously, to turn something comforting into something terrifying.

Maybe Joan Fontaine was imagining things, but Hitchcock made sure we shared her suspicion.

The view over the canyon was indeed remarkable — the crystalline blue sky with white cirrus smudges, the raked bristles of pine forest blanketing the folds and ripples and gouges of the mountainside, the boiling pristine waterfall far below.

The wind howled and bit.

"That's the Devil's Punchbowl down there. And that's Crested Butte. Imagine driving this, huh?"

Danny paused for a few seconds. "Lot of fun, I bet."

Galvin laughed again, one sharp bark. "This is an old wagon road built to connect a couple of mining towns. Hacked and blasted out of the mountainside over a hundred years ago. I've driven it, and let me tell you, it's an asshole-puckering experience."

They stood there in silence for a long moment. Galvin at the edge of the cliff and Danny ten or twenty feet away, not far enough.

"Don't do this, Tom."

Galvin didn't reply. A long silence passed. Maybe it was only a minute, but it felt like four or five.

Then he said, "I know you went to the back of the mountain, and you saw I wasn't skiing. You saw me with someone."

"I got hit in the head. I don't remember anything."

Galvin inhaled, exhaled. "You know about the Parsis in India, what they do when they die?"

Danny shook his head.

"The Parsis believe that earth and fire and water are sacred elements that must never be defiled. So they prohibit cremation or burial."

"What do they do instead?"

"They take the bodies of their loved ones to a place they call a Tower of Silence, and they put them on a marble slab for the vultures to eat. A couple of hours later, the vultures are fat and happy and the flesh is gone."

"Leaving only the bones."

"That goes to feed the soil, I think. I forget. Anyway, so a while back, the vultures in India started dying out. And it turned out that the hospitals in India were administering painkillers to patients. Painkillers that are toxic to vultures. So you kill pain in humans, you kill the vultures." He paused. "But we need the vultures."

"The circle of life."

"Like this road, sorta. You can be the best professional driver in the world, but one slip, and you're over the side. Or there's a rock slide. Or a boulder comes down at you. Or your brakes get wet. You do everything right, but there's always a factor out of your control."

"What's your point, Tom?"

"I need to come clean with you," Galvin said. "I'm in serious trouble."

50

"What kind of trouble?" Danny asked. He felt his body start to uncoil.

"Ever think about just, you know, disappearing? I mean like, go off the grid."

Danny nodded, didn't know what to say.

"Just disappear forever," Galvin went on. "Leave all this behind. Shuffle off this mortal coil. Erase your digital footprints and go somewhere like Belize or Madagascar or New Zealand and start over."

"Sure," Danny said slowly. "Sometimes." But he had the feeling Galvin wasn't speaking hypothetically. "Of course, it's probably not so easy to do anymore. With everything online and all . . ."

"There are books about how to do it. People who specialize in it. I've thought about it a lot. I'm out on my boat and I slip and fall over the side and my body's never found."

"And you're alive and living in Madagascar."

"Like that."

"A fantasy, sure. But you can't do it. You have a wife and kids. We have people who depend on us."

Danny turned to look, but Galvin seemed to be peering into the chasm. "Tom," Danny said quietly. He paused for a few seconds. "You almost sound like you're planning to kill yourself."

"Remember I told you I was just a lucky son of a bitch?"

A smile played on his lips, but not a happy smile. Danny watched and waited. Galvin was still peering down at the yawning chasm below their feet. "Look up *right place, right time,* you're gonna see my picture, right? Well, my luck finally ran out."

Danny nodded. "Your luck . . . with, what? — Money? Business?"

He shook his head. The wind howled. It stung Danny's cheeks and ears.

His mind raced. Was Tom Galvin about to unspool some elaborate lie to explain what Danny had seen? When in fact Danny had seen nothing more than a meeting, two men in a slopeside shack. Galvin, though, seemed to be agonizing over something, struggling.

"About twenty years ago," he said, "I went

371

down to Cancun to scout out an investment opportunity in Playa del Carmen. A couple of Mexican businessmen had a vision for a high-end, luxury resort on the Mayan coast near Tulum. I thought the business plan looked great, the location was perfect. The lead partner was this guy named Humberto Parra Fernández y Guerrero." Galvin pronounced the name quickly and fluently in his native-sounding Spanish. He paused for a long time. "The guy seemed to be loaded. Someone told me he used to be the governor of the state of Michoacán before he went into business. I guess that's one way to get rich in Mexico — get elected to political office and then make a bunch of deals."

Danny nodded.

"So Fernández and his associates wined and dined me, showed me a good time. They knew I was working for one of the biggest mutual fund companies, so I represented a hundred billion in assets. And they really seemed to want me to invest some of that money."

"Okay."

"I went back home. Told my bosses I thought we were onto something that might really work big-time. I convinced them to make the investment. A month later I went back down to Playa del Carmen, and we closed the deal." He paused. "Mexicans are big into family, you know? Fernández invited me to have dinner with his wife and his daughter. His beautiful daughter."

Danny smiled. "Celina."

"I asked her to join me for dinner the next day, and we totally, you know, clicked. Head over heels. I stayed down there in Mexico and we started seeing each other. Really fell in love. When I first met her, I spoke a little high school Spanish, but, man, did I learn the language." He laughed ruefully. "After I got back to Boston, I started making up reasons to fly back to Mexico. I had to see her. I couldn't stop thinking about her. Lina would fly to Boston, or we'd meet here, in Aspen, or go to New York for a weekend. Four months later we got married.

"Well, I guess her dad saw something in me he liked. I was family now, but that wasn't the main thing. He saw I had a good head for deals. I was a young guy on the make, and he liked that. He gave me some money to invest on my own, not with Putnam — half a million US dollars — and I guess I did all right. More than all right. Good timing, good picks, whatever whatever — and I more than doubled it in five months. So he gave me more cash." He shrugged, turned back to Danny. "What can

I say? When you're hot, you're hot. I didn't double it in five months again, but I beat the market easily. He said no one in Mexico even came close to what I was doing. Pretty soon he was one of my biggest private clients.

"And then one day, I told him I was thinking about leaving Putnam and going off on my own, starting my own investment-management firm, and he said he had a proposal for me. He had a hundred million dollars for me to invest."

"Jesus."

Galvin nodded slowly, as if remembering his own amazement. "He said he'd see how I did after a year, and if I kept performing the way I'd been performing, there'd be more. A lot more."

"Amazing. So he wasn't just rich, he was *super*-rich."

Galvin made a funny head movement, half nod, half tilt, accompanied by a shrug. "Or so I thought. But the money came with one condition. He had to be my *only* client. I had to agree to invest no other money besides his. So I had this huge decision to make. Do I leave Putnam and go off on my own with one client? Who happened to be my father-in-law?" He turned slowly and said, "Let's walk, okay?"

Danny followed Galvin along the middle of the road. It was off camber, sloping down toward the outside edge. The surface was dirt and loose gravel, caked with snow and ice and scattered with the detritus of broken rock.

Galvin pointed. "If you look over there, you can see the old mining town. It's a ghost town now."

"You've really driven this road?"

"Sure."

"Not in the Suburban, though . . . ? The wheel base is too long."

"No, I used to have an old Land Rover Defender 90."

"Love those trucks."

"I miss it."

"But I wouldn't call this a road."

"Not here it's not. It's barely a trail. Forest Service wants to close it. They're losing too many tourists." He kicked a rock, sending it over the edge. It rolled wildly downhill, accelerating, and then launched into the air and plummeted down toward the stream.

Danny couldn't hear the rock hit ground. It was too far away.

"So obviously you made the deal," Danny prompted.

"Here's the thing. I'd been working for

Putnam for five years by then, and I was making around three hundred grand, maybe three fifty. And I'm thinking, why in hell should I bust my butt working for chump change when I could be making real money?"

"Sure." Danny winced inwardly — three hundred fifty thousand dollars a year didn't sound like chump change to him — but he said nothing.

"I was tired of being a lackey. Working for idiots in a giant bureaucracy. The only reason to keep working there was job security. And, I mean, you want job security, go work for the post office."

"Sure."

"Here, finally, was a chance for me to prove how good I really was. Put myself on the line every single day. And I ran the numbers. I figured, if I run my own fund, I'm gonna make two and twenty — two percent management fee, twenty percent of the profit, right? Assuming I make twenty percent and I don't splurge on fancy office space, whatever whatever, I'm taking home five mil. *In one year,* Danny. Five million bucks in my first year."

"Not bad for a plumber's boy from Southie."

"And get this: Worst-case scenario, if I

screwed up and *lost* money, I'd still pocket a million bucks! How could I say no to that?"

"You couldn't."

"I couldn't. A no-brainer."

"But you strike me as the kind of guy who always does his due diligence."

Galvin looked at him, surprised to find Danny a step ahead, then gave a sly smile. "You really are a smart SOB, aren't you? But look, here's the reality: A guy offers you a hundred million dollars to play with, the chance to set up your own shop, how close are you really gonna look? You think Putnam or Fidelity asks all their investors how they made their money? Right?"

"Of course not."

"Anyway, my first year, I beat the S&P by eight points. The guy was happy. His partners were happy."

"Partners?"

"Turns out my bride's dad wasn't your run-of-the-mill entrepreneur." He paused for a beat. He looked at Danny. He waited a few seconds longer.

Maybe he was being dramatic. Or maybe he knew that once he told Danny, nothing would ever be the same.

Galvin let out his breath. "Turned out I

was working for a Mexican drug cartel," he said.

PART FOUR

51

When it finally came out, Danny was surprised at how matter-of-fact it sounded. How undramatic.

And what a relief it was to have this confirmed.

"Whoa," Danny said softly.

Did he sound convincingly shocked? He hoped so. After all, it wasn't entirely contrived. He was astonished that Galvin had just revealed something so explosive, so dangerous. That he trusted Danny enough to tell him.

But the question still remained: *Why* was he talking about this?

"Lina's dad was what you call a *pez gordo* in the Sinaloa cartel. A big fish. A *jefe*. I guess he was sort of like their chief financial officer."

"You had no idea until then?"

"I had a pretty good idea something was squirrelly. But like I say, I didn't look too hard. Maybe I didn't want to know." Galvin furrowed his brow and scowled as he talked, as if it pained him to speak.

"You're telling me you're a . . . you launder money for the cartel?"

"No," Galvin said firmly, almost with distaste. "I don't *launder money.*"

A distant sound of a motor revving, big and throaty. A long way off, but it seemed to be coming from where they'd parked. Galvin turned around. It didn't sound at all like the Suburban. Maybe just a passing truck.

Galvin gave Danny a quick, puzzled look, but then he resumed walking down the middle of the path, and Danny fell in alongside.

"They don't need me for that anyway. They've got major banks for that."

"In Mexico?"

"Here. In England. All over the place. You can Google the HSBC bank in London and the Wachovia bank here. Famous cases."

"Then what did they want from you?"

"Their own money manager. Their own private equity investor."

"The *cartel* did?"

Galvin nodded. "Lina's dad was a smart dude. He saw all the cash they were generating — billions of dollars a year, and most of it sat in warehouses or locked away in suitcases. And he wondered why they couldn't do something with all that money. Invest in real estate or restaurant chains or the stock market. Grow it, right? That's what they wanted me for."

"Why are you telling me this?"

He kept walking a while longer, as if he hadn't heard.

"Tom," Danny said.

Finally, Galvin stopped. He stood close to Danny. "I can't have a private conversation at home. They've got it bugged. In Boston, too. They monitor my phone calls. They read my e-mails. Out here there's no mobile phone reception, so no listening devices."

"The cartel, you mean? They monitor you because they don't trust you?"

"Oh, it's nothing personal. They don't trust anyone. They want to make sure I'm not cooperating with the FBI or the DEA, selling them out. I run two billion dollars of their money. They have to be careful."

"I'd think you're the one who really has to worry. You could go to jail."

Galvin's expression was inscrutable.

"Is your car . . . safe? To talk in, I mean?"

"Not in Boston. This one I just leased, so they wouldn't have had time to wire it up. But the driver listens."

"Your driver . . . ?"

"Works for them, not for me. He's not just a bodyguard, he's a minder, too. Golden handcuffs, Danny. Golden handcuffs."

"But . . . I still don't get why you're telling me all this."

"Because I know you've seen some things, and I don't want you poking around and asking questions. For my sake, and for your own sake. You saw me on the mountain. I don't know what else you've seen, but I want to protect you." He paused to watch a hawk, black with a yellow bill and a white-banded tail, gliding on the wind, tilting and swooping and searching for prey. "And something else. I'll be honest, I'm scared out of my mind, and I don't know who else to talk to."

Surprised, Danny looked at him. Galvin's face was strained and creased.

"Scared of what?" Danny said.

"You understand you can't tell a soul? I can't emphasize that strongly enough. For your own sake. And Abby's."

Danny nodded. The mention of Abby's name clutched at his insides.

"The cartels have sources in US law enforcement like you wouldn't believe. Especially the DEA — that place is riddled with moles. A couple of weeks back, the cartel got an internal DEA report about a new informant. Someone who was giving the DEA extremely in-depth information on the Sinaloa cartel. Names of contacts in the US, cell phone numbers, e-mail addresses. The name of a logistics company I helped create that we use as a shell, mostly to move cash around. Information that could only have come from me, they decided."

Danny swallowed hard. It tasted bitter, metallic.

"So they did a sweep of my office. The house, my cars, even the plane. Everything."

"And?"

"At first they thought the informant had to be Esteban, my driver."

"Esteban? But why?"

"I'm not entirely sure. But they said it had to be someone who had access to my home office. Not my office downtown. I've got close to a hundred people working for me, but as far as any of them know, they're working for a family office. I'm the only one who knows the truth. I'm the only one who's in touch with cartel leadership. I'm the only one who has their personal e-mail addresses and cell phone numbers. So it had to be someone who had access to my home computer or my BlackBerry."

"And that's why you had to fire him?"

"Danny, the truth is, *I* didn't fire him. I told you, he didn't work for me. He worked for them. One day he was just . . . gone. I'm pretty sure they killed the guy."

Danny closed his eyes. That image of Esteban, mutilated so horrifically, came to mind. "Wow," he said at last.

"You know what kind of retirement package these boys offer? An all-expenses-paid one-way trip through the wood chipper. Understand? But that didn't plug the leak. The information kept flowing." He paused for a long time. "Now they think it's me."

"You mean your own father-in-law would have you whacked?"

He shook his head. "Who knows. He might have, if he was still alive. But he's been gone a while. He had a stroke ten, twelve years ago."

"So you have no protector anymore."

Galvin nodded.

"But why the hell would *you* cooperate with the DEA?"

Galvin was silent for a long moment. He looked uncomfortable. As if there was something he couldn't bring himself to say. After a few seconds, he shrugged. "That's their theory. They think I made a deal. That I'm cooperating with the DEA to stay out of prison. That I sold out to save my own ass."

"But . . . that's obviously ridiculous." Danny shook his head.

It took all the composure he could muster to keep up the façade. Inwardly he was racked with guilt. Danny knew that *he* was the DEA informant whose existence must have somehow leaked, setting off alarm bells at the top of the Sinaloa cartel. And while Galvin was spilling his guts, revealing the deepest, darkest secret he could possibly have, Danny wasn't saying a word.

While putting Galvin and his entire family in peril.

Tom Galvin, who was a friend. Was that an exaggeration? Maybe they hadn't been before, but they'd become friends, sort of, as much as men their age were capable of making new friends. Danny needed to sit down. Somewhere, anywhere. His heart was knocking wildly.

He argued with himself. He told himself he'd had no choice about cooperating with the DEA. He'd been cornered, blackmailed into it. He hadn't even given Galvin a thought at the time. He'd barely known Galvin.

But that didn't make it feel any better.

"Is it so ridiculous?" Galvin said. "I've

387

been at this a long time. Long enough for the DEA to dig down deep into what I've been doing. And trap me. Force me to flip. That doesn't seem crazy, does it?"

"No," Danny admitted. "But it's not true."

"Of course not. But that was why we were meeting in Aspen. They demanded it. They almost never meet with me in person — way too risky. That was who I was meeting with on the mountain, when you followed me. Their North American chief of security."

"He's able to enter the country?"

"He's a naturalized US citizen."

"Well, they didn't kill you. They just talked. That must mean something, right?"

"It means either they're not *sure* I'm the source — too much contradictory information — or they need me alive a little while longer. My bet's on the second theory. They want me to transfer assets and provide financial records. Until I do that, I'm too valuable to them. Then the wood chipper."

"Jesus, Tom, I . . ." Danny found himself agonizing, arguing with himself. He couldn't keep up this lie. He couldn't do this to his friend.

"So while we were meeting, Alejandro was patrolling the north sector, and that was when he — well, he obviously didn't recognize you. I assume you remember that."

Danny nodded. Galvin thought he'd seen Alejandro's face. No sense in pretending otherwise.

"I'm sorry about that," Galvin said. "It was a stupid mistake. As soon as I saw your face, I told them you'd innocently followed me down the back of the mountain. Which happens to be true."

He paused. Danny nodded.

"Basically, I was vouching for you, and they took me at my word. For the time being, anyway. But we had to abandon the meeting and call for help."

"I guess I was in the wrong place at the wrong time," Danny said.

"It could have ended a lot differently. Fortunately, it didn't."

Danny nodded uneasily. "Fortunately."

"Danny . . . I gotta ask you something. This — this is really important to me."

Danny turned and saw that something — was it agony? — had come over Galvin's face. He didn't recognize it at first, because he hadn't seen it before, but Galvin was overcome by emotion. "Of course — what is it?"

"Listen, if anything happens — to me, to me and Celina . . ." He fell silent.

Danny nodded, encouraging him to go on.

"Will you promise me? — promise you'll

take care of my kids. Especially Jenna."

"Well, I mean — um, of course —"

"Danny, I need this. I need to know. I've got nowhere else to turn."

52

As they wound their way back along the cliffside road to the car, Danny felt light-headed, woozy.

He glanced to his left, at the chasm below. Here and there the jagged rock face was dusted with patches of ice and powdered-sugar snowdrifts. The sight made his head swim with vertigo.

"Okay," Danny said, because he didn't know what else to say. He nodded. Galvin was trapped just like Danny was trapped.

"Brother?"

Danny turned. Galvin was looking down.

"Danny, I'm trusting you like I've never trusted anyone in my life. It's a relief just to be able to talk about it. You know, to know I can trust you."

Galvin's words sliced into him. Danny was almost overcome with guilt. All he could manage to say was, "Of course."

The Suburban was parked in the same

place it had been. But Alejandro the driver wasn't behind the wheel. Galvin stopped ten feet or so away and peered warily around.

"What the hell?" he muttered.

The car was there, but not the driver.

"Maybe he went to take a piss?"

Galvin, who had a stricken look on his face, shook his head.

Danny took a couple of steps and looked. The ground in front of the Suburban was stained dark, in a large irregular oval, like an oil slick. The snowdrifts and ice-crusted ruts were stained with red. Strewn here and there were gobbets and streamers of wine red and greasy tangled cords of sickly yellow.

It looked like the kill floor of an industrial slaughterhouse.

Danny whispered "No" and came closer and saw a carcass on the ground, too small to be human. The body of a horribly slaughtered animal. A dog or a fox, maybe?

Galvin followed Danny around to the front of the Suburban — Alejandro must have moved it while waiting for them — looking perplexed. "What the hell is this?"

Even stranger, the carcass appeared to be fastened to the front of the truck. A stainless steel winch cable had been tied around the hump, which was in turn looped into a galvanized hook fastened to the trailer hitch behind the front bumper.

The hump moved. It was still alive.

Danny looked at Galvin, who suddenly pitched forward and vomited, the splash audible.

"Jesus," Danny said and took another step closer.

Once out of the shadow, the carcass began to take on a recognizable contour. It was too small, indeed, to be a human body; it was maybe half the length of a body, and now it became clear why.

A chuff and a ragged breath and then a keening, an animal whimper.

What he saw he knew at once he'd never forget.

Something scrabbled in the blood-soaked earth, something attached to the hump, and he saw fingers, human fingers, twitching and wriggling.

"Oh, dear God in heaven," Galvin whispered. He lunged for the door handle on the driver's side, doubling over, then struggling up to grab the handle, steadying himself.

Danny, too, vomited, and the keening filled his ears and he stared dully at the crab-scuttling fingers.

Galvin yanked the car door open. All the while he was gasping and gagging and moaning. "My God, my God," he said, again and again.

Galvin now came around the front of the car, a black pistol in one hand. He thumbed the safety, racked the slide like a seasoned hunter, and then he pulled the trigger and shot his chauffeur in the head. Finally, thank God, the desperate clawing fingers were still.

53

Danny knew now what had happened.

His understanding came in waves. Isolated details aligned and then realigned themselves into new patterns like a kaleidoscope turning.

Ten feet from the Suburban's grille the tire tracks of a much larger truck rutted deeply in the ground. It was where the other truck must have parked and spun forward, Alejandro's legs yoked to its rear bumper. He must have been gagged so that neither Danny nor Galvin could hear his screams.

He knew from his web searches that what had just happened there was a type of execution favored by the Mexican drug cartels in certain instances.

He wondered whether the cartels knew they were reenacting one of the most macabre executions of the medieval era, reserved for those found guilty of high treason. He'd read once about a Frenchman named François Ravaillac, who assassinated King Henry IV of France, for which he was punished in a particularly gruesome manner. Each of his arms and legs was roped to a different horse in the Place de Grève. The horses were then whipped to run in four different directions, tearing the man apart, literally limb from limb. Drawn and quartered.

The Mexican drug cartels preferred the brisk efficiency of two cars or trucks driving in opposite directions, though. Lacking a key to the Suburban, they'd obviously used just their own vehicle.

But it did the job.

"We have to dump his body," Galvin said. "No choice." He looked around wildly, pointing the weapon. "Can't involve the cops." Danny looked around as well. Whoever had done this might still be in the immediate vicinity. He saw no one.

Galvin beckoned him over. Danny moved like a sleepwalker, as if hypnotized. Slowly, like wading through a pond.

The lower half of Alejandro's body had been dumped on a snowbank a ways down the road. Galvin waved Danny over. Danny followed the broad swath of blood on the ground that had gouted from the man's dismembered legs and torso.

Wound around his feet and ankles was more steel cable, also attached to a galvanized hook. On the feet were black leather boots. On the legs, dress slacks. Above the belt tumbled loops of glistening viscera.

He said, "Oh, dear God," and was sick again.

"Do you have gloves?"

Danny shook his head.

"Me neither. Just —" Galvin leaned over and grabbed the steel hook, which was dappled with blood. He tried to lift the ruined body, but it was too heavy. Instead, with concerted effort he dragged it along the ground as if it were a side of beef, toward the cliff road. His mouth was set, his face drawn.

"You're going to throw it over?" Danny asked.

When Galvin didn't answer, Danny said, "Why?"

"For the vultures, damn them," Galvin said.

Danny looked at him. He was gritting his teeth in exertion. "At least it'll slow down the identification of the body."

"Someone's going to see all that blood and the . . . and call the police."

"Luckily, it's snowing. Maybe that'll cover this up. Buy us some time. You take the other . . ." Galvin gestured with a nod toward the Suburban, toward the horror that had been his driver's head and hands and torso. He had gone quickly from a near catatonic to a man firmly in control.

In any other circumstance, Danny would have refused. To cover up a crime was to be implicated. But now he assented without a word. He went to the front of the Suburban and reached down and unhitched the galvanized hook from the bumper.

"Oh, good God," Galvin said, looking away from the torso. "They carved a *Z* on him."

"A *Z*? What's that — for?"

But Galvin just shook his head.

The shadows cast on the mountains had grown longer and more distinct, midnight blue in the clefts and hollows. The jags and promontories were bathed in amber light. The sun hung low in the sky, a fat orange globe against the deepening blue. Above it, streaks and ribbons and whorls of clouds, charcoal and white, seemed to be lit from within. Opposite the sun the narrow pink smear of alpenglow glimmered over the mountaintops.

It had grown cold.

"We have to get the hell out of here. Get

the hell out of Aspen, I mean."

"Who, all of us?"

"All of us, right. Back to Boston."

"You think — the women are in danger?"

"Maybe. It's possible."

"How are we going to explain it to them? Does your wife . . . ? No, of course she knows."

"We'll tell them I have an emergency meeting in Boston that just came up. I have to fly back, and since I've got the plane, everyone's going with me. It's a bummer we have to cut the weekend short, but they'll deal."

Danny nodded. "The girls won't be happy."

"Call your girlfriend and tell her to pack up," Galvin said. "Your stuff, too. And Abby. Tell them we need to leave immediately."

54

Galvin noticed blood spatters on the front bumper and grille. He pulled out a handkerchief and tried to wipe them away, but couldn't. The blood had frozen on the metal.

"Shit," he said. "We have to hose the car down or something. I can't have blood tying this thing back to me."

"I saw a car wash back in Carbondale," Danny said. "You think we'd have time to stop?"

Galvin grimaced. "No, not really. But we don't have a choice."

After they'd gotten into the Suburban, and Galvin was behind the wheel, he tore open the Velcro closure of the left-hand pocket of his parka and took out his phone.

"Curtis," he said. "Change in plans. I need the jet fueled up and ready to go in an hour. Can you do that?" A pause. "And file the flight plan. Ninety minutes, then. That's fine. Thanks." He disconnected the call without looking at the phone.

Galvin was driving crazily. He gripped the steering wheel so tightly his knuckles were white. A few times, on the winding narrow road, he nearly slammed into the guardrail.

"Jesus, Tom — slow down."

Galvin just muttered to himself. The car veered off the side of the road and hit a snowbank, then swerved back onto the road. Danny caught his breath and gripped the door handle for support.

"Holy shit! Let's get there in one piece."

Galvin groaned. "Great choice of words." He sighed in frustration. "We gotta get home, make sure they're okay. And make sure they hustle."

Danny waited until Galvin's driving was less frantic, then he called Lucy.

"What happened to you?" she said. "Where'd you go?"

"For a ride with Tom — listen, Tom needs to get back to Boston right away, which means we have to fly back with him."

"Huh? Did something happen?"

"An important meeting just came up. An emergency."

"We can't stay on, the rest of us?"

"He's taking the plane."

"Okay, right. Well, that's a shame. Baby, are you sure you're okay? You sound — I don't know, different, somehow. After that head injury —"

"Just bad reception. I'm fine. We'll be back soon — maybe half an hour or so. Just — hurry." And he ended the call.

"There it is," Galvin said, pointing to a car wash up ahead on the right. Tires squealing, he pulled into the lot. It was open, with no other customers around.

A minute or so later, the Suburban bumped along the conveyor track through the clear vinyl panels and into the tunnel, with Danny and Galvin inside.

Danny interrupted the tense silence. "What happened back there, Tom? This is the second driver of yours to be targeted. That I know of."

Galvin said nothing for a few seconds. He seemed distracted, but maybe he was just scared. "I told you, they're not just drivers," he said finally. "They're babysitters. Minders planted by the cartel. To watch me — and to watch out for me. Which also makes them convenient targets."

The car moved through the mitter curtains, hanging flaps of cloth that slapped the car's exterior, swishing and wriggling back and forth. It crawled along at what seemed an excruciatingly slow pace.

"So who did it? Your bosses, the Sinaloans?"

"No . . . Remember that *Z* carved into his . . . abdomen? Tells me it's Los Zetas."

"Zetas? What — ?"

"That's another cartel," Galvin said. "There's seven major cartels. Biggest players are Sinaloa — my guys — and Los Zetas. Some people say the Zetas are the most sophisticated, the most dangerous of them all. And that thing with the body and the two cars? That's a Zeta signature."

"But why would a rival cartel target your driver?"

He shook his head. He shrugged. "I don't have any carthly idea," he said, looking at Danny, fear in his eyes.

Danny thought of Alejandro standing outside the coffee shop that morning. He'd seen Danny meeting with the DEA guy, Slocum. Obviously, Danny couldn't say anything to Galvin about it, but he couldn't help but wonder: Did Alejandro's murder have something to do with his seeing Danny that morning?

His BlackBerry played "Sweet Home Alabama."

"Sweetie," he answered. *"Querida."* He launched into a hurried conversation in

Spanish. Danny could make out only a few words. *Inmediatamente.* And *protección.* And *peligro,* which he knew meant "danger." Words like that. He was telling her what had just happened, maybe. Telling her they had to leave.

The high-pressure nozzles assaulted the Suburban's windows and its flanks. It was like driving through the worst rainstorm ever.

He hung up and for a long while he said nothing, just watched the hot air blast from the nozzles on either side, blowing the droplets away, the wind from a dozen hair dryers.

"My time is up," he said finally. "I have to vanish."

"Vanish?"

"And only you and my wife can know about it."

55

Graciela Arriaga had worked at the Drug Enforcement Administration headquarters in Arlington, Virginia, for almost eighteen years.

She was a file clerk in the Records Management Unit. She knew her colleagues mocked her behind her back, considered her humorless, uptight, rigid, rules-bound. A stiff. They called her Debbie Downer.

The truth was, she was none of those things. She was a woman who just wanted to do her job and do it right, keep her head down, earn a living, be left alone.

Somehow she had to support a daughter and a granddaughter on a GS-6 salary and the negligible survivors' pension the VA paid for her husband, Luis, a Vietnam vet who'd died more than a decade ago.

Her daughter, María Elena, worked in customer service at Marshalls in the Snowden Square Shopping Center. Her take-home pay barely covered day care for her two-year-old boy, Jayden, with just enough left over for food and clothing.

So María Elena and Jayden lived in the second bedroom of Graciela's apartment, on the fourth floor of the ugly dun brick building on Columbia Road, in Columbia Heights, Maryland. Graciela's son, Raúl, was in prison in Hagerstown for boosting a Zipcar.

Graciela was not the type of person ever to do anything that might put her job at risk. Yet there were all the money problems. And there was Tía Yolanda, back home in Mazatlán, and her nine children and twenty-four grandchildren. They needed whatever money Graciela could spare to send them.

Life did not always give you choices.

Wearing a long puffy charcoal-colored down coat with gray pants and simple black shoes, she climbed to the fourth floor and keyed open the top and bottom locks and then the police lock. Graciela had high cheekbones and wore prim black glasses and had once been considered reasonably pretty. Now she was generally regarded as matronly.

Her tabby cat, Señor Don Gato, meowed loudly when she entered, and brushed up against her leg. That was unlike him. Most days he scarcely bothered to rouse himself from the sofa.

Graciela sniffed. The kitty litter needed changing. She hung up her down coat on the wall hook next to little Jayden's snow pants. She noted with disapproval the dishes still in the sink. She was always asking María Elena not to leave the breakfast dishes unwashed.

Then she lit the flame under the kettle to make herself a cup of tea and selected her favorite mug from the cupboard: WORLD'S BEST MOM.

"Make two cups, if you don't mind."

The voice — a soft baritone — startled her. She turned, saw the silhouette in the shadowed recesses of the living room.

"You know who I am, don't you?"

She nodded mutely. The mug slipped from her hand and thudded to the linoleum floor of the kitchenette, where it bounced but didn't break.

"I hope you have something for me," the man said.

56

"Anything you need," Danny said. "I'm here."

"I'm going to need you to vouch for me."

Danny looked at Galvin curiously. "Vouch for you? How do you mean?"

"Well, not to put too fine a point on it, brother: I'll need you to lie to law enforcement after I disappear. Back up an alibi for me. When the FBI question you — and they will, believe me — just say I told you I was flying down to meet some business contacts in Mexico."

"Where will you really be?"

"Probably best you not know. Belize, at first. Then somewhere else. Cuba, Venezuela. Maybe Kazakhstan or Croatia or Dubai." He was driving less erratically now, though just as fast. "There's this remote fishing village in New Zealand Celina and I discovered on our honeymoon. It . . . it's the town that time forgot. On the west coast

of the South Island, in the middle of nowhere. The landscape's out of *Lord of the
Rings.* Maybe a dozen ancient stone houses,
green rolling hills dotted with sheep. You sit
there eating the greatest fish and chips from
a little shack on the water's edge. Watching
the dolphins playing and the fishing boats
bobbing in the bluest water you've ever
seen."

Danny nodded. "You're taking your
plane?"

"Right. But as I told you, it's chartered. I
don't own it. Means I have to file a flight
plan. Which I will, but it'll be a bogus one.
I'll be requesting one particular pilot, and I
know he'll cooperate. He'll fly me wherever
I ask. For a briefcase full of cash."

"So you want US law enforcement to
think you were meeting with cartel officials
and were abducted. Something like that?"

Galvin nodded.

"So what's — what's your plan? Just fly
away one day?"

"Pretty much."

"Do you have a fake passport or something?"

"No. A real one."

"I don't get it."

"If you know the right people and you
have the right kind of money, you can buy

an absolutely one hundred percent genuine US passport under a different name."

"Jesus, Tom. You sure it's real? It's not counterfeit — not something that might be flagged and get you arrested?"

"It's absolutely authentic. And it was extremely expensive."

Danny went quiet for a moment. Neither man spoke. Then Danny said, "You're talking about leaving your family behind?"

He nodded. "It's for their own protection."

"Would you . . . will you . . . tell them?"

"Just Celina. She knows this may happen someday. As for the boys and Jenna — I couldn't burden them with the knowledge. When the time is right, I'll say good-bye to them as if I was just going away for a week or so on business."

"And then just disappear."

"Right."

Another long silence. "I don't understand."

"What don't you understand?"

"How you can actually do this. The way you love your kids . . . the way you love Celina . . . how you could bring yourself to decide one day you'll never see them again."

Galvin exhaled slowly. Then he replied, hesitantly, stumblingly. "I can't — I mean

— I mean, consider the alternatives! Having their father in prison for the rest of his life? Having their father killed by the cartel? And *them* in jeopardy, too?"

"So why is this any better, Tom? Leaving your kids to think you just ran off one day? Or that you were abducted and killed. But never *knowing*?"

Galvin sounded weary, even defeated. "They'll figure out in time that I had to leave, that I had no choice. Maybe they'll hate me for it. But they'll know this was the only way to protect them. Anyway, they all have money in trusts. They'll be taken care of."

Taken care of, Danny thought: What a phrase. When the one thing his kids *wouldn't* be was taken care of. They'd have money, like they'd always had. But to have their father just be gone one day without a word of explanation? It was difficult to think of anything harder or more painful than losing a mother to cancer, as Abby had. But losing a parent without closure, without ever knowing how and why? That would be painful beyond words.

"Well," Danny said softly, "I just can't imagine it."

"I've had twenty-some years to think

about this. Though it doesn't make this any easier."

Danny looked at Galvin's gun resting on the console between the seats. It was matte black and had a seal stamped on its handle that read R. BERETTA. He picked it up. It was cold and heavier than he'd expected.

He didn't like guns particularly — they made him nervous — and didn't own any. But his father had taught him to fire pistols and shotguns at the Nauset Rod and Gun Club on the Cape. He knew how to use one if he had to.

"Careful," Galvin said. "That's loaded."

Danny nodded. "The safety's on."

"You know something about guns?"

"Enough. Do you have another one?"

Galvin looked away from the road, gave Danny a searching glance, then turned back. "There's another one under your seat. Could you pull the trigger if you had to? I mean, and shoot someone?"

Danny was silent for five or six seconds. "Yeah," he replied. He swallowed hard. "I could now."

57

Danny reached down and felt something flat and hard. A metal flap. He pulled it open. Inside the compartment, he felt the cold smooth steel carcass of another gun and a small cardboard box. He slipped out the gun and the box. An identical Beretta. The box contained Cor-Bon jacketed hollow-point high-velocity ammunition and felt heavy.

He checked the magazine and saw it was full. The gun was loaded.

"What happens if they send a bunch of cartel guys with AK-47s after us?" Danny said. "A pistol's not going to be much help."

"If they send anyone after me, it's not going to be what they call a *fusilado*. More like a *tiro de gracia*."

"Translation, please?"

"A single shot. Not a firing squad. If and when it comes to that, I mean. They're not going to send a bunch of goons with submachine guns after me. Not here. Not back in Boston, either."

"Why not? They have the manpower, right?"

"They have armies. But they don't need it, not for one guy. And they're limited by the surroundings. Around here, a truck full of scary Mexicans with tats and Uzis isn't going to blend into the background so easy. And something else: Even if they want to kill me, they're not going to do it right away."

Galvin paused, and Danny looked at him. He shrugged. "I don't follow."

Galvin tapped the side of his head with a forefinger. "There's too much up here they need. Passwords to bank accounts and such."

"Meaning they'll torture you first."

Galvin nodded.

Danny felt a wave of revulsion. He tried to keep those goddamned Internet videos of beheadings and castrations from playing in his mind.

"Oh, Jesus," Danny said.

Galvin said, "But I don't plan to give them the opportunity."

Danny nodded.

"For now, I'll just need you to keep a watch at the house. We have to get the women to the airport and onto the plane uneventfully. And make sure Abby and Lucy have no idea anything's wrong, okay?"

"I'll do what I can, but —"

"You're a good friend. None of this has anything to do with you. You could just walk away if you wanted, but you're not. I can't tell you how much that means to me."

If you only knew, Danny thought, but he just shrugged.

As they pulled into the long driveway in front of his house, Galvin said, "See the window over the garage?"

Danny nodded.

"Do me a favor and keep a watch from that room while everyone's getting packed. That's probably the best vantage point. You see someone with a gun drawn, shoot 'em."

"Got it."

When they came inside, Galvin clapped his hands like a grade school gym teacher and said, "Let's go, girls. We need to be at the airport in half an hour. Less, if we can. We've all got to hustle."

The girls were on the landing, on their way upstairs. "Well, this totally sucks," Jenna said.

"Right?" Abby said. They were both still wearing their ski attire, their faces rosy from hours on the slopes.

"We don't even have time to take a shower?"

"No."

"Is what's-his-name, Alejandro, going to come up and get our stuff or do we have to bring it down?"

"Alejandro isn't working tonight," Galvin said without a pause. "Bring your own stuff downstairs and I'll load the car."

"You're not even packed, are you?" Celina asked her daughter. "Upstairs and pack. Now."

"They're not packed yet?" Danny said. "Come on, Abby, *move* it!"

The girls trundled loudly up the stairs. Celina bustled around the big main room, picking up miscellaneous items the girls had scattered about. Jenna's iPad, a phone charger, lip gloss. She didn't look at her husband. She wasn't wearing any lipstick, or else it had worn off, and her eye makeup was smeared. Her eyes were bloodshot. She'd been crying.

Lucy wasn't there. She was probably upstairs packing.

"Come on," Galvin said, following the girls up the stairs. He stopped at one of the first doors off the long hall that led to their guest room. He switched on the light. The room had the faint solvent smell of newly installed carpeting. It was much smaller than the room where Lucy and Danny had spent the night. The only furniture in here was a queen-size bed with a chenille bedspread, a couple of end tables, and a bureau. Galvin pointed at the window.

"You should be able to get a good angle from here without standing directly in the path. If you have to fire through the window, do it."

"Understood," Danny said.

Galvin turned and left quickly without closing the door.

Passing headlights bloomed and faded on the road at the end of the driveway. They came by at the rate of around one car or truck every minute. He shifted from one foot to the other, tense.

"Danny?"

Lucy's voice. He turned, saw her standing in the hallway, her blond hair gleaming in the overhead light.

The gun in his hand.

"Danny, what are you doing?"

58

Danny carried the Beretta onto the plane in the pocket of his down parka.

It went just as Galvin had promised. No going through security. No metal detectors or wands or pat-downs. He just walked right onto the plane as he'd done in Boston. Galvin had told him to keep the gun with him.

The seating arrangement on the plane was slightly different on the way back.

Celina sat next to her husband. They spoke almost continuously, in low voices, alternating between Spanish and English. Danny couldn't hear what they were saying, but Celina looked worried and upset, and Galvin seemed to be trying to placate her.

The two girls sat next to each other on the couch at the back, as before. Jenna was reading the book Abby had just finished, John Green's *The Fault in Our Stars.* Abby was reading a novel by Jodi Picoult.

Danny took the seat near Lucy's, but she appeared not to be speaking to him. She hadn't said a word in the Suburban on the way to the airport, and as soon as the plane took off, she'd opened her Cleopatra biography. A couple of times he'd caught her eye, or took her hand, only to get no response. An averted glance, a limp hand.

She smoldered. He'd never seen her so angry. In fact, he could barely think of times when he'd seen her angry at all. Nothing more than momentary irritation. But this was different. She was angry, and she was frightened.

She'd seen him holding a gun, and there hadn't been an opportunity for him to explain without someone else overhearing. It must have freaked her out to see a gun in his hands.

"Hey," he said softly.

She arched a brow, turned a page. "Hmm?"

"We need to talk. It's important."

She closed the book on her index finger. As if to say: *I'll give you a minute, no more.* "Important enough to involve me? And maybe your daughter?"

Her voice sounded high, constricted. Indignant. A faint tremble.

She looked at him, eyes hooded, a hostile

expression that said either *I really don't care* or *I don't believe a word you're saying.*

"Oh?"

"I can't talk about it here. But as soon as we get home. I just want to say I'm sorry."

She shrugged, returned to her book.

The horror he'd witnessed that afternoon on the mountain pass had changed everything.

For far too long, he'd kept the real situation from the woman he loved.

It was time to tell her the truth.

■ ■ ■ ■

PART FIVE

■ ■ ■ ■

59

He waited until Abby had gone to bed that night.

In the old days, not so long ago, that meant tucking her in and reading to her and talking and eventually turning out the light. Often he'd fall asleep before she did and later stumble out of her bedroom in a stupor. Now it meant she closed the bedroom door and put on her headphones and listened to music and "chatted" with friends on Facebook.

Danny kept his voice low, just in case Abby wasn't wearing her headphones and had her ear against the wall.

"Baby, something happened this afternoon," he began. "But it began a while ago."

He started with Galvin's loan and the meeting with the DEA. He told her how he'd planted a bug in the Boston College medal and how it was somehow discovered. He told her about Esteban's mutilated body.

About how he furtively downloaded Galvin's BlackBerry at the Plympton Club. And finally about the nightmarish event earlier in the day. Had it been only a matter of hours since they'd discovered the mutilated body of the bodyguard? It felt like days.

Mostly, she listened. After the first few minutes, she stopped interrupting him with questions. Her mouth came open a few times, an understandable response to the shock. She gasped at his descriptions of what had happened to the two driver/ bodyguards.

When he finished, she was silent for a long time.

Her eyes were filled with tears, her jaw tight.

"So basically you decided to secretly cooperate with the DEA against a Mexican drug cartel," she said. "And put your life in harm's way. And your daughter's. And mine, too." He was surprised by her tone, flat and cold and bitter.

"That's not how it happened, Lucy. I told you."

His cell phone made the plinking sound of a secure text message. He ignored it. He knew what it was: They wanted his photos of whoever Galvin had met on the Aspen mountainside. Well, they could wait.

She sat up in bed very straight. "No, that's exactly how it happened. You didn't tell me in the beginning because you knew what I'd say. You knew how I'd react."

He shook his head. "Come on." But he knew she was probably right.

"Because keeping me in the dark would keep the bad guys away. Like that? Is that what you thought? You know, we shrinks call that magical thinking."

"Lucy."

"Because you didn't want to have this very argument?"

"I wanted to keep you safe. You and Abby both."

She shook her head slowly.

She was wearing an extra-extra-large T-shirt that said KEEP CALM AND CARY GRANT on the front. A spoof of an old British wartime poster you now saw parodied everywhere: KEEP CALM AND CARRY ON. A silhouette of Cary Grant in *North by Northwest,* running from a crop duster. Danny had forgotten whether he'd given it to her. She loved old Hitchcock movies. She insisted they didn't make movie stars like Cary Grant or Spencer Tracy or Gregory Peck anymore.

"I figured, the less you or Abby was

involved, the better. Safer to keep you out of the loop."

"So one day Tom Galvin would get arrested and — what, the Mexicans would leave us all alone and say, 'Rats, I guess we're just going to have to file an appeal'? And 'Oh, that guy who's responsible for us losing billions of dollars, that guy who funneled the information to the DEA, we'll just leave him alone, because them's the breaks of the justice system'? Like that?"

"There's no need to raise your voice."

She swung her feet out from under the covers and onto the floor. "What the hell were you *thinking*? That they'd go away quietly? Because they always do that, right? Just walk away and throw up their hands. These people who behead their enemies and butcher them, and . . . and you just thought you were going to work against these cold-blooded killers and they'd leave you and your daughter alone?"

He made a palms-down gesture, patting the air, trying to calm her, get her to keep her voice down. "You don't really think I'd deliberately do anything that might cause harm to you or Abby, do you?"

She folded her arms across her chest. "So when you told her she couldn't go over to the Galvins, and I asked you if there was something about them you didn't like, and you said no . . . ?"

"Yes. That was a lie."

"And the reason you didn't want her being driven around by Galvin's chauffeur — when you said you were just uncomfortable —"

"That was also a lie."

"The old friend who wanted publishing advice, the Jay Gould letters at Wellesley —"

"I lied to you over and over again. I did. I'm deeply, deeply ashamed of it. But everything I did was about protecting you and Abby. Lucy, come on, keep it down, Abby can hear."

"And all because you can't deal with confrontation." Her cheeks burned deep red. "Well, that's something I really can't fix. This is such a disappointment, really."

He no longer recognized her. The mask of anger had lifted away, and what remained was terrifyingly unfamiliar. A woman who looked at him like he was a stranger. Her eyes stared, her expression oddly neutral, impassive.

"You didn't want to have this fight, so you decided you knew best."

"I didn't —" He faltered. He didn't know what to say, because he knew she was right.

She fell silent, and so did he. There didn't seem to be anything more to say.

He got up from the bed. He saw tears in her eyes. She spoke so softly he could barely hear. "You take care of that girl, and tell her I love her so much and I'll say good-bye to her another time. Right now I can't."

"Lucy," he said.

But she'd closed the bedroom door behind her.

He lay awake for what seemed like hours.

He wept.

At four in the morning, when the sky was dead black, and daybreak seemed impossibly far off, he had an idea.

He selected ChatSecure on his iPhone and texted the DEA agents: Need to meet ASAP.

"It really sucks that I have to go to school today," Abby said the next morning. "Instead of being in Aspen."

"I know. Life's tough."

She seemed to relent a bit. "I know. Jenna calls it a first-world problem. Lucy left already?"

"She had to leave early."

A beat. "You guys were fighting last night."

"We were talking. Did we wake you up?"

She shook her head, then shrugged.

His iPhone, in his pants pocket, vibrated and bleated the distinctive tritone of a secure text message.

"Is that yours?"

He nodded, slipped it out of his pocket. Entered his passcode. The message read: Busy on another case. Can't meet until tonight or tomorrow.

"That from Lucy?"

"It's business. Boring."

"You changed the text alert sound? It sounds different."

"I don't know. You want some coffee?"

She gave him a quick look of surprise. "Yes, please." She looked at him and smiled.

"Just this once," Danny added. He rose and got down a Winnie-the-Pooh mug from the cabinet and filled it three-quarters of the way with coffee. "You can add your own milk and sugar."

"Okay." She poured some Lactaid milk until it was as light as coffee ice cream. She stirred in three teaspoons of sugar. "You sure you guys weren't fighting?"

"We're fine," Danny said. He'd tell her when it felt less raw. "Get a move on. You don't want to be late."

"Let's go," Danny called out fifteen minutes later.

He jangled his car keys. Abby was still in the bathroom, doing whatever teenage girls do in the morning that takes them so long.

"Boogie, move your butt."

The bathroom door opened. Abby's face was different. It was twisted in what at first looked like intense curiosity, but something about her expression made Danny look twice. Anger?

"Where's her toothbrush?" she said.

"What are you talking — ?"

"Lucy. Lucy's toothbrush. Her makeup. It's gone. It's all gone."

Danny couldn't think of what to say beyond, "It is?"

"You broke up." An accusation.

Danny sighed. "Can we not get into this right now? You're going to be late for school."

"You lied to me!"

"It's not your business."

"Not my *business*? All the times you've told me to treat her like a member of the family? 'She loves you, Abby. She's part of our family, you should treat her like that.' And now you're freaking *lying* to me?"

"Abby. Boogie. We'll talk later. Not now."

"No!" Abby threw something at him, something small and hard. A hairbrush. It missed him by a couple of feet.

"Hey!" he shouted. "Abby, what the hell are you doing?"

"Sure, why not lie to me the same way you lied about Mom."

"Huh?"

"You said she had an infection. An *infection.*" She was crying now, her face red and distorted.

"Abby —"

"You made me go to camp!"

"You *wanted* to go to camp. *Mommy* wanted you to go to camp."

"I was kayaking and swimming when Mommy was *dying.* Oh my God." Her voice had gotten high and tiny and constricted.

"Baby," he said. He went to hug her and she pushed him away. He went numb.

Tears dripped from Abby's cheeks. Her nose was running. It tore Danny apart to see her like this. "Like it wasn't my *business* Mom had breast cancer. Like I couldn't hear the truth."

Crying now, too, Danny said, "Abby, sweetie, no. That wasn't it at all. Mommy wanted you to be happy for as long as possible."

She said something, but Danny couldn't make out the words. All he heard was *"happy?"*

"Honey," he said. "I lied to you because

431

Mommy asked me to."

And then it was out.

Pass the buck right back to your dead wife, he thought. Blame her. She's not around to defend herself.

Did it make any difference that it was true?

This time when Danny tried to hug her, Abby didn't fight him. She didn't hug back, not really, but she allowed herself to be hugged for a long time. His shirt was hot and damp from his daughter's tears.

Ten minutes later he called Jay Poskanzer, the criminal defense attorney.

"Jay," he said, "I need a little help."

"On what?"

"It's about the DEA guys I've been dealing with."

"Uh-oh."

"Yeah. I want out."

60

The terror Danny had felt in Aspen at the side of the mountain had scarcely lessened its grip on him.

Whatever the reason behind that nightmarish mutilation, it might as well have been done for his sake alone. It was a warning, that's what it was. A glimpse of his future.

But it was Abby's tears that had finally decided it for him: He had to get out. The DEA agents would not let up until he met an equally grisly end. To them it made no difference; he'd be a casualty of a long and brutal war.

He could predict what they'd say. *No turning back now. Toothpaste's out of the tube. Hang in there; keep the faith. We'll take care of you.*

They'd say whatever it took, make whatever threats they could, to keep him reporting on Tom Galvin, trying to incriminate him. But he couldn't, wouldn't, do it anymore. He couldn't be responsible for putting the guy in prison. Or getting him murdered, more likely.

A loving father of three kids who'd never done him any harm, who'd tried to bail him out, who was himself trapped like Danny was trapped. Lucy was right. He'd made a terrible mistake.

And now he had to undo it.

Force the DEA to back off. However he had to do it.

So he sat in front of Jay Poskanzer's desk and tested out the solution he'd finally come up with.

Poskanzer toyed with a miniature baseball bat, a Red Sox souvenir. He leaned back in his expensive-looking office chair. "What do you mean, you want out?"

"I want to stop cooperating with them."

Poskanzer's eyes narrowed. His wire-framed glasses were clouded, as if begrimed by fingerprints. His frizzy reddish-gray curls came to a point on either temple like ram's horns. "You signed an agreement. It's a binding legal document."

"Yeah, well, I want to get out of it. I want it nullified. I want to stop cooperating with the DEA. Simple as that."

The sun shone through one of the plate-glass walls of his office, flooding the place with light, glinting off the glass-topped desk. "Dude. Not so simple."

"If it were simple, I wouldn't need to hire you."

"Are we on the clock?"

"I'll let you know in a couple of minutes." Poskanzer shrugged. "On what grounds do you want to get out of the agreement?"

"Professional misconduct."

He chuckled nervously. "What does that mean?"

"Threatening to leak to the Sinaloa cartel that I'm cooperating with them."

"They wouldn't — You don't actually believe they'd do that, do you?"

He nodded. "Sure. It wouldn't surprise me. I take them at their word."

Of course, all they had to do was take a deposition and put him on the witness stand and the cartel would put out a hit on him. It was a wholly unnecessary threat. But they'd made it.

"You got proof? An e-mail, maybe?"

He shook his head.

"Voice mail? A note? Anything?"

He shook his head some more.

"What are their names, again?"

Danny told him. Poskanzer wrote them down. "So it's your word against two federal agents'."

"Not if we get them on tape."

"Wait a second." Poskanzer held up his hand like a traffic cop. "You're not talking about recording it yourself, I hope."

"Why not?"

"It's illegal, for one thing? In Massachusetts, both parties have to consent."

"Yeah, well, I don't think they're going to consent."

"Right. And I can't counsel you to break the law. That's against the Massachusetts lawyers' code."

"Well, I didn't ask your counsel on that, did I?" he said with a smile. "We're talking about a massive, multibillion-dollar investigation into the Sinaloa cartel. So I broke the law by making an illegal recording. That'll be a slap on the hand. A goddamned *speeding* ticket."

Poskanzer shrugged. "I . . . I didn't agree to this."

"Got it. So noted. Now, let's say I get proof. Then where do I go with it?"

"You take it to the Department of Justice's Office of Professional Responsibility. Hold on." He swiveled his chair and batted out something on his keyboard. "Okay, here's their website, okay . . . it says . . . here we go: *Jurisdiction* . . . yada yada ya . . . *investi-*

436

*gate allegations of misconduct by law enforce-
ment personnel.* Yep, these are the folks you
want."

"And they'd really go after a couple of
DEA agents? Not just cover it up?"

Poskanzer exhaled a long sigh of what
sounded like frustration. "Here's the deal.
This is what they do, investigating official
misconduct. But they won't open an investigation unless they think they can win it.
Which brings us back to proof. You don't
have any."

"Not yet," Danny said, and he stood up.
"But I will."

He'd gotten three secure texts from the
DEA agents demanding to meet. They
wanted the photos, the ones he'd failed to
get in Aspen. He'd avoided their texts.

But he was ready to see them now.

61

In front of the Hancock Tower, Danny grabbed a cab to Government Center.

He still hadn't answered the DEA agents' text messages. He wanted to surprise them. Catch them off guard. Provoke them into making threats again, if need be. Anything.

The afternoon sun was melting the snowdrifts. Water seemed to be dripping everywhere. A truck plowed through an immense gray puddle on Cambridge Street in front of One Center Plaza, splashing everything within ten feet, including Danny's shoes and socks. He cursed aloud.

Standing outside the ugly façade, he took out his iPhone and selected one of the recording apps. He recorded a sample and played it back. It seemed to work fine.

Then he started it again and began the recording: "My name is Daniel Goodman," he said. "I live at 305 Marlborough Street in Boston, Massachusetts." He gave the date and the time. Keeping the recorder on, he slipped the phone into a front pocket. For evidentiary purposes, Poskanzer had told him, he had to make one continuous uninterrupted recording.

He took the elevator to the second floor. His cell phone rang. He saw BATTEN SCHECHTER on the caller ID. Jay Poskanzer.

He debated taking the call. Then decided against it. He'd already begun the recording by stating his name and the date and time. The iPhone was recording. He could talk to Poskanzer when he was finished with the DEA.

He found room 322 and recognized the stain on the carpet. This was definitely the place.

He turned the knob and pulled the door open and looked to the left. The receptionist, strangely, wasn't at her desk. The L-shaped mahogany-laminate desk was still there, but that was the only piece of furniture in the reception area. The row of chairs was gone. There was an empty cardboard box on the floor. The DEA seal, which had occupied a place of prominence on the wall, was gone. So were all the Most Wanted posters.

No.

"Hello?" he called.

He advanced farther into the room, pulled open the door to the inner corridor where he'd met with the DEA men.

It was empty, too.

A snowdrift of Styrofoam peanuts across the hallway. Another empty cardboard box. The wrapper from a ream of Staples copy paper.

Nothing here. No one.

The quietly bustling office was no more. It had been disbanded, broken down like a stage set at the end of a run.

He stood there, dazed, looking around. His cell phone rang. Batten Schechter again. He picked it up.

He knew what Jay Poskanzer was going to say before he said it.

"Hey, what's the deal?" he said. He sounded angry. "I talked to my pal at the US Attorney's office. There's no special agents named Slocum or Yeager on the DEA payroll. They used to work for DEA, couple of years ago. But no longer."

62

Danny felt a coldness settle over him, icy tendrils reaching inside, freezing and palpating his guts.

If they weren't DEA, then who were they?

Maybe they were real DEA agents using cover names. That was certainly a possibility. He'd covertly taken a picture of one of them, Slocum, and he mailed it to Jay Poskanzer and asked him to forward it to the DEA. The real DEA.

Poskanzer called back twenty minutes later. "It gets better," he said. "These guys used to work for the DEA in Mexico, in Nuevo Laredo, and got caught up in a corruption sting. They each got fired seventeen months ago. They're bad apples."

"Well, they made pretty convincing DEA agents."

"Probably because they've had practice. Question is, what's their game? What are they up to? What are they doing it for?"

Danny didn't reply. He didn't know.

But he would find out.

His cell phone chimed: a secure text message. "Hold on," he said. He held it away from his ear, read the message.

From AnonText007@gmail.com: 6 p.m. Home Depot parking lot, South Bay.

South Bay was a shopping center between the South End of Boston and Dorchester, just off the Southeast Expressway.

"Slocum" and "Yeager" were ready to meet.

63

Wallace Touhy's knees hurt like hell.

When the doorbell rang, he got up from the couch and lumbered to the front door. It took him a good minute or so. He groaned. He'd planned to hold off on the knee replacement until he retired, but now he wasn't so sure he could make it another four months. The soft knee brace didn't do a damned thing, and the steroid injections were worthless. He gobbled Motrins like popcorn. His doc told him if he lost thirty or forty pounds, it wouldn't hurt so bad, but he knew better. It was those four years of serious wear and tear, playing football for the Billerica Memorial High School Indians half a century ago. That was what did it. Everything else was just the cherry on the cake.

"Agent Touhy?"

The man at the door was tall and lanky and appeared to be Hispanic.

Touhy elbowed the storm door open. "Yeah, yeah," he muttered. "Come on in. Hernandez, right?"

"Thanks for seeing me."

"I don't know if it's gonna be worth your while, but okay." He flapped a hand toward the living room. "I'd make coffee, but believe me, I'm doing you a favor not making it. Your stomach will thank me later."

"Oh, that's perfectly fine," the man said. "I suspect you'll enjoy this more than coffee anyway."

He handed Touhy an elegant box containing a fine bottle of whiskey.

"Pappy Van Winkle, huh?" Touhy's mouth came open.

"I hope my intel was accurate. I'm told you love bourbon."

"I do."

"That's a small-batch bourbon that's —"

"I sure as hell know Pappy Van Winkle. Just never had it before. Can't find it around here. Awful generous of you. This is a first for me."

"They were out of the twenty-year, but the fifteen's supposed to be quite smooth."

"Much obliged, Agent Hernandez."

"David. Please."

"All right, David. Have a seat over there. I'll get us a couple of glasses."

Touhy broke the seal on the bourbon bottle and glugged a couple of fingers into two highball glasses. He hobbled over to the visitor and handed him a glass. "Neat okay?"

"The only way."

Agent Touhy looked easily a decade older than his fifty-seven years. His white hair had a yellowish tinge to it. He had a large, jowly face. His cheeks were taut and shiny and scarlet, evidence of a bad case of rosacea, though years of heavy drinking might have broken a bunch of capillaries, too.

A large flat-screen TV was on, some sort of reality show about two men fighting to survive in the Amazonian jungle.

"So," Touhy said, sinking with a deep sigh into his favorite chair. He reached for the cable remote and hit the MUTE button. "Any reason this couldn't wait till tomorrow?"

"I apologize for the inconvenience, Agent Touhy. I have to fly back to San Francisco tomorrow morning."

"Right, right, you said that." Touhy took a sip of the bourbon. "Not bad. Not bad at all."

"So glad you like it. I'm sorry I didn't give you any advance notice."

"Yeah, well, you really cut into my social life." Touhy laughed rumblingly and coughed. "Smoke?" He held out a pack of Camel Lights.

"Not for me, thank you."

"I don't think I'm going to be able to go back to Wild Turkey after this." Touhy tapped out a cigarette and put it in the corner of his mouth and picked up a red Zippo lighter from the end table. He thumbed the Zippo, lit the cigarette, took a deep crackling lungful of smoke. "Trudy never let me smoke inside the house. Now I grab my little pleasures where I can."

"I'm sorry about your wife."

"It was a blessing, believe me. The last couple of years were no fun. I wouldn't wish ALS on my worst enemy." He blew out a white plume. "So you work out of S.F."

His visitor nodded.

"How'd you like Mexico City?"

His visitor smiled. "You've done your homework. Mexico City was no walk in the park."

"It's where the action is. At least you speak the language. My Spanish is crap."

His visitor shrugged, took a tiny sip from the highball glass.

"I don't know how much I can tell you," Touhy said. "I just keep the source files in my office."

"You're too modest. You're the division

security officer. You keep the files on the confidential sources updated."

"There's barely any updating to do. Which CS are you interested in?"

The visitor pulled a little spiral-bound notebook from his jacket pocket and consulted it as if he couldn't remember. "SCC-13-0011."

"That's one of ours, all right. Number eleven, did you say?"

"That's right."

"What kind of background are you looking for?"

"Any criminal background, for example. Anything that might disqualify him. We want to send a team out here to do a joint debriefing of the CS, but I'll be honest, my ASAC thinks it's a waste of resources."

Touhy took a large swallow of bourbon. "I don't know what I can tell you that might make a difference."

"Well, I'm not going to ask his name, of course, but maybe you could give me a rough sort of sketch of the man. Some details. What kind of job he has, where he lives, his standing in the community, all that."

Touhy filled his lungs again with smoke and narrowed his eyes. Then he exhaled slowly, a narrow stalactite of smoke escaping through his pursed lips. "How's Renny Haberman doing these days? Still a practical joker?"

"He's great. Yes, still the office cutup."

"Will you give him my best? We did basic agent training together."

"I most certainly will."

"Huh. Renny Haberman is my orthopedic surgeon. He's not in the DEA."

A long, long silence.

"Agent Touhy," Dr. Mendoza said sadly. "I really wish you hadn't tried to be clever."

64

The old man had put up quite a fight, lunging toward the console by the front door, where he kept his DEA-issued .40-caliber Glock 23.

But age hadn't been kind to him. His knees were fragile as glass, and the bourbon had slowed his reflexes.

Dr. Mendoza subdued him well before he got anywhere near the Glock.

Now the man struggled on the wall-to-wall carpeting near the TV. Flex-cuffs bound his wrists and ankles, duct tape over his mouth. A nasty purplish welt appeared on the supraorbital ridge where Dr. Mendoza had struck him with the leather Denver sap.

In the struggle, Dr. Mendoza's hairpiece had come loose, but he no longer needed to look like a DEA agent named Hernandez in the San Francisco field division.

It was always preferable to extract information by means of social engineering. He never enjoyed the rougher methods and considered having to resort to them an admission of failure.

But when it was necessary, he was good at it.

He'd dragged the DEA agent's body, with great difficulty, into the nearest bedroom. It was a guest room that appeared to get little or no use. The only furniture in the small room was a queen-size bed covered in a dark blue polyester-blend spread, two small unmatched end tables, and a bureau. The floor was covered in turquoise wall-to-wall carpeting. A fine layer of dust coated the furniture. Agent Touhy was a widower and lived alone, probably had no housekeeper. Maybe he did a quick run-through with a vacuum cleaner every couple of weeks.

Agent Touhy bucked and struggled, which only made it harder to get him onto the bed. Not impossible, though: Dr. Mendoza was strong. By struggling, Agent Touhy made it necessary for Dr. Mendoza to handle him roughly. He had to pull at the DEA man's arms, wrench him this way and that. This caused pain.

The pain was nothing compared to what he was about to experience, though, if he did not cooperate.

Once he got Touhy onto the bed, he

flipped him over with one hard tug. Face-down, Touhy bucked some more and then gave up. He tried to shout through the duct-tape gag, but the noise was nothing more than stifled, strangled nonsense. He was not going to be cooperative, which was too bad.

Touhy fought some more and tried to turn over, but Mendoza held him in place with one knee. Hog-tied with flex-cuffs on his ankles and wrists, the agent was not difficult to maneuver.

"Agent Touhy, you can make this all go very easily for yourself, simply by telling me the real name of confidential source number SCC-13-0011. That's all I require. Once you give me the name, there's no point in causing you any harm. I will leave you here, unhurt, until I've finished my work. I think you'll agree this is the preferred resolution. Just a name. That's all I ask."

Dr. Mendoza waited for some signal of agreement. A nodding of the head, some-thing. But Touhy simply breathed heavily through his nostrils, his face down on the coverlet. Dr. Mendoza decided to give the man a chance to agree and make things easier. He braced the back of the man's neck with one hand and carefully pulled off one end of the duct tape.

Agent Touhy blurted out an obscenity.

Dr. Mendoza smiled. This was nothing more than the powerless tantrum of an infant. "You know the identity of all active confidential sources in the Boston division. Number eleven was just queried yesterday by the San Francisco office. The name is quite fresh in your mind."

"You're not Hernandez, you slimy little mother —"

Dr. Mendoza, latex gloves on each hand, replaced the flap of duct tape over Agent Touhy's mouth. He disliked obscenity and had no use for personal slurs in any case.

From his coat pocket he withdrew a small rectangular nylon case. He unzipped it and opened it flat on the side table. He opened a sterile cotton gauze pad and squeezed a few drops of Betadine onto it. Force of habit: Even when he did his work for the cartel, he always maintained a sterile surgical field. He painted an orange oval on the back of Touhy's neck.

The DEA agent struggled even harder, torquing his body from side to side. He knew something bad was coming; he knew many of the techniques employed by the *sicarios* for the Sinaloa cartel. Dismemberment, say, or decapitation.

But Dr. Mendoza didn't use chain saws. His methods were more sophisticated and far more effective. And far less bloody.

Agent Touhy continued to struggle violently. He was not going to make this easy. Unfortunate for him, Mendoza thought. But so be it. Mendoza was prepared for all eventualities. He selected a single-dose vial of Amidate, twenty milligrams of etomidate. He carefully pointed the hypodermic needle at the carotid artery on the left side of Touhy's neck. Behind his duct-tape gag, Touhy roared, but the etomidate worked rapidly. In less than a minute, Touhy lay flat on the bed, calm and compliant.

Now Dr. Mendoza was able to do his work with his accustomed fastidiousness. He untied the agent and then removed his blue button-down shirt, unbuttoning the placket carefully. Now the man's torso was exposed.

Two more injections, the first a delicate job. He used a Whitacre needle, three and a half inches long, and injected it at the C4 level of Touhy's cervical spine, about three centimeters deep at the back of his neck. There was a small yet distinct *pop* as the needle point penetrated the dura.

Then he injected the fluid, a local nerve block called ropivacaine.

He stood up, returned the syringes to his zippered travel case, and selected a conventional hypodermic. This one could be injected nearly anywhere. He chose the same carotid artery where he'd injected the etomidate. The damage had already been done. This hypodermic contained naloxone, an opioid inverse agonist. Naloxone was sometimes used to counteract heroin or morphine overdose. Inject it in the bloodstream of someone floating on a heroin high and it would bring him crashing down, make him scream in pain. In a normal person it heightens the sensation of pain.

It would put Agent Touhy into a nightmare from which he could not awaken.

Dr. Mendoza rolled the agent over onto his back. His chest was pale and doughy. Wispy gray hairs garlanded his nipples. His eyes fluttered and then opened as the drug began to take effect. Dr. Mendoza peeled the duct tape back so the man could talk.

"What the hell are you — I can't — I can't —"

"You can't move," Dr. Mendoza said gently. "You are paralyzed."

"Oh, Jesus. Oh, Jesus."

"The pain you are about to experience will be unlike anything you've ever felt before. Normally, if you were to drop a brick on your foot, say, or accidentally hit your thumb with a hammer, you'd feel intense pain, but then the pain would subside. Your body secretes endorphins that dull the pain and make it bearable. But the drug that is now in your system blocks those endorphins. You will feel pain with an intensity that human beings are simply not meant to experience."

He took a number 11 disposable scalpel from the nylon travel case, pushed its blade through the sealed foil pouch, and without hesitation flicked it precisely down the DEA man's areola and nipple, splitting the nipple cleanly in half. Bright red blood wept from the wound.

Agent Touhy bellowed, his eyes wide, his mouth contorted.

Dr. Mendoza replaced the tape over his mouth. It flapped open, allowing Touhy to emit a full, ear-rending scream of pain. The adhesive had disintegrated, so Dr. Mendoza ripped off another length of the silvery tape and placed it over the agent's mouth.

The screaming did not stop, but now at least it was muted.

Dr. Mendoza put his index finger to his mouth and made a shushing sound. "You see, the pain does not subside, does it? Sadly, it will continue as long as the naloxone courses through your blood vessels."

The duct tape wrinkled and belled but stayed affixed.

"If I do nothing, the pain will begin to diminish within five minutes. It will be a very long five minutes, but it will come to an end. If, however, I inject another bolus of naloxone, you will experience excruciating pain. Before long, either your heart will give out or you will simply lose your mind."

Agent Touhy's face was purplish red and his eyes bulged. He snorted in a lungful of air.

"Agent Touhy, you have the ability to make the pain go away. All I want is one name. Right now it doesn't seem a frightfully high price to pay, does it?"

Agent Touhy held out less than one minute more.

65

Danny had no choice. He had to meet them.

If he didn't show up, they'd become suspicious. He had to keep things as normal-seeming as he could.

But what if this were a setup?

And if they knew he'd learned the truth?

If they'd cloned his iPhone and could monitor every call he made or received, they'd have listened to his conversations with his lawyer.

If they had, then this meet was going to be an execution.

Or maybe he was just being paranoid. They had to take physical possession of the iPhone in order to clone it, right? Then maybe they thought nothing had changed. That Danny still believed they worked for the DEA.

But how was this different from playing Russian roulette, spinning a revolver's chamber and pulling the trigger?

Was there a round in the chamber, or not?

He looked at his watch. In about half an hour he was supposed to pick Abby up from school and take her home. But if "Slocum" and "Yeager" knew he knew, then Abby wasn't safe. Anywhere, really, but especially not at his apartment.

He needed to talk to Tom Galvin on a phone he could trust.

He bought a ten-dollar Samsung Trac-Fone and spent another twenty bucks on a card offering sixty minutes of call time.

It was a truly craptastic phone. You had to put in a battery and slide in the metallic-look plastic back panel, then hook up the power cord to charge it. The instructions were half in English, half in Spanish. On his laptop he went to the TracFone website and activated the phone. He put in a fake name — Jay Gould, because why not? And a fake e-mail address, and the serial number of the phone from the brochure in the phone's box. He scratched the silvery stuff off the back of the phone card to reveal the airtime PIN, and he entered that, too. Eventually, he got the phone to work, even though the website kept chiding him in red type that the phone number wasn't verified. That didn't seem to make any difference; the phone worked anyway. He wondered how a strung-out meth head or cokehead was able to set up burner phones and make it through the complicated registration process. Maybe they didn't bother, either. Maybe you didn't have to.

But whatever: He now had a disposable cell phone that wasn't cloned or traceable.

He couldn't call Galvin's BlackBerry — that was out — and he wasn't sure about Galvin's office line. Maybe that was safe, maybe not. He had Celina's cell phone number. The DEA guys probably did not.

When she first answered, she sounded guarded, not recognizing the incoming number. Then, when she recognized Danny's voice, her voice warmed a bit.

"I was wondering whether Abby could go home with Jenna today. I'm going to be out for the afternoon."

"I'm sure that would be fine with Jenna."

"Is your driver picking Jenna up?"

She was silent for several seconds. Then: "Tom changed drivers."

"Okay." Meaning what, exactly? Another dead chauffeur/bodyguard? The only job with less security was managing the Red Sox.

"He replaced Diego with someone he hired himself."

Good. He'd followed Danny's suggestion.

"One more thing. Did my number come up on your caller ID, the number of the phone I'm calling from?"

"I — let me — yes, but I don't recognize — this isn't your normal number."

"Is Tom there?"

"He's gone into his office."

"Okay. Do me a favor. Call Tom and give him this number. But don't call him on his BlackBerry or his office phone. Give this number to someone else to give to him."

"What — ?" she began, but then, understanding that everything had changed and that bad things were happening, she said, "All right."

On his iPhone he texted Abby and told her that the Galvins would pick her up and that she should go to their house after school. He didn't offer an explanation. Abby's text came back quickly: OK!

No argument there.

A few minutes later, the disposable Samsung trilled.

"Danny?" It was Galvin. A number Danny didn't recognize. "Everything okay?"

"Use this number from now on."

"Understood. Same with this one."

"I asked Abby to go home with Jenna today."

"Right, Lina told me. Did something happen?"

"Let's talk later. Is your house safe?"

Galvin sighed loudly. "As we agreed. I've hired private security."

"Just outside the house?"

"The perimeter as well. The entire property. What happened?"

"Later," Danny said, and he disconnected the call.

66

He got to the South Bay Center twenty
minutes early. The giant parking lot
swarmed with cars pulling in and out and
circling and jousting for spaces. It was rush
hour, and this was a shopping center of big,
busy chain stores: Bed Bath & Beyond,
T.J.Maxx, OfficeMax, Old Navy, Marshalls,
Target, Best Buy, Stop & Shop. Home
Depot. The good old Home Despot. An
Applebee's and an Olive Garden. Pretty
much Danny's idea of hell. That and shopping at Whole Foods late on Sunday afternoon.

He found a spot a few traffic aisles away
from Home Depot, closer to Old Navy,
fifteen rows back. He sat in his car and
awaited further instructions: a call or a text.
They'd said only the Home Depot parking
lot. But it was a big parking lot and he had
no idea whether they'd be on foot or in
some vehicle.

Under the front seat he'd stashed the Beretta Galvin had given him.

In his pocket, his iPhone.

He took a few deep breaths. Tried to steady his nerves. He'd asked for this meeting before he'd discovered the truth about them. Or if not the truth, at least he'd discovered the lie about them: that they weren't working for the DEA.

But who were they, and what were they after?

The best theory was that they were ex-DEA agents running some sort of long con. They'd been fired in Mexico on grounds of corruption. Then maybe they'd tried to cash in. They'd run across the name of a cartel money man while working for the DEA, but instead of reeling Tom Galvin in, maybe they'd decided to scam him.

Or maybe they were working for another cartel.

Whatever they might be up to, there was only one way to shut them down: Bring the FBI down on them.

Jay Poskanzer knew people at a high enough level to make this happen. But he needed something tangible, he'd said. "Get me something on them we can give the FBI," Poskanzer said. "A place. A location where these two grifters can be confronted and questioned and apprehended by FBI. Once we've got something, we hand it over to the FBI and let them go to work."

He knew what he was about to do was risky. Maybe extremely so. He tried to relax, calm himself.

What he was about to do required thinking and acting on a whole new level.

He checked his phone for text messages, just in case he hadn't heard the secure-text alert. Nothing. He switched off the ringer and slipped the phone back into his pocket.

He waited.

Then it came, that unusual, electronic plinking sound of ChatSecure. Rear lot, row 5 white van, the message read.

At the back of the parking lot, at the end of an aisle that ran perpendicular to Home Depot, he spotted a white van labeled INTERSTATE FOOD & BEVERAGE. Sitting behind the wheel was Slocum, the wiry rat-faced one with the shoe-polish-black hair. He glanced at Danny briefly, scowled, and glanced away. Danny heard a door open, and Yeager, the bald squat one, came around the hood of the van.

He beckoned Danny to follow him, then went to the rear and opened the swing-out doors. Danny hopped up inside. Cargo racks lined the walls of the interior. Gray

464

powder-coated steel modular shelves. Apart from a few toolboxes and an extension cord, most of the shelves were empty. It smelled of machine oil and old cigarettes.

"All right," Yeager said, "just stand still a moment."

He took some oblong black object from a shelf, the size of an old-model cell phone, switched it on, pulled out a telescoping antenna, and began waving the thing up and down against Danny's sides. It emitted a tinny squeal like a metal detector, its high-pitched tone swooping low to high, soft to loud.

This he hadn't expected. Something had made them suspicious of him. Almost as if they *knew,* somehow, what he was up to. But that wasn't possible, was it?

"What's this about?" Danny said.

Yeager ignored the question, tapped the outside of Danny's left front pants pocket.

"That a cell phone?"

Danny felt his insides seize. He shrugged with feigned casualness. "Good guess."

Yeager lay his hand out flat. As in: *Hand it over.*

But the iPhone had been set to record, a big fat red RECORD button on the home screen. As soon as Yeager saw it, Danny would be busted.

There was nothing to do but give it to Yeager. Danny pulled the phone out and placed it, with an impatient sigh, facedown on Yeager's beefy palm. When Yeager flipped it over, Danny's heart clanged.

The screen had gone dark.

Without another thought, Yeager set it on a shelf next to a black plastic DeWalt drill case and resumed running the bug detector along Danny's lower back, over the seat of his pants, down to his shoes, back up to his wristwatch. He nodded. There was nothing else.

"You forget something?" he said.

Danny just blinked.

"The pictures from Aspen. Where the hell are they?"

Danny shook his head. "I got nothing for you."

Yeager looked momentarily surprised, but his expression quickly turned into grim amusement. "That's a real shame," he said, beginning to massage the fist of his right hand.

"That's why I wanted to talk. They grabbed the camera."

"They? Who?"

"How do I know? Whoever Galvin's working with. His security guy."

"You didn't make a backup?"

"Did you not hear me? They took my camera. There wasn't anything to back up. I didn't have a chance. They caught me trying to take pictures on the mountain at Aspen."

"What do you mean, 'caught' you?"

"Someone knocked me out. Literally, like" — Danny pantomimed a sap clocking his own head — *"bam."*

"And you couldn't tell us this via e-mail?"

"I got caught, you get it? That means Galvin's onto me. *They're* onto me."

Yeager stopped rubbing his knuckles. "How'd you play it?"

"When I came to? Like I was just skiing."

"And the camera?"

"No one said anything one way or another. It was just gone. I assume they took it."

Yeager shook his head. "With no questions, like why did you have a camera with you when you were skiing?"

Danny shook his head. "Right. No questions, nothing."

"And you're sure there weren't any pictures on the camera?"

"Like I told you."

"Then maybe you were just Wildlife Cameraman, taking artsy pictures of the snow and the trees. Well, we're just going to have to figure out another way for you to get what we need —"

"Actually," Danny said, cutting him off, "no."

Yeager laughed. "No?" He cast a glance at Slocum, in the driver's seat way up front. "You believe this guy? *'No'?*"

"This turns out to be a dangerous job, and the rules are changing. Now I'm going to require hazard pay."

Yeager had opened his mouth to speak, maybe to scoff, but he stopped midsyllable. "You're a funny guy."

Danny leaned back against the wall of the van. "No joke. I've done everything you've asked me to do, and the smart thing for me to do is to walk away. But I'm willing to try again. If I get compensated for my efforts."

"The DEA doesn't pay informants."

Danny smiled. "Come on, Glenn, you think I don't do research? You underestimate me. DEA pays, and sometimes you pay really well. I read about a Guatemalan drug dealer the US government paid nine million bucks as a source. But you're in luck this morning. I'm willing to offer you a deal. A special low low price."

"In your dreams."

"Thing is, I have something you want pretty desperately. And I'm willing to get it for you. On my terms."

"Your . . . terms?" Yeager was looking at him differently. Was it a newfound respect?

"An authorized payment. In writing. A million dollars in cash."

Yeager burst out laughing, a strange, hollow sound that rumbled from deep in his chest.

"I'm willing to accept payment in four installments," Danny said. "The first two hundred fifty thousand dollars is due no later than ten o'clock tomorrow morning." He paused to let it sink in. Yeager didn't reply. Stunned silence, perhaps. "Now, why don't we discuss what you want from me."

Yeager shook his head slowly. He gave a thin smile. "I don't think you understand," he said. "You're not in a position to negotiate. You're out there all by yourself at the end of a limb, and you're sawing away at it. Not smart, Danny. Not smart at all."

"You think?"

"I know."

"Well," Danny said, "you and your partner have a decision to make. You know how to reach me." He turned around and yanked open the van's rear doors and hopped out.

Leaving his iPhone behind.

Not by accident.

67

Danny sat in a groovy café on Newbury Street called Graffiti. The walls were lined with paintings for sale, done by students at the Museum of Fine Arts school. The ceiling was pressed tin, the floor was tiny white hex tiles, and the coffee was "single-source." And expensive. A cappuccino cost six bucks. The baristas were clean-cut, with neatly trimmed beards, wearing white button-down shirts.

No one at a table seemed dislodgeable, so Danny ordered a six-dollar cappuccino and sat at a banquette, placing his laptop on one of the shellacked tree stumps they provided for the tableless to set down their cups and plates.

He signed into their Wi-Fi. No password required. He had to assume the phony DEA agents had found a way to tap into his Internet at home.

He went to iCloud.com, Apple's cloud

storage and computing service, and entered his Apple ID. There he found a green radar-screen-looking icon for an application called Find My iPhone. It showed his iPhone. Up came a big Google map of Boston, centered on the Back Bay, where he was. Then the map swooped toward the western suburbs, and a tiny green pinhead appeared on an orange road marked I-90, the Massachusetts Turnpike.

The green pinhead was slowly moving westward along the turnpike.

He was tracking his own iPhone, and with it, the bogus DEA guys, Yeager and Slocum. The idea had come to him while he was standing inside the van. His iPhone was more useful to him as a tracking device than a tape recorder.

Maybe Yeager would realize Danny had left his iPhone behind. In fact, he probably would. But he'd assume Danny had forgotten it in the heat of the moment.

Would he and Slocum toss it? Not likely. They'd want to mine whatever intelligence from it they could — call logs, text messages, phone numbers. Not that they'd find much of use; Danny had deleted quite a bit.

Or maybe they wouldn't even notice he'd left it. He'd turned off the ringer and the vibrate mode.

Now the green glowing pinhead had turned off 90 and was headed north on Route 128.

A couple of sips of bitter cappuccino later, the pinhead had turned off onto Third Avenue in the town of Waltham, heading south.

Where they were going, and why, he hadn't a clue.

A few minutes later, the green glowing pinhead had stopped moving.

He clicked the + button on the map to move in closer. Now he was in Google's Street View. The green dot was in a parking lot behind a building that was marked AM-BASSADOR SUITES.

He Googled "Ambassador Suites" and "Waltham" and found a website for an extended-stay hotel for businessmen.

Residentially inspired suites. One-week minimum occupancy. Fully furnished mini-kitchen, light housekeeping.

The temporary home for two ex-DEA agents.

Time to pay them an unannounced visit.

68

Half an hour later, Danny pulled into the parking lot of a generic-looking redbrick three-story motel-like structure.

The Ambassador Suites Extended Stay Hotel of Waltham.

No white van in sight.

He parked and switched off the engine. In front of the hotel was a portcullis over a concrete T that led to the main entrance. The grand entrance. It was a dismal, antiseptic-looking place. It pulsed with loneliness and desperation and transience. Most of the guests here, he figured, were midlevel business executives from places like Oracle or Raytheon or Biogen Idec who'd just "relocated" to the Boston area and were searching for housing. Or maybe visiting "teams" from Google or Microsoft or Genzyme here on some short-term project for a couple of lonely weeks. Skilled construction engineers working on a job, here for a month or two, away from home.

But what about a couple of ex-DEA agents running some sort of scam? Were they here?

A gray Mini Cooper came around the side of the hotel and pulled out into the street. And he realized there was more parking behind the hotel. He started up the car again and moved around to the back. Two rows of parked cars, broken in the middle by the rear entrance to the hotel and a lane perpendicular to the cars that led to a street. Directly across the street from the hotel was a big concrete and steel parking garage, almost a block long.

In the back row of cars on the left, nestled among the rented-looking economy sedans, was a white panel van with INTERSTATE FOOD & BEVERAGE on the side.

They were staying here, at this hotel, and they were probably in their room. This wasn't an area where anyone walked any-where. There were no sidewalks, and the distances were too great. If they'd gone out, they'd have taken the car.

They were here.

He parked, slung his laptop bag over one shoulder, and walked under the portico into the main entrance. The lobby was small and dimly lit and smelled of burnt coffee and fast food. The reception desk was small, with a marble-topped counter. Fluorescent light flickered. No one seemed to be behind the counter.

There was a bell, the kind you hit to make it go ding. No one, not even Pavlov's dogs, likes being summoned by a bell. He called out, "Hello?"

A bulky young man, midtwenties, trundled out. His name badge said MATT.

"Can I get a room just for the night, Matt?" Danny asked. Maybe the one-week-minimum policy was flexible. He shifted the bag on his shoulder. It bulged on one side with the mass of Galvin's pistol, but the shape wasn't obvious. Still, he couldn't help feeling self-conscious.

"Sure," the clerk said. Simple as that. Plenty of vacancies and the policy goes out the window.

"Got anything at the back of the hotel?" *Where the white van was parked,* he thought.

The clerk hunched over a keyboard that was a little too low for comfort. *Tappa tappa tap tap tappa.*

Danny's chest felt tight. He was on the verge of doing something pretty damned dangerous. But it was better not to dwell on the odds.

It was like a Wile E. Coyote moment

where you fall if you look down: the cartoon laws of physics.

So don't look down.

"That'll be one hundred four ninety-nine."

Danny handed him a credit card, held his breath. After a moment, he saw the charge had gone through okay. This one he'd paid down. There was room on the credit line. He exhaled.

The clerk took a sheet of paper from the printer and slid it across the counter. Danny signed it.

"Help you with your bags, sir?"

"I'll bring them up later."

His room was on the second floor. It was entirely possible that he'd bump into Slocum or Yeager or both, and he had no explanation prepared.

If they saw him, he was pretty well screwed.

The room was small and efficient. A queen-size bed, a desk, and a chair. A kitchen area with a dishwasher, refrigerator, coffeemaker, two electric burners. Everything a relocating executive could need to make his lonely little home for a few weeks.

The window looked out over the back of the hotel and the double rows of cars.

The white van was still there.

Slocum and Yeager were in the hotel. But where? In which room? There were ways to find out. Pretexting, it was called. Pretending to be someone you're not, or pretending that something had happened.

But maybe he didn't need to go that far.

He unzipped his laptop bag and took out his PowerBook, and plugged it in, and he signed on to the free Wi-Fi service.

He took out the prepaid Samsung Trac-Fone. Then he took out Galvin's Beretta and a box of ammo and set it on the desk next to the laptop.

The Beretta smelled of gun oil. It didn't smell like it had ever been fired, or at least not recently. It was new-looking and un-scratched. He popped the magazine release and pulled out the magazine. It was still loaded with fifteen rounds. He picked it up and held it in a two-hand grip the way his father had taught him and sighted on the right bedside sconce. Then he turned and aimed it out the window at a blue Prius. A traditional dot-and-post system, a half-moon rear sight with a red dot, and a front post with a red dot.

The pistol felt substantial in his hands, heavy yet balanced. It was a serious gun — was there such a thing as an *unserious* gun?

— and his aim had always been decent. Nothing great — he was no sniper — but not bad for a guy who fired a gun no more often than every couple of years. At most. And that was standing in the range at the Nauset gun club with his dad. In controlled, artificial, ideal circumstances.

In the real world, he was a rank amateur.

Facing off against someone who used weapons on a regular basis? Forget it. Danny would be dead. Facing off against a semiautomatic assault rifle? Don't even think about it.

So what did he need the Beretta for? Could he in fact use it, under duress?

He put the thought out of his mind. It was simply better to have the thing than not.

He could call Jay Poskanzer now and have him give the FBI this address. The exact location of two former DEA employees who were pretending to still be on the payroll, impersonating law enforcement officers.

But as long as he was here, he could get a lot more.

Beginning, he realized, with the license plate number of the white van. He looked out the window.

Just in time to see Slocum and Yeager getting into it.

69

The elevator was too slow in coming, so he raced down the stairwell to the lobby. His footsteps clattered and echoed. He slowed to an unhurried pace as he entered the lobby.

He caught a glimpse of Matt, the rotund desk clerk, behind the counter. Danny went to the glass door at the rear of the building and, standing to the side, looked out.

The white van was gone.

He circled back to the front desk. He smelled French fries. "Those guys who just left in that van?"

"Excuse me?" Matt was still chewing. He tilted his head politely.

"Man, did I screw up," Danny said. "I hit their van when I was parking earlier, and I wanted to leave them a note. You know who I'm talking about? The white van?"

Matt swallowed. "Um, I don't know anything about a white van, sir. I don't really notice what kind of cars guests drive." A shred of lettuce nested among the hairs of his goatee.

"The two guys who just left — the skinny one with the black hair and the squat bald guy? Just walked out?"

He nodded. He knew who Danny was talking about. "Would you like me to leave a note for them?"

Danny shook his head, looking horrified by the idea. "I can't take that chance. I mean, if they see the damage and file a claim against — well, I'm just screwed, because I'm driving this company car without going through all the paperwork, and I could lose my job. Will you be around later tonight?"

"Tonight? No, my shift is over at five, but Leslie will be here."

He probably worked an eight-hour shift, nine to five. Of course he wouldn't still be here at night. Danny was counting on that. "All right, let me write down their room number." Not *What room are they in?* "I'm going to have to get an insurance form and a personal check, and — I'll just slide it under their door when I get back here tonight."

Matt hesitated. He inhaled. His expression looked like he was about to apologize.

To say something officious and bureau-cratic. *I'm sorry, sir, we're not allowed to give out room numbers of hotel guests. It's hotel policy.*

But then he noticed the twenty-dollar bill that Danny was sliding across the counter.

"That's — that's not necessary, sir," he said with an embarrassed smile.

"I know it's not much. My job's worth a lot more than that. But . . ."

Once Matt snapped up the bill, the deal was sealed. It wasn't the twenty bucks that did it, of course. It was Danny's despera-tion. It would have been churlish to refuse to help.

Matt *tap-tap-tapp*ed away and said quickly, quietly, "They're in rooms 303 and 304. I really can't give you their names, though."

"Oh, that's not necessary. All I need is the room number. Thank you so much. You have no idea what a huge help this is."

70

Danny wandered the third-floor hallway in search of a housekeeper. He finally found one in room 307, where the door was propped open with a cart.

"Excuse me," he said. "Like an idiot I locked myself out of my room. Three oh three — could you let me in, please?"

The housekeeper whirled around, eyes widening. "Oh! Sir? What happen?"

He held up a Lucite bucket. "I stepped out to get some ice." He shook his head, scowled. But not apologetically, not really. More annoyed at the hotel. At the unexpected speed with which his room door had slammed shut. The hotel's fault. Not his.

"What room you say?"

"Three oh three." He shook his head, the disgruntled hotel guest.

She approached, pulled a clipboard on a string from a well in her cart. "Eh, what is name?"

"Yeager."

She looked down the list of hotel guests. Shook her head. "I'm sorry?"

They'd probably checked in under different phony names. "I'm in three oh three. Could you hurry? I've got an important conference call in a couple of minutes."

"Yes," she said with a brisk nod. "Room 303." She said it as if confirming it to herself.

He followed the woman out into the hallway. She smelled like a fabric softener sheet you'd toss into a load of laundry in the dryer. Or like a room deodorizer spray. It was mixed with the odor of her perspiration, the sweat of a hardworking woman. It wasn't an unpleasant smell, but it was the miasma in which she spent her workday.

She led him briskly down the hall. She had a slight limp.

When she got to room 303, she pulled out a master key card and inserted it into the electronic card reader in the lock set unit. It probably opened all the rooms on her floor.

"Thank you so much," Danny said as she pushed open the door. He handed her a twenty-dollar bill.

"Oh, *gracias, gracias,* señor. Eh — you want I get you ice?"

■ ■ ■ ■

The room was a near-exact replica of Danny's and looked like it had just been cleaned.

A metal Rimowa suitcase rested on a luggage stand, closed. He tried to open it, but it was locked. A suit and a blazer hung in the ample closet next to the bathroom. Nothing in the kitchenette had been left out. Just about the only indication that someone lived here, apart from the locked suitcase, was the desk.

A black Toshiba laptop was open on the desk, next to a neat sheaf of papers. He pulled Galvin's gun from the small of his back and set it down next to the computer.

A psychedelic screen saver swirled and undulated, a rainbow of streamers in a starry night sky.

He tapped the keyboard, and the screen saver vanished and a password prompt came up. He stared at it for a few seconds. Hit RETURN, just in case it didn't really require a password.

PASSWORD INCORRECT.

He typed the word *password* and hit ENTER.

PASSWORD INCORRECT. Well, it was worth a try. He typed *12345678* and hit RETURN.

PASSWORD INCORRECT.

He typed *abc123.*

PASSWORD INCORRECT.

He hesitated. Maybe the machine would lock up after a certain number of wrong tries. He typed *999999,* then paused, then added two more 9s, for a total of eight.

PASSWORD INCORRECT.

Hold on, he told himself. *You don't need to access their laptop. Leave that to the computer experts at the FBI.* The laptop would have all sorts of compromising information on these phony DEA agents. It would be serious leverage. It would enable him to make an excellent deal with the Department of Justice.

Just take the damned thing.

He closed the laptop. Picked up the neatly stacked sheaf of papers. On top was a printout of an e-ticket. A boarding pass, actually:

```
Flights 401/2470 Flight 2470
operated by AEROLITORAL DBA AER-
OMEXICO CONNECT

Depart:
12:45 AM
New York, NY (JFK)
```

Arrive:
8:20 AM
Nuevo Laredo, Mexico (NLD)
Connect in: Mexico City

The ticket was in the name of Arthur Duncan, and the flight departed in three days. Maybe Arthur Duncan was the real name of one of them, or maybe it was an alias. The destination was a place in Mexico called Nuevo Laredo. Jay Poskanzer had said that Slocum and Yeager had been working there for the DEA when they were fired. But why Arthur Duncan was going there now was a mystery.

He folded the paper in quarters and slipped it into a pocket.

The door to the room came open.

Danny picked up the gun and spun toward the door.

It was Philip Slocum.

71

Slocum pushed slowly into the room. His eyes widened as he took everything in. Then he smiled. The door slammed shut behind him.

"That's it," Danny said. "No farther."

With his right hand he aimed the Beretta at Slocum's chest. At center mass. He'd read somewhere that aiming for center mass increased the odds of hitting your attacker, especially if you weren't confident in your aim. He thumbed the manual safety off. The gun was solid and fairly heavy, maybe a pound or two.

Slocum stood no more than fifteen feet away. It would be hard to miss.

If he could bring himself to pull the trigger.

He brought his left hand up to steady his grip. "Hands up."

Slocum seemed to be calculating something. He hesitated, looked twitchy. He seemed to be contemplating making a run at Danny.

But he shrugged and lifted his hands as high as his chest, grudgingly, palms out, a tolerant grin on his face. As if Danny were an annoying child who insisted on playing patty-cake. As if the whole thing amused him and he was putting up with it just to be a good guy.

"All the way."

Slocum exhaled. Lifted his hands up. His smile had morphed into something closer to a sneer. He didn't look as nervous as a guy who had a gun pointing at him should.

"Step around to the side. That way." Danny indicated, with a wag of the pistol, the armchair by the window. The reading chair. Next to it was a standing lamp with a big white cylindrical shade. "Sit over there."

The TV in the adjoining room came on, muffled but audible through the thin walls. The other impostor, Yeager, was home now, too.

"Maybe you're not aware that killing a federal law enforcement agent is a capital offense," Slocum said, standing defiantly.

"Yeah? What's the penalty for killing a *former* law enforcement agent who's gone bad? Sit down."

Slocum nodded and grinned and remained standing. Their secret was out, and he knew it.

"Twelve feet away and you probably think your chances of hitting me are pretty good," he said. "Well, guess what. You're more likely to drill a forty-caliber round through the drywall and kill or maim an innocent civilian. A hotel guest you can't even see. An employee, maybe. That's why police are instructed never to fire a gun in circumstances like this unless they're absolutely certain of the stopping range. *Are* you, Danny?" He shook his head. "You haven't really thought this through, have you?"

The surge of adrenaline was making it hard to collect his thoughts. What should he do now? He wasn't going to shoot the guy, and he had no name or phone number of anyone at the FBI. Call the police? By the time the police got here, Danny would be long dead.

Suddenly, Slocum lunged at him, hands outstretched like claws. Danny sidestepped, then swung the Beretta hard. Gripping it tightly, he slammed it into the side of Slocum's head. Slocum grunted and yowled in pain and then sprawled backward to the floor. Blood seeped from his eye. "You just screwed up big-time, you pathetic bastard," he snarled.

Behind him Danny could hear the faint metallic clunk of the door to the adjoining room coming open.

Danny turned and saw Yeager coming through the doorway. "Oh, Daniel, this is not good," he said as he trundled in. A gun drawn.

On Danny's left, Slocum was scrambling to his feet. Rivulets of blood streamed down one side of his face. The gun had apparently gashed the skin just below Slocum's eye. Danny turned and pointed the weapon at Slocum, then moved it around to the right, aiming at Yeager.

"Put the gun down, Daniel," Yeager said patiently. "Don't be foolish."

"Back off," Danny warned Slocum, jerking the gun at him.

"Daniel, I see you hurt Phil," Yeager said. "Looks like you kicked ass beyond your wildest dreams. I salute you for that." He tipped a hand to his brow, making a salute. "Sure, you could try to shoot my friend here, which would be ill-advised. You'd be shocked at how quickly I can put you down. Which I really don't want to do, because frankly you're far more useful to me alive than dead. So please, let's both lower our weapons so we can have a civil conversation. We have some things to discuss."

Slocum swiped a hand over his bloodied face. He gave Danny a poisonous glare. As if he'd go after Danny if Yeager weren't there.

Yeager was utterly calm. He could have been discussing football scores.

"Daniel, if we wanted to kill you, you'd already be dead, I *promise* you."

He was right: They still needed him. It wasn't in their interest to kill him. This was pointless.

He lowered the gun.

"Thank you," said Yeager. "You're doing the right thing."

"I'm onto you guys," Danny said. "You're frauds. You don't work for the DEA anymore."

"Busted," Yeager said. "You're right. We're not with the DEA. You should be so lucky."

"All your threats about sending me to prison — they were all lies."

"Also true. We're not going to send you to prison. No, Daniel, if you don't cooperate, you'll *wish* you were going to jail. It will be far, far worse. Am I making myself clear?"

Danny stared. He'd begun to feel cold.

"You mean to tell me you still haven't figured out who we work for? I'm disappointed in you. Here, here's a hint." He pulled something from his jacket pocket and tossed it at Danny. He grabbed it with his free hand: a necklace of green and black beads with a pendant of a robed woman holding a scythe. "Look at all familiar?" Yeager said.

"That — that —" Danny had last seen that necklace around the neck of Galvin's driver in Aspen. He'd thought it was the Virgin Mary. But it wasn't. With that scythe it looked more like the Grim Reaper.

A few of the beads were crusted with something dark that was probably blood. Danny dropped it in revulsion.

"That's right. Consider it a gift from us. You don't mind if it's pre-owned, do you? That's Santa Muerte. Saint Death. A non-canonized saint. South of the border, some people wear it for protection. It's supposed to bring you luck."

"I'd say this one's had sort of a mixed record," Slocum said.

Yeager chuckled. "It didn't turn out so well for Alejandro, that's true," said Yeager. "But hey — you never know. Maybe Daniel could get lucky."

And Danny knew then that either they'd been the ones who'd murdered Galvin's driver in Aspen or they worked with the people who did. The room seemed to tilt.

So who did they work for? A cartel, was it

possible?

That e-ticket he'd found: One of them was flying to Mexico, back to the city of Nuevo Laredo, where they'd been fired by the DEA. Was a cartel based there?

"Phil," Yeager said, "could you cue up the home movies?"

Slocum moved to the desk and tapped away at the laptop. Then he turned it so that it was facing Danny. He hit a couple more keys on the laptop, and a window on the screen opened. It took him a minute to recognize the image.

The blood drained from his face. He felt dizzy.

Lucy wore a pastel blue T-shirt and navy gym shorts, doing something in a room that looked like her own kitchen.

Making coffee. The image was grainy. It looked like surveillance video.

"Want to know why she always smells like smoke?" Yeager said. "Not because of the bums she hangs around, I'm sorry to say. I know, she told you she quit smoking. But I'm afraid your ex-girlfriend is what you call a chipper — she borrows cigarettes from friends, never buys her own. Phil, pull up the next channel, could you?"

Another video window came open on the screen. With terror, Danny recognized the family room of his childhood home. His father was leaning back in his favorite chair, the Barcalounger. His mother sat in her customary place on the plaid couch. Both watching TV.

"It's cute," Yeager said. "Mom and Dad go together to Stop & Shop in Orleans twice a week. Your dad insists on buying the day-old bread, and your mom hates it, but she puts up with it. In a long marriage, I guess you gotta make all sorts of compromises, you know?" He cleared his throat. "Yeah, there's your teenage daughter, too, but we don't do kids unless we really have to. Which I hope doesn't come to pass. I have a daughter myself."

"You son of a bitch," Danny said, crackling with anger. "You goddamned son of a bitch."

"So here's the thing, Daniel. You asked for two hundred fifty thousand dollars in cash by tomorrow morning at ten, and that's not going to happen. But I appreciate your directness, and I'm going to be just as direct with you. Thomas Galvin keeps all of his account numbers and passwords in one cloud-based encrypted site. Which is locked by means of a single password. That password generates a random key and a random vector initialization and blah blah blah. So you, my friend, are going to get us that password by ten o'clock tomorrow morning. Your own deadline. If you *fail* to give us that password, you're going to become an orphan. And that will be just the beginning of your troubles." He brightened. "On the other hand, give us that password, and all of these problems go away. Life becomes good again."

Danny stared.

"Are we clear?" Yeager said.

Danny nodded. His pulse raced and the room had gone bright. "Yes," he said. "We're clear."

"Good. One more thing?" Yeager said.

Danny turned.

"Please be careful with that gun. You might hurt someone."

72

His tires squealed as he swung through the Lyman Academy's wrought-iron gates, barreling past the teacher's parking lot — Hyundais and Nissans and Ford Fiestas — and careening around the semicircular pickup lane. Two hours before school got out, and his was the only car parked in front of the main entrance. He hummed with anxiety. Everything was too bright and seemed to move like a jagged stop-motion video. Adrenaline pulsed through his bloodstream.

Their assurance that children were off-limits — that was meaningless. What they, or their colleagues, had done to Galvin's driver in Aspen bespoke a limitless violence. If abducting his only child was the way to force his obedience, they wouldn't hesitate.

He had to get her out of here, keep her away from all known locations, which included Lyman and his apartment. Wellfleet, staying with his parents — that was out of the question now, since the cartel had them under surveillance.

There was only one safe place right now, and that was the Galvins' house in Weston. It was a target, yes, but a hardened one. The property was fenced in, and Galvin had assured him he'd brought in private security. Not manpower provided by the Sinaloa cartel, but real security guards. If she'd be safe anywhere, she'd be safe there.

He sprang out of the Honda and raced through the school's front doors.

Leon Chisholm, the school security guard, looked up from the chair where he was reading the *Globe,* and said "Hey, Dan —" but Danny kept running through the hall and up the stairs, no time to talk. Mrs. Gifford, the school secretary-receptionist, gave him a perplexed smile that quickly turned into alarm. "Mr. Goodman, is everything all right?"

"Where's Abby?"

"She didn't sign out —"

"What class is she in?"

She lifted her reading glasses from their chain around her neck and peered at the computer monitor. "She's in Mr. Klootjes's precalculus class. Do you need me to get a note to her? Is there something wrong?"

"Where's the class?"

"Mather 29, but —"

"Which way?"

"I can send a message, but parents can't
—"

"Thanks," he said, and he vaulted into the corridor in search of Mather Hall.

In his peripheral vision he saw Mrs. Gifford get up from her desk chair and heard her call after him, "Mr. Goodman?"

His shoes slapped against the terrazzo floor and rang in the hallway. The damned school was a maze of halls and cubbyholes and lockers and short flights of stairs and blind turns.

It took him a good five minutes to locate Mather. Room 29 was a modern-looking classroom, at least by Lyman standards: whiteboard walls instead of blackboards or greenboards, M. C. Escher posters, inscrutable diagrams. Danny stared into the classroom through the window in the door. Fifteen bored-looking students sat in burgundy tablet-arm desks staring dazedly at Mr. Klootjes, an obese bearded redhead with grimy wire-rimmed glasses and a soporific teaching style, scrawling a tangle of digits with green marker on a whiteboard. Danny had met him once, at a routine parent-teacher conference, and understood at once why Abby detested the man.

Abby was in the back row apparently struggling to stay awake. He didn't see Jenna; maybe she wasn't in the same math class.

Danny yanked open the classroom door. Mr. Klootjes turned around slowly, squinting. "Um, hi . . . ?"

"Abby, come on," Danny said, beckoning with an urgent wave.

Abby looked up at the door, alarmed. "Daddy?"

"Let's go, come on, now!" Fifteen girls were staring at him, a few tittering. He heard one of them say, "Abby's dad."

"Excuse me, sir," said Mr. Klootjes.

"Abby, let's go, this is important," Danny said.

Mortified, she slunk out into the hallway. "What's going on?" she said.

"Let's go, we'll talk in a minute."

"I need to get my stuff from my locker."

"No time for that."

"It's close, it's just in Burke —"

"We can get stuff from your locker another time."

"What? What's going on? What *happened*?"

"We'll talk in the car.

"Wh-why are you doing this? Did something bad happen?"

"We'll talk in the car," he said again.

Abby slammed her car door. "Oh my *God,* this is so *embarrassing*! What the hell is so *important* that you have to pick me up now? What'd I *do*?"

"You didn't do anything." He couldn't tell her the truth, couldn't tell her what was going on, what exactly the threat was. "I'm taking you over to Jenna's house now."

"Jenna's — for what? How come we're going there now?"

"Just . . . just *listen* to me, please," he snapped as he maneuvered the car out of the main gates of the school and onto St. Agnes Road. "You're going to be staying at the Galvins' for a couple of days."

"The Galvins — ?"

"At their house. Just for a couple of days."

"Why?"

"You're not complaining, are you? I would have thought you'd be thrilled."

"I can't — I mean, all my stuff's at home!"

"I'll get it for you later on today."

"You don't know what to get! You don't know where I keep all my stuff."

"It's not a big apartment. I'll find whatever you need."

It wasn't as if Danny could give her an

explanation that would make any sense to her. *I'm afraid something might happen to you. I'm afraid someone might take you hostage. You'll be safer, far less vulnerable, in a house in the suburbs surrounded by fenced-in acres and armed guards than in a second-floor apartment in the city with a couple of flimsy locks between you and them.*

No reason to terrify her.

"What is the big *rush,* are you going to *tell* me?"

"No," he said. "Not now. Later."

73

The regular security at Galvin's house had seemed elaborate enough, with the eight-foot-high wrought-iron fence and the electric swing gate that opened only once you identified yourself.

But Galvin, at Danny's urging, had hired a private security company that provided trained ex-soldiers and ex-policemen to corporations and wealthy individuals. And now the property had the look of a military base. The two uniformed guards who stopped Danny at the gate didn't look like the run-of-the-mill, rent-a-cop variety. They looked fit and professional and had walkie-talkies and were armed. A third appeared to be patrolling the perimeter on foot.

One of them came over to Danny's car. Danny rolled down his window at the guard's stern behest and handed over his driver's license.

"I'm a friend. Daniel Goodman."

"Yes, sir, we're expecting you," he said, consulting a clipboard. The guy stared at Danny's license, handed it back, and nodded to his partner. The gate slowly came open.

"What is this?" Abby said. "What's with those guys?"

Danny didn't answer. He couldn't tell her the truth, but he didn't want to outright lie. He drove up the long tree-lined road that wound through the woods to the house.

"Are you going to *tell* me what's going on?"

He pulled over and put the car in park, the engine running. "Boogie, listen. One of Mr. Galvin's clients has been threatening him and his family."

She squinted, frowned. "So . . . what does that have to do with me?"

"The thing is, they're probably targeting close friends, too. Anyway, that's what Tom's security company tells him, and we don't want to take any chances."

Her mouth came open. "But what — what about Jenna?"

"She's being picked up separately."

"Holy crap!" she said. "I don't believe this. You mean we can't leave the house?"

"Just for a couple of days. Until this blows over."

They pulled up to the house.

Celina answered the door, looking beautiful as ever, in jeans and a beige silk top, but her radiant smile was gone. She wore no makeup and looked a little haggard. She gave a perfunctory smile; she wasn't hostile so much as remote, guarded. Her life had been rocked by the carnage at Aspen and its aftermath here at home. Everything had changed, and was about to change even more drastically, and she was frightened for her family.

"Abby, would you like to go to Jenna's room? She's on her way back right now." The little rat dogs skittered around them, swarming them, wheezing and rasping, their nails clicking like tiny tap shoes.

"Torito! Loco! Enough!" she said.

She placed both hands on Abby's shoulders. "Abby, *querida,* you and Jenna will have a nice time this weekend. Maybe you and Jenna can help make dinner tonight?"

Abby blinked and nodded. "Okay, sure," she said, unenthusiastic, giving a quickly disappearing smile.

"There's nothing to be scared about," Celina said.

But Abby didn't look convinced.

■ ■ ■ ■

A few minutes later, Tom Galvin and Jenna came through the front door, followed by a stocky black man in a navy sweatshirt, his gun holstered on the left side of his belt. In his ear was the coiled wire of a security earpiece. He stood in the doorway.

Galvin looked ill. His shoulders seemed stooped. He was pale, with beads of sweat on his forehead. "We're all set, Dennis," Galvin told the guard, who nodded and left, pulling the door closed behind him.

"Mamá!" Jenna gasped, her eyes wide. "Will someone tell me what is going on here? Are we, like, prisoners here? Is anyone going to *explain*?"

"Celina," Galvin said flatly. "Have a talk with the girls. Danny, you and I need to have our own talk."

"What about College Night?" Jenna said.

"Huh?" her father said.

"Tonight at school," Abby said. "College Night. Everyone has to be there."

"Sorry," said Galvin. "Change in plans. College Night's been canceled. You girls can stay here and have a party."

"We don't have a *choice*," Jenna told her

father. "It's not, like, *optional.* We have to go."

Danny shook his head. Celina said, "It's not good time."

"Dad, every single girl in the class is going to be there," Abby said. "There's going to be admissions reps from Yale there, and Princeton and Brown, and the college counselors will be telling everyone what we have to do, and answering questions. It's not a choice. I have to be there. We both do."

"Not tonight," Danny said. "Sorry."

"You think I *want* to go to College Night?" Jenna said to her parents. "Abby really wants to go, okay? I mean, it's not like I'm even going to get *into* college. Not unless you buy them a gym."

Galvin looked stung. "Don't say that, honey. The right college will be lucky to get you."

"Lucky to get *you,* you mean. Anyway, you can't force us to stay here. We're not prisoners."

"Actually, I have bad news for you. I *can* force you to stay here. Last I looked, I'm your father."

"And I wish to hell you weren't!" Jenna shouted. "You're a goddamned Nazi, you know that?" The sharp edge of her banked fury was blunted only by her tears.

Galvin was quiet for several seconds. Then he shook his head, as if all the fight had gone out of him. "Don't talk that way," he said softly.

"I hate you!" Jenna said. "You're ruining my life."

"Your father loves you, *chica*!" Celina said. "Don't say like this!"

"No!" Jenna shouted, and she stormed upstairs. A moment later, Abby followed Jenna.

Galvin muttered something to Celina in Spanish. Then he said, "Right now, Danny and I need to have a talk of our own."

The two men headed toward Galvin's office.

"I've got to show you something," Galvin said.

"It's gonna have to wait," Danny said.

Galvin looked at him.

"I think you haven't been honest with me," Danny said.

"Oh, yeah?"

"Yeah." At the door to Galvin's study, he folded his arms.

Galvin looked at him sharply. "About . . . what?"

That was when Danny knew for certain

he was right. "About how you're working with the DEA."

74

Until he learned the truth about Slocum and Yeager — that they were grifters — Danny had believed he was the leak, the confidential source of damaging information about Galvin that had so alarmed the Sinaloa cartel.

But he'd assumed wrong. Since they were frauds, someone else had to be the leak.

And that someone was Galvin himself.

It defied the odds that Galvin could have served as Sinaloa's chief money man for so long without the DEA finding out and trapping him.

Galvin had as much as said so.

I've been at this a long time. Long enough for the DEA to dig down deep into what I've been doing. And trap me. Force me to flip. That doesn't seem crazy, does it?

Now Galvin looked at Danny for a long time. He blinked a few minutes. "You're a smart son of a bitch, you know that?" he said at last. "I'm going to put all my cards on the table. The simple, ugly truth is, the feds got onto me about a dozen years ago. I should have expected it — the whole arrangement was too good to last. An agent with the DEA showed up at my office and started asking me questions. I guess they had a team of accountants poring over Mexican cartel cash flow out of the HSBC bank. And he had a theory that pointed right to me."

"Which you denied."

"Of *course* I denied it," he said with a shrug. "Until I figured out that someone high up the chain of command in the cartel must have turned. They had me. I had a choice of cooperating or fighting it. But this one DEA guy — name of Wallace Touhy — was too smart. Or his sources were too good. He had me."

"You didn't . . . try to fight it?"

Galvin shook his head. "What was the point? You can't prove a negative. I couldn't prove to them I wasn't cooperating with the DEA — they'd *assume* I was cooperating. Or that eventually I'd break down and give them up. Then they'd have no choice but to kill me. They'd write me off as just another cowardly gringo who'd sell them out."

"You became a confidential source for the DEA."

"They gave me a choice. Twenty, thirty years behind bars — or help them out. Tip them off. Hand them the occasional Sinaloan, as long as I could do it without the cartel suspecting me. That was the trick — you never know who inside the DEA might be secretly working for the cartels. So Touhy agreed to run me off the books. A silo operation. The only way to make sure the cartel didn't find out. He locked up my file in a cabinet somewhere — I mean, there's always documentation. Has to be. He assigned me a number, and that was about it for paperwork. I must have given up five or six high-ranking Sinaloans over the years."

"And how do you think the Sinaloans found out?"

He shrugged. "Ever seen that World War Two poster of a guy drowning, says, 'Someone Talked'?"

Danny nodded.

"I guess I'm just lucky I got away with it as long as I did."

"This DEA guy can't help you now?"

Galvin scoffed. "The DEA? What are they going to do, put my whole family in witness protection? I mean, short of giving me plastic surgery and stashing me in North

Dakota, there's nothing the government can do, once the cartel has it in for you.

"For days now, I've been trying to reach out to Touhy. They gave me a number; I call it, he answers twenty-four/seven. Always. Except not this time. I've been calling him. No answer."

Danny felt a fresh panic rising. "And?"

"And I just found out why. I got a source in the state police. Touhy's dead. Murdered, brutal. Like, tortured to death. And if I don't act now, I'm next."

"You say this like you're certain."

"I am. And I know who they're sending."

75

"I need to show you a picture," Galvin said, nodding toward his open laptop.

The image that filled the screen was of a man in a dark overcoat. Danny leaned in closer. The image was slightly blurred, like a still from a surveillance video. The man was entirely bald and had rimless glasses and appeared to be sitting in a vehicle, his head turned toward the camera. Looking directly *at* the camera, in fact.

"Who's that?" Danny asked.

Galvin turned away from the screen, his eyes red-rimmed and bloodshot. His face shone with sweat. It occurred to Danny that he looked as if he'd recently been sick to his stomach. He wiped a hand over his face.

"*El ángel de la muerte.* The angel of death, they call him. He's the guy they send."

"Who? Send to do what?"

"The cartel. Sinaloa. His name is Dr. Mendoza. That's all I know — Dr. Mendoza, no first name." He paused, took a deep breath. "He specializes in . . . coercive interrogation."

"You mean like 'enhanced interrogation techniques'? Torture?"

Galvin shrugged. "Whatever you want to call it. I'm next on his list."

"But how do you know he's coming?"

"This picture was taken about an hour and a half ago, from a security camera on my fence. The guy was just sitting in a car across the road, watching and waiting. Like he was biding his time."

"So you think your guy — Touhy? — was tortured and gave up your name, that it?"

Galvin nodded. "And maybe we're safe as long as we stay on the property. But I can't stay here indefinitely. I've got to vanish. At some point soon I need to leave."

"And then what? He's gonna . . ."

"You know the videos on the Internet of those guys with chain saws cutting off people's heads and all that? The ones you see in your nightmares?"

Danny exhaled audibly, nodded. He didn't trust himself to speak. "Oh, yeah."

"Well, this is the guy who gives *those guys* nightmares."

"Oh, Jesus," Danny said, and for a long time he was silent. Then: "What does he want from you?"

"Account numbers, access codes, every-thing."

"Was he behind what happened in Aspen?"

"No, I don't think so. That was a Zeta signature. And that's what I still can't figure out."

"What can't you figure out?"

"Blood in the water brings out the sharks. I get that. My guys — Mendoza — they're Sinaloa. But I don't know how the Zetas got involved. Or why they're coming after me."

He turned and looked at Danny curiously. Something in his expression seemed almost accusatory. As if he knew Danny was holding something back.

And Danny could no longer keep Galvin in the dark about the ex-DEA agents. No more. Keeping that secret from Galvin had become unbearable.

"Now I need to tell you something," Danny began.

76

The air in Galvin's study was thick with cigar smoke. It hung in the air like clouds, like suspended jet contrails. A cigar smoldered in a big glass ashtray on the desk in front of him. The husk of another one sat blackened in the ash.

Galvin had listened to Danny's story in silence, barely reacting.

"I knew you were ensnared in something," he said when Danny had finished. "I've known it since that squash game."

Danny winced. "I don't even know what I can say to you. How I apologize."

"You think I'm gonna judge you? After what I've done? Come on, man."

Danny fell silent for a moment. "Do you . . . you think they're working for Zeta?"

He shrugged. "Could be. I'd say it's likely. They're apparently ex-DEA contractors, and we know at least one of them was in Aspen. I told you, that obscenity in Aspen

— that looked and smelled like the work of the Los Zetas cartel."

"And that ticket to Nuevo Laredo — isn't that where Los Zetas is based?"

"Right. Tell you something else. This is exactly how Zeta operates. They're — like hermit crabs."

"Meaning . . . ?"

"Know how the Zetas got their start? They were all members of Mexico's special forces, who were hired by the Gulf cartel to do security, enforcement. But after a while they decided, why be just the hired muscle — when they could make as much money as their bosses? So they broke off and started their own cartel. Kinda like the way hermit crabs find empty seashells and move in."

"So in this case they're trying to take over . . . what, the whole Sinaloa cartel?"

"They want what I built for the cartel. The entire financial structure. Account numbers and passwords and the keys to the kingdom. Cut to the head of the line. They colonize. They take over. Forget hermit crabs — they're like cancer."

"They want your master password by ten o'clock tomorrow morning, or . . ." He shook his head, didn't want to let his mind even go there. "I mean, is there even such a thing? Do you have one master password?"

"How would they know that?" Galvin said with a curious half smile.

"Do you?"

He nodded. "Look, I'm no computer guy, but I'm smart enough to hire smart people, and they set me up with the most sophisticated password-management system you can get. All the most sensitive information — the entire list of account numbers and passwords and contact names and numbers — is encrypted and stored on a cloud-based service and blah blah blah. If you want to unlock that directory, you need to enter a passphrase, not a password. It's actually a lyric from a Lynyrd Skynyrd song."

"I'll bet I know which one." "Sweet Home Alabama" was a fairly safe guess.

"I'll bet you do."

"But it's not going to do me any good. It's not like I'm going to give them the passphrase and they're going to say thanks and shake hands and leave me alone."

Galvin grimaced. "I'm sorry you got into this."

Danny looked at him for a long time. What did Galvin have to be sorry about? He didn't get him into this. Danny did, himself. "There's pretty much nothing I can give them that will guarantee my safety or the safety of my family," he said softly. A gloomy desperation was settling in. "The best I can do is buy a little time."

"I wish I had the answer," Galvin said, "but I don't."

"And what about you? You disappear with however many billion dollars of their money, they'll look for you forever."

"Of course. Which is why I'm only taking the profit."

"The profit?"

"The cartel owns real estate and shopping malls and fast-food franchises and a whole range of companies. All owned by a holding company. Plus a lot of cash."

"You're taking their cash?"

"Uh-uh. I always knew this arrangement had an expiration date. I knew the time would come when I'd have to disappear. I've been squirrelling away nuts for years now."

"Meaning what? You've been ripping the cartel off?"

"Not at all. It's money I've earned. A couple of hundred million dollars in an array of offshore accounts. Management fee."

"So you're going to sail to, what, the Caribbean and disappear under the name of that one hundred percent genuine US passport you bought?"

Galvin nodded once.

"And the couple of hundred million bucks — that's in the same name?"

"No. All the offshore accounts are in a different name. You have to keep the passport name and the account name completely separate. I've done the research."

"And what happens when US law enforcement starts pulling at the loose threads? They're getting good at it, aren't they? A lot of these Caribbean countries are starting to cooperate with the US."

"Some are more than others, but that's beside the point. My money's in something the accountants call a walking trust. Meaning that the moment law enforcement opens an inquiry into one of my accounts, the trust is automatically dissolved. The funds are wired out immediately to another account in another country. Believe me, they're not going to find me."

"There's no guarantees. Even if you do something elaborate like faking your death, they won't be convinced. They won't believe it."

"You're right. But there's nothing I can do about that."

"Maybe not. Unless there is."

"This is not for you to worry about. You just need to take care of your family."

"Well, you're protecting my daughter.

That means a lot to me."

Galvin bit his lower lip. "You and Lucy are — over, right?" It sounded like he'd been wanting to ask about her for a while.

Danny nodded.

"You did it to protect her."

Danny just blinked a few times. His eyes were moist. "She walked out."

"But you didn't stop her."

Danny nodded again.

"You did the right thing."

"It wasn't up to me."

"But you let her go. You're letting her walk away because you love her. I get it."

Danny winced, nodded. "What about you?"

"What?"

"Walking away. You're just going to, what? Get on your boat and sail off the grid?"

"Pretty much."

"What about your family?"

"My being gone is their best protection. You think it doesn't rip my heart out?"

"Of course it does. But it's not enough. It's only half an exit strategy."

"I've got my walking papers and my walking trust. What else is there?"

"I'm a biographer. Trust me on this. You need a narrative. A story."

Galvin peered at him, shook his head, not

comprehending.

"The answer's been staring me in the face this whole time," Danny said.

77

Galvin looked at Danny, shrugged. "What?"

"What would Jay Gould do?"

"Huh?"

"Jay Gould. The guy I'm writing a book about — industrialist, robber baron, whatever?"

"Right."

"So we play one off against the other. That's the only way we're going to survive this."

"How?"

"A double cross."

"Explain."

"I'm starting to have a real appreciation for Jay Gould. He was a shrimpy little guy. Frail, often in poor health. Had a lot of enemies — just about everyone on Wall Street. But he was just light-years ahead of anyone else. And the way he did it, the way he got so rich, was by playing a far deeper, far more sophisticated game than anyone else."

"Okay . . . ?"

"The way he went after Western Union. Back in his time, the telegraph was like our Internet. And the big gorilla in the telegraph business was Western Union. So naturally, Jay Gould wanted to own it. But their board of directors wouldn't even let him in the door."

"Okay." Galvin was listening closely now.

"So he scammed them. Made them think he was going into business against them. Started buying up shares of the competition, the Atlantic and Pacific. And he knew that Western Union monitored the telegrams sent by their competitors. So he sent telegrams that made it *look* like he was planning to build a rival company. Sure enough, Western Union read those telegrams, and of course they didn't want competition. So they bought his company. But the whole thing was just an elaborate scam, because he'd jacked the stock price way up. He made them pay ridiculously inflated prices for the stock. Like a poison pill. So Western Union stock tanked. And then Gould moved in, striking quick like a rattlesnake, and — presto — he owns Western Union."

"What's the connection?"

"It may be a bit complicated," Danny began. "But I think it should work quite nicely. You have a bunch of companies in your portfolio — I mean, the cartel's portfolio. Right?"

Galvin nodded.

"Are any of them, say, construction companies?"

"Sure."

"Any of them around here?"

"We own Medford Regional Construction & Engineering. Nothing in the city."

"That may do it."

Galvin looked puzzled.

"Let me explain," Danny said.

For the next thirty minutes, he laid out his idea. Galvin listened and made notes and occasionally argued. He made a few calls.

In time they had come up with something that seemed feasible.

Not a sure thing, and not easy.

But possible.

78

As Danny pulled out of Galvin's estate, he gave a quick wave to the hired guards outside the gate. One of them waved back. The other stared at Danny's car, as if inspecting the interior. Maybe looking to confirm there was no one else in the car besides the driver.

About half a mile down the road he noticed, in his peripheral vision, a large black vehicle pull out of a turnout just behind him. It was a black Suburban. The only other car on the road. He glanced into his rearview mirror. No one he recognized. Some musclehead behind the wheel and another one in the passenger's seat.

When he entered the Mass Turnpike and the black Suburban was still behind him, he was fairly certain he was being followed. The Suburban stayed a car length or two behind, maintaining a consistent speed, never overtaking Danny's car. When Danny exited at Copley Square, the Suburban did the same.

The men in the Suburban had that vacant-faced, stolid crew cut blandness that Danny had always associated with federal agents, Secret Service or FBI or whatever.

Then again, they could just as easily be private, though — working for, or with, Slocum and Yeager. If they were, it wasn't clear what they were going to find out by tailing him. Galvin's house and his Back Bay apartment were the two places he was sure to turn up. What was the point? Maybe nothing more than keeping the pressure on, letting him know that wherever he went, his movements were being observed.

So let them follow him. He was keeping up the appearance of a normal, predictable routine.

Because in less than an hour, he was going to depart from his routine. And make a trip someplace where it was vitally important he not be followed.

He found a parking space on Marlborough Street, across the street from his apartment. The black Suburban had followed him, not bothering with subtlety. It kept going past his parking spot, half a block away, then stopped and double-parked, putting on its flashers. They were going to wait for him.

Let them wait.

Once inside his apartment building, he pulled out his apartment keys. He could hear Rex whining softly, scratching at the door, desperate to go out. His tail thumped against the hardwood floor.

The bottom lock wasn't locked.

He'd locked both locks when he was there last. He was absolutely certain of it.

Rex whimpered softly. "I'm taking you out now, boy," he said.

The overhead light in the foyer had been left on, and he knew he'd turned it off.

They — probably Slocum and Yeager, the ex-DEA grifters, again — wanted him to know they were here.

Rex whimpered some more and struggled to get up. "You poor guy, you've been so patient." Danny reached down and attached collar to leash — a red grosgrain Lyman Academy dog leash Abby had talked him into buying, at a fund-raiser for a school that didn't need funds — while Rex licked his hand in gratitude.

As far as his observers could tell, Danny had driven in to the city to feed the dog.

Just part of his regular routine.

Rex hobbled the block or so to the Commonwealth Avenue Mall to relieve himself on the grass. While Rex circled to find a choice spot, Danny took out an index card on which he'd written down a few important numbers. He pulled out the disposable cell phone and punched out the phone number for Leon Chisholm, the Lyman Academy security guard.

Leon was expecting his call.

"You're in luck," Leon said in his low, smoky voice. "I still got friends on the job."

"Excellent. Boston Police, or — ?"

"Yep, BPD."

"How much advance notice will you need?"

"The more, the better. But half an hour, forty-five minutes ought to do it."

"I'll call you soon. You're the best."

"And don't forget it," Leon said.

Five minutes later he got back into his Honda. The black Suburban was now double-parked even closer, about twenty feet away.

Waiting for him.

It pulled into the street right behind him, as if it were part of a convoy. Or an escort. They expected him to return to Galvin's house, the way he always went, taking the turnpike to exit 15. So that was exactly what he'd do. At the end of Newbury Street, he crossed Mass Ave and entered the turnpike, the Suburban following close, and conspicuously, behind.

It was three thirty, half an hour before the start of rush hour, but the traffic was already heavy and grindingly slow. The old Accord had a fairly zippy pickup, so he was able to pass a few cars and leave the Suburban four cars back and one lane over. He wasn't trying to lose his pursuers, not here. Just trying to show irritation. To let them believe he was annoyed, maybe a little spooked, which was the natural reaction.

It took almost forty minutes of driving through sluggish traffic to reach the Weston exit, sixteen miles away, a drive that normally took half that time. As he approached exit 15, he put on his right-turn signal and glanced in the rearview. The Suburban was still following him, maintaining a steady distance, always a few cars behind.

Instead of taking the exit for Weston and Galvin's house, as he normally would, he pretzeled around onto Route 128 heading north.

He wasn't going to Weston.

He had to get to Medford, a town not far from Boston. But without his followers knowing where he was going. That was critical. If they saw what he was doing, his entire plan would come crashing down.

Only by getting to Medford and making the transaction without being seen did Danny have any chance of staying alive.

As he sped north, he looked in the mirror again and saw the gold Chevrolet bow tie nameplate and its menacing front grille like the bared teeth of a wild animal. He caught a glimpse of the crew cut passenger.

They were still there.

He had to lose them or else scrap the meeting in Medford. Up ahead was the exit for Route 2. He signaled and took it, and the Suburban followed. Now he was heading east in the direction of Boston, and also Medford. The highway here was wide, four lanes each way divided by a steel guardrail. On one side was a sheer cliff face, the rock out of which the road had been blasted. On the other was a high concrete wall. Even though it was now rush hour, the traffic here was moving at a good clip, sixty to sixty-five miles per hour.

The Suburban was two cars behind. When he slowed down, it slowed. He pulled into the right lane, and it moved over to the middle lane, always staying back, but always in view.

There was nothing furtive about it: The guys in the Suburban wanted him to know he was being followed. They were doing the automotive equivalent of breathing down his neck. Anywhere Danny drove, he'd know they were on his tail.

Up ahead was a sign for exit 60. It said LAKE STREET, EAST ARLINGTON, BELMONT. He signaled right, and the Suburban did the same. He took the exit, and the Suburban followed. The road veered around hard, doing a complete one-eighty, past a chain-link fence and some trees and all the way around to a traffic light.

At the intersection, the road forked. On the right it took you back to Route 2. The lane on the left took you into a densely settled old residential neighborhood in Arlington. He'd driven around here before and knew it well enough. The traffic light showed a red left arrow. A couple of cars were waiting in the left-turn lane ahead of him, a U-Haul van and a VW bug. He slowed down to a crawl as he approached, the Suburban right behind him, clinging like a barnacle.

He had a choice to make: left or right.

He flicked on his right-turn signal, and the Suburban did the same. Suddenly, he jammed one foot down on the brakes while keeping the other foot on the gas pedal. His car rocked to a halt, its engine revving like crazy. As the Suburban slammed to a halt behind him, Danny cut the wheel hard left and floored the Honda's accelerator, blasting through the intersection, through the red light, swerving around the U-Haul van, narrowly missing it.

The van honked and braked and skidded sideways. The VW bug, trailing too close behind it, clipped its rear bumper, sending both cars spinning into the center of the intersection. Danny saw this in his rearview mirror as he gunned it down the tree-lined road.

He took a quick right turn, so fast that he felt the tires on the left side nearly come off the road, narrowly averting a collision with a Subaru station wagon pulling out of a driveway. Two blocks more and he turned left, then another right.

Sirens were blaring, two police squad cars heading the other way — toward the accident, he assumed. The accident he'd caused. He glanced left, saw the pileup — and no Suburban. He'd left it behind. It was massive and ungainly and top-heavy, and a sharp turn might tip it over.

Meanwhile, Danny took advantage of the crucial few seconds of lead time to hang a left, once he was sure he was out of the Suburban's sight. He'd entered a short road with two houses on either side that ended in a T. There he took a right. The houses here were small, pristine brick buildings, all the lawns neatly mowed. He went to the end of the next street and took the first left and immediately realized he'd entered a cul-de-sac. Not good. He didn't want to get stuck. So he pulled into the first driveway he came to. A pink tricycle sat in the driveway, silver fringe hanging from its handlebars. A brightly colored play structure on a postage-stamp-size lawn. Someone pulled back the curtain in the front window.

He backed out down the street and went on to the next one.

He was on a main thoroughfare now, much more heavily trafficked. A jeweler, a travel agency, a RadioShack, a Chinese restaurant. Two more blocks and he'd hit Route 60, which would take him straight to Medford. He glanced at the rearview —

And his heart sank. There, turning onto the street, was a black Suburban. Gritting his teeth, Danny sped up and swung around into a narrow alley next to the Chinese restaurant. On the left side was a Dumpster, heaped with black trash bags. He cut the wheel and pulled up just past it, the Honda right up against the brick side wall.

Had they seen him make the turn? Would

they be able to make out the car from the road? He'd pulled into a blind alley, a dead end. All he could do now was wait. Wait, and hope. He was fairly certain he couldn't be seen from the street. He looked in the rearview mirror, watched and waited.

He was still holding his breath a minute later, when the Suburban came into view. It moved slowly, the sun glinting off its shiny black hood. Moving slowly enough that he could make out the crew cut driver, now wearing mirrored sunglasses.

No question about it. It was them.

He breathed out slowly. Took another breath. Waited.

The Suburban kept going. Drove right past.

He waited a few minutes longer, just to be sure. A scuffed steel door in the alley came open suddenly and a tired-looking middle-aged Chinese man emerged, jolting Danny. He spun, his fists up — and then he saw the man hurl a trash bag up into the Dumpster, and Danny started laughing, uncontrollably, with relief. The guy glanced in Danny's direction, shook his head, and went back inside, slamming the door behind him.

Five minutes later, Danny pulled back onto the street.

Half an hour later, he arrived in Medford.

He pulled into a large dusty lot sur-
rounded by a chain-link fence topped with
coils of razor wire. Signs on the fence said
NO TRESPASSERS and KEEP OUT. A sign at
the entrance gate said MEDFORD REGIONAL
CONSTRUCTION & ENGINEERING/
EMPLOYEES ONLY/TRESPASSERS WILL BE
PROSECUTED.

The gate was open.

79

Medford Regional was one of several Massachusetts companies owned by the Sinaloa
cartel, with Tom Galvin the titular CEO.
Danny wasn't sure whether the cartel owned
them for any reason other than that Galvin
considered them a good investment. The
company's officials, according to Galvin,
had no idea who their real owner was.

But they knew the name of their boss on
paper and were happy to accommodate.

He drove through the gate and stopped at
a construction trailer.

Danny got out and climbed up a few steps
into the trailer. On the trailer's front door
were a US Marine decal and a Boston
Strong ribbon sticker. He opened the door
and said, "I'm looking for Paul."

The guy at the desk stood up. He was a
short, heavily muscled guy with full-sleeve
tattoos and thick steel-framed glasses.

"I'm Paul," the guy said, glowering.

"I'm Dan."

The guy suddenly turned friendly. He stuck out his hand.

"The orders I got — this can't be right."

Danny had expected such a reaction. "It's right," he said.

"You got an end-user certificate?"

Danny pulled out the document that had been e-mailed to Galvin and handed it over. Paul looked at it briefly, then looked up. He shrugged. "Long as my ass is covered, I'm good. Where's all this stuff going?"

Danny pointed to his Honda.

"You're gonna want to pull up to the last trailer. But first, you got a bunch of forms to sign."

80

Though it had been several hours since Dr. Mendoza had learned the identity of the DEA's confidential source, he was still astonished by the revelation.

Thomas Galvin, one of the cartel's American employees, had turned.

Dr. Mendoza would never have expected *el dedo,* the snitch, to be someone at that high a level. Galvin had become immensely rich through his dealings with Sinaloa. He wouldn't have terminated the business relationship unless he'd somehow been compromised. The DEA must have obtained actionable intelligence on the man. There was no other plausible explanation.

But the explanation was far less important than the solution.

The cartel wanted him silenced. For that, of course, they didn't need Dr. Mendoza. A simple hit team would do. The cartel could dispatch a unit comprising local talent, to take Galvin with brute force, neutralizing his minimal private security presence. There were, after all, only four security officers standing guard at Galvin's estate: three patrolling on foot and a fourth in a vehicle circumnavigating the perimeter.

Easy.

But the cartel also needed Galvin's full cooperation. They needed access to the accounts he ran for them. They needed a full transfer of owner documents. To kill the man would only create vast bureaucratic problems for the cartel. Galvin had to be questioned before he was killed.

Dr. Mendoza sat in his rented Nissan Maxima and watched the front gates of Galvin's property and thought for a moment.

Galvin had barricaded himself and his family inside his estate. But that was merely a desperation move. Dr. Mendoza had compiled a hasty psychological profile of the family based on little more than credit reports, financial statements, and a few cartel files. Galvin's wife was a regular shopper with a regular, if small, social life. She was likely to insist on leaving the property soon. But she was the child of one of the cartel's founders, so she was off-limits. Galvin had a school-age daughter who didn't have a driver's license. She would not be leaving the premises on her own.

But he was confident that Galvin himself would be leaving, and soon.

And then he would set to work.

Galvin would crack, as absolutely everyone Dr. Mendoza worked with cracked, without exception. He would volunteer passwords and codes and so forth. No doubt about that.

What worried Dr. Mendoza was not Thomas Galvin. It was the others who were trying to get to him first.

The former DEA agents.

A few quick calls had established that they had been hired by the Zeta cartel. Los Zetas had been trying for quite some time now to penetrate Sinaloa's security, and they had failed. Then they found a soft spot: Thomas Galvin.

If they captured Galvin, they would capture, in one swift move, the ownership of billions of dollars of invested capital. Seize it from Sinaloa. It would be a catastrophic loss, and it had to be stopped.

A black Chevrolet Suburban had been circling the perimeter of Galvin's estate for the better part of an hour. They were hoping, as Dr. Mendoza was, to grab Thomas Galvin.

But they had to be stopped. Dr. Mendoza had to get to Galvin before they did. That was crucial.

Suddenly came the unmistakable sound of a police siren. A squad car roared up the road half a minute later, all of its lights flashing.

Was it possible . . . ?

Yes. The police cruiser pulled right up to Galvin's front gates. Dr. Mendoza could see through his binoculars one of the security guards checking the policemen's badges and then waving it through.

The police car was entering Galvin's property for some reason. Was Galvin about to be arrested by local law enforcement? The sirens wouldn't have been activated for a routine visit.

Something very strange was going on.

After the police cruiser had been on Galvin's property for almost five minutes, Dr. Mendoza heard the sirens again, and the squad car came rocketing back out through the gates.

In the backseat, a passenger was visibly handcuffed.

It was Thomas Galvin. He had just been arrested.

81

Sixty-five minutes later, the Honda was hurtling down Atlantic Avenue, past the North End, along the Boston waterfront.

Danny turned into a narrow lane posted with a NO VEHICLES ALLOWED sign, slowed to ease over the speed bumps, and pulled up to a gate labeled BOSTON YACHT HAVEN.

The gate was unlocked. The marina was open twenty-four hours, but it was slow this time of year. Most of the slips were unoccupied. There were a couple of cars in the front lot, probably belonging to marina staff. A guy in a short-sleeved blue polo shirt and holding a clipboard came out and circled around to the side of the clubhouse, looking preoccupied.

A few hundred feet away, Atlantic Avenue snarled and rumbled with rush-hour traffic, but here on the waterfront, it was oddly tranquil. A pair of seagulls soared and coasted on the breeze and then one of them dove suddenly to the surface of the water when it spied something.

Tom Galvin's beloved boat, *El Antojo,* was moored on the right side of the clubhouse, where the water was deepest. It glinted in the late-afternoon sun. It was truly a beautiful ship. Danny could understand why Galvin loved it so. It was the biggest boat in the marina for now, but not for long. When the summer season began, there would be far bigger, more ostentatious boats.

Danny had downloaded the blueprints of the Ferretti Navetta 26 Crescendo, Galvin's boat, and knew it was eighty-six feet long and almost twenty-three feet across. He knew it had twin MAN V8-900 engines and a fuel tank that held more than three thousand gallons.

He knew it could go as far as the Lesser Antilles without stopping to refuel.

Danny looked at his watch. He had very little time before Galvin arrived. Half an hour at most.

With Galvin's key card, he unlocked the gate that led to the gangplank down to his boat.

Most of the wiring had been set up for him by Paul, the foreman at Medford Regional, back at the yard. Paul was a master electrician. It didn't look particularly complicated. Now all Danny had to do, really, was put things in the right places.

Everything else was outside of their control. It would happen, or it wouldn't.

It took him no more than twenty minutes. The sun was orange and plump on the horizon as it set. The sky was the purple of a bruise. The outside lights were coming on.

He heard the squall of a police siren approach, nearby. He cocked his head. The siren was getting louder and closer. He stepped off the boat and went up the gangway, through the locked gate, and around to the side of the yacht club.

The police car had pulled into the lot, its lights and siren now off. Leon Chisholm trundled out slowly, favoring one leg. He looked around at the clubhouse, at the water, and then he opened the back door.

Tom Galvin emerged in jeans and sneakers and a gray sweatshirt. His eyes were bleary and bloodshot. He looked like he'd been crying.

82

"Yes, sergeant, that's correct," Dr. Mendoza said. "The name is Thomas Galvin. I'll wait."

He had taken note of the squad car number as it pulled away from Galvin's house. Only later had it struck him that it was a Boston Police car, not a Weston one. On his laptop in the front seat of the rental with its wireless connection, he had Googled the district number from the car and was startled to learn that District C-11 was Dorchester, part of the city of Boston.

Why was a police car from Dorchester arresting someone who lived in the suburb of Weston, Massachusetts? It didn't seem logical.

The desk sergeant from District C-11 came back on the line. "No paperwork here on a Thomas Galvin. What's your name again?"

"John Ryan," he said. "With Nutter Mc-

Clennen."

The sergeant probably didn't even know that was the name of a real Boston law firm. He certainly didn't ask Dr. Mendoza to prove he really was a defense attorney representing Thomas Galvin.

"Look, Mr., uh, Ryan, I got no Thomas Galvin brought in at all today at any time. Not for questioning, not booked for arrest, nothing."

"Ah," he said. "Very strange. My apologies." If Galvin had been taken into custody, for some reason, by a police car from Dorchester, he'd have been booked at the Dorchester station house. How could they have no record of him?

Unless . . .

"Oh, one other thing, Sergeant. Mr. Galvin gave me the number of the squad car. It was number 536. That's a District C-11 car, is it not?"

The desk sergeant sighed loudly. "Hold on."

He came back on the line two minutes later. "You got that wrong, too. That car's out for repair. Hasn't been in service for almost a week."

83

Tom Galvin set two duffle bags down on the pavement.

"Thank you, Leon," Danny said.

"It was worth it just to find out my old uniform still fits," Leon said. "Now, if you gentlemen are all set, I need to get this back to the garage before someone reports it missing. Then I got to head over to school. I'm working tonight — College Night, you know."

"Sorry we're not going to be there," Galvin said.

Danny wondered whether Galvin had ever had occasion to speak to Leon before today. Maybe not. But not from snobbery, he knew. They were just two circles that never overlapped.

"Your family gonna be all right?" Leon asked Galvin. "Or are those Russians after just you?"

"Just me," Galvin said. He took out his wallet.

Leon shook his head. "No need. Any friend of Danny's is a friend of mine."

Galvin pulled out a wad of bills and pressed them into Leon's palm. Leon looked embarrassed, but he took the money. "You let me know if I can do anything else." He shook Galvin's hand, then Danny's.

When Leon Chisholm had left, Galvin handed Danny one of the duffle bags. Danny zipped it open and quickly checked its contents. "Shoes?" he asked.

"Boat shoes. Sperry Top-Siders."

"Sure, why not. Underwear?"

"Check."

"I need a wristwatch, too," Danny said.

"All I have is what I'm wearing. I left the other watches . . . behind. At home."

"I'll need it."

"Christ," Galvin said. He unbuckled the brown leather strap of his Patek Philippe and gave it to Danny. "This wasn't cheap. How'm I supposed to check the time?" He seemed to be complaining almost by rote. His heart wasn't in it. He looked distracted, tentative. As if he'd been hollowed out.

"Use your BlackBerry," Danny said. "I'm sorry. Now we need to check cell phone reception."

"I get a full five bars here."

"Out on the water," Danny said. "I need to know how far out you can go and still get at least two bars of signal. You need to be making and receiving calls on your BlackBerry when you're offshore."

Galvin nodded. "I'll take her out into the harbor. I got nothing to do but wait."

Danny looked at his own watch again. "Not much longer," he said. "You need to get on the boat. You shouldn't be standing around here. Where's all your stuff?"

Galvin gestured with a toss of his head. Just the one remaining duffle bag.

"Is this it?" Danny said. "All your worldly possessions?"

"It's an interesting exercise, packing for the rest of your life. How much do you really need? What do you absolutely have to have with you? And you realize pretty quickly that you can't pack everything, so instead you pack almost nothing. You can't pack for years, so you pack for a few days."

"Probably better not to bring much of your old life with you. The fewer things to connect you to who you were, the better."

"I never thought it was going to be easy to leave my family," Galvin said slowly. "I just didn't expect it to hit me so hard."

"It'll probably hit you even harder later on."

Galvin nodded. His eyes were rimmed in red and glistened.

"Even harder because they don't know," Danny said.

"Just Celina. She knows. Jenna asked why I was making such a big deal out of a business trip."

"Sweet Home Alabama" blared tinnily, and Galvin pulled out his BlackBerry.

"Lina, *querida,*" he said softly. Then, louder: "What?" His eyes widened. "You're kidding me. Hold on." To Danny, he said, "You have any idea where the girls have gone?"

"What?"

"Celina went upstairs to get them for dinner, and they're gone. Both of them."

"They — they must be somewhere in the house. It's big enough to get lost in."

Galvin shook his head. "No. Celina's Range Rover is missing, too."

"Christ. I assume Celina called Jenna's cell phone."

Galvin nodded brusquely. "No answer."

"Try again. I'll try Abby's."

They both punched speed-dial numbers on their mobile phones.

"I told her not to shut off her phone when

she goes somewhere," Danny said, more to himself than to Galvin.

"No answer," Galvin said. "Until I know where they are, I'm not getting on my boat. Not until I know for sure my girl is okay."

Abby's voice mail came right on after a single ring. "Same here," Danny said.

"Jenna, it's Daddy," Galvin said into his phone. "Your mother and I are worried about you. I told you, we all have to stay inside the house until this all . . . blows over. Now, you — call me as soon as you get this message. Please."

Danny didn't bother leaving a message. He disconnected the call. The last time Abby had disappeared and gone radio silent, she'd gotten her nose pierced. How utterly benign that now seemed.

"I'm going to find them," he said.

84

Dr. Mendoza looked around the grand room, admiring its wainscoted walls of deep, rich oak. All around the room were hung large gilt-framed oil portraits of the school's headmistresses, going back to the founder, Miss Alice Lyman, in the early nineteenth century.

In his well-cut serge suit and red tie, he knew he looked distinguished and prosperous. He looked like a Lyman Academy father. In fact, several parents and administrators had nodded and smiled at him, not sure who he was but never questioning that he belonged.

He peered pleasantly around as if looking for his wife or his daughter.

The problem was that he had no idea of his target's appearance.

He knew, of course, what her father looked like. But the father wasn't here.

It had been a stroke of luck that he'd seen

the girls driving out of Galvin's property. A gift, really. They were here somewhere; they had to be. But where?

The students and their parents, he noticed, were socializing separately, parents with parents and girls with girls. He sensed a great deal of nervous energy in the room. He could see it particularly in the overwrought expressions on the parents' faces, their frantic good cheer.

He stopped one of the girls. In his most solicitous tone he said, "Where can I find Abby Goodman?"

The girl pointed toward a small cluster of students.

"Ah, yes, there she is!" Dr. Mendoza said. "Thank you so much."

85

There was no direct route from the yacht club to the Lyman Academy, so Danny had to navigate the Honda through a maze of city streets, from Commercial Wharf to Tremont Street, poking along maddeningly, a sclerotic steel artery of rush-hour traffic.

He cursed aloud. *"Move, goddammit!"* Every few moments he alternated redialing Abby's and Jenna's phones. Each call went to voice mail. After the first few, he stopped leaving messages.

When he was still a few miles from school, Jenna picked up. Danny was so startled he almost sideswiped a cab.

"Um, hi, Mr. Goodman," Jenna said tonelessly.

"Jenna! Is Abby with you?"

There was a long silence. Then: "I mean . . ." and another long pause.

"Look, your dad and I know you left the house. Where the hell *are* you? Are you at school?"

Jenna didn't reply. He understood what had happened: Abby didn't want to miss College Night, and Jenna wanted to take her there.

"Jenna, please put Abby on right now!"

Jenna sighed loudly. "I just dropped her off, like, ten minutes ago. I couldn't find a place to park. I'm still, like, circling around."

Lyman's grounds were large, but for some reason it was always difficult to find parking on busy nights. Several small parking lots were nestled among the trees, attractively landscaped and unobtrusive. But never enough spaces.

"She went into the College Night assembly?"

Silence.

"Jenna, this is important. You guys have to get back home. It's not safe. Now, tell Abby to call me immediately."

"I mean, you tried her phone, probably, right?"

"I'm on my way into school. Where are you right now?"

"I'm just circling around, like —"

"Call Abby for me, can you do that? Please!"

Then Danny hung up.

86

"Excuse me — Abby?" Dr. Mendoza said. "Abby Goodman, yes?"

"Yes?" The girl looked at him warily.

"Oh, thank goodness. Your father needs you at once."

"Um, w-wait, who are you?"

"He's okay, but your father's been in a terrible accident." He took her by the elbow and gently escorted her toward the hall. "Come this way, please. Quickly."

"What?" the girl cried. "Oh my God!"

"He's at Mass General, and he's been asking for you. My name is Dr. Mendoza. I'm a Lyman father, and I just got a text from a colleague of mine at the hospital."

"Oh my God oh my God. What happened to him?"

"Please — quickly!" Dr. Mendoza said. He began striding rapidly toward the exit. Daniel Goodman's daughter now hurried alongside. "There was a multiple-car collision on the pike not far from Weston."

Dr. Mendoza was careful to use the right words, the right abbreviations. The *pike,* not the *freeway.* And *Mass General,* not *Massachusetts General Hospital.*

The girl cried: "But is he — oh my God, you said he's okay — he's okay, right? He's not hurt? Or *is* he?"

The hall was deserted and dark. Once the door to Founders Hall had closed behind them, they were alone, with no one around to see. Their footsteps echoed.

"Is he hurt?" the girl asked again, louder. "Oh my God, please tell me!"

"Your father needs you," Dr. Mendoza simply said.

87

Danny pulled his car up to the curb directly in front of the school, which was MARKED NO STOPPING/NO STANDING. *Let 'em tow,* he thought.

He slammed the door and jogged into the main entrance of the school.

Leon Chisholm was sitting on a chair inside the foyer. "Danny boy, I thought you weren't coming —"

Danny shrugged. No time to explain. "You see my daughter, Leon?"

"No, 'fraid not, but all the girls and the parents are in Founders Hall. If she's anywhere, she's there."

"Thanks," Danny said, hurrying away.

"If I see her, I'll tell her —" Leon called out.

But Danny was already out of earshot.

Founders Hall was the large, grandly appointed assembly room where the big school meetings took place. Back-to-School Night, when parents met with their daughters' teachers, began with the parents assembled here. On College Night, juniors and their parents gathered as a group to listen to a few selected admissions officers, usually from one of the Ivy League schools or exclusive small colleges, tell them what colleges were looking for.

When he reached the set of doors that led to Founders Hall, he stopped. Through the round glass portal windows in the double doors, he could see that everyone was seated in chairs listening to a red-haired, freckle-faced young woman holding forth.

". . . could fill the freshman class with students with 4.0 GPAs and 2400 SATs," the woman was saying. "Several times over, in fact. But we're looking for that certain special 'plus,' that something extra that makes the application pop."

From this vantage point, he could see only the backs of people's heads. He couldn't make out Abby or Jenna. So he walked down the hallway to the next set of doors, and from there he could see faces. At this angle, he could see roughly half of the audience. He combed the crowd, row by row, looking for Abby or Jenna, not seeing either one.

Then, as he raced along the corridor to the other side of Founders Hall, where he'd be able to see the rest of the audience, his iPhone gave a text alert.

He stopped, glanced at the phone's screen, and was surprised to see a text from Jenna.

Did u find her?

He texted back: No, is she w. u?

I'm here in Founders, don't see her anywhere. Thought she was with you.

Please come out & talk w. me, he texted back.

A pause. Then her text came through: OK.

He resumed jogging down the corridor toward the far side of the room. He heard a thunder burst of applause and then a rising cacophony. The presentation was over. By the time he got to the entry doors, people were getting up from their seats, talking loudly to one another. The Yale admissions rep was standing at the front, engulfed by a huge jostling crowd, a honeybee queen surrounded by worker bees. A knot of parents stood near the door, obstructing Danny's view.

He pushed the door open and entered, now searching only for Jenna. He had to push through a throng gathered around the tired, pillaged display of red grapes and Jarlsberg cheese cubes.

The chatter all around him seemed to break into unconnected fragments of speech like confetti scattered into the air. A woman was saying, "But if she gets in early decision, she *has* to go, and then what happens if she gets into Williams, regular decision? I mean, it's a nightmare, right?"

A man was saying, "They don't even do on-campus interviews anymore, just alumni interviews, and everyone knows those're a joke."

He saw a small, pudgy dark-haired girl who looked sort of like Jenna, wearing a Lyman Lacrosse sweatshirt. But it wasn't Jenna. "Excuse me, have you seen Jenna Galvin?" Danny asked her.

The girl motioned with a jerk of her head. "I saw her back there."

He was jostled by a woman who was saying, "Sure, but it's not even in the top ten on the *U.S. News* ranking."

A man was muttering to another one, "You do know that the school for war orphans their daughter allegedly founded in Rwanda was actually underwritten by her father, right?"

Suddenly, Danny glimpsed Jenna and exhaled with relief. He pushed his way toward her. When he got closer, she saw him and said, "I don't know where she is. Is my dad here?"

"No. Did anyone see Abby at all tonight?"

"Well, yeah, a bunch of people saw her come in. Then Jordan and Emily saw her walking out with this guy."

"What guy?"

She shrugged. "I don't know, like someone's dad?"

"Walking out of the *building*?"

She shrugged. "I guess. I thought maybe she'd gotten in trouble or something."

"You haven't heard from her — message, call, nothing?"

"No —"

"She's definitely not in here?"

"Definitely not. I texted her —"

"Well, you guys both need to get out of there. Get back home. And if you do hear from her —"

"I know, I'll tell you."

She'd walked out with a man who looked like someone's dad.

He felt a rising panic. Abby had walked out of the building with someone, a man Jenna didn't recognize.

But she wouldn't go anywhere with someone she didn't know. She wouldn't do that. Even here, in the safe environs of the Lyman Academy, she knew not to trust strangers. That was drilled into kids these days.

He jostled a couple, trying to squeeze past. "Well, her older sister got Z-listed at Harvard. They definitely played the Eliot card."

"Aren't they Eliots, like *that* Eliot? Like President Eliot of Harvard, those Eliots?"

"Hey, Danny," he heard someone say. He felt a tap on his shoulder. A fellow Lyman dad he saw at school events and liked. "Man, you look as nervous as me! I mean, is this Tension City or what?"

Danny turned to look at him, a million miles away. "Yeah," he said thickly. He gave an unconvincing smile. Sidling away, he took out his iPhone and hit speed dial for Abby once again.

It rang once, twice . . . and — that was different: It didn't go directly to voice mail.

It rang a third time, and then someone said, "Hello, Daniel."

A male voice.

"Who's this?" he said, his heart suddenly racing.

"I'm sorry. Abby cannot come to the phone right now."

"Who *is* this?"

"I am your life raft," the voice said. "And you are a drowning man."

88

"Who the hell is this?"

Danny became aware that the background noise on the other end of the line was identical to the background noise in the hall, and he felt a shudder.

The man on the phone was here, somewhere, in this room.

"You have something I want, and I have something you want," the voice said.

"How the hell did you get my daughter's phone, you bastard?" he burst out. It was all he could think to say.

His eyes desperately searched the room, scanning back and forth, looking for someone speaking on a phone. Someone who wasn't a Lyman parent, someone who didn't belong.

"Neither one of us has time to waste, Mr. Goodman. Your daughter is in the care of an associate of mine who has instructions to take good care of her."

"An associate . . . *Who is this?*"

A knot of parents momentarily parted, and Danny saw a bald man with mocha skin and rimless glasses holding Abby's red LG mobile phone against the side of his face.

Their eyes locked.

It was the man from the surveillance image Tom Galvin had shown him. The man sitting in a car outside Galvin's house. The man sent by the cartel to . . .

"If you cooperate," the man was saying, "nothing will happen to her. There's no need to worry about that. It will be quick and painless. But if you refuse to cooperate, or you are slow about it, I need only call my friend. And then, what happens to your daughter . . . well, I'm afraid she will never be the same."

Galvin's words came rushing back to him. *You know the videos on the Internet of those guys with chain saws cutting off people's heads and all that? The ones you see in your nightmares? Well, this is the guy who gives those guys nightmares.*

And: *His name is Dr. Mendoza. That's all I know — Dr. Mendoza, no first name. He specializes in coercive interrogation.*

"Let us step outside, Mr. Goodman," the voice said.

89

Heart thudding, nearly dizzy with adrenaline, Danny stood at the rear of the school's main building, off to the side.

Waiting for Dr. Mendoza.

His skin prickled. A parking light fixture buzzed loudly. In the distance a car started.

Everything had taken on an eerie clarity, a feeling of heightened reality.

Then he heard the scuff of a shoe on gravel and the man named Dr. Mendoza loomed into view.

"Well, then —" Dr. Mendoza began to say, but Danny lunged.

"You bastard!" he roared. "You goddamned bastard!"

He grabbed hold of Dr. Mendoza's shirt collar, the knot of his necktie, and Dr. Mendoza made a tight strangled sound as Danny slammed his full weight against the man's chest. But the man came back upright with surprising strength.

Dr. Mendoza's rimless glasses were knocked askew.

He looked at Danny with an amused arrogance as he straightened them. "I am sorry you've done this," he said, and he blinked several times. "You have just made a grievous mistake."

"Where the hell is my daughter?"

"Please back away," Dr. Mendoza said patiently. He pursed his lips.

Blood roaring in his ears, Danny unsteadily stepped back. His fists clenched and unclenched at his sides.

"Mr. Goodman, you are overwrought. I will permit you this one outburst, because you are clearly unable to control your emotions. But let us be blunt. If you so much as lay a finger on me ever again, you will only harm your daughter. She will experience pain of a type and a magnitude that killing her will be a mercy, one she will beg for."

"What the *hell* do you *want*?"

"I want to know where Thomas Galvin has gone."

"And what makes you think I have the slightest idea — ?"

"Oh, dear. This is a shame. You are risking your daughter's life with your silly games. What I am proposing is a very simple trade. Your daughter for Thomas Galvin."

"I don't know where he is."

Dr. Mendoza shrugged. "This game doesn't benefit either one of us, and it doesn't help your daughter. Abigail, is that right? Abby?"

It took all the restraint he could muster to keep from lunging at the man again. Danny clenched his fists and bit his lower lip. He actually trembled with anger.

"How do I know she's okay?"

"You have my word."

"Your — *word*?"

"I'm afraid that's the best you can do. But you'll see that I am a man of my word."

Danny swallowed. He heard distant laughter, a girl's squeal. "Okay, listen. If you let my daughter go — and if you absolutely guarantee my daughter's safety — I'll — I'll try my best to find Galvin."

Dr. Mendoza smiled. "You'll try to find him? This is your notion of good faith? You disappoint me. Good night." Straightening his tie, Dr. Mendoza began to walk away.

"Wait —"

Dr. Mendoza stopped, made a half turn.

"Hold on," Danny said. He swallowed again. His face was taut, burning. Agonized, he said, "He's on his boat."

"Thank you," Dr. Mendoza said. "And where is that boat?"

"Where's Abby? Give me my daughter and I'll tell you where his boat is."

Dr. Mendoza sighed and shook his head.

"This is a game you really want to play? A game with your daughter's life? No, this is how it will work: You will take me to Galvin. Then I'll tell you where she can be found."

Danny looked around wildly, trying to regain some semblance of control. He swallowed, closed his eyes.

"All right," he said at last.

90

Danny sat behind the wheel of the Honda. In the passenger's seat next to him sat the man in the suit, tall and lanky yet powerfully built.

"Place the call," Dr. Mendoza said.

"He's on his boat. I don't even know if a call can get through."

"For your sake, for your daughter's sake, let us hope it does."

Galvin was on his boat, waiting for Danny to give him the all-clear signal.

But this call would change everything.

Once again, Danny felt a terrible clarity. His daughter's life depended on this. He remembered the morning when Sarah and he had strapped their tiny baby into a car seat and drove her home from the hospital. A howling snowstorm outside, and they'd covered her face with a pink-and-blue-striped baby blanket to protect her from the snow during the dash from the hospital to their car. He drove as if the baby was made of glass, as if the baby's life was in his hands, and it was.

As it was now.

The most precious thing in the world to him.

His stomach was roiling. He was frightened and alone and his baby's life depended on him. Abby or Tom Galvin — was that even a choice?

He punched the numbers for Galvin's BlackBerry. It rang once, twice, three times, and he thought: *What if he doesn't answer? What will this monster in the seat next to me do?*

On the third ring, Galvin answered. "Danny?"

"Tom — don't leave yet. I have — something to give you."

"Danny? What, did you say — give me — ?"

"Don't go anywhere," he said, and he ended the call.

"Where is Galvin?"

"Boston Harbor," Danny said softly.

"The faster you take us there," Dr. Mendoza said, "the faster our business will be concluded."

"What are you going to do to him?"

A long silence. "That will be determined

by his behavior."

Danny drove like an automaton. Not another word was exchanged between the two men on the way over. His chest was tight. He found it hard to breathe. He was acutely aware of Dr. Mendoza's presence next to him. It burned his cheeks and ears like he was standing next to a raging fire.

Traffic had gotten light, and they made it there in twelve minutes.

He pulled the Honda into the Boston Yacht Haven parking lot. He got out, his legs leaden, a prickle at the back of his neck.

As they came around the side of the clubhouse to the dock, Dr. Mendoza drew up close to him. "Do I need to tell you that if anything happens to me, if I do not place a call to my associate within an hour, harm will befall her?" He glanced at his wristwatch, a large white face with gold numbers and a brown leather strap. "You will see I am not in the business of making idle threats."

Danny nodded. He felt light-headed, thick and slow. He moved as if through sludge.

"And where is his yacht?" Mendoza demanded.

El Antojo wasn't tied up at the dock. Its berth was empty.

He pointed. Galvin's yacht had left shore.

It was a few hundred yards off, its running lights illuminating the ship with an orange glow as if lit from within.

"He's left?" Mendoza said. "This is most unfortunate for you."

"He's out there. I told him not to go anywhere."

Danny could taste the salt in the air. He heard the scuff of a shoe against pavement nearby, but when he turned he saw nothing.

"You had better persuade him to turn back now."

Danny looked at Mendoza, then looked at the water. He said nothing.

"Let us be clear, you and I," Mendoza said. "If he does not return to shore, your daughter is dead. It is as simple as that. If you cannot persuade him, your daughter is dead. It all rests on you."

"Christ!" Danny said. His nerves felt stretched taut. He took out his cell phone and was about to hit REDIAL.

But then he stopped. Shook his head.

"Make the call," Mendoza said.

"No."

Mendoza's eyes flashed. For the first time, Danny detected anger in the man's face. Anger was good. Anger revealed vulnerability.

"You give the order to release Abby,"

Danny said, "and I'll get Galvin back here. But you'd better do it now, or you'll lose Tom Galvin forever. Once Galvin's out of cell range, it's too late for you."

"You do not make the rules of this game."

"Let her go and I'll make the call. You want a hostage, you have me. But let her go now. I want to hear her voice. Then I'll give you whatever the hell you want."

Mendoza gave Danny a basilisk stare. Taking a small mobile phone from his suit jacket, he spoke quickly in Spanish. Danny understood nothing of what he said.

Mendoza handed the phone to Danny.

"Daddy?" Abby croaked into the phone.

"Abby!" Danny said, tears in his eyes. "Baby. Where are you?"

"They tied me up! I think there's a furnace? It's like the boiler room — the basement of the school."

"Did they hurt you?"

"He just left, Daddy, he's gone. He cut off the things, the — those, like, plastic things for handcuffs?"

"You can move?"

"Yeah. I just want to get out of here. I —"

"Call Lucy. Right now. Ask her to pick you up at school. Can you do that?"

"Yeah. I —" She started crying. "Daddy, I'm sorry. I love you. I'm sorry —"

"Boogie. Sweetie. Just call Lucy, would you do that for me?"

He hung up the phone.

Mendoza nodded, and Danny nodded back.

"As I have said, I am a man of my word," Mendoza said. "And now it is your turn."

Danny dialed the number for Galvin's BlackBerry. It rang once, and then Galvin came on the line.

"Danny, what the hell is it?"

"Please, Tom, listen to me. You need to return to shore. Come back in. This is important."

"What's going on?"

"Just — it's important. I'm here on shore. Come back." He clicked off.

Mendoza, he noticed, had suddenly flinched. Danny turned to look and felt an iron grip on his left upper arm and something cold and hard pressing into the side of his head and he knew it was a gun. He froze.

He heard another scuffing sound and saw someone was holding a gun to Dr. Mendoza's head as well. They were flanked by two men who smelled of cigarettes and body odor and whose bulging arms were tattooed down to their wrists.

In front of them stood Glenn Yeager. At

his side he held a large stainless steel pistol. He wasn't bothering to point it at Danny and Mendoza. He didn't need to. His muscle was taking care of that for him.

"Well, Daniel," Yeager said. "Looks like you've brought us a Sinaloa legend. Dr. Mendoza, it's good to finally make your acquaintance."

Mendoza stared straight ahead.

Danny looked back at Yeager, dazed.

"Oh, yeah," Yeager said, smiling, "and thanks for the tip. As always, we're three steps ahead of you. Forgot about Galvin's BlackBerry, didn't you? Forgot we were listening in to everything you and Galvin said. Well, you enjoy your new babysitters. Phil and I have some business to transact with your friend Tom Galvin. And, Daniel?"

Danny looked at Yeager. Yeager smiled. "I knew you'd do the right thing."

Danny saw where Yeager was heading: down the ramp to the lower level of the pier where some of the smaller ships were tied up. Down there, Philip Slocum and several other guys with guns were boarding what looked like a large black inflatable raft with an outboard motor. Slocum had a large assault rifle slung around one shoulder.

Then the inflatable's motor roared throatily to life. Danny turned instinctively to the loud noise, and he felt Mendoza's left arm twitch.

Suddenly, Mendoza torqued his body to his right, whipping his free left hand around. Something caught the light, something glinting and lethal and slashing. In almost the same instant, the man on Mendoza's right turned questioningly toward Mendoza. Around his throat was a thin red seam. As the man moved, the seam in his throat gaped open and a geyser of blood spewed forth, and the man's knees buckled and he sank to the sidewalk.

Then Mendoza spun to his other side as Danny jumped out of the way. The man who a moment earlier had been holding a gun to Danny's temple now lurched away from the blade concealed in Mendoza's left sleeve.

The blade whooshed in the air, missing its target. Danny dove to the ground, taking cover behind a tall concrete planter.

What happened next took no more than ten seconds, but it seemed to take minutes, as if time had somehow slowed.

Dr. Mendoza juked behind a broad wooden column, a large gun in his hand. He moved with balletic grace. The other man fired, the muzzle flash a tongue of orange flame, and a shot splintered the wood a few inches from Mendoza's head.

Another muzzle flash and a bullet zinged against the brick sidewalk near Danny. He could feel sharp fragments sting the side of his face. He crabbed on his knees toward where Mendoza was crouching behind the column, and with one forceful lunge, he shoved Mendoza, hard.

Mendoza lost his balance, sprawling out from behind the column, and a bullet exploded in his abdomen. Mendoza gasped. Then suddenly came another muzzle flash, and a bullet whizzed, striking him in the chest. Holding his gun level in a perfectly steady grip, he squeezed off one more shot. There was a scream, and the shooter's weapon crashed to the ground.

For a moment, there was just the whine of the outboard motor.

Mendoza's white dress shirt bloomed red. He'd been badly wounded. He reached down with one hand to feel his abdomen, and his pistol slipped from his hand and clattered to the sidewalk.

A moment later, he seemed to list to his left and then toppled slowly, tripping over the chain-link barrier, plummeting headlong with a great splash into the black water.

A frenzied splashing in the water as Mendoza struggled to stay afloat . . .

Then nothing. Just the growl of the motor.

A distant shout from the water.

Danny lay flat against the brick. He waited for another gunshot, but nothing more came. He waited some more. Then he turned toward the harbor and saw the inflatable racing toward the *El Antojo*.

Danny scrabbled to his knees, then onto his feet. His ears rang. Transfixed, he watched the speedboat pull up alongside Tom Galvin's yacht. Its motor sputtered and died.

The former DEA agents and their cartel associates began boarding the yacht, intent on killing Tom Galvin.

Danny found himself praying. All was now beyond his control. He had done his best. He had done everything he could.

He took out his disposable cell phone and hit the only number he'd programmed into it. He listened to it ring precisely three times and then stop.

He waited. Three, four, six seconds . . .

And then the night lit up with an immense flash of fire, as if somehow the sun had suddenly climbed back up over the horizon, bleaching the sky, and a second or two later came the explosion, an enormous deafening boom, seemingly out of sync, like a badly dubbed movie, and the *El Antojo* had become a vast ball of fire. The sky was ablaze with orange and red and plumes of black smoke, a great roaring inferno.

And as he sank to the ground, he kept watching the burning yacht, and he felt an emotion he did not at first recognize because he hadn't felt anything like it in such a long time.

It wasn't despair and it wasn't elation.

It was, quite simply, relief.

AFTER

He became aware of a bright light and a throbbing in his eyeballs and an insistent beeping, a cacophony of beeps from everywhere. Voices murmuring; someone groaning in pain. Shapes floated across the scrim of his closed eyelids. His eyes felt glued shut. It hurt when he opened them. He saw a ceiling, a curtain rod, became aware of commotion, the hubbub of many voices.

He was in a hospital bed.

He swallowed and his throat hurt immensely. He groaned aloud.

"Baby?" A woman's voice. "Danny?"

Lucy's. He smiled. "Luce?"

"He's awake," she said. To him? He wasn't sure. Why was she here? He didn't want to ask.

"He," Danny said, "has a headache." It took effort to speak. He felt drugged, slow and gauzy and a thousand miles away. "And the worst sore throat in the world. He tried

to smile. "You finally got me in a hospital. You know I hate hospitals."

"I figured it was better to leave the trauma surgery to the experts. If I could have taken the bullet out myself, I would have."

Danny squinted, thinking he'd misheard. "I didn't get shot."

"Yeah, you did. You're gonna be fine, but you're going to have a nasty scar on your shoulder."

He struggled to sit up, felt a burst of pain. An alarm began to sound, a different sort of beeping, rapid and high.

"Where's Abby?"

A nurse yanked open the curtain. "What'd he do now?"

"Where's Abby?" he repeated.

"Abby's at the Galvins'," Lucy said.

The nurse pulled the sheet away, tugged something off his chest, ripping chest hair painfully. She adjusted whatever it was — an adhesive lead, he saw — and pressed it back down on his chest. "Please don't try to sit up again, Mr. Goodman."

"Can I get a glass of water? I'm really thirsty."

"Not until your blood pressure stabilizes, and not until we see some urine. Lie back down and please stop moving."

He shrugged and felt the pain shoot down

his right side.

"Abby's doing fine," Lucy said. "Shaken up, obviously. She was pretty traumatized, but she seems to be doing okay."

"I want to see her."

"She was here for a bit while you were asleep. Now you're going to have to talk to the FBI."

"FBI? Wait . . ."

"There's two of them, but the nurse will only allow one in here at a time. They say they just want information. They're sitting in the waiting room. I could tell them to come back."

"But why . . ."

"The explosion, sweetie, remember? Getting shot, everything at the dock?"

Danny closed his eyes, felt it coming back to him now. The gunfire, the blat of outboard motors, the immense, deafening blast.

A minute or two later, he heard the scuff of a chair on the floor nearby. "Mr. Goodman, I'm Agent Steve Nocito with the FBI, and I was wondering whether I could ask you just a few questions."

Danny, lying down, turned his head to one side. He remembered the elaborate con perpetrated on him by the impostors Slocum and Yeager. "Can I see some ID?"

"Of course." The agent handed him a

587

black leather folding credential wallet. Danny glanced at the badge and ID — it felt heavy, substantial. He handed it back.

"Mr. Goodman, you were at the scene of the . . . explosion last night."

"Mm-hmm."

"Why were you there?"

Why *was* he there? Ah, yes. How much could he say? As he thought — his brain was working far too slowly — he remained silent.

"Did you know the deceased, Thomas Galvin?" the FBI man prompted.

The words hit him in the gut. *The deceased.* "I did."

"Were you a friend?"

Danny thought a long while. "Yes. I was."

"Was he planning to flee the country?"

He thought some more. What was supposed to be known, and what wasn't?

"Yes, I believe he was," Danny said.

"Do you know where he intended to go?"

Danny shook his head.

"Might it have been Anguilla? He and his family used to vacation there regularly."

"Could have been. Yes, I think so."

"Did he have enemies?"

Danny could hear one set of beeps accelerate as his heart sped up. "Of course."

Agent Nocito waited for more, but Danny

had fallen silent. After a moment he went on: "Our preliminary investigation indicates three other deaths in the explosion. Two of them are former employees of the Drug Enforcement Administration. Were you familiar with them, by any chance?"

What was the right answer? He guessed: "No."

"Do you know whether they were associates of Mr. Galvin?"

"Not that I know of."

"I see. Now, your . . . your daughter was taken hostage for a short while last night."

"That's right."

"Do you have any idea why?"

"The man wanted to know where Galvin was."

"The man being . . ." The agent took out a sheaf of photographs and flipped through them. He pulled one out and showed it to Danny. "This individual?"

Danny nodded. The bald head, the rimless glasses, the mocha skin. Looking at Dr. Mendoza's face made his stomach go cold.

"You told him where Galvin was."

"I didn't really have a choice. My daughter —"

"I understand. She'd been abducted. Did the man who abducted her — this Mr., uh, Mendoza — did he say what his connection was to Galvin?"

Danny paused. "I believe he was employed by the Sinaloa cartel."

"You don't have any proof of that, do you?"

"No."

"Then that's not really something you want to speculate about. This is a sensitive area for a lot of parties."

Danny, head turned toward the side, couldn't quite make out the FBI agent's facial expression. "That's what Tom Galvin thought."

"Did he have any proof of that?"

He looked at the FBI man, and for a moment their eyes locked. Nocito's head moved imperceptibly, a gesture of — warning? Then he leaned in and whispered in Danny's ear. "Be very, very careful how you answer this, do you understand?"

Danny realized he was holding his breath. Nocito sat back in his chair, a neutral expression returning to his face. He repeated his original question.

"Do you have any proof of this? Anything beyond mere speculation, about . . ."

And Danny understood suddenly. It was like a puzzle piece falling into place. Something he'd known all along, in his gut, without ever quite realizing he'd known.

Galvin had been a confidential source for the DEA. Mistakes had been made, things were being covered up. Powerful people didn't want to be embarrassed.

"Mr. Goodman, do you need me to repeat —"

"No, no — there's no proof. Not sure why I said it. My head . . ."

"Yes, I understand. You're disoriented, not thinking clearly. It's best for a lot of reasons to keep your theories to yourself. Not least Mr. Galvin's survivors. His family."

"My memory, it's not so good."

Danny watched Nocito's stern gaze melt away, like an actor on cue. The agent now smiled benignly, stood. "That should cover it, then," he said. "Thanks for giving me a few minutes of your time, Mr. Goodman. Feel better, okay?"

Danny had drifted off to sleep. When he woke up, the FBI man was gone and Lucy was sitting in his chair. He saw her and smiled.

She said, "You weren't telling him the truth."

Danny was silent. He felt the blood pressure cuff tighten on his left arm, heard its gasp and wheeze.

"About . . . what — ?"

591

"Quit it, Danny. The FBI guy. You weren't telling him the truth. I want to know why. Will you tell me?"

He told her about Jay Gould and the telegrams. How Gould knew his telegrams were being read by Western Union, and how he'd used this to his advantage. Presenting falsehoods he wanted them to believe as true. And believe it they did.

In the same way, Slocum and Yeager, the two ex-DEA employees who'd planned to extort Tom Galvin for billions of dollars, had cloned Galvin's phone. Assuming Galvin to be unaware of this, they naturally believed everything Galvin and Danny said over the monitored line had to be true. Which was why they believed that Galvin was on his own boat preparing to sail away.

And that once they learned that Dr. Mendoza hoped to get to Galvin first, they had no choice but to kill the man.

And in this way, Danny and Galvin had set up Galvin's enemies to neutralize each other. Which was exactly what happened.

The Medford Regional Construction & Engineering Company later reported to the Bureau of Alcohol, Tobacco, Firearms and Explosives that eight one-pound blocks of C-4 plastic explosive had been stolen from its inventory, along with a quantity of fifty-grain-per-foot detonating cord and an electric blasting cap. Medford Regional kept stores of such equipment to raze buildings.

Had agents from the Sinaloa cartel targeted their own financier before he could escape? Had the events in Boston Harbor in fact been the result of an internecine battle between two warring Mexican drug cartels?

Investigators from the Bureau of Alcohol, Tobacco, Firearms and Explosives and the Boston Police bomb squad later determined that the C-4 had been placed in three locations on Thomas Galvin's yacht: near the forward cabin, aft of the engine room, and on the fly bridge. Most experts agreed that Thomas Galvin had been standing on the fly bridge, piloting his yacht. Because the fly bridge had been completely destroyed, nothing of Galvin's body remained. Just some clothing and shoes and his Patek Philippe watch.

Lucy watched Danny explain, and when he had finished, they were both silent for a long while.

Too many elements within the US government had a vested interest in keeping things quiet. Mistakes had been made. Danny had told Lucy everything, and now she understood the sort of pressure he'd been under.

"When I heard you'd been shot, I was worried out of my mind," she said. "I'm sorry it took something like that to make me realize."

"Realize?"

"How much I still care for you. How much you were dealing with. Some of the choices you made were, I don't know . . ."

"Wrong?"

She shrugged. "Not for me to say. Sometimes life gets complicated, and the answers aren't so easy."

They were both quiet a moment longer. Finally, Lucy asked, "Does this mean you're safe? That we're safe?"

He nodded. "I think so."

A week later, there was a memorial service for Tom Galvin at St. Brigid Parish in South Boston, where he'd been baptized and confirmed. He was eulogized as a brilliant investor and generous man who'd never forgotten his roots.

A lot of old friends of Galvin's from Southie showed up. A much smaller group of friends from his later years sat uncomfortably on one side of the aisle. Celina Galvin wore a long black dress and a veil and looked dazed and small and lost. His daughter, Jenna, wept quietly throughout the service. Abby sat next to her and tried without much success to comfort her. His two sons looked awkward and forlorn in their dark suits.

Danny noticed a couple of men in business suits sitting near the back of the nave who looked particularly out of place. They actually didn't appear to be mourning. They seemed to be studying the mourners. He recognized one of them as the FBI agent who'd paid him a visit in the hospital.

Danny and Lucy were married in August. The ceremony was performed by a justice of the peace in the Boston Public Garden. The only attendees were Abby Goodman and Lucy's son, Kyle. Afterward they all repaired to Legal Sea Foods for a late lunch.

It took Danny a good six weeks before he was able to sit at a computer keyboard and type comfortably, but once he could, he experienced a great surge of productivity. He finished the book in three months, and his agent, Mindy Levitan, sold the book to another publisher. For more money than even his last publisher had paid.

Eighteen months after the explosion in Boston Harbor, *Genius: The Controversial Life of Jay Gould* was published to universally glowing reviews. The first one ran in *The New York Times* on a Tuesday, the book's on-sale day, and it was enthusiastic enough to spur a six-week run on the *New York Times* bestseller list.

The book party was held at an art gallery in the South End owned by a friend of Lucy's. Shortly after Danny had said good-bye to the last guest, he gave Abby a hug.

"Hey, Boogie. Luce and I have decided to spend Christmas in Turks and Caicos. Sort of a celebration of the book being finished and all that. How about you come with us? Maybe with Jenna, too, if she's free."

Abby looked at Danny with incredulity. "Seriously? Doesn't that seem like kind of . . . I don't know, a waste of money?"

"I thought you always wanted to go to the Caribbean."

She and Jenna had each decided to put off college for a while, spending a gap year volunteering at an orphanage in Guatemala.

"Come on, Dad," she said, and in her eyes a teasing smile sparkled. "Keep up."

As they left the gallery, Danny got a message alert on his phone.

It said, SNAPCHAT FROM LYNYRD.

"Who is it, Dad?"

"Not sure, Boogie." He stepped away, touched in his passcode.

596

On the screen before him was a photo of an ancient stone house in an emerald field next to a flock of sheep. Beautiful, timeless, like a picture postcard — except he knew it wasn't a postcard. On the top right of his phone's screen, a number was counting down from 10.

Danny had never been to New Zealand, but this looked a lot like the way Tom Galvin had described it. The scene was lovely and still and remote and it filled him with a deep sense of calm.

He studied the picture, staring intently at it, wondering if it contained some hidden message. It looked like a good place to live a peaceful life off the grid.

"What is it, Dad? Let me see." She leaned in close; an instant later, the picture was gone.

"What the heck? What —"

"Oh, Dad," Abby said. "You're so clueless! That's Snapchat. You take a picture and send it to your friends and then it's gone after a couple of seconds."

He nodded. "And it just — disappears? Forever?"

"Forever, Dad." Abby laughed. "Anyway, that was pretty — who's it from?"

"No one," Danny said. "Just an old friend."

ACKNOWLEDGMENTS

A number of people were particularly helpful to me in researching and writing this novel. For details on the workings of the Drug Enforcement Administration, my thanks to Mike Braun (former chief of operations of the DEA); John Arvanitis (Special Agent in Charge of the DEA's Boston office), and former DEA agent Paul Doyle. Former DEA agent Heidi Raffanello was immensely helpful. On money laundering, I thank Matt Fleming, Don Semesky, and, most notably, Jack Blum. My legal advisers included Jonathan Shapiro of Stern Shapiro Weissberg & Garin, Isaac Peres of Altman & Altman, George Price of Casner & Edwards, and especially Jay Shapiro of White and Williams.

Once again, Jeff Fischbach helped extensively with details on computer forensics, as did Kevin Murray with surveillance techniques and Jay Groob on investigative methods. For details on Mexico and Mexican culture, I thank Fred Feibel, Janet Lapp, and particularly Patricia Leigh-Wood. For medical advice: Dr. Tom Workman; Dr. Franklyn Cladis; Dr. Carl Kramer; Dr. Fred E. Shapiro, president of the Institute for Safety in Office-Based Surgery; Dr. Mark Morocco; Dr. Doug Lyle; and my brother, Dr. Jonathan Finder. For a little inside color on Aspen, I'm indebted to Lisa Holthouse. Bruce Irving helped me design Tom Galvin's Weston house; Justin Sullivan advised me on Galvin's plane; and Alyssa Haak, Steve Doyle, and Kevin Lussier of Boston Yacht Haven helped me with his boat. J. Mark Loizeaux kindly shared some of his endless expertise on controlled demolitions and explosives; Tony Scotti and Jon Schaefer suggested some clever evasive techniques; and Frank Ahearn counseled me on Galvin's disappearance. George Kurtz of Crowdstrike helped on security and passwords. Sharon Bradey advised me on Danny and Galvin's squash game. Margaret Boles Fitzgerald and Eileen C. Reilly told me about Boston Healthcare for the Homeless, a remarkable organization. I'm grateful to Seth Klarman for sharing some discerning insights. Thanks as always to my website manager, Karen Louie-Joyce, and my editor/researcher and social mediaite, Clair Lamb. My assistant, Claire Baldwin, is invaluable and irreplaceable. My agents, Simon Lipskar and Dan Conaway, at Writers House, were my champions at an important time, and I'm indebted to Ben Sevier for his enthusiasm and vision.

The Lyman Academy is entirely fictional and bears no resemblance to any real-life private schools in the Boston area. Really. Finally, I'm grateful for the steadfast loving support of my wife, Michele Souda, and the immeasurable awesomeness of our daughter, Emma J. S. Finder.

— **Joseph Finder**
Boston, 2013

ABOUT THE AUTHOR

Joseph Finder is the *New York Times* bestselling author of ten previous novels, including *Vanished* and *Buried Secrets.* Finder's international bestseller *Killer Instinct* won ITW's Thriller Award for Best Novel of 2006. Other bestselling titles include *Paranoia* and *High Crimes,* both of which became major motion pictures. He lives in Boston.